"I want to taste you, lass," he murmured, bending to brush his hot, raspy tongue across one engorged nipple. Gillian shuddered at the touch. Her breath hissed between her teeth, and she closed her eyes to the sky and mountains so every sense might give itself over to the magic he wrought. Gently he pressed her back in the grass and bent over her.

"So bonny," he murmured, running his hand over her flesh, leaving a fiery trail wherever he touched. She opened her eyes and gazed at him, a golden giant shimmering in the sunlight, then he lowered his head to nestle his face between the full orbs of her breasts and his greedy tongue licked a path to one soft nipple. . . .

**Doubleday Book Club —
July 1997 Alternate Selection**

By Peggy Hanchar
Published by Fawcett Gold Medal:

THE GILDED DOVE
WHERE EAGLES SOAR
CHEYENNE DREAMS
FANCY LADY
WILD SAGE
SWAN NECKLACE
THE SCOTTISH BRIDE
LADY OF THE MIST

LADY OF
THE MIST

Peggy Hanchar

FAWCETT GOLD MEDAL • NEW YORK

A Fawcett Gold Medal Book
Published by Ballantine Books
Copyright © 1997 by Peggy Hanchar

http://www.randomhouse.com

Library of Congress Catalog Card Number: 96-91021

ISBN 0-449-14867-X

Manufactured in the United States of America

First Edition: May 1997

10 9 8 7 6 5 4 3 2 1

To my husband, Steve, and my sons, Steve, Jim, and Dr. Bob, and to my daughter, Laura. To Nancy and Janis and Janice. To Jenny, Candi, Stef, Jackie, and Eric. To Elsa, Lyn, Mary, and Bob, all of whom give me so much love, I'm able to write my stories with a full heart.

Author's Note

THE MACGREGORS AND the Campbells are two well-known clans in the history of the Highlands. The MacGregors, whose motto "Royal is my race" indicates a claim to descent from Griogar, King of Alpin in the eighth century, received the lands of Glenorchy, Glenstrae, Glenlyon, and Glengyle for service to the king, Alexander II, in his conquest of Argyll. They maintained their possession of this land by right of the sword and earned themselves a reputation for being warlike. Sir Walter Scott called them Children of the Mist.

The MacGregors were proscribed at various times, a process that stripped away their titles and lands and caused their very name to be banned. They were forbidden weapons or the right to gather in numbers more than five. A bounty was placed on their heads, their leaders hanged, their women branded, and their children taken away and given to other clans. The Campbells were very much a cause of the proscriptions described in this book and were ruthless in squeezing lesser clans from their lands. Unlike the MacGregors, however, the Campbells did not use force so much as they made use of their growing influence with the crown.

The fortunes of the MacGregors turned, however, and they won favor again. They fought for the Stuart cause and sheltered the fugitive Bonnie Prince Charles and were stout defenders of the Highland Gaeldom.

Kilchurn Castle was a holding of the Campbells', as was Edinample Castle of the MacGregors'.

As for the attitude of superstition and fear regarding witches in Scotland, King James was especially militant in trying to rid his country of witches, even going so far as to write his tract, *Demonology*, in which he outlines the mystery of witchcraft and espouses women as more susceptible to magic and the "grosse snares of the divell, as was overwell prooved to be trew, by the serpent's deceiving of Eve." It's interesting to note here that John Knox himself, the great father of Protestant Reformation in Scotland, was thought to be a wizard by Scotland's Catholic Church.

Unfortunately many who were accused of witchery were old women with no means or family to protect them. They were tortured until they confessed, then burned on Castle Hill in Edinburgh. Oftentimes their children or anyone known to be associated with such women were also accused of witchcraft and tortured into confession. Witches were thought to have a secret mark in their eyes or the mark of a cloven hoof on the roof of their mouth.

LADY OF
THE MIST

Chapter 1

"*T*HANE, YOU MUST not go there. It's the witch's lair!"

"I fear no witch." Thane Campbell's roar was considerably less than it might have been if he'd not been weakened by the loss of blood. He clasped the ragged edge of his wound and fixed his men with a baleful glare. Sweat stood out on his brow as he turned to Duncan Burnhouse, his commander and trusted friend.

"Aye, Duncan, I don't believe in witches, lad. Take me to Old Hannah's hut or my death'll be on your hands." His eyes darkened with pain. Drawing a deep, shuddering breath, he sagged over his steed's neck. His face was dead white, and without the fierce, burning gaze that spoke too eloquently of Thane Campbell's iron will, his spirit seemed crushed. Many a man there thought he'd breathed his last, and trembled and crossed himself. If such a man as Thane Campbell proved mortal, after all, then what hope had the rest of them?

"Thane, you canna die, man," Duncan cried as he spurred his horse so it brushed against the side of Bhaltair, Thane's devil-black steed. The stallion reared his head and whickered a warning. "Whoa," Duncan soothed. "I'll not hurt your master." He gripped the reins and held the stallion still while he leaned from his saddle to push the thick wheat-colored hair from Thane's pale face.

"He breathes, lads," he grunted, "but he's little time left in this world if we canna find help for him. If he trusts the old crone Hannah, then, by the gods, we'll take him there." Leading Bhaltair behind him, he turned his own mount toward the smoke spiraling above the treetops, the only indication that another human existed in the vast Forest of Glenartney. The men were silent as they rode behind, exchanging uneasy glances, yet willing to follow their chief faithfully into the bowels of hell itself if such were required of them.

The trees grew close about the stone hut, nearly obscuring the low, ragged thatched roof. A single window set deep within a stone wall gave off the slightest illumination. Duncan brought the two stallions to a standstill before the wooden door, which was firmly latched.

"Hail to those within," he cried out, and waited. The horses stamped their feet impatiently against the damp earth. The men seemed to hold their breath. He raised his voice. "Come out, I tell you. We mean you no harm. We've a wounded man here who needs your help."

The sagging wooden door creaked on its leather hinges as if someone had opened it a crack to peer out. "Who are you?" a rough voice came to them. "I know you not. You be strangers to me," the voice answered, disembodied and whispery from behind the stout door.

"I'll wager you know the name Campbell well enough," Duncan roared. "Would you close your door to such?"

"What d'ye seek here?"

"We have need of the services of Old Hannah. Now, open the door and give us your hospitality or you'll carry the death of the laird upon your hands. Even now his blood flows into the ground, and I fear 'tis already too late."

At these words, the door was thrown open and a short

figure emerged, scuttling crablike into the clearing. A sharp, piercing cry emerged from behind a ragged red beard.

"What in God's name is it?" Evan MacGibbon swore as the hunched figure darted among the horses, causing them to rear.

"Hold them steady, lads," Duncan ordered. With a gleeful laugh the shapeless figure leapt upon a tree trunk and repeated the fierce cry that raised a chill up each man's neck.

"Lachlan, be still," a lilting voice called, and a golden glow filled the doorway of the cottage. The light seemed to come from some unearthly source. The men yanked at their reins, and the horses stamped the ground and backed away. Every man present had heard Porta's tales of an evil lamp filled with hare's fat, which when lit was thought to move men to madness and had been known to cause women to cast aside their clothes and dance naked as long as the light burned. They feared, one and all, that they'd lose their senses if they stared into the flame, so they turned their gazes to the ground.

"Dinna look at the light," they called to one another. Stealthily the ray moved forward, revealing the misshapen hunchback. His ragged, unkempt hair and knobby features were so ugly that men turned away. The little man sensed their disgust and lunged at them, uttering half-formed words and shrieks.

"Steady, lads," Duncan called, and remained unflinching although his pulse thundered in his ears. All his life he'd heard tales of the witches who took up residence in the trees and hollows of the Forest of Glenartney. Hiding themselves away from decent folks, the evil creatures practiced their black witchcraft, bringing death and disease to man and beast alike. Many a witch had been discovered and burned on the Castle Hill of Edinburgh. Yet Old Hannah had escaped such a fate, for there were some who believed her to be a white witch, and because she'd kept herself hidden away in the wooded glen between Loch Earn and Loch Tay so even those who'd tried could not find her.

The men held their breath and waited. Slowly the light moved out of the darkness of the hut and they saw it was an innocent enough looking lamp held high by an arm uncommonly graceful and youthful. They blinked as the lamp was put to one side upon a tree stump and its bearer turned to greet them. Their breath whistled from between their dry lips as they stared at the vision before them.

This was no pockmarked hag in tattered rags and matted hair, reeking of rotted flesh and brimstone. The lithe, slender form was of a young woman of such beauty that could not speak. Her hair, as black as a raven's wing, tumbled about her shoulders in wild, shiny disarray, framing the pale oval of her face. Witch-green eyes peered back at them with uncanny poise. Her full lips, wide and generous, were as pink as the wild berries that grew on the sunny slopes of the braes at midsummer. She stood before them in her simple linen shift as regal as a queen and with such uncanny stillness, each man was mesmerized by her presence. Duncan recovered himself first.

"You be Hannah?" he asked uneasily, for he'd heard the hag Hannah was old and painfully ugly. Had she taken on this beauteous form to trick them?

"Nay, I'm not Hannah," she replied, and her voice was soft as a silvery brook tripping along the stone-strewn ground. Her glance fell upon Thane Campbell draped across his saddle and her lips formed a circle of alarm before she looked away and forced her features to reflect no emotion. "I canna help you, sirs. I beg you, be on yer way. There is a village if you but follow the waning westward light. There is a goodwife there you may call upon to bind your wounds."

"Nay." Duncan shook his head. "My laird will not make it to the village, and the light fades even as we speak. We must camp here for the night and ask for your help."

She cast a wary glance at the party of men. "I canna help you. You must leave."

Thane moaned and raised his head. For a moment his eyes opened, brilliant blue against his fevered skin, and he stared at the girl, his gaze seeming to reach deep inside her. She shivered and made to turn away, back to the safety of her hut. Her hand trembled as she took up the lamp, then, against her will, she stepped forward to the black stallion that bore its wounded master. Bhaltair sounded a shrill warning and pranced nervously. Immediately Lachlan leapt forward as if to protect the girl.

"Careful, lass, he be a devil with strangers." Duncan called the warning, his clasp on Bhaltair's reins tightening, but the girl placed her hand on the stallion's muzzle, speaking in a low voice. Bhaltair ceased his rearing and stood quietly, listening to the silky croonings. The men exchanged significant glances. Even Duncan was flummoxed by the maiden's way with the beast.

Oblivious of the men who watched, the girl placed her fingertips against the faint pulse that throbbed beneath Thane's sun-burnished skin. Her quick glance took in the blood-soaked leather binding and the bare muscular thigh exposed beneath the short skirt of plaid.

"What has happened to him?" she asked in that same low, clear tone that settled Bhaltair.

"He was gored by a wild boar," Duncan replied, remembering the jubilant laughter of his chief as he bounded out of his saddle and bent triumphantly over the stag he'd just downed with an arrow. Suddenly an enraged boar ran forward, head lowered. His horn caught Thane's thigh, ripping through flesh and muscle until the white of the bone was revealed. Then, turning with a speed remarkable in one so squat and ungainly, the boar ripped at him again, tearing a long slash across his chest. Dark blood gushed with every heartbeat, testifying that the wounds would be fatal if something weren't done at once.

"Can you help him, lass? Call the old witch. Whatever spell she must cast, tell her to do so. I'll see she's not punished for her witchcraft."

Once again the green eyes turned to him, then contemplated the wounded man. "Hannah is not here now," she replied almost reluctantly. "But I will try to help him. Bring him inside."

"Nay, Gillian," the ugly hunchback cried, hobbling forward.

"Be still, Lachlan," the girl whispered. "He's mortally wounded and will die without our help. Hannah would not have turned him away."

"Hannah would not have bid me open the door," the little man mumbled, and drew back into the shadows. The girl faced the men once more.

"Bring your laird inside," she instructed, and turned toward the door, carrying the lamp with her. Duncan nodded to two of his men, but they wouldn't budge.

"I'll lend my hand," Evan MacGibbon said, and swung out of his saddle to join Duncan as he eased Thane from Bhaltair's back and bore him inside.

In a land that bred giants, Thane's well-muscled frame stood taller than most, so the two men strained under the weight of their young chief.

"Put him there on the table," the girl said, hurrying to clear away a wooden bowl. Duncan and Evan did as she bade, then stepped back, studying the man who'd earned their allegiance and love. Even unconscious he exuded power, his broad, muscular shoulders filling the width of the table, his long legs hanging over the end. The girl seemed hesitant to touch him, so all three stood staring at the unconscious man until Duncan turned away and took in the interior of the small hut.

Roughly hewn beams blackened by the soot of countless fires rested on sturdy rooftrees, and round about the

stone walls sat simple crofters' plenishings. A stool of
bogwood stood in one corner, a small wooden chest
rested beneath the single window, and a draped curtain
hid what must have been a simple cot.

Though bunches of dried flowers and plants hung sus-
pended from the rafters, no dead frogs, newts, or toads
fouled the surroundings. A kettle bubbled merrily over
the small peat fire, but from the odors wafting from it,
Duncan suspected there was nothing more noxious there
than a plain stew. The coziness of the hearth and cottage
pleased him. They'd not eaten since early morning, and
Duncan's stomach rumbled with hunger as he turned
back to the table where Thane lay.

The chief's face was even more pale than before, and
his body seemed unnaturally still, for Thane was a man
who moved with coiled strength and speed.

The girl had untied the leather pad from his thigh. With
the pressure removed, blood welled from the serrated
flesh. She gasped and said nothing, quickly replacing the
pad and turning to a side table, where she opened several
leather pouches.

"Can you help him?" Duncan muttered, suddenly
fearful that the man who lay so still, the man he loved as
a brother, might be lost to them forever.

"I will try," the girl said, drawing handfuls of dried
herbs from the bags and placing them into a mortar.

"Here now, none of yer devilish concoctions," Evan
cried, grabbing hold of her shoulder and jerking her
around so the mortar tipped and the contents spilled
across the earthen floor.

"I hope to make him well again," the girl said evenly,
"but I canna work if you're at my shoulder, accusing me
at every turn."

"Leave her be, Evan," Duncan said wearily, numbly
accepting that his beloved chief and friend would die and
there was nothing he could do about it. Suddenly he
longed to be outdoors. "Do you have need of us?" he

asked the girl, noting how her hands trembled and she jerked away from them when they came too near. Dear God, she was as frightened of them as they were of her.

" 'Twould be better if you waited with your men," she said, nodding toward the door and the sounds of men settling themselves for the night. Duncan stared at her for a moment, wondering if he should leave Thane unguarded in her care. She seemed to read his thoughts.

"I'll not willingly harm him," she said softly. "I canna promise I can make him better. He's lost much blood."

He paused in the low doorway and turned back to the girl. "The hunchback called you Gillian. Be that your name, lass?"

"Aye, I am so named," she answered quietly, and waited for them to leave.

Duncan's gaze grew stern. "Be he dead or alive, if you use your black magic on him, I'll tear your heart from your body with my bare hands," he warned. "I would take him back to his kinsmen all of one piece."

Gillian regarded the giant that loomed in her doorway. In the dark eyes she read the truth of what he promised. Yet, behind the violence of his warning, she saw the love and grief he felt for his fallen leader. She smiled briefly and Duncan blinked at the fleeting image, for the smile had brought a radiance to her beautiful, serene face.

"I have told you true, sir. Ye need have no fear of me."

Duncan studied her face for a moment longer, then ducked his head and left the small cottage.

Alone, Gillian worked quickly, pulverizing the bark of a wild plum and flinging a handful into the pot of water she kept boiling on the back of the hearth. Cutting away the makeshift leather dressings and the bloody shirt beneath, she set about cleansing the wounds with the boiled herb water. She feared a lung might have been pierced. Conscious of the breadth of the giant's chest, she placed an ear against his side and listened to his breathing. Though thin and reedy, there was no sound of bubbling. The deadly horns had mercifully bypassed his lungs.

Though her touch was gentle and sure, the blond giant rolled and moaned in agony. When she was certain the wound was purified with the herbal wash, she packed it with the powdered inner bark of a hemlock and bound it tightly.

Her patient tossed in fevered delirium, so she bathed his brow and cheeks with cool herb-scented water and forced into him a decoction of catnip leaves. Her quick, slender hands slowed in their task as she studied the face before her. Never had she seen a man of such beauty, so like a special gilded creature from some mystical place, a god caught on earth with only her to help him.

His mouth and nose were chiseled to perfection, his chin jutting and firm, his neck column long and graceful, his shoulders and chest thick with muscles. Her eyes traveled over his body to the slender hips and strong legs, and she wondered what he looked like beneath the thick woolen plaid left buckled at his waist. Her cheeks grew pink at the thought, and she turned away, her fingers suddenly clumsy as she fumbled with her bags of herbs.

She prepared him a potion to calm him for the fight against fever and pain, then dribbled it against his lips from a clean rag. When she was sure he'd had enough, she covered him with a woolen plaid, her hands going of their own accord to his brow to smooth back the golden hair. The thick strands reminded her of sunshine pouring itself into Loch Tay with careless abandon on a summer's day. His skin was hot and supple to her touch. Her fingertips trailed down his cheek, startled at the contrast in the smoothness of his skin and the sudden rasp of whiskers on his clean-shaven jaw. She couldn't resist the feel of him. Never had she been so close to a man, though she'd studied them from afar. Even then she'd never seen such a specimen as this. He was all tawny muscles and latent power. Even his smell was different from that of Hannah and herself and even Lachlan.

He moaned and stirred in his delirium, rolling his head from side to side. Suddenly, with a bellow, he pushed himself upward, nearly toppling from the table. She shoved him down again, her fingers splayed on the broad, tawny chest, her palms sensitive to the heat of his body. He lay back, spent by his effort. His eyes opened, blue sapphires rimmed with dark golden lashes. They seared her soul as they had before, and she felt unable to breathe.

He gazed beyond her for a moment, then his vision seemed to clear, and he stared at her as if seeing every detail of her features. His face took on an expression of wonder, his lashes dipped, and he slid backward into the healing darkness her herbs had made for him.

Gillian stood for a long time, her stomach quivering, her thoughts scattered and uncertain. He was a High-lander, and Hannah had said such men were dangerous. She was to run anytime she saw one. Yet she felt no desire to run from this golden warrior. His very glance held her speechless, while her body shook as with the ague. She tentatively touched his shoulder. There was no response. His breathing was deep and even.

Her fingers glided over his shoulders and down onto his broad chest. She had thought a man to be rough and grizzled like old Darach, the woodcutter from the village. He'd stopped once when Hannah was alive and asked for a cup of milk from their cow to go with his bread for supper. When Hannah had filled his cup, he'd gone on his way. She thought of the village men she'd observed from a distance and the Highlanders who sometimes passed through this part of the forest. None had possessed the beauty of this man.

She pushed her thoughts backward to that other time and place, when her life had been different, to a time when uttering the name of her clan was not forbidden. There had been many handsome, strong men around then, and none as strong and handsome as her father. Angus Michael MacGregor! The name came unbidden to her mind, though she tried to shut it away. Hannah had said she must never think of those days again, must never say that name, and she never had, but she couldn't control the wayward memories that conjured up the sight of a giant of a man, nearly as broad and tall as this one who lay on her table. What had his men called him? Thane!

Gillian drew the bogwood stool closer and sat down so she might watch over her patient through the night. Leaning her head against the table, she dozed in fits and starts, rising often to wipe his fevered brow with a cooling cloth and to force sips of water between his dry lips.

Near dawn she woke with a start and leapt to her feet, fearful her patient had died while she slept. His chest rose and fell evenly, but his breathing was shallow. His face was pale and damp and his brow burned with fever. He would live and needed only time to regain his strength. She should go tell his men so they could return him to his castle, yet she lingered, reluctant to give up this close contact with him.

She'd been lonely since Hannah died. More than that, she'd had strange, unnamed yearnings, yearnings that this man's very presence had further awakened. There was a new awareness, a blossoming within herself, half-formed, uncertain, as timid and shy as a spring wildflower hiding on a hillside. Why should this man, handsome and powerful as he was even in sleep, have such a power over her emotions? Was it always so between men and women? Was she wicked to feel this curiosity? She thought of his manroot lying flaccid in its bed of golden hair. Why had glimpsing it made her feel warm, as if she blushed all over?

She ran a slender finger along his jaw. She liked touching him. Touching him made her body tingle. Would he tingle also if he were to waken and touch her in the same caressing manner? Would she like his touch?

She took hold of his hand and placed it against her bare
arm. Except for the warmth of his hand, there was no life
and therefore no answering emotions. Having a man
touch you was not nearly as disturbing as touching a
man yourself, she decided, and placed his large hand back
at his side. Her gaze fell on his lips, and without thinking
she leaned forward and placed her lips against his. His
mouth was unresponsive, yet she felt a warmth spread
through her. His lips were firm but soft beneath her own.
Just as she was about to withdraw, she felt his lips move,
mastering her own, tasting her, drawing her deeper into a
maelstrom of unexplored passions. A tongue, raspy and
hot, brushed across her lips, and she drew back, gasping
with surprise.

The sapphire eyes were open and staring straight into
hers. He was awake! Nostrils flaring, cheeks tinged with
color, Gillian fought to hold his gaze. He was silent for a
moment, his gaze moved from her around the humble hut,
over the fire, and finally back to her.

"Hannah?" he croaked.

"Nay, m'lord. Hannah is dead these twelve months."

"Who be you, then?" he demanded.

"I am called Gillian," she replied.

"Are you a witch?" His bright blue gaze was like a
beacon reaching deep inside her, and she wished to cry
out a denial.

"Some say I am, m'lord," she answered in a low voice,
her head held proud and high.

"Are you from the Campbell clan?" His glance was
sharp upon her face.

"Nay, m'lord. I canna tell you the name of my clan."

"Why not? Don't you know?"

She remained mute, lashes lowered over her eyes.

"Whoever you be, you're bonny," he said, and the
rasping edge of his voice raked along her nerve endings.

"So are you, m'lord," she blurted out, and blushed at
her own boldness. He seemed not to mind. He chuckled,

then grimaced at the pain such an act brought him and fell back against the table with a groan.

"Are you hurting, m'lord?" she asked, going forward to tend him.

"Aye," he gasped.

"I'll give you something to ease your suffering," she cried, hurrying to mix a new potion for him. Her hands trembled as they hovered over her carefully hoarded supply of herbs, barks, and roots.

"Here, drink this, m'lord," she urged, raising his head against her shoulder and holding the cup to his mouth. He gulped a great swallow of the brew and grimaced.

"God's Passion, what is this poison ye give me," he cried, dashing the cup to one side.

"Not poison, m'lord," she answered calmly, ignoring the pain of the hot brew as it sloshed over her fingers. "It will dull the pain and help you heal. You must drink it." She held the cup to his lips. His eyes, the stubbornness he felt reflected in them, studied her face over the rim of the cup. Then he nodded and swallowed the contents without further demur.

When the cup was empty, he lay back and stared at the soot-covered beams overhead. A movement brought his attention back to the girl.

"D'you live here alone?"

"Nay. There's Lachlan." Her heart beat fast in her chest, and she could not turn her gaze to meet his.

"Is Lachlan your husband?" Thane asked, the tempo of his words slowing as the medicine began to take effect.

"Lachlan is my friend," Gillian answered, then continued in a rush of words. "He's a dwarf, a foundling, left abandoned in the woods. Hannah took him in and raised him the same as she did me."

She glanced at the warrior on the table and saw that his eyes were closed and his breathing deep and steady. He hadn't heard her words. Just as well, she thought, for Hannah had said she must never reveal such details about

herself. Gillian knew it was for their protection against
strangers intent on doing evil.

The fever returned, robbing Thane of his senses,
leaving him delirious and weakened. Gillian tried every
scrap of knowledge Hannah had taught her. Still the ague
claimed him, shaking his body until she thought he would
fall off the table. Time and again he cried out incoher-
ently, his voice harsh and raspy. Duncan and his men
came to the door, demanding to see their chief, and
Gillian let them in.

"What spell is this you've put upon him?" Duncan
demanded.

"None, my lord. I swear by all that's holy," Gillian
answered, frightened by the men's fierce expressions. She
knew swift and deadly was a mob's passion. Duncan's
men seemed well-disciplined enough, but she feared what
they might become if her visitor were to die.

For three days Gillian worked feverishly over Thane
Campbell. For three days Duncan and his men camped in
the forest, impatient and anxious, tempers frayed. For
three days she bathed her patient and tended his needs,
her hands coming to know the texture and shape of his
body as surely as she knew her own.

At last she fought back the vapors that had tried so hard
to claim him, and he slept quietly. His rugged body was
mending, though it would be some time before he
regained his strength from the loss of blood.

The time had come to let him go, she thought reluctantly, her hands automatically smoothing the coverlet
over him, her fingertips following the curve of his
shoulder, the sculpted contour of his broad chest. She
leaned over him, feeling the warmth of his breath against
her cheek. Placing her nose against his neck, she drew in
the heady scent of his body, now so familiar. She had no
wish to see him go, yet she heard the impatient demands
of his men from beyond her door. Drawing a last sigh, she

placed her soft lips against his, and as before, though he did not waken, his lips moved beneath hers, responding in a manner that would have been bold and frightening if he'd been awake.

A knock sounded against the stout door. They'd come for him as she'd known they would. Slowly she drew away, and with a final glance at her golden warrior she left the cottage through the trapdoor and hid herself in the woods. With a bellowing cry the man called Duncan threw open the door to the hut and entered, calling out to her, but she remained silent and hidden. She knew her safety depended upon this, for their need of her was done and she feared what they might do.

"By the saints, she's not here," Evan MacGibbon called out.

"She must be, man. She did not leave the hut by the door, and there is no other way." Duncan tramped into the small hut and looked around.

"What is this witchery?" he demanded when he saw no sign of the girl. He and Evan looked at each other, neither daring to voice the fear that claimed him. A moan sounded from the table, and they turned shoulder to shoulder to tend their chief.

"Thane. Are you with us, man? Or has the witch stolen your mind from you?" Duncan asked fearfully.

"Nay, Duncan. No such thing. She's not a witch."

"Can you travel, Thane? If so, we'll take you from this place." Duncan hovered over his chief, his heart grateful to see the blue eyes were clear of the signs of fever.

"I would see the lass, Gillian, first," Thane whispered.

"She's gone, my laird." Evan MacGibbon spoke up.

"Wh-where?"

"We don't know, laird. She dinna leave through the door as do regular souls. Perhaps she went up the chimney like smoke. What better sign than this that she is indeed a witch?"

"Nay, lad. Be brave of heart. She's but a lass." Thane's whisper died away. Weakly he closed his eyes.

"We'll take you home now, laird," Duncan said, signaling Evan to help carry him out.

"Wait, Duncan." Thane stirred himself to grasp Duncan's tunic. "Find the lassie for me. Bring her to Edinample."

Silently Duncan glanced at Evan. Thane's hold became more demanding.

"Promise you'll find her," he commanded. "P-promise me."

"Aye, Thane. We'll find her for you." Duncan nodded, and the men bore Thane from the hovel out into the green-tinged sunlight and placed him gently on Bhaltair's back. Duncan stood looking about the clearing. The rain had halted the day before and birds sang sweetly in the warm air. Sunlight flooded the small clearing. There was nothing fearful here, yet Duncan felt a shiver along his spine, for there was no sign of the girl and none had see her leave. Duncan thought of his promise to his chief, and with a final shake of his head told his men to mount. Quickly they left the clearing behind them, moving through the trees with only the sound of their horses' hooves against the rocky ground marking their passage.

Gillian remained hidden in the trees till long after all sound of their departure had ceased. The sunlight paled and a gentle rain began to fall once more, pattering against the broad leaves of the quaking aspen and the ash. The smell of earth and pine and rain came to her, but it brought her no comfort. Her solitude closed around her more cruelly than anything else life had dealt her, even the passing of Hannah. She was alone in the great forested glen without the sound of human voice or the warmth of another's touch.

She came out of her hiding place and made her way to the cottage. The coverlet she'd used for the golden warrior was left behind. She hugged it and buried her face in it, drawing in the scent of the man she'd healed. Would she ever see him again? She bowed her head, and tears rolled unchecked down her cheeks. Outside the cottage the twilight gathered and the rain dripped onto the leaves.

Chapter 2

"**W**HY DIDN'T YOU bring her with you, man?"
Thane glared at his friend. "I canna see why
you failed t'do as I asked, even if she objected. She was
but a wee bit of a lass." Restlessly he paced his room,
crossing to peer out the window, then turning to scowl at
Duncan and the room in general. His face was still pale
beneath its weathered tan, but his lean body moved with
the same animal grace and energy he always displayed.
Two days he'd remained in his room, lying abed, waking
only to take the thin gruel the servants had brought him.
His thoughts had centered on the beautiful face that had
hovered over him in his delirium and now invaded his
dreams. He had to see her again.

"You've no stomach for finding her, you're that afraid
she may be a witch," Thane scoffed.

"Aye," Evan agreed readily enough. "I'll not back
down from any man, Thane, as well you ken, but I've a
dread of witches, and a witch she be."

"She's but a lone woman living in the woods! She can't
have disappeared into a mist." One golden eyebrow
arched above an ice-blue gaze as Thane regarded him.

"Nay, Thane, she's not alone." Duncan came to Evan's
rescue. "She lives with a crouchie, a crook-backed dwarf

18

of such ugliness of face, he alone would turn the bravest man back."

"Bah!" Thane strode across the room.

"And," Duncan said, "there was no door in the hut save the one facing us, and I had a guard posted there at all times, yet she disappeared."

"Your guard must have slept."

"Not so, Thane," Evan cried. " 'Twas I who stood on guard those last hours. I had no trust for the witch or her hunchbacked monster."

Thane paused and gazed from one man to the other. The lowering sun shone through the open window and gilded his fair, thick hair. He sighed and slumped onto the window seat. Duncan and Evan were good men and true. They would not tell him false, nor would they fail in their duty, so fierce was their pride. Accepting that they spoke the truth, he must consider that the lass was indeed bewitched and that she had bewitched him as well, for a fever burned within him to gaze into the emerald depths of her eyes again and smell the sweetness of her warm breath as she leaned over him.

In his dreams he imagined her moving out of the mist to reveal herself to him. She bent close, her silken black hair brushing against his chest as she pressed her lips to his. He could taste her kiss, feel the heated softness of her breast pressed against his shoulder. Such thoughts tormented his nights and haunted his days. The memory of her willowy body and her soft hands on his own fevered flesh, taking away the pain, caused him to harden with a desire he'd never known with any of the country wenches he took so readily. Aye, he was truly bewitched.

Still, he could not give up.

"Tomorrow you will try again," he said.

"Thane, 'tis time and effort wasted," Duncan protested.

"You'll try again and I will ride with you."

"Man, you're in no condition t'ride," Evan protested.

"Tomorrow I ride wi' ye. You have no need t'ride with

me," Thane said, and so quiet was his tone that they had to strain to listen, so adamant his glance, they looked away and sighed with frustration. Thane would not be thwarted in this.

"If you're set on finding the witch, Thane, I'll ride wi' you," Duncan said.

"Aye, and me!" Evan echoed.

Duncan combed his red beard with his thick fingers as a wolfish grin spread across his face. "If you're well enough t'ride, are you well enough for a little drinkin' and whorin' this night?" he cried.

Thane looked at him in surprise. He'd thought so much of the witch that he'd had no desire for anything stronger than the watered wine ordered by Shadwell, the castle physician. Mayhap what he needed to put these teasing images from his mind was a cup of stronger spirits and a buxom lass on his lap. He met Duncan's expectant gaze and laughed. Leaping up, he clapped both men on the shoulder.

"Aye, you've hit upon a cure, Duncan," he declared. "Let's go down to the hall and order the prettiest wenches and the strongest ale." Laughing in agreement, the two men followed him down to the great hall. Soon a group of the best Campbell Highlanders were gathered around the stout trestle tables, quaffing cups of ale and consuming great chunks of cooked lamb and beef. Serving girls, their eyes flashing coquettishly, hurried to keep cups and platters filled, their skirts tucked into their waistbands so their ankles showed.

Thane sat at the head of one table, his platter of food barely touched, his cup drained yet again as he sought to still the images of eyes that changed like the green shadows of the forest, and skin so fair and smooth, his hand itched to caress it. In his spirit-fogged mind, the witch smiled at him and he responded in kind.

A plump-bosomed girl sat down on his lap. Gaily she pulled his earlobe and leaned forward. "Ye've a bonny grin to ye, Thane." She'd unlaced her bodice and the tops of her breasts were creamy and full, their rosy tips barely covered by her shift. She moved so they were mere inches from his mouth. If he were so minded, he had merely to open his lips and suck her through the cloth. He knew from the gleam of anticipation in her eyes that she expected him to, but he could not. The memory of a willowy figure made this wench's overblown charms a mockery of desirability.

"Ah, now you've gone and stopped smiling," she cried, playfully tickling his cheek.

"I'm sorry, Bridget. It was Bridget, was it not?"

"Aye, milord, Bridget it is," she whispered, and pressed her full breasts against him.

"You're a bonny lass, Bridget, but I fear I'm not good company tonight."

"Aye, milord, you are," she said quickly, bouncing on his knee a little so her breasts jiggled. "You've just been ill, 'tis all. You need some time t'recover your hungers. That's what I'm here for." She smiled provocatively. "I ken how to give a man a powerful hunger and how to satisfy the hunger once it's awakened."

"I've na doubt you can do all that and more, lass," Thane said, and put an arm around her waist so he wouldn't dump her on the floor when he stood, "but I'm not of a mind to have a hunger tonight. Mayhap another night." Turning away, he ignored her gasp of outrage and her mouth hanging open in surprise. He'd gone no more than a few steps, when her cry of fury sounded so that everyone in the hall turned to look at them.

"Aye, you should have told me you had no need of a woman tonight and I could ha' spent my time with someone else," Bridget called sassily. "I'm not used to having ma bed empty if I'm not of a mind to."

Chuckling slightly, Thane turned to face her. She stood with her hands on her ample hips, her golden hair tousled and lying along her shoulder and across one full breast.

"I have only to look at you, Bridget, t'know 'tis true," he said. "The loss this night is mine and mine alone."

Mollified, she swished her skirts and grinned around the table before turning back to him, unwilling to give up on her opportunity to spend the night with the handsome young heir to the earldom of Argyll. "Then you want me t'come wi' you to your chambers?" she teased, certain he would not refuse in front of all the onlookers. Once she had him in bed, she was certain her skills would win him to her so she would hold a special place in the castle hierarchy. But Duncan saw the distress and fatigue in Thane's face and spoke up.

"There'll be no bouncing tonight, Bridget. Can't you see the fever's upon him?"

"Aye, and the fever's upon me." Bridget's ribald sally was answered by a hoot of laughter. Emboldened, she threw herself against Thane, making sure he felt the lush fullness of her breasts. "You canna turn yer back on what I offer, Laird Thane," she purred. "Otherwise I'll be thinkin' you've a taste for boys instead."

The onlookers laughed at her challenge and called out a few suggestions as to what Thane must do with a lass as fully giving as Bridget. Thane listened to their high jinks, and pushing aside the memory of a sweet, pale oval face framed in a tumble of raven-black curls, wrapped an arm around Bridget's waist.

"Never a man accused me of preferring a boy over hot womanly flesh," he growled, and bent her backward in a passionate embrace that brought about cheers of approval from his men. Thane's tongue breached Bridget's half-hearted defenses and dueled with her sassy tongue until she moaned with desire. Greedily her hands reached beneath his plaid, and she rubbed herself against him in shameless invitation.

"Nay, lass, I've no desire t'take you in the public rooms." Grabbing her hand, he pulled her after him toward the stairs.

"My, but you're in a rush of a sudden, milord," Bridget laughed, following willingly. Once they were inside Thane's chambers with the door closed behind them, she tore at his clothes. Without preamble they fell upon each other in the bed. No coaxing was needed, no preparing required. Bridget was an experienced wench and knew what she wanted, and more, what was expected of her in return. She gave as good as she got, and when at last they'd achieved a mutual satisfaction and lay sated and sweating upon the covers, she wound her arms possessively around Thane's waist and fell into a deep sleep, signified by the robust snores she emitted.

Thane lay silent and awake beside her. He'd had no real desire for this woman tonight. He'd performed because he'd thought it might drive the spell from him, and that for a little while he might forget the witch with her green eyes and red lips. What had she called herself? Gillian. His lady of the mist. The name ran through his mind like a siren's song. He must find her, he thought restlessly. He must find her and end this spell she'd cast over him, lest he never have peace of mind again. Tomorrow, he consoled himself. Tomorrow he would ride into the Forest of Glenartney and find the hut and look into her eyes again and see that she was but a mere woman with no more charms than most. Tomorrow.

At dawn he was awakened by a pounding on his door. Duncan rushed in, his hose and breeches undone, his hair tousled. His face, still dulled by sleep, displayed shock and dawning anger.

"Thane," he cried. "Some bloody bastards've been at our stock down in Glen Ample. They've driven away more than half the herd and burned a village."

"Was it the bloody MacPhees again?" Thane cried, springing out of bed and reaching for his shirt and plaid. Bridget moaned a sleepy protest and sat up, rubbing her eyes.

"I dinna ken," Duncan answered, barely sparing the wench a glance. "The raiders gave no warning and left no witnesses."

Thane paused in donning his shirt. "You mean men were killed?"

"Aye, the murderin' bastards. Some of the villagers were killed as well, women and children." Duncan turned away, not wanting to see the flare of fury in Thane's face.

"The MacPhees haven't been given to killings," Thane said, snatching up his weapons. His nimble fingers belted his sword at his side and he stuffed a pair of German pistols into his waistband. He jerked up his head and glared at Duncan. "D'ye ken any other enemy who would seek to attack us like this, to hate us so much as to kill our women and children?"

"Nay, Thane." Duncan shook his head. "The Campbells are feared and hated by many, but none would dare go against the king and defy us like this."

Thane shook his head, then stirred himself to action, striding purposefully toward the door. "First off, we'll visit the MacPhees," he declared. "Bevan MacPhee had best have a convincing story, or, God's Passion, I'll break his clan."

Following Thane to the courtyard where Evan had seen to it that men were saddled and waiting, Duncan thought his chieftain had never seemed more like his father than at that moment. The power and might of the ruthless, ambitious Campbell clan had broken many a smaller clan who'd dared to challenge them.

He thought of the MacGregors, who had defied the Campbells, trying to keep their lands by arms, only to be outmaneuvered in the courts. By order of King James himself and through the instigation of the Campbells, the fierce, unruly MacGregors had paid a stiff price indeed. In theory they no longer existed. MacGregor land had become Campbell land.

"I've been thinkin', Thane," Duncan said, bringing his

mount alongside Bhaltair when they'd slowed to a walk to rest the horses. "To make such an attack doesn't seem like a thing the MacPhees would do."

"Aye, so I've thought," Thane said, casting a glance at Duncan. He'd always been impressed by his friend's quick intelligence and fair nature.

"This act seems more like something the MacGregors would have done years back."

Thane nodded. "But their leaders were killed some years ago, when I was but a lad myself. The clan was broken."

"Aye, so they were." Duncan nodded. "But would na some of them have escaped into the hills, aided by sympathetic clans?"

" 'Twas always the talk," Thane answered, his expression thoughtful. "Ask about it among the men, Duncan, but don't be obvious. We don't want t'raise tales of the legendary MacGregor clan if we can help it. Let them stay buried."

"Aye, I've no wish to waken that sleepin' dog," Duncan replied. They rode on in silence and soon came to the eastern borders of Argyll, where they entered the land of the MacPhee clan and rode swiftly to confront the Highlanders.

" 'Tis not wise t'go into the village, Gillian. Remember Hannah's warnings?" Lachlan perched on a tree stump so he might peer into Gillian's eyes, so great was his need to convey his sense of disaster should she ignore Hannah's warnings.

"Aye, well I remember," Gillian replied gently. "And I have no wish to defy you, Lachlan, but I've a need to be among people. Since Hannah died I'm fearsomely alone." She didn't tell him her sense of isolation had been tenfold since the golden warrior's men had carried him away. However, the dwarf guessed at the reason for her melancholy.

"Don't I count, then, lassie?" Lachlan demanded, his ugly, bumpy face screwing up in offense.

"Aye, you count, Lachlan. I don't know what I would have done without you, but you're not Hannah and I've a need to talk to someone of my own kind." She saw his crestfallen expression and hurried to ease the hurt she'd unintentionally inflicted. "Aye, you're a man, Lachlan, and you canna understand the ways of women." At her words the dwarf grinned and leapt down from the trunk. Galvanized to action by his own shyness, he turned somersaults and landed upright before her, his chest puffing out in pride. Gillian laughed.

"Aye, Lachlan, and you're a divil," she teased. "Someday you'll find a fair lady who'll tame you to her hearth."

"Aye, that'll be the day," Lachlan said cockily, then his grin faded. " 'Tis not so, Gillian, and well you know. I am but a freak to the eyes of women. None would ha' me at their hearth."

"Don't say that, Lachlan." Gillian sighed, running a hand over his rough cap of hair.

"Why not? 'Tis true. I'm but an oddity, a curiosity just as ye—" He caught himself and looked away. "I'm sorry!" he mumbled.

"There's no reason t'be," Gillian whispered. She wiped at the tears that rolled down her cheek, rejecting their quick release from her sorrow and loneliness. "But it doesn't have t'be that way, Lachlan. We could go to the village together. You could take your carvings and sell them in the booths and I—I will take some of my herbs and plants and sell them as Hannah did."

"She warned us never to go there."

"But she went herself, Lachlan. If she were able to come and go wi'out harm, why can't we?"

"I've seen the ways of the villagers," Lachlan said, shaking his head. "They are not kind or tolerant as Hannah was."

"Mayhap some of them will be. We must try, Lachlan," Gillian responded, "else we are doomed to spend our lives here in these woods, in this cottage, and speak to no one. I canna bear such a thought." Her wail of despair was so heartrending, Lachlan put aside his fears.

"Mayhap ye be right about this. I will go with you."

Gillian's face brightened and she scrubbed away the tears. "Will ye truly, Lachlan? And will ye take some of yer carvings, the little birds and forest creatures. They are the best."

Reluctantly Lachlan nodded. His carvings were something he held dear and had no wish to share with others, who might laugh at his renderings, for despite Gillian's encouragement and praise, he had no real faith in his skills. He had no way of knowing that the delicate wooden figures that emerged from the knife his short, thick fingers wielded were indeed masterpieces.

They emerged from the woods and onto the edge of the village before Gillian was prepared for it. She stopped and gasped, blinking at the sights before her, not certain whether to be disappointed or awed by what she saw. The cottages were small and humble, but there were so many, she could not conceive of people living side by side as the villagers appeared to do. In the back of each cottage was a small patch of garden, and flowers bloomed on windowsills.

A distant memory came to her as they went to the village square. Once she'd stood frightened and alone, defiant and nearly savage in her grief in this place. Only one person had stepped forward to offer her a home: Old Hannah the witch. The pain of that moment came back with such blinding clarity, she almost cried out and sank to her knees. Only Lachlan's grip on her arm saved her.

"I must put away these thoughts," Gillian told herself, but her ebullience had ended and she crept down the street toward the square. When they entered the square she blinked, her mournful memories momentarily pushed back by the bustle and hue and cry of a market-day fair. Booths had been erected along one side of the square, and farmers called out a litany of their wares— plump chickens, fresh cheese, new potatoes, and much more.

Gillian wandered along the line of booths, forgetful of her own basket of wares as she marveled over the variety of goods, fresh produce, beeswax candles, fine wool plaids. Running her fingers lovingly over the wools, Gillian considered a new linen for herself and a new cloak for Lachlan. Perhaps she could sell her herbs for enough coin to buy the wool needed. With new purpose she moved among the villagers, calling out a list of her herbs. No one bought from her, and she'd just about given up, when a woman furtively beckoned her closer. Her lean face was weary and careworn. Once she must have been beautiful, but drudgery and hardships had taken their toll on her. A flaxen-haired girl not more than six clung to her skirts, peering with fearful eyes at Lachlan, who stood only a little taller than she.

"Be ye the girl who lives with the old witch Hannah?" the woman demanded, shoving the little girl behind her.

"Aye." Gillian nodded and smiled tentatively. If this woman remembered Hannah, she must be a friend. "I'm Gillian, and this is Lachlan."

The woman glanced at the hunchback and quickly turned away, furtively crossing herself. "Ha' ye brought some of yer magic potions and spells?" She kept her face averted as if fearful of meeting Gillian's eyes.

"Aye, I've brought some healing herbs," Gillian said, offering the basket of goods. "Of what d'you suffer? Maybe I've a cure for it."

The woman cast a quick glance around, and seeing that no one was openly observing them, began to speak, her eyes downcast so she might not be afflicted by the evil eye. "I would buy a bit of lady's mantle from ye," she whispered.

"I've not brought any with me," Gillian answered, perplexed, for she could not remember any afflictions for which lady's mantle was a known cure. "Tell me what you suffer. Perhaps something else would work."

At Gillian's first words the woman had moaned in distress, so Gillian thought her in extreme pain. Mentally she ran through the herbs she'd brought—heartsease for heart problems, pine leaves boiled with vinegar for toothache, lungwort for chest complaints, carpenter's herb for healing wounds.

The woman stared at her with growing anger while a deep flush blossomed on her weathered cheeks. "My husband's eye has wandered," she whispered. "I—I've a wish to appear young again. Hannah told me once that lady's mantle would restore youthfulness and beauty, no matter how faded."

"Oh," Gillian said, for she knew such a claim was not true and that Hannah had sold such potions more to soothe the vanity of those who sought them than with any real hope of their working. Now she stood considering what she must do, for the woman looked unhappy beyond all reason.

Perceiving Gillian was safe for the moment and involved in business that was of no interest to him, Lachlan moved away to study some fine horses being offered by a farrier.

"I have no lady's mantle, but I know of something that will work nearly as well," Gillian offered. "You must soak wild tansy in buttermilk for nine days, then wash your face in it three times a day. Your complexion will come out fair as a milkmaid's."

"I've tried that," the woman cried. "There must be something else, some spell, some potion."

"I don't know any other," Gillian said, feeling some alarm, for the woman's hands had fastened clawlike upon her arm.

"Ye lie!" the woman cried. "Ye're a witch. Ye ken all things."

"That isn't true," Gillian cried. "I am but a woman like you. I have no witches' spells." Frantically she looked around for Lachlan, but he was nowhere in sight.

"Tell me the secret," the woman hissed, her eyes were wild-looking.

"I can't help you," Gillian cried, pulling away and turning to run.

Lachlan heard the high-pitched edge of her voice and appeared at her side. "Leave her be, ye hag," he cried, pushing at the woman.

"Witch! There's a witch among us," the woman cried in her shrill voice. Her daughter screamed and set up a wail, grasping her mother's skirts. The woman's abrupt movements sent her daughter sprawling in the muddy road, which only increased the child's anger. She cried so hard, she couldn't catch her breath, and arched backward in the mud, her eyes rolling upward until only the whites showed.

"Aieeyh! She's cast a spell on my daughter," the woman cried. "She's bewitched my Lisbet! Save us, oh, save us all, Lord." The woman crossed herself repeatedly and raised her eyes to the heavens. A crowd gathered around her.

"There she is," someone cried, pointing at Gillian and Lachlan. "There's the witch and her devil's spawn. Get them."

"No, you're wrong. I'm not a witch," Gillian cried. "I came only to sell my herbs." She held out her basket to show how innocent were her wares, but a young woman stepped forward and dashed the basket from Gillian's hands. All the carefully dried herbs fell into the mud. Suddenly a clod of mud flew through the air and hit Gillian's cheek. She cried out and put her hand up against the sting of it. Emboldened now, more villagers scooped up mud and rocks and hurled them at her, striking her in

the chest and shoulders, so she reeled from the pain and
nearly fell.

"Come, Gillian," Lachlan cried, tugging at her hand.
"We must flee." Gillian stumbled after him. Howling
their rage and fear, the villagers followed, continuing to
pelt them. Suddenly the sound of horses could be heard
and riders swept into the village square.

"What goes on here?" a voice called, and despite her
fear and Lachlan's urgency, she peered over her shoulder.
The golden warrior, Thane Campbell, sat astride his great
black horse, his golden head flung back, his brows drawn
into a straight line of anger over his searing blue eyes. She
recognized the man known as Duncan as well as some of
his other men.

Subdued by their chieftain's appearance, the villagers
crowded around him, eager to explain their actions and to
tell him of the witch in their midst.

"Hurry, Gillian, now is our chance," Lachlan urged,
and she turned to follow the little dwarf through the
narrow streets. Behind them they heard the angry voices
of the villagers and the abrupt questioning of the Campbell chief.

"Quick, Gillian, hide in here," Lachlan ordered, pushing
her toward a cow byre. "I'll lead them away."

"But they'll catch you, Lachlan. Ye can't run fast
enough with your bandy legs, and they've horses."

Lachlan grinned. "Even wi' horses they can't catch
me," he boasted. "Put your head down. I'm away." He
leapt down the path and quickly disappeared from view.
The sound of hooves against the stony ground made her
draw back into the shadows of the byre. A black horse
flew past, carrying the proud figure of Thane Campbell.
How often she'd dreamed of seeing him again, but not
like this, not with him and his men hunting her down like
a criminal. Miserable, Gillian drew herself into a ball and
huddled down to wait.

The sun was sinking low in the sky when at last Thane

and his men gave up the hunt. As he'd boasted, Lachlan had managed to elude them. Through the slats of the byre Gillian watched as the men gathered in the square.

"There is no sign of them, Thane," Duncan said. " 'Tis as I've told you. She disappears at will, like a ghost among the trees."

"But she is not a ghost, nor a witch," Thane snapped. His gaze raked the villagers and he raised his voice so all might hear. "A gold coin to any of you who bring me the witch."

Chapter 3

THANE RODE AHEAD of his men. So close! He'd come so close to having Gillian within his grasp. For one instant he'd glimpsed her fleeing from the village, her black hair flying behind her like the glossy wings of a raven. He'd seen her pause and look over her shoulder, her face pale with fear, her green eyes wide and startled as they met his. He'd heard the villagers calling out accusations of her witchcraft, of the spell put upon the child, and he hadn't believed it, couldn't believe it, for he remembered the gentleness of her touch on his fevered brow. Such gentleness would not turn to wickedness against a helpless child. So he'd reminded the mother, who'd stopped her wailing. The child had quieted herself and clung to her mother's neck, no more the worse for her experience.

Somewhere in the Forest of Glenartney sat Hannah's cottage, and there she would be if he could but find his way back. Why could he not? Was this in itself part of the bewitchment? Thane cursed beneath his breath and strove to push her from his mind, but she would not go. His nostrils quivered with the remembered scent of her hair, his fingers tingled to touch her satiny skin, his mouth hungered for her soft lips.

They'd spent the past two weeks riding to the holdings of neighboring clans, seeking an answer to the attacks on their villages and cattle. None of the clans admitted to being the perpetrator of such acts, and Thane was inclined to believe them. But if not neighboring clans, then who continued to ride out of the darkness, setting fire to cottages, killing families, and stealing Campbell cattle? The men had begun to mutter among themselves and offer their own opinions. The attacks had begun after Thane had been nursed by the witch. Catch the witch, they declared, and the raids would stop.

The men were silent as they made their way to Edinample Castle. Evening was falling across the land, painting the shadows on the distant hills a deep purple, while the sky sent its blazing red-orange rays across the horizon in one last, defiant display. The castle sat on a gentle knoll overlooking Loch Earn, its hammered stones softened by age, its regal lines undaunted by the passage of time. Once it had been the MacGregor stronghold; now it was one of the Campbell clan's outlying holdings. Built to hold back its enemies, Edinample's crenellated towers soared as majestic as the distant Highland hills. Thane could have made his home base at Kilchurn Castle, his familial holding, but something in the defiantly regal walls of the sturdy castle appealed to him.

"M'lord Thane!" A lookout hailed them from the wall. Lost in thought, Thane started and glared up at the man.

"Why do you bellow my name across the countryside?" he demanded. "Can you not wait until I've come inside and dismounted?"

A figure appeared beside the lookout, and a youthful face peered down at him. "Nay, cousin, quit yer foul temper," Aindreas Campbell called down. " 'Tis I who've set the lookouts t'warn me at first sight of you."

"Aindreas, why're you here?" Thane cried, his spirits lifting at once. He spurred Bhaltair toward the lowered gate and rode across in a thunder of hooves as his men followed. Aindreas had left the ramparts and gained the inner bailey by the time Thane drew his black stallion to a halt.

"Have you come to play a bit of mischief on us, cousin?" Thane demanded good-naturedly, dismounting to stand towering over the young man. As always, Aindreas was garbed in the latest fashion with a waist-length doublet of blue velvet and matching slops tied at the knee with fringed sashes. His striped hose were of bright yellow and black, and his black leather shoes sported silk rosettes on the toes. Thane bit back a grin.

"I'll wager your father's sent you here as punishment for mischief you've done." He slapped Aindreas on the shoulder in a manner of camaraderie, for he'd always liked his cousin.

Aindreas's brown eyes sparkled with good humor, and he impatiently patted an unruly auburn curl away from his face before nodding sheepishly. "There was a bit of outcry over who planted the seed in the belly of Farmer Drummand's birdie."

"Little Finola?" Thane remembered a gawky, long-legged child with enormous eyes in a thin face.

"Aye, Finola." Aindreas nodded. "She rounded out devilishly well. I was not the only rouge scratching at her gate, and Finola, bless her soul, fully enjoyed her new-found comeliness. Without a doubt she became rather bluffle-headed about her charms and shared them willingly enough. I honestly can't say the child she was about to bear would ha' been mine."

Thane shook his head. "Poor Finola!"

"Poor Finola, my arse!" Aindreas exclaimed. "She came out right enough for her waywardness. Father found her a suitable husband, much better than Drummand could ever have wrangled for her, and she's lordin' her new status over all the women in the village. I'm the one he's decided t'punish by sending me here to this godfor-saken outpost."

"Have a care, cousin, lest I take offense at you," Thane growled, though his eyes danced with blue laughter and he slapped his hand against Aindreas's shoulder in rough affection. "You can stay at Edinample, but only if you show proper respect for my home and if you promise any maiden you get with child won't have a sour father to raise objections. I've no need for more problems now."

"Edinample is a veritable jewel of a castle, cousin," Aindreas answered with the crooked smile that had charmed far too many village maidens and even a married woman or two. He clamped an arm around Thane's shoulders and walked beside him to the stables. "You're far too serious, cousin," he teased. "Didn't you ever find pleasure between a maiden's thighs simply because she was willing enough?"

"Aye, Aindreas, you're not the only libertine in the family, but I would not have my very life changed for such dalliances."

"Not all of us Campbells are set on gaining more land than we'll ever need," Aindreas answered.

Thane halted and whirled to face him, a stern rebuke on his lips, for this was not the first time Aindreas had dis-missed his calling so lightheartedly. Yet so open was the glow of good humor on the younger man's face, he didn't have the heart to argue with him. He clamped his shoulder.

"I will na debate you over this matter, Ain," he said. "No woman's worth more than a tumble between the sheets unless she brings land with her." A visage of Gillian's pale face mocked his words.

"I'll be sure to apprise Lady Juliana of your view when next I see her," Aindreas teased, falling into step beside Thane.

"You've seen Juliana, then?"

"Aye, I came by way of Cawder Castle."

"But why, man? That's far to the north."

Aindreas laughed, and turned his head to hide a blush. "Aye, but I did a favor for your mother, who sent an invitation to Sir Robert and his daughter. Besides, I'd a wish to see your bride-to-be for myself. When she and her father visited Kilchurn Castle in the spring, I found her to be a bonny lass indeed, though she's still little more than a child. At any rate, Sir Robert has agreed to stop by Edinample on his way to Edinburgh when your mother plans t'be here as well. I think I've imparted all of the family news. What of yerself, cousin? You look peckish. Have you been ill, or are you in need of a lassie or two yerself?"

"Enough talk of women." Thane stomped away, Aindreas following. With sure, quick movements he divested Bhaltair of his saddle and gear and began rubbing him down with clumps of hay. "How many men did you bring with you?" he asked.

"Only a handful," Aindreas replied nonchalantly.

"For your own safety you may want to keep them with you when you ride out," Thane advised. "We've had raiders and we don't know who they may be yet. They've burned out villagers and killed many."

"Raiders? Dear me." Aindreas stared at him with some consternation. "We may already have crossed paths with your raiders."

"What?" Thane demanded.

"We'd paused on the trail down near the Ample burn to water our horses and such, when we heard men moving through the woods. Naturally we fell silent and watched them pass us by. I thought them local men, except that they were taking some care not to make noise."

"Bigod, why didn't you tell me when I first arrived?" Thane demanded. "Which way were they headed?"

"East, toward Ben Earn," Aindreas said decisively. He'd grown up in the Argyll region and as a young boy tagged along after his cousin. "I had no glimmer of your problem or I would have ridden fast away t'let you know."

"Aye, I'm sure you would have," Thane agreed, and turned to bellow to his men. "Duncan, saddle up. We ride again. Aindreas has given us our first direction to the mysterious raiders." He turned back to his cousin, who stood with his mouth gaping. "What plaid were they wearing?"

"None that I was that familiar wi'," Aindreas confessed. " 'Twas of a red color changing to a deep wine and striped in green."

"The MacNabs wear such a plaid," Duncan said. He'd come to join them during Aindreas's description.

"Aye, and if the raiders were heading north toward Ben Earn, they came from the south and the MacNab holdings," Thane said, his lips tightening with anger. "Do you ride with us, Aindreas?"

"I would not miss this even for another tumble with Finola herself," Aindreas cried gamely, and ran after the two men as they went to saddle their mounts.

"We'll ride toward Ben Earn in case the raiders have thoughts of attacking another unsuspecting village. If they're not there, we'll backtrack all the way to MacNab lands if we must." In little time the men were mounted and headed out of the castle walls, pushing their horses hard to make the most use of the waning light.

Aileen Tannoch was a goodly wife, though given to the vapors a bit and prone to whine about imagined illnesses. Her earlier beauty had quickly waned with the birth of her child, Lisbet, and so had her passion, which had seemed to her husband, Doire, to be lukewarm at best. Still, Doire loved his wife in the haphazard, careless manner of many men who've come to take their marriage and their mate for granted. He loved her for the good suppers she put on his table and the clean shifts she had ready for him every

Sabbath day. Most of all, he loved her because she'd given him Lisbet. He marveled at his child's beauty and delicacy. Philanderer though he might be, causing his wife unintentioned pain with his infidelities, Doire never wanted to do anything to hurt his daughter. By the same token, neither would he take lightly any event that threatened Lisbet's well-being.

So it was that when Aileen returned from market day and related to him the spell cast upon his beloved daughter by the witch, his face had blanched and he'd grabbed Lisbet up so fiercely that it frightened her to the point that she set about sobbing hard, and began to lose her breath and hiccup with the effort to regain it.

Speechless and enraged, Doire rushed from his cottage and sought out his friend, Farlane.

"We must stop the witch," Doire declared after telling the events of the afternoon.

"Aye, look what else she's done of late," Farlane cried. "My milk cow has given me no milk for a fortnight now. Only a witch could cause my faithful, my good Machara not t'give down her milk."

"We must stop her!" Doire repeated. "Are ye afeerd to go wi' me?"

Farlane blinked.

"I know where the witch's lair is. I've seen it when I've been in the woods. I'm going there to burn her out."

"Ye're going to burn her?"

" 'Tis the only way to stop the enchantment."

"But what of the gold coin the laird offered?"

"He dinna say we had to bring her t'him alive."

Farlane let the words sink. "Aye, he dinna."

"Will ye go wi' me, man?"

"Aye, and that I will, Doire."

The two men gathered up their axes, shovels, and flints and set off. Farlane was nervous and jumpy in the dark forest, for he seldom went there, and it seemed to hold endless mysteries. Doire had played there as a boy, trap-

ping hares and an occasional grouse for his family's
cookpot. Even at that he lost his way several times, and so
the moon had begun to wane when they finally stumbled
into the clearing before Gillian's hut.

"God's Passion," Farlane swore, and turned to run.
Only Doire's hand hard on his arm halted his headlong
flight.

"Good. There's no light," Doire said, peering through
the trees at the outline of the small, dark building.

"If the hunchback be in there with the witch," Doire
said at last, "then we'd best bar the door from without, so
neither can escape."

"Aye, good plan," said Farlane, who was perfectly content to let his friend take charge. "How ye going t'do it?"

"There's a tree stump back there aways," Doire
answered. "We can use that to block the door."

The two men tugged the stump forward into the small
clearing and set it against the door. "No one's coming out
of there," Doire whispered with satisfaction. "Gather
some kindling and lay it against the walls." They gathered
dried twigs and branches, then lit the brush and stood back
while hungry flames gained strength to race up the dried
vines clinging to the stone walls to the dry thatched roof.

"Thane, look yonder!" A glow lit the eastern sky.

"The bastards, they're burning Kirkcaldy," Thane
cried, and bellowed to his men to follow. Setting his spurs
against Bhaltair's sides, he urged the great stallion forward. Though they had already traveled a goodly distance
at a punishing pace, Bhaltair did not fail him. They
topped a ridge and thundered down on the burning village. Men and women scurried from well and spring with
staved buckets, trying their best to quench the flames.

"Thane, the raiders!" Aindreas shouted, pointing to a
distant ridge. Men on foot were climbing the mountains.

Thane reined Bhaltair to a halt. "Duncan, take half the

men and help put out the fires. Aindreas, you and your men follow me!" He spurred after the raiders fleeing through the fog.

Tirelessly Thane pushed his men onward, noting that the raiders seemed to have turned south toward MacNab lands. Deep in the Forest of Glenartney Thane cursed the weather that had proved so beneficial to their enemy. Suddenly the fog swirled away as if blown by the hot breath of some great mythical god. He could see the shape of the tree trunks now and the cushioned forest floor. He caught a movement from the corner of his eye and whirled. A lone man stood with drawn claymore held in both hands, his gaze fixed on Thane. His muscular shoulders were broad, his feet planted firmly on the ground as if he had readied himself against a rushing attack. The mist cleared enough so Thane could see the red of his beard and the plaid he wore.

"What clan are you, man?" Thane demanded. "And why did you burn my villages and steal my cattle?"

"Your villages? Your cattle?" the man called in a scoffing voice. "Are you a MacGregor, then?"

"Nay."

"My feud is not with the MacGregors," the man answered.

Thane felt the temper flare higher within him. "If you've a feud with me, then I would know the name of my enemy."

The stranger regarded him for a moment. "You'll know the name soon enough. In the meantime, you might call us"—he glanced around as if looking for a name—"children of the mist."

He bowed and leapt backward, and before Thane's very eyes seemed to disappear in the fog. Sword at the ready, Thane spurred Bhaltair forward, but search as he might, the red-bearded stranger had disappeared. Thane made his way back to his men.

"We'll never find them in this fog, Thane," remarked Aindreas.

"Aye, you're right." Thane nodded. "We'll bed down here tonight and try again in the morning. The men unsaddled their mounts and rubbed them down with moss, then rolled themselves in their plaids and lay down on the ground. Along with the lookouts he'd posted, Thane sat awake, thinking of the mysterious stranger and the "children of the mist" until exhaustion claimed him and he fell into a troubled sleep.

Danger! She was in danger! She should wake up and flee. She must not sleep, yet she was so tired, so tired. She couldn't breathe. Her heart beat wildly, as if she'd run a great distance and she was in the same place. She drew a deep breath, trying to draw air into her aching lungs, but the air was smoke-filled and made her cough. She tried to open her eyes, but something heavy lay on her lids. She was covered with a warm, heavy blanket that smothered her. She lashed out with her arms, trying to throw it off so she might breathe.

With a gasp she came awake and found the cottage was filled with smoke.

"Lachlan!" she cried out, leaping off her cot, but there was no answer. Above her head was the crackle of flames making a swift path across the dry thatch. The cottage was on fire! She had to get out. She ran to the door, but it wouldn't open. Even the shutters at the window wouldn't give beneath her frantic pounding. She was still dreaming, she thought wildly. Soon she would waken and the nightmare would be ended. But this was no dream, nightmarish as it seemed. She threw herself against the door. Something held it closed. The secret passage! She turned toward the cupboard that held the hidden passage, but fire had already claimed that side of the cottage. She was trapped. The door was the only way. Frantically she beat against it.

"Help me," she cried. "Is anyone out there? Help me, please."

"Listen! God's Passion, and it's the witch," Farlane whispered, and shivered with fear.

"Nothing can save her now. She'll na be puttin' any bloody spells on anyone again." The men fell silent, watching the hungry flames claim the cottage. "Listen to her scream," Doire said with some satisfaction, for despite his fears, he'd bested the witch after all.

"It fair gives me the chills down my back," Farlane muttered. "I'm leaving this unholy place." He turned and made his way back through the woods.

"Wait, ye goat's arse," Doire called, but he hurried to catch up with his friend. He had no wish to stay alone in the woods.

Thane lay still on his pallet. Something had wakened him, but he couldn't determine what, so he waited. There were no sounds; all was silent in the woods. Still, something wasn't right. It took him a while to realize that what had troubled his dreams and brought him awake was the smell of smoke. He raised his head and sniffed again. The smell was stronger now. He nudged Aindreas, who moaned and turned over.

"Do you smell something burning?" Thane muttered in a low voice.

"Nay, I was but caught up in a dream with a fair country maiden, and only the smell of her all ripe and sweet filled my nostrils."

"There's a fire out there somewhere," Thane said, leaping to his feet and grabbing up a weapon. "Mayhap our raiders have thought themselves safe enough to start a bonfire. Wake the men and be silent."

Aindreas was alert now and did as Thane ordered, instructing the men to take up their weapons and follow. They moved on foot through the forest. The smell of smoke became stronger.

"Look there, through the trees," Aindreas cried.

"Something's aflame, and it's not a bonfire."

Thane's sharp gaze caught a glimpse of two men moving away through the forest. "Halt," he cried out, and ran forward. Only when he neared the fire did he hear the screams and realize a cottage was ablaze.

"Someone's trapped inside," he cried, turning aside. He raced toward the door.

"Help me, please, help me. Holy Mary, Mother of God," came the cries from inside.

Thane wasted precious seconds trying to open the door before he discovered it was blocked. "Quick, give me a hand here," he called to his men, and the stump was tugged away. Thane flung open the door and flinched at the wave of heat that rolled over him. No one could be alive inside that inferno, he thought, yet remembered the faint cry for help. He moved forward, but a hand at his elbow halted him.

"You can't go in there," Aindreas cried. " 'Tis too late for the poor sot who's there."

"I have to try," Thane said, and flung off his cousin's hand. Taking a deep breath, he stepped inside the cottage. His eyes watered and he couldn't see. He blinked against the stinging smoke and finally saw a figure lying on the floor. Clad in a white shift, her black hair spread around her head like a dark halo, the girl he'd been searching for lay still as death. Her face was pale and lifeless.

A small flame reached with greedy fingers for the hem of her shift. She made no sound. Grief welled within Thane. Ignoring the flaming roof, he scooped up her limp form and blindly turned to the door. A shower of burning thatch rained down on them as he ran through the fire and reached the blessed cool air of the clearing. Hands slapped at their clothes and hair, putting out the flames that smoldered about them.

Thane lowered Gillian to the ground. Her lids, blue-veined and delicate, did not flicker. Her pale face was smudged now with soot. Her fingers curled delicately against her palm, making her seem all the more vulnerable.

"Is she alive?" he cried as Evan knelt and felt for a pulse in the slender throat.

"Nay, she's not breathing, Thane," he said softly. "The witch is dead."

Chapter 4

*T*HANE STARED AT the slight form on the ground. She could not be dead, not now, not when he'd just found her again! "No!" he bellowed. He raised his fists to the sky, his face contorted by fury. "You cannot have her!" His defiance vanished as quickly as it was born, and he swayed over the motionless girl. She had saved his life. He had not been able to save hers. Beside himself with anger and grief, he laid his cheek beside hers.

"I'm sorry, lass," he whispered through a sting of tears. He slid his arms beneath her shoulders and lifted her up against his chest. Her hair, silken and glossy, tumbled over his arm and swept the ground. He stared at the delicate lines of pale features and felt like weeping at the loss of such beauty and gentleness. He was unaware of the tears that flowed unchecked down his cheeks.

His men saw and were dismayed at this sign of weakness in a chief who was so fierce and brave. They turned away, troubled at such a display of emotions over a woman he barely knew and one that was thought to be a witch. Her enchantment lasted even after death, they thought.

Thane's gaze was fixed on Gillian's face, and one big hand smoothed the glossy wings of hair from her temple. "I'm sorry, lass," he murmured over and over. Suddenly a small moan came from her throat. The men stared at her, thunderstruck. Thane seemed to be holding his own breath, willing her alive. Her body jerked, and with a sharp cry she gasped in air. Her lashes fluttered on her cheek but her lids did not open.

"She's alive!" Thane cried to them. "She breathes."

"Aye, she does," Aindreas answered. "What witchery is this that she can bring herself back from death's door?"

"Not witchcraft, Aindreas," Thane said sternly. " 'Tis a miracle from God himself. You're too young yet to have seen men thought dead on the battlefield come to life again."

" 'Tis so, I have not seen it for m'self, but I heard my father speak on it. Still, I cannot believe this is not some evil magic. I'm telling you, Thane, I felt for a pulse m'self and there was naught. She was dead."

"She is not dead now," Thane said pragmatically, "and we must get her back to the castle, where Shadwell can care for her."

"You'd take her t'the castle?" Aindreas said, shocked.

Thane ignored him. "We mount and ride," he ordered, and gently placed Gillian on his own bedroll while he saddled Bhaltair. Without waiting to see that his men were ready, he swung into his saddle.

"Hand the lass up t'me, Aindreas," he ordered, and despite his better judgment, Aindreas did as he was ordered. She was feathery light, almost ethereal. Before handing her up to Thane, Aindreas gazed upon her face and felt his heart stir within his breast.

"If you've looked yer fill," Thane growled, "hand her up to me." He bent low in his saddle, plucked Gillian from Aindreas's arms, and settled her against him, his strong arms forming a cradle for her shoulders. Her head rested against his chest.

Aindreas stared up at his cousin, his young face gone pale beneath its mop of sandy hair. "Leave her, Thane," he pleaded, although he knew full well his cousin would not. It was too late! The witch had claimed him, made him hers, and Thane was not even aware of it. Thane cast him a derisive look and nudged Bhaltair's sides. As the big stallion moved away, Aindreas crossed himself, uttering a litany of prayer.

The sweetness of her! Thane stared down at her. She must be a witch to ensnare him like this, he thought, and knew he would willingly surrender to her spell if he could but continue tasting her lips and explore the slim body with all its mysteries.

So caught up was he in his fantasies that it took him a moment to realize that she'd opened her eyes and was gazing at him in puzzlement.

"You!" she whispered. "How did you come to be here?" She looked around and sat up in alarm. "Where am I?" Her eyes flashed with terror.

" 'Tis my castle. You're safe here." Thane began to reassure her, but her expression remained fearful and she looked around frantically, her dark curls swirling over her face and shoulders. In her distress the green of her eyes was nearly black.

"Lachlan!" she cried out with such pain that Thane felt alarm.

"Who is Lachlan?" he inquired, but she was too panic-stricken to speak. Thane took hold of her shoulders, all too aware of the warm softness of her beneath the shift.

"Who is Lachlan?" he repeated, shaking her slightly. The panic left her face.

"Lachlan is—is my friend," she stammered.

"Was he there in the cottage with you?"

"No, I don't think so. He didn't come home last night."

Thane relaxed. He hadn't seen anyone else in the cottage. The flames and smoke had obscured his vision, yet he felt certain she'd been alone in the hut.

"Do you know where Lachlan is now?"

Slowly she shook her head. "He didn't come back after the villagers chased us," she said. "I don't think he was captured by them. He's far too clever."

"He is, huh?" Thane grunted, studying her face. She seemed to set great store by this Lachlan. He twinged at a feeling he'd never known before. "I'll have my men keep an eye out for him," he offered.

"It will do no good," she said. "If he doesn't wish you to see him, you won't."

"He's that good, is he?" Thane said, and couldn't repress a grin. This enchanting creature was alive and here in his castle, in the bedchamber next to his very own, and he knew with a certainty deep in his soul that within a fortnight his fantasies about her would become realities. She stared back at him, then blushed, obviously uncomfortable at his scrutiny.

"Are you hungry?" he asked, taking up a cup of broth left warming on the hearth.

She shook her head, her gaze darting to his broad shoulders, then to his long, straight legs. In a dream she'd rested against those shoulders and ridden through the forest on the back of a great black beast. It had been a beautiful dream, and she hadn't wanted to waken from it.

He spooned a portion of the broth into another cup and crossed the room to stand by her bed. She realized she'd been staring at him overly long and lowered her lashes, fixing her gaze on her hands, where they twisted in her lap.

After an awkward moment Thane sat on the edge of the bed and took up the spoon to feed her. Never had he done such a thing in his life, but to do so now seemed right.

"You're very kind, m'lord," she whispered, "but I canna swallow. My throat is too painful."

"That's from the smoke," he said, setting aside the broth and pouring a glass of wine. "Sip this. I promise it will take away the pain." When she hesitated, he held the cup to her lips, tipping it so she was forced to drink. A rivulet of wine escaped, ran down her chin, and dripped on the white shift just above her breasts. Glancing down, she saw how clearly her breasts were outlined, how boldly her nipples pressed against the thin cloth. Gasping, she crossed her arms over her chest.

Her cheeks were flushed, her eyes emerald green when she glanced up from beneath her lashes to see if he'd noticed. Discerning her modesty, Thane looked away, pretending to be absorbed in setting down the wineglass and taking up the broth again.

"And now, lass, ye must eat something," he admonished her, and held out a spoonful of broth. Unable to move without revealing herself, Gillian made no protest, but obediently opened her mouth.

Slowly, tenderly, he fed her, and so warm and solicitous was his gaze, so natural his tone and words, she soon relaxed in her vigilance and even forgot to cross her arms a couple of times, so he was afforded yet another tantalizing glimpse of her primly covered bodice. He thought of Bridget and how boldly she displayed herself and could not help but smile indulgently at this beautiful lass's shyness.

He'd never met a wench who blushed so easily. Yet her green eyes held sparkling depths when she chanced to raise her dark lashes and meet his gaze. There was a refreshing naïveté about her. She'd had little contact with other people, he perceived, and certainly with men. By the gods, she must be virginal! He drew back and gazed at her so fiercely, she shivered.

"M'lord. Have I done something wrong?" she cried.

"Nay, nay, lass," he said. But he remembered her anguish when she'd called out for Lachlan. Was Lachlan a lover? Better if it were so. He had no wish to seduce a virgin, and seduce this wench he intended with all the expertise and skill at his disposal. So what of Lachlan? Was he a suitor, a guardian who would one day call Thane out for dallying with this bewitching creature?

Nay, she'd called him a friend, but she'd blushed and stammered when she said it. Was she promised to him?

"Is Lachlan a suitor?" he inquired more abruptly than he'd intended, for he perceived that if he were to woo this shy creature, he must do so gently, patiently. She gazed at him, her eyes filled with alarm at his tone. He smiled to allay her fears and was rewarded with a tentative response that lit her face into a thing of blazing beauty so that he caught his breath and stared at her, mesmerized.

"Ah, lass," he murmured. "If 'tis so he is your suitor, I shall have to fight him for your favor, and so I shall."

"Nay, m'lord," she cried, growing alarmed again. "You must not fight Lachlan. He is but a poor cripple, unable to defend himself, although he'd be hurt to hear me say such. I fear one day, in his attempt to protect me, he will bring disaster to himself."

Ah, the hunchback! Thane considered her words and smiled at the realization that Lachlan would not be a rival for this beauty's affections. "I vow he'll come to no harm at my hands, dear lady," he said, taking her hand and bringing it to his lips. Though delicate, her slender hand was roughened and work-worn. She had not lived the life of a lady, he guessed, which led him to consider several other problems.

"I'm afraid all your belongings burned in the fire," he said. "I'll have Bridget look for something for you."

"Thank you, m'lord," she said softly. "You've been most kind to me."

"I but return the favor of my life, lass," he reminded her. "Do you know who set the fire?"

Dark brows drew downward over her eyes and she shook her head. "I don't know. I may have dreamed that I heard two men whispering outside the cottage." She frowned. "They spoke of collecting a gold coin promised them if they captured the witch."

Thane cursed at his own foolishness. He should have guessed such an offer would bring outrageous measures by greedy men intent on receiving such a coin. His offer had been meant to aid in finding her, instead, he'd nearly cost her her life.

"You may stay here at Edinample Castle as long as you wish," he said.

"Only until I'm feeling better, m'lord," she said firmly. "Perhaps tomorrow I'll be strong enough to go on my way."

"Nonsense, I insist you are to stay here," he said with such an air of authority that she held her tongue and did not argue. Believing he'd won the argument and seeing the droop of her lashes, he rose and placed the empty cup on a side table. "I'll leave you now so you may rest."

"Thank you, m'lord." Sliding down, she pulled the coverlet up to her chin. Her green eyes were wide and compelling as she gazed at him.

"I would have you call me Thane, as you did when you nursed me," he said softly, his blue eyes warm as a summer sky.

"Thane!" she repeated. "I can't, m'lord. I—I—you're a great laird, a chief. 'Twould not be seemly."

"Didn't you call me Thane before?"

"Aye, but I didn't know then that you were such a great laird."

"No?" His gaze pinned her, made her squirm. She had to look away.

"Well, yes," she admitted, her voice small. "But you were wounded and helpless. You didn't *seem* like a great laird then."

He leaned over the bed, his broad hands planted on either side of her, his strong, muscular arms holding him mere inches from her. "Nay, Gillian, I'm not a great lord when you're about. I'm as helpless as a babe mewling at his mother's teat," he said in a voice strangely guttural, as if it were hard for him to admit such things. "You truly are a witch."

His accusation might have frightened her, for she knew such words only brought death. Hannah had warned her of the dangers, reciting the tales of women forced by torture of the cruelest sort to confess witchery and then were burned in spite of their innocence. But she felt no fear of harm from this man. She was all too aware of the lean, hard body poised just scant inches above her own. Images of that golden body beneath her healing hands came to her, and she swallowed.

His eyes darkened, holding promises and mysteries and something else she could not name, but it awakened a response in her like the great rushing of a bird in flight. Her body ached from it, her breasts and groin tingling in a way that brought first pleasure, then a sweet yearning. She was far more sickly than she realized, she thought fleetingly, and then she became mired in the prisms of his gaze and could not think again. Her whole body felt feverish.

"I—I fear I am not yet recovered from events, m'lo— Thane," she whispered, putting a hand to her brow, for she could not bear to gaze into his eyes and feel the urgent longing aroused by his nearness. He drew back and stood smiling down at her.

"Rest well, lass," he murmured. "We'll talk again when you're well."

Swallowing hard, she nodded and watched as he left the room.

To walk away from her, all soft and womanly in the warmth of her bed, was much harder than anything Thane had ever done. He'd longed to throw aside his garments and stretch out on the bed with her, to cradle her body against his and watch the greenness of her eyes turn to black as he taught her the delights between a man and a woman, for he was certain now she did not know such things.

Thoughts of her, the sound of her voice, the heated smoothness of her skin beneath his fingers, the sweetness of her lips, stayed with him as he descended the stairs and gave orders to his men. Not only did he intend to patrol his borders, he wanted to find the men who'd sentenced Gillian to such a cruel death.

"First to Tayside," he shouted, and led the way on Bhaltair. The village was only a few short hours' ride from Edinample. Men and women glanced up in surprise as Thane and his men galloped through the streets. Thane entered the square and brought Bhaltair up short while he gazed around. Not one villager came forward to offer him goods or a greeting. There was a furtive air about them all.

"They already know that you've taken the witch t'the castle," Duncan said beneath his breath.

"How could they?" Thane demanded.

"They know everything that takes place here."

"Then they'll know who set the fire in the forest." He edged Bhaltair forward and looked around the square. "Hear ye all," he called. "Last night a fire was set in the Forest of Glenartney. A woman who once saved my life was nearly killed. Even now she recovers at my castle. I would have the names of the men who set this fire."

Once again his gaze swept around the square while he waited for someone to speak up. The villagers were silent, their eyes cast down to their rough, muddy boots.

"Come now, there's a reward in it for any man who'll speak up about what he knows." Still no one spoke, but at one cottage poorer than the rest a woman threw an apron over her head and turned aside. Her small daughter clung to her skirts. Thane remembered the woman from the day before, but his gaze didn't linger on her.

"The reward is there for whoever remembers something," he said, and motioned his men away from the square, marking well the cottage where the woman and her daughter lived.

"They won't give up one of their own," Duncan said as they rode away from the village.

"Aye, well I know," Thane answered. "But I think I can guess who's guilty of such a crime. Tonight I want you and Evan to ride quietly into the village. Go to the third cottage on the east side of the square. There you'll find a woman and child. Leave them be, but bring the man of the family to me at the castle."

"Do you think it's wise to pursue him? To the villagers he's no doubt a protector for trying t'kill the witch."

"She's no witch, Duncan, and I'll not have her called one again. You may call her Gillian, for that is her name."

"And of what clan is she, laird?" Duncan dared to ask.

Thane's expression lost some of its belligerence, and he sighed. "I don't know what clan claims her. I know only that she's a fair lass who saved my life. Can I do less than repay the favor by protecting her from those who would harm her? You saw the way the doors and windows had been blocked. Whoever set that fire meant to burn her alive."

"That's what is done to witches," Duncan said, then shifted his feet at his laird's glare. "I only meant they obviously thought her a witch t'want t'burn her like that."

"Aye, 'tis true," Thane acknowledged. "And they'll not rest as long as they think she's alive and helpless. I will become her guardian, Duncan. I can hardly do less. And any man who seeks to do her harm will answer to my sword. I want that fact made known to all throughout Argyll."

"I'll see t'it, Thane," Duncan said, and set his jaw so that he might not say more. He dropped back to speak to the troops of Highlanders who followed, but in reality to give himself a chance to chew on the words he'd not been able to utter to his chief. Thane understood and rode alone at the front of the column.

He had his own thoughts, and they were all of Gillian. Everything about her was a mystery, but Duncan had raised a very good question. Where had she come from? She hadn't sprung from the loins of Old Hannah, and whatever poor, misguided soul who might have mated with her. Hannah had been past childbearing age when his father was a young rogue. No, Gillian was not Hannah's child. There was a fineness to the lines of her face and figure, and her wit was quick, indicating a ready intelligence. She was not of lowly birth.

Who was she, then? What clan name did she claim? How had she come to live in the woods with Hannah? He had to put these questions to Gillian herself, he decided, and pressed forward more quickly.

He was delayed first with the needs of his villagers who'd suffered at the hands of the raiders and then by the apprehension and questioning of the two men Duncan brought to him that night. Impatiently he ordered the men taken to Edinample and there, in a rage, ordered them strung up from the castle ramparts.

"Thane, you can't do this t'yer people. They acted in good faith," Duncan argued.

"There is no good faith in burning someone alive. They set a gruesome fate for the girl, and now I would have them suffer as well so she might see them and rejoice."

"Please, m'lord," Doire sobbed, falling on his knees in the dirt of the bailey. "I didn't act out of evilness. My child, my wee little Lisbet, was put under the witch's spell. I sought only t'free her, m'lord. I am not an evil man. I work hard, I try to be a good husband and father and I serve you, m'lord, with all the loyalty I possess. Please, m'lord. Have mercy on me. Who will take care of my good wife and my little daughter? Who?"

Thane tried not to be moved by the man's words, but he heard within them the same desire to protect loved ones that he felt within his own breast. Yet he could not back down before his men and appear too lenient. He glared at the two men.

"Hang them!" he snapped. Doire's eyes widened. Farlane began to sob. Thane stalked away, but over his shoulder he called final instructions: "Hang them by their heels."

Gillian woke from her long, restful slumber and lay watching the low, slanting rays of the sun make a pattern over the floor. It seemed very strange to waken in a place other than her simple cot in the hut. She gazed around at the elegant furnishings. Something about the room reminded her of a time long ago, a time she'd tried hard to forget. Hannah had told her she must forget or face being branded or hanged as her father ... She thrust the memory from her. She would not think of that horrible morning when she'd stood watching the bright sun rise over the rugged peaks of Ben Earn and heard the last choking gasps of the men who had ruled her world. If such powerful men could be so easily destroyed, their very existence wiped from the face of the earth as if they'd never been, then what dangers awaited her, a small, powerless child. She had heeded Hannah's warnings well.

Shaking aside her melancholy thoughts, Gillian leapt out of bed, pulled the thick dressing gown over her thin shift, and stepped into a thick pair of padded leather slippers several sizes too large. The velvet dressing gown was meant for a man, obviously Thane Campbell, for the arms hung over her hands.

Shuffling to the window, she threw open the shutters and gazed down on the bailey below. At first the sinking sun, brilliantly golden, was blinding after the darkness of the bedchamber, but she blinked against its glare and soon her sight adjusted so she could see the details of the castle walls and the bailey. As she took in the sight of the familiar stone walls and thatched roofs, a numbing horror filled her.

She knew this place, knew the grassy slope of the middle bailey, the towers, and the gateways to the lower and upper baileys. She'd climbed up on the parapets and dared walk their edges to the terror of her father and nursemaid. She'd collected pigeons' eggs and watched the blacksmith until he'd sent her scurrying away. She'd even played on the drawbridge though it was forbidden, and every morning upon rising she'd sat in this very spot and watched the activities below, eager to be on her way and join all the castle workers who were her friends and greeted her cheerily, although before the day was out they knew they'd shout at her for being in their way. Edinample, her home. She was home!

A smile curved her lips, and tears slid down her cheeks as she thought of those happy days so long ago. So caught up was she in her memories, she didn't at first notice the cluster of men who rode into the bailey below. She was unaware of their presence until she heard a man scream and saw two bodies being pulled through the air to dangle on ropes from the ramparts. Then the memories she'd tried so hard to repress came back to her, memories of the day the king's soldiers had come and arrested her father. Angus MacGregor and his men had been promised clemency by the king and so had laid down their arms and gone to Edinburgh, but in the end they were brought back to Edinample and hanged from the ramparts. That was the last time she'd seen her father. Hannah's words came back to her:

"You've enemies here, child, greedy men who take what they want and they'll not take no for an answer. If they can't get what they want one way, they do it another. Never forget, child, the Campbells are yer enemies, and should you ever find yerself caught in their snare, run. Run as fast as you can, for they mean you no good."

Thane Campbell owned Edinample now, which meant he and his clan had caused her father's death and the transfer of his clan's holdings to the Campbells. The handsome giant who'd towered over her that morning, with his easy smile and flashing blue eyes as innocent and candid as a summer sky over the loch, was her enemy. That smile merely hid some evil intent toward her. In her confused mind the dangling figures became her father, and he hung not by his heels but by his neck. The terrors had begun again! She must escape, she must! The shrieks of the men in the bailey fed her terror. She turned to run, became entangled in the thick velvet folds of the long dressing gown, and went sprawling across the floor.

Lurching to her feet, she flung off the encompassing gown and padded slippers. On bare feet she crept out of the room, pausing to listen for sounds of anyone approaching before proceeding. Instinctively she knew the way through the twisting corridors and down the twisting stairs. She knew the niches where a child or a small woman might hide from servants moving about on their business, and she knew how to leave the castle without using the main gates. Hundreds of times she'd slipped away from her nursemaid's watchful eye to go wandering alone in the woods or along the banks of the River Ample. She took that way now and turned eastward toward the Forest of Glenartney only when she was well away from the castle. If she could make the forest, she would be safe. She knew how to hide there. She hugged her arms about her, for already the evening shadows were touching the hollows and a chill lay over the land. Her thin shift would be little protection against the coming night. She shivered. Even freezing was better than being prisoner to the hated Campbells.

Chapter 5

"MAN, HOW COULD a wee small lass like her get past without being seen?" Thane stormed at Eanruig Shiels, the captain of his castle guards. When his anger had cooled over Doire and Farlane, he'd ordered them hauled down from the ramparts and released. They'd limped away toward Crieff, casting hasty glances over their shoulders. Thane had finally sought out Gillian, but she was not in her room, and upon inquiry he'd found she'd vanished. The castle and grounds had been searched, but she'd disappeared without a trace.

"M'lord, I tell you, she didn't leave by either gate. My men would have tried to stop her and they would have reported it t'me," Eanruig asserted.

"I can't believe no one saw her," Thane answered, stalking back and forth across the great hall with angry strides. He'd thrown aside his doublet and weapons and was clad only in his linen shirt and plaid. Eanruig Shiels regarded his laird's broad shoulders and forbidding expression and tried not to show his dismay. He'd seen Thane Campbell toss a man twice his size over those shoulders. He knew the strength and energy in that huge body when the chief was roused to anger, as he seemed to be now.

"What of the servants?" Aindreas cut in. He'd been

silent to this point, quietly sipping his ale and regarding his cousin's display of bad temper. "Didn't they see anything?"

"They claim they didn't, blast them!"

"M'lord." Eanruig spoke up tentatively. "My men have even now moved beyond the castle walls and are searching the hills beyond. We're bound t'find her. There's no place else for her to go."

"Aye, there is," Thane snapped, whirling to face his man. "She may have tried to flee back to her home."

"The hut?" Aindreas asked in some doubt. "But it's a burnt-out shell and no good t'anyone."

"Aye, but she may not be considering that," Thane said, striding across to the fireplace and strapping on his claymore.

"Thane, why not let her go if she's of a mind t'return t'the only life she knows? T'take her away from it against her will seems a cruel way to repay your debt to her."

Thane chose to ignore Duncan. "We'll search for her there in the direction of the Glenartney forest." Without waiting to see if they followed, he hurried out of the hall and strode toward the lower bailey, where the stables were located. He made no notice of the commotion that arose behind him.

"M'lord!" Eanruig ran after him. "They've found her!"

Thane whirled and faced his panting captain. "They've found her? Where, man? Don't keep me in suspense."

"Well, they have not actually found her yet," Eanruig stammered upon seeing the eager look on Thane's face. "They've found footprints leading away from the bridge gate. 'Tis only a matter of time."

Thane's face darkened with anger so that Eanruig stood stiff to keep from flinching. Thane seemed not to notice him. His gaze was turned toward the castle gates. "Aye, 'tis only a matter of time. Lead the way, Eanruig." He clamped a hand on Eanruig's shoulders and eagerly turned to the stables, where Bhaltair was already saddled and waiting for him.

They found her footprint along the riverbank, a delicate mark of her passing that might have gone unnoticed except for the sharp eye of one of the Highlanders.

"Ach, she goes barefooted," Thane noted in some alarm. He raised his shaggy golden head to study the path ahead, his eyes narrowed and unblinking. Carefully he followed the trail, sometimes losing it, sometimes finding an unexpected print on some crushed moss or in the soft mud of the bank. He lost the trail for a while and had to double back. His men spread out in an ever-widening circle, until Aindreas sighted a torn fragment of linen on a gnarly branch.

"She's heading toward the forest, as you predicted, cousin," Aindreas observed when Thane had dismounted to examine the torn cloth.

"Aye, and 'tis growing dark," Duncan said, casting a look at the lowering sky. A mist was moving down from Ben Earn. "We'll not find her in this."

"So I fear," Aindreas remarked.

"If she has no shoes and no warm plaid, she'll suffer mightily this night," Thane said. "We'll go on looking for her." He turned in the direction of Glenartney, unable to end the search, though he felt it was hopeless. His men cast uneasy glances at one another, loath to follow him into the mysterious forest at night, yet not one of them would turn back to the comfort and safety of Edinample, for they could not bear to have their chief consider them cowardly. They rode their horses into the forest's dark interior and soon had to dismount and walk, leading their horses behind them. So black was the night, they could not see the trees looming ahead and feared injuring their valuable steeds or themselves.

"Thane, we must pause for the night. We could pass her by without knowing it," Duncan called, and finally Thane had to heed his friend's advice.

"We'll camp here," Thane ordered. "Build bonfires and keep them burning high throughout the night. She might be out there close by and see them."

With some relief the men hurried to find wood and build the fires as directed, for the heat would drive away the chill and any forest creature who might be intent upon mischief. Restlessly they settled themselves on the ground and fell into slumber. Thane lay tense and anxious far into the night, recalling his last conversation with Gillian and wondering what he'd done or said to frighten her so, she had to run away.

She had never been afraid of the forest, but this part of Glenartney was strange to her. For all her wanderings in search of plants, she'd never come this far, nor had she ever roamed at night. The green-gold rays of sunlight shining through the branches had formed great gleaming arches and made her think fancifully that the Forest of Glenartney was God's own personal cathedral. Therefore she'd always walked in awe and humbled respect that she was allowed to set foot there.

But now dark shadows gathered around the twisted trunks and a mist moved among the boughs, bringing darkness that much sooner. The thought came to her that this was not a place of God, but then, hadn't he made all of Glenartney just as he had made all of Scotland? She tried to take comfort in that, to utter a prayer to reassure herself and God that her faith was absolute, even though it was taught at the knee of a woman everyone else considered a witch.

Gillian remembered the tales of witches and fairy people who lived in the woods and worked their evil deeds on unsuspecting trespassers, so she moved cautiously, trying to bring her terrified thoughts to the task of determining the direction back to the hut. Burnt out as it must surely be, the stone walls would afford her some protection.

The cold mists settled around her shoulders, and she shivered as with the ague while her brow was fevered. Her breath came in short gasps and her chest ached with the effort. She'd not given herself enough time to recover from breathing the smoke of the fire, she thought dimly, then wondered what else she could have done. She had been in the hands of the greedy Campbells, the enemy of her clan. She'd had no choice but to flee.

Still, moving through the dense black forest in the cold night was an ordeal far greater than she'd imagined. Many times she stumbled over a root and fell sprawling onto the ground. Her bare feet were bleeding from the scrapes they'd sustained, and each step was agony. She pressed on, shivering in her thin shift. The mist had dampened the fine linen so that it clung to her body in clammy folds that only added to her misery.

What was she to do? she thought numbly. Whom could she turn to when all in the world seemed intent on harming her? Even the Campbell warrior with his kind words and soft touches that set a fire racing through her veins had proved to be her enemy. Aye, he most of all was her enemy, for what would he do if he learned her true identity? Yet how sweet to be at Edinample once more.

She pushed the thought aside and pressed on, becoming more hopelessly lost. Finally, in that dark hour before dawn when the cold lies over the land more cruelly than at any other time, she stumbled to her knees and could find no more strength to go on. With a groan of despair she crawled to a mossy place beneath a mammoth oakwood tree and curled up against its trunk, her knees drawn up for warmth, her weary head resting on them. Before a minute had passed, her eyes closed and she slept, finding comfort and warmth at last.

She woke with a thirst such as she'd never known before. Forcing herself up on shaky legs, she stumbled to a tiny burn and drank deeply, but the water did not quench her thirst. Catching a glimpse of her reflection in the eddying stream, Gillian was startled to see her pale face and leaf-matted hair. She blinked, thinking her vision would clear, for even her eyes felt hot and feverish. Each breath she drew came with a gasp and a cutting pain in her chest. Such was the way of it for Hannah before she died.

Suddenly, lying alone on the side of the burn, too weak to rise and help herself, Gillian wept, for she didn't want to die, not there in the great forest where no man might find her and where the crows or some great beast might feed upon her. But even the weeping weakened her, so she closed her lids against her aching eyes and drew a deep, painful breath. The sounds of the forest faded from her consciousness. The burn tumbled over her outstretched hand and ran merrily on its way.

Thane and his men had risen at first light and renewed their search, covering the ground inch by inch at times, searching for a small footprint, a scrap of linen, a black hair caught in a branch, anything to show a slender young girl had passed that way, but there was not a sign of her.

" 'Tis impossible, Thane. We'll never find her." Aindreas paused beside him and wiped the sweat from his brow. Though the night had been devilishly cold, the day had warmed with the rays of the sun. "The forests are too big, and some beast might have claimed her by now, either that or she's made her way back to that burnt-out hut."

"Nay, she's not had time to travel that far yet," Thane said. "She's here somewhere in this part of the forest. I can feel her nearby. Tell the men to keep searching."

Thoughtfully Aindreas looked at his cousin. Never had he seen Thane in such a dither. They searched through the afternoon, pausing only to rest the horses and eat the last of the cold bannocks they'd brought with them.

Thane looked at the slanting sun. "Only a few hours of daylight left," he observed with a sense of panic. "She'll not last a second night without shelter or warm clothing."

"Mayhap she didn't want us t'find her," Duncan pointed out.

"Why, man? She'd have no reason to flee from us. She seemed well content to be at Edinample. Something happened to cause her to flee." Thane rose impatiently and prepared to mount Bhaltair. The sound of rustling in the brambles brought him up short.

"Who goes there? Come out!" he demanded, drawing his claymore and setting his feet. His thoughts flew back to that other time, when he'd relaxed his guard and been wounded by the boar. Now he waited to see what emerged from the wooded cover. At his command Duncan and Aindreas sprang to their feet, drawing their swords and running to stand beside him. The low brush rustled again.

"If you don't come out, I'll run you through with my blade," Thane warned, and with those words uttered, the bushes parted and a hunchbacked dwarf pushed forward, his chest out, his chin raised in a show of bravado.

"Ye don't scare me," the hunchback bragged. "Ye'd have t'catch me first before ye run me through." He flipped over in a somersault and disappeared behind a tree.

Duncan looked at Thane and ran to search behind the tree. "He's not here," he shouted, turning one way and then the other, as if he expected the little man to leap up behind him.

"That's because I'm over here," a voice called, and the men swung around to the other side of the campsite. The dwarf grinned arrogantly. "See, ye can't run through what ye can't catch."

"Do you know the woman called Gillian?" Thane demanded.

"Aye, m'mighty Laird Campbell. I know her well," the man answered smugly.

"And what are you called?" Thane asked.

"D'ye wish my given name or what the villagers call me when they chance to see me?"

"I'll have your name," Thane said without a flicker of pity in his cool blue gaze.

Satisfied by the laird's manner, the dwarf nodded once again. "I'm named Lachlan of Badenoch of the Clan Cuimean, a once-proud old clan that was broken by Robert the Bruce himself."

" 'Tis a pleasure to make your acquaintance, Lachlan of Badenoch. Now, tell me do you know the whereabouts of the woman known as Gillian?"

The dwarf studied them with a wary gaze, his red-brown eyes of the same color as his beard and hair. "Aye, I know where she be," he answered slowly, and his humor was gone. His misshapen face grew serious. Impatiently Thane took a step forward, and instantly the little man jumped backward.

"God's Passion, man, will you tell me? Where is she? Is she well? Did she find shelter?"

"Why d'ye wish t'know these things about a simple lass from the woods?" the little man asked, belligerent now that he was being pressed to reveal her whereabouts.

"I rescued her from her hut when men sealed her in and set fire to it, and I took her to Edinample, where I left her to recover. But something spooked her, for she fled from the castle yesterday and we can't find her."

"And ye've had all these men out here searching for her?" the dwarf asked in some surprise.

"Aye! She saved my life. I owe her the same," Thane answered.

Lachlan looked up at the towering Campbell chief. Such a man he had yearned to be, with long, sturdy legs and a powerful body and a keen wit. He took his time measuring the man's character before he finally nodded.

"I'll show ye where she be. She spent a poor night of it in the forest and she's come down with the fever. I'm feared she'll not make it."

"Take me to her," Thane demanded, and mounted and gazed down at the bowlegged dwarf with the ugly face. The eyes that gazed back at him were filled with intelligence and a fierce pride born of years of mockery and rejection. Thane held out his hand to the little man. "Take hold," he ordered. "You'll ride behind me."

The dwarf hesitated for only a moment as if disbelieving of such kindness, then without any help from Thane he leapt up on Bhaltair's back. "Turn toward the sun," he directed, and grasped the belt at Thane's waist to steady himself.

With Lachlan leading the way, they rode through the dense forest until they came to the site of a small burn rippling through the tangled roots and stones. On its banks Gillian lay still and pale in her tattered shift, her hair spread around her matted and tangled. Her feet were bruised and torn. Thane lifted himself out of the saddle before Bhaltair had come to a complete stop and ran to kneel beside her. Gently he raised her head, his hand smoothing back the tendrils of hair and leaves.

"Gillian, lass," he murmured. "Are you alive, or have you gone to meet the shades of heaven?"

Lachlan had alighted from Bhaltair's back and stood staring at Thane as he bent over Gillian. For a man so large and overpowering, he was surprisingly tender, Lachlan noted with satisfaction. The gods had been kind in leading him to Thane Campbell.

Thane was unaware of Lachlan's scrutiny. He threw off his plaid and wrapped it around Gillian's slight figure, then carried her to Bhaltair and swung up in the saddle as effortlessly as if he carried no burden. Cradling her gently in his arms as he had done before, he turned toward Edinample. But when he'd gone a few yards he turned back in search of the dwarf.

"Duncan, see that Lachlan of Badenoch has a ride back to Edinample," he called.

"He's disappeared, Thane," Aindreas said, riding up to

join him. The two men sat looking around the forest. There was no sign of the small man, no flash of a red beard or a cheeky grin.

"Aye, so be it. He saved Gillian. That's the important thing."

"Aye." Aindreas nodded, looking at the pale face swaddled in the green and black plaid. The girl looked defenseless and utterly beautiful despite the dirt and scratches. He could see why Thane had lost his heart.

Silently they rode back to Edinample and reached the gates before nightfall. A stable boy came forward to take Bhaltair's reins and lead him away. For the first time in Bhaltair's existence, Thane did not tend to the black stallion's needs himself and Bhaltair jealously neighed his protest. Thane carried Gillian into the castle and up the stairs to the room she'd had before. Once again Shadwell was summoned and came, clucking his tongue and shaking his head.

"She has a fever," he said to no one in particular as he raised one of Gillian's eyelids and peered into her eye.

"Aye, and even I know that," Thane snapped. Shadwell cast him a jaundiced glance and remained silent while he continued to examine his patient.

"She'll not be waking up this night," Shadwell said. "So you might as well go on your way and let me make her better on my own."

"Nay, I'll not do that again," Thane protested. "The last time I did, she ran away."

"You need have no fear she'll do that tonight. She's too weak for much of anything. I'll give her some broth and yes, one of my remedies for the fever and we'll see how she does."

So offhanded was the physician's manner that Thane took offense and grabbed hold of his shirt. "She will live, will she not?" he demanded, his blue gaze piercing.

"I can't say for sure, Thane, and ye can't hold me to such a promise. She's weakened by her exposure t'the night air, and I fear she might suffer permanent damage to her lungs."

"Do something for her," Thane said, shaking the slight physician by his shirtfront.

"Aye, I'll do the best I can, Thane. That's all I can promise. It's what I'd do for you or your men. If you can't trust me after all these years—" He shrugged.

Thane released him. "I'm sorry, Shadwell," he muttered, turning away. "I don't know what's got into me since I first set eyes on this bit of a lass. The men think I'm bewitched, and mayhap I am, but I cannot bear the notion of her dying."

"With God's help, I'll do all I can," Shadwell said. Thane nodded and wearily left the room. After a quick meal he returned.

Shadwell looked up when Thane entered. He'd been packing his bag, preparing to leave the patient and order a servant to sit with her the rest of the night. Now he regarded his chief's expression.

"She's resting now, although she seems prone to have the night demons torture her."

"What do you mean? Is she in pain?"

"Not of the sort I can alleviate," Shadwell said. "The lass has had many a fright in her life, and tonight those come back to haunt her."

Thane regarded the slight figure on the bed. Except for the shiny ebony of her hair, she was as colorless as the bed linen. "Is she any better?"

Shadwell shook his head. "She might be better except for the demons."

"Have you nothing to drive them from her?" Thane demanded.

"Aye, and I've given it t'her. Still she rants in her sleep."

"She's silent now. Perhaps your potion works," Thane said hopefully.

"Morning will tell the tale." Shadwell snapped the lid

on his medicine chest and carefully locked it. "I was about t'go below for a bit of supper. I'll send a maid-servant up t'watch over her."

"Never mind," Thane said curtly. "I'll stay with her for a spell."

"You?" Shadwell asked in surprise.

"Aye. I've no mind to join the men in drinking and wenching tonight. I'll sit beside her."

"As you wish," Shadwell said, and picking up his case, quit the room.

Thane sat far into the night studying the clean, delicate lines of Gillian's profile, wondering what it was about her that drew him to her, that made him chase through the Glenartney forest in search of her and made him sit there mooning over her like a lovesick puppy. He'd never been a man to allow a woman that much importance in his life.

His first love had been Cora, one of his father's serving maids, a generous, fun-loving woman twice his age who'd taught him well the intricacies of passion between a man and a woman. He'd soon gotten over his infatuation for her and gone on to other women, younger, prettier, but never kinder or more entertaining than Cora had been. The only woman who had held his respect was his mother, Lady Joan, and Juliana Cawder.

He was a fool! He sprang to his feet, meaning to go to his own bed, when a cry sounded. Whirling, he gazed down at Gillian. She was still asleep but the serenity of her face was gone. Her features were drawn into an expression of horror and fear.

"Nay, nay," she cried out, thrashing with her arms. "Papa! Papa! I want Papa!"

Thane stepped to the bed and took hold of the slim shoulders, shaking her slightly. "Who is your papa?" he demanded. "I'll bring him to you."

Her hands fluttered to her lips as if to hold them shut. "I can't tell you," she whispered. "You'll hang him." Her eyes were wide open now, but he guessed she did not actually see him.

"Nay, Gillian, I will not harm your father. Tell me who he is."

Her eyes widened and she stiffened in his hands. "The flames," she cried, batting at herself with her hands. "I'm burning. I'm burning!"

"Nay, lass, you're safe here at Edinample. Nothing will harm you here."

"Edinample?" she whispered, staring at him. "I'm at Edinample Castle?"

"Aye. You're safe."

"No. I must leave here." She struggled to get out of bed. "Don't hold me here. I will surely die. I must escape to Glenartney. Please, I beg of you, let me go. Let me go!"

"Gillian!" Thane shook her slightly. "You're but dreaming. Wake up now and see that you're safe."

"The flames are burning me," she screamed, fighting against him. "Put out the flames."

"Here, lass, let me," Thane said, and slapped her clothes as she had done, then he pulled her against his chest. "There. The flames are out. Nothing can harm you now." He cradled her against his chest, smoothing her hair back from her flushed cheeks. "You're safe. I'll not let anything harm ye, lass."

"Papa, I was so frightened," she whimpered. "I dreamed they hanged you in the bailey below."

Thane was taken aback that she should mistake him for her father, and worse, that she'd misunderstood the harmless lesson he'd sought to teach her tormentor and his accomplice. He made no effort to set her straight, but he vowed to tell her the truth at the first opportunity.

"I'm here, lass," he murmured against her temple. His lips brushed her smooth skin, and a hunger grew from that touch. He kissed her brow, her cheeks, and finally took hold of her chin to raise her head so he might have access to her lips. He swirled his tongue against the soft petals, breathing in the scent of her, feeling the heat of her body against his. His own body responded with a need that was instant and more intense than any he'd ever felt before.

He wanted to taste her deeper, to tear away her clothes and taste her nipples, to kiss the valley between her breasts and lick a path down her velvet stomach to the juncture between her legs where he might taste the sweetest of fruits.

She whimpered in his arms, and he was reminded that she was feverish and half out of her mind. To take her then would be unthinkable, scurrilous. As great as his need, he could not take her like this, when she had no power to protest or to respond to him. Nay, he was not such a lout as to that.

Slowly he lowered her back onto the bed and sat beside her, smoothing her brow with his large, sun-browned hand and muttering wordless, soothing sounds that seemed to calm her fears. When at last she slept peacefully, he went back to his chair beside the fire and sat thinking of the woman Gillian. More than ever he wanted to know from whence she came. Who were her people? He would find out, he vowed. By all that was holy, he would know this woman's every secret before he was done.

Chapter 6

$\mathcal{S}$HE SHOULD RISE and flee, Gillian thought, but somehow over the past fortnight the urgency to do so seemed to have vanished. Nothing had changed except her own desire to run away. Thane, her gentle blond giant, came to her room morning and night to sit beside her bed and hold her hand and smooth her hair from her brow. Always he touched her and always his touch was gentle yet troubling, for it awakened uneasy responses within her that she knew she must deny with every fiber of her being. For this giant and his people were the instrument of her father's death and the destruction of their clan.

She rolled over in the wide bed and pulled the covers over her head. Her fingers brushed across the fineness of the linen coverings, enjoying the smooth feel. She was becoming far too used to such luxuries, she thought, and hated herself for being so frivolous, so easily seduced by the trappings of her enemy. She threw away the covers and rolled to her other side, yet her troubled thoughts pursued her.

The seduction was not being wrought by satiny sheets, she acknowledged, but by the warmth of a man's touch and the fervor of his gaze. Thane Campbell was casting a spell upon her, making her forget that she should fear and

74

hate him. His tenderness was but a ruse, she reminded
herself, for she'd seen evidence of his anger toward a servant who'd neglected her in his absence, and she'd heard
his voice below in the bailey, berating his men for their
failure in some duty. But most cruel of all was the
hanging of the village men. Yet the piercing gaze he was
capable of turning toward one in anger was always softened when he looked at her. And she? When she looked
at him her heart fluttered in her chest like a bird startled to
flight.

Flight! She must regain her strength and leave this
place. She gazed around the room, so dearly familiar.
Once the room had been hers, with her nursemaid
sleeping on a cot nearby and her father and his latest para-
mour sleeping in the next chamber. She had felt secure
there. She'd been happy as only a child can be. She'd
lived an enchanted life, abruptly ended.

Restlessly she threw aside the covers and rose on
unsteady legs. She would not regain her strength by lying
abed. She made her way across the room to the window
seat and sank down on the cushion. Throwing open
the mullioned windows, she leaned out and enjoyed the
breeze freshened by the loch. Sighing, she gazed at the
glitter of sunlight on water.

Tears filled her eyes and rolled down her cheeks. How
often she'd dreamed of Edinample and longed for it when
she first went to live with Hannah in the forest. At first
she'd been frightened of the dark forest and afraid to
leave the hut until Hannah had taken her by the hand and
led her out into the golden-green world of Glenartney.
Patiently the old woman revealed the wonders of that
forest world, and Gillian lost her fear and grew to love
that place nearly as much as she had Edinample, which
she'd very nearly forgotten.

But now, as she gazed at the loch in the distance, and
the rolling foothills, and beyond that the rising peaks of

Ben Earn, she felt a welling of passion and knew she'd never stopped missing her home.

Thane found her by the window, her gaze turned outward, her cheeks wet with tears.

"Why do you weep, lass," he asked tenderly, taking hold of a slender white hand in his own and smoothing tendrils from her cheeks. "Are you feeling poorly still?"

Unable to speak, her heart was so torn, Gillian merely shook her head. "I weep for the men you hanged from the castle wall," she whispered finally, and he had no notion she spoke of her father and his officers. He chuckled and her head came up, her eyes wide with outrage.

"Do you find it humorous to take a man's life, m'lord?"

"Nay, lass, if that were what happened, but I did not take those men's lives, though they well deserved it, for they were the men who set fire to your hut."

"But I heard their screams as they dangled above the bailey."

"Think well, lass. If they were hanged by their necks, they would not have uttered a sound, the bite of the rope would have seen to that. I had them hung by their heels for a time to teach them a lesson. They'll think twice before attempting to take a life in Glenorchy, for they know that next time the rope *will* be about their necks."

"They're alive!" Gillian pressed her fingers to her mouth and blinked against the sting of tears.

"Why do you weep now, lass?" Thane asked in puzzlement.

"I'm happy with you, m'lord," she said. "You are truly a kind and wise man."

"You should not be here in the draft," Thane said, and rising, scooped her up in his arms and carried her back to the bed. Tucking pillows behind her back and smoothing the covers about her as tenderly as her old nursemaid might have done, he smiled down at her. "Are you hungry, lass?"

Gillian shook her head.

"If you don't eat, ye can't regain your strength."

"Aye, I must regain my strength," she murmured. "And then I must leave Edinample." Her lashes were cast down, so she didn't see the alarm that swept across his face.

"Nay, lass, you've no need to leave. Your home burned down. You've no place to go. I would be honored if you stayed at Edinample."

"I can't!" she answered with such ferocity that his golden brows drew down in a scowl that usually sent kitchen maids scuttling from his sight. This was the true Thane Campbell, she thought, and quickly looked away.

"Why can't you stay here?" Thane asked in some perplexity. "Have you family who would worry about you, who need to know your whereabouts?" He couldn't imagine this was so, otherwise why would she be living in that deplorable hut in the forest? Still, she might, for clans could ban someone from their midst for a time as a punishment. Perhaps such was the case with her. If so, he wondered what deed she could possibly have committed.

"I'll send word to yer family that you're here at Edinample. What is the name of yer clan?" He waited, an expectant smile on his face.

Her gaze flew to his in wonderment. His eyes were guileless. He truly did not know who she was, though he waited for her to tell him. He must never know, she thought with some dismay.

"I can't tell you my clan name," she answered, looking at the fire so he might not see her evasion for all it was.

Thane was taken aback by her words, then chuckled indulgently. "You wish to remain always the mysterious lady?" he teased.

So cheerful were his words, she couldn't resist a glance and refrained from smiling in response to the sparkle of humor in his blue eyes. Her gaze was drawn to the finely chiseled mouth and the strong chin.

"D'ye see me as a woman of mystery, m'lord?" she asked, glancing up from beneath her lashes.

God's Passion, she's flirting with me, Thane thought, and couldn't repress another rich, deep chuckle.

"You're laughing at me," she said.

"Nay, lass," he said, tugging her hand into his. "I'd never laugh at such a bonny lass as you, but being with you makes me feel like laughing, the way a spring morning with mists rising from the ground and burning away on the slopes of Ben Vorlech make me laugh with the sheer joy of being alive."

Gillian gazed at him in amazement. "I know that feeling, m'lord," she cried. " 'Tis such a lifting of the spirits that you must make some noise so the good Lord knows how pleased and grateful you are by His gift."

They smiled at each other, suddenly reserved after the sharing of such confidences.

"I would not have my men know," Thane began. "They'd think me bedundered."

"They could never think that of you, m'lord," Gillian answered, her eyes sparkling with laughter. She was unaware of the fact that her hands gripped Thane's as innocently and eagerly as a child's. She felt a kinship with this man. He'd saved her life, not once but twice. He couldn't mean her any harm, especially since he didn't know who she really was. In that moment, looking into his warm blue eyes, she decided she'd never tell him the name of her clan or that she'd once lived at Edinample.

Thane saw the light leave her eyes and was reminded of the gist of their conversation before they'd become sidetracked. "Do you not remember who your kinsmen are?" Thane inquired, dismayed at the thought. He clasped her hands again with some urgency, forcing her to meet his gaze.

"I—I—aye, m'lord," she said, hating to lie to him, but knowing she could do nothing else. "I can't remember them. I—I was taken to live with Hannah when I was but a child." Gillian lowered her lashes and drew a deep breath. "You need not worry about me, m'lord. As soon as I've regained my strength, I'll be on my way."

"You'll not go anywhere," Thane answered so peremptorily, she was taken aback. "Edinample shall be your home, and we'll be your kinsmen."

Gillian smiled bitterly, though he misinterpreted the twist of her lips. "Will you be my brother, then, m'lord?" she asked.

"Nay, Gillian," Thane cried, taking hold of her elbows and shaking her gently. "I've something quite different in mind."

Gillian's cheeks grew flushed as she gazed into the sparkling blue depths of his eyes. So intense was his passion, so intense was her response that she had to look away quickly or she would fling herself against his broad chest.

"I've embarrassed you and I have no wish to do that."

"Nay," she protested, although his words were true. Her heart hammered in her chest so quickly, she feared she might faint, and her cheeks were hot as with a fever.

"If I am to consider your people my own, then tell me something of your clan," she said. "Did you always live here at Edinample?"

His brows drew down in one of his scowls, which were becoming more familiar and therefore less fiercesome to her now. "Nay, it was once the stronghold of the murderin', thievin' MacGregor clan." Gillian wanted to protest his words but remained silent, dismayed to hear an outsider's assessment of her kinsmen.

"Were they a clan without honor, then?" she asked quietly.

"Some would think so," Thane answered. "Certainly my father considered them a turbulent clan. I was not here at the time of their feud, being away in France for my schooling. However, Mother wrote to me of the disagreement. When I returned, the MacGregors had been proscribed by the king and their lands confiscated. King James awarded my father the lands in return for services rendered the crown."

"How fortunate for your father," Gillian commented innocently, "that the lands were there to be given away."

"Aye, my father would have been aware of that and seen that King James was fully apprised of his interests. Such is the way of things. Once Glenorchy was owned by the Campbells, but then it was bestowed on the MacGregors by Alexander II in his conquest of Argyll. It was always Father's wish to regain Glenorchy and Argyll, so he did."

"Your father must have been a powerful man," Gillian prompted, sadly fascinated by this bit of history.

"Some said of him that he was cunning as a fox, wise as a serpent, and slippery as an eel." Thane stopped talking and sat silent for a moment.

"You must be proud of him," Gillian said.

Thane's lips twisted into a bitter grimace. "Aye, one must love one's father and feel pride in him."

"And is he as proud of you?" Gillian prodded, sensing there were old wounds festering between father and son.

Thane turned his attention back to her. "You're far too astute for a lass so young," he said. She thought he meant to go no further with his narrative of his family, but he sighed. "Nay, my father thought me too soft."

"Too soft? Is he daft?" The words were out before she could stop them. "He didn't see you endure the pain of your wound or the way you command your men or—or—"

"Whoa, my little spitfire." Thane laughed. "Would you defend me, then?"

"Aye, m'lord," she answered, color rising to her cheeks despite her attempt to hide it. "I will tell your father, should I ever see him."

Thane's laughter died away. "You never shall, lass. He was killed in Glenlyon last year, trampled by his own horse."

"Oh, m'lord, I'm truly sorry. To lose one's father is the most painful of all things."

"I thought you had no memory of your father," Thane said.

Gillian was stunned, caught in her lie already. "I don't," she said quickly, "but I used to imagine my father was there beside me, comforting me and protecting me. When I was forced to face the reality that he was not, I used to weep with longing." Again she had spoken the truth from the depth of her feelings.

"I'm sorry for your loss," Thane said, seeing the sadness dim the emerald lights of her eyes. Lines of weariness had etched themselves around her lips and her face had gone pale. "I've overtaxed you. I'll leave you to rest." He brought her hands to his lips and kissed them fervently. "Have no fear here, Gillian," he said, staring into her eyes gravely.

He left her then, casting one last glance at her. Gillian sighed. He had lied. She was not safe here, not as long as he gazed at her so fervently and her own heart responded so traitorously. Still, she felt better after having heard his side of the feud with her clan. He had not even been in Scotland. He'd been abroad. His father had been the one who destroyed her kinsmen and brought about her father's death.

In the days that followed, Gillian's strength returned rapidly and she progressed from taking her exercise from bed to window and back again to other rooms of the castle and finally out into the bailey. These were perhaps the happiest days for Gillian, for she spent them rediscovering her home. There were many improvements, she noted, and all of them enhanced Edinample's regal beauty.

She explored the additional guest rooms and library, where a great desk held household ledgers and shelves along one wall held hand-illuminated manuscripts of such rare quality, Gillian was fearful of touching them. Still, she ran her hands along the leather spines and ornate gold clasps before moving on to the newer books published on a printing press. With these she lingered, struggling to read the words, and was able to recall letters of the alphabet.

She'd had a tutor when she lived here as a child, but during the years in between she'd had no reason to practice her skills, so they'd grown rusty. Now, as she pondered over the symbols, old knowledge came back to her and she began to make out the words.

With each passing day her presence became more accepted by the castle servants. They began to speak to her and she learned their names. Awed by the industry of all who lived within the castle walls, she sought to help at their tasks or offer some advice from her own knowledge, recommending shepherd's purse, an herb that would help her kidney complaint, to old Edra Richardson or fevertwig bark for an ointment for Katie Jack's son, who had acquired a nasty burn on one leg while working as an apprentice to the blacksmith. Now, as Gillian wandered through the bailey, old Edra came out of her laundry shed to talk to her.

"Gilly-lass," she called. Her hands were red from the hot water and harsh lye soap she used in her washing. "The shepherd's purse worked. No more pain in my kidney."

"I'm so happy, Edra," Gillian said, going to stand outside the shed in the sunlight. Edra's grandson, Peter Krochmal, was digging nearby.

"Good morning, Gillian," Muriel Krochmal called, coming to join them. "Mother told me of the shepherd's purse and how it eased her pains. My Peter has a sore on his foot which will not heal. Can you recommend anything?"

"Aye, let me think," Gillian replied, all too happy to be of service. She liked the young woman for her cheerful, forthright manner and found Peter, for all his mischief, a delight. "Do you know the pilewort?" she asked finally. " 'Tis a pretty little plant with nine pointed petals of brilliant gold. It blooms only seven hours on sunny days and its roots must be gathered then. Grind it down and make a poultice for Peter's foot. It should be better in a day or two."

"Aye, I'll try that," Muriel said.

"Ma." Peter threw down his shovel in disgust and kicked at the ground.

"What is it, lovey?" Muriel called, going to her son, a mother's pride and love evident on her face.

"I can't find any worms t'go fishing," he whined, and kicked at the ground again for good measure.

"I know how to find worms, Peter," Gillian exclaimed. "It takes a bit of magic."

"Oh, Gilly," he cried, leaving his mother and the overturned earth. Laughter bubbled within Gillian as she thought of the trick she'd once seen Lachlan perform. So pleased was she at the prospect, she didn't notice Muriel's frown or the glance she exchanged with her mother.

"May I borrow this pail and a bit of your washwater, Edra?" Gillian asked, taking up a staved bucket.

The old woman nodded uncertainly. "Aye, go ahead, if ye'll na be dirtying my water."

"Nay," Gillian said, and dunked the pail into the vat of hot, soapy water. Pouring it over the ground, she closed her eyes and waved her hands over the wet ground.

"Under the garden wall / Forward and back / Come all the little worms / And spring into my sack," she sang.

"Mother, look!" Peter cried. "The worms are coming out as she commanded."

Filled with glee that her trick had worked, Gillian opened her eyes and gazed around happily. Muriel's face was white, her lips compressed into a line, her dark eyes snapping with anger. Edra stood to one side, nodding her head, as if unable to think of anything to say.

"Look, Mother," Peter cried, kneeling to gather the worms.

"Nay!" Muriel cried, jerking him upright and hiding his face against her bosom. She glared at Gillian with hate-filled eyes. "I've heard about you," she said, "but I didn't believe what they said."

Gillian's courage faltered in the face of such hostility. The old helplessness settled over her. "Do you mean the tales of my being a witch?" she asked in a low voice. "I swear by God himself that it isn't so."

"Go away from us," Muriel cried. "And don't come down here again or I'll tell the laird of your treachery. Go away from us."

Holding Peter behind herself, she charged toward Gillian so she had no choice but retreat. None of the other servants seemed to have noticed the interchange, for they went about their business as before. Gillian knew if she tried to explain any more to Muriel, a scene would ensue that would only bring her to the attention of all present. She couldn't bear to see the suspicion and hatred grow in their eyes as it had with Muriel.

"I'm sorry. I meant no harm to you or your child," she whispered, then, uncertain of whether she'd been heard, she turned and raced back toward the castle keep. Tears coursed down her cheeks, and she gasped in an effort to hold back the sobs. So enclosed in her misery was she that she didn't notice the tall shadow looming before her until she plowed into the hard, muscular wall of Thane Campbell's chest.

"Here, lass, where do you go in such a rush?" he teased, taking hold of her shoulders to steady her.

Gillian kept her head averted in hopes of hiding her

tears, but Thane was not to be fooled. He took hold of her chin and turned her face up so he might study it. One rough thumb wiped at a tear. "Why do you cry, lass?" he asked.

Wordlessly she shook her head, then swallowed hard against the bubble of pain that clogged her throat. " 'Tis nothing, m'lord," she gulped. "I've gotten a bit of dust in my eye, 'tis all."

"Which eye?" he asked, and leaned closer. Hesitantly Gillian pointed to her left eye, then her right. Thane grinned. "Which is it, lass?"

"B-both," Gillian gulped again, blinking rapidly. "But I've got it out now." She pulled away from him. She would have fled but for the heavy hand that weighted her shoulders.

Thane studied her closed expression. "Are you certain 'tis only dust that brought your tears?" he persisted. "You look too melancholy for only that."

"Nay, I—I have been a little melancholy. I—I miss my friend Lachlan. When I was sad, he could always make me laugh."

Gillian turned away. "If I knew where he was, I could go to him and he would take care of me. I would no longer be a burden."

Thane turned her around to face him again. "Didn't we talk of this, Gillian? You'll never be a burden to me. Now, we'll have no more of such talk."

"Aye, m'lord."

"And no more of that," he instructed, shaking her slightly. "You're to call me Thane."

"I can't, m'lord. What will your servants think?"

"They will think you're a friend and peer," he answered blithely.

She stood, considering him. He'd exchanged his plaid for a velvet doublet and close-fitting breeches. A fine gold belt and chain and pendant set off his vest, and his wheat-colored hair had been brushed smooth. He was breathtakingly handsome. He smiled at her silent perusal.

"And as my friend, my kind lady Gillian, will you join me for supper tonight in the great hall?"

"Nay, m'lord. I can't."

"I insist. You've taken enough meals in the solace of your room." She saw the determination in his gaze.

"Aye, m'lord, if you wish my presence."

"Aye, I do, lass. I do."

"Until tonight, then, m'lord," she said, and hurried away before he could berate her for the use of his title. Her heart beat with trepidation over the coming supper with Thane and over the reaction of Muriel and Edra over the worms. What had Muriel said? She'd heard tales of Gillian being a witch, but she hadn't believed them until then.

Gillian sat on the edge of her bed and held her head in despair. Even now the evil lies followed her, putting her in danger and destroying her peace of mind. And tonight she must join Thane Campbell in the great hall before all his servants and his men. How many of them had heard the same tales and considered her a witch? She could not bear to walk among them and feel their hatred and disgust.

Her gaze settled on the ragged skirt of the servant's gown she wore. She must do something to make herself more presentable for tonight, she thought in dismay, and ordered bathwater be brought to her. She hung her shift out the window to air and settled into the tepid water to wash her hair and body with the perfumed soap provided. She wished for a new gown, even a clean servant's shift to don, but would have to make do.

She'd finished her toilet and was sitting before the fire, wrapped in a linen sheet from her bed, combing her long hair, when a knock sounded at the door.

The servant called Bridget stood on the other side, her lips curling with disdain, her eyes snapping with anger.

Had she talked to Muriel, Gillian wondered helplessly. Was that why she showed such hostility?

"I've been told to bring this t'ye," she said without preamble and without a customary curtsy. Across her arms lay a beautiful rose-colored silk gown with petticoats beneath. Gillian forgot about Bridget's animosity when her fingers smoothed across the satiny folds.

" 'Tis for me?" she asked in wonder, lifting the gown and holding it up.

"Aye," Bridget said bitterly. " 'Tis a gown the laird gives to all his trollops to wear. He'll want it back when he's had his way with ye."

"Oh, I don't expect to keep it," Gillian answered innocently. Only later, when Bridget had swung around and marched off down the hall, did her words come back to Gillian. Was she to be considered Thane Campbell's current trollop, then? Angered that all within the castle must think that of her, she thought of not going down to the great hall, but the shimmer of rose silk and the anticipation of seeing Thane's eyes when he first glimpsed her in it made her put aside her pique and don the beautiful gown.

It fit her almost as if it had been made especially for her, with a tight waist and a low, ruffle-edged neckline that displayed far too much of her breasts. Gillian tugged at the dainty ruffles that barely covered her nipples, uncomfortable with the naked swell of her breasts. She could not appear below in such a gown.

And the skirt! Ah, she'd seen such skirts on rare occasions when she'd gone to the edge of the village on market day and caught a glimpse of some fine lady, but she never dreamed she'd be required to wear something so ridiculous. The skirts were held away from her body in a wheel-like affair that brought up her skirts so her ankles showed. Indecent!

She was incensed that Thane Campbell would expect her to wear such a gown in public. No wonder the servants thought her a *baille*, a mistress. In anger she cast the beautiful silk gown from her and drew on the ragged servant's gown. Then, her heart pounding, she made her way downstairs and under the censorious eyes of all Thane's men walked to the head table to join her host.

Chapter 7

THE ROOM FELL silent as Gillian made her way to the head table, where Thane Campbell sat. His expression fell when he saw her still dressed in the worn servant's clothes.

"Didn't Bridget bring you the gown I sent?" he demanded, setting down his cup and staring at her with displeasure. Gillian might have been intimidated if she weren't so offended.

"Aye, m'lord, she brought the gown to me," she said serenely.

Thane waited for her to go on. "Didn't the gown fit?" he prodded when she offered no further explanation.

"Aye, it fit quite well, m'lord," she answered. "Do you wish me to sit here, m'lord, or below the salt?"

"Sit here, of course," Thane said, leaping to his feet to hold the chair for her. When she was seated and had spread her dingy skirts as elegantly as if she did indeed wear the silken rose gown, he signaled a servant forward to pour wine and another to bring a platter of meat from which he chose the choicest morsels and placed them upon her plate. When she was served with some of everything at the table so that her plate ran over with rich food, he leaned back in his chair and regarded her. She'd dressed her long black hair in a plaited coronet atop her head with the thick, glossy tresses in the back swirling down her back like a silken veil. The style was at once innocent and provocative, for her slender neck and brow were revealed in all their perfection while tendrils curled fetchingly at her temples. The color was high in her cheeks and her lips were red and slightly swollen, as if she'd worried her bottom lip with her small white teeth. Thane thought he'd never seen her look more beautiful. He couldn't help imagining her in the rose gown he'd sent with her pale white shoulders revealed. He scowled. He wasn't used to being thwarted; still, he forced himself to patience as he leaned toward her.

"Tell me, lass, why have you chosen na to wear the gown I sent you?"

"I thought it far too grand for me, m'lord," she answered calmly, and took up a piece of meat and daintily placed it in her mouth. Her green-eyed gaze met his, and she smiled, looking somehow mischievous and angelic at the same time. "I did not wish to rise above my station, m'lord."

Thane regarded her for a moment as if sorting through the things she'd said. "Since you don't remember the origin of your clan or any of your people, why would you think you would be rising above your station by simply wearing a gown?" he inquired with a little less patience than before.

"Oh, I know full well, m'lord, that I was not meant to wear the gown of a common trollop!" She used the word Bridget had thrown at her so contemptuously, and her voice rose with anger. "I may be a woman without a clan name, m'lord, but I am not a trollop, nor will I become yer *baille*." So saying, she rose from her chair and turned to leave the great hall. Everyone sat in stunned silence. Never had they heard man or woman speak to Thane Campbell, laird of Glenorchy, in such a manner. They waited expectantly for his response, certain it would be a terrible thing to see.

Gillian, unaware of the magnitude of her deed, marched head high, back stiff with pride, straight for the door and paused only when she heard Thane roar her name. So fierce was the sound, she jumped with fear, then, pulling her courage and anger about her, she turned to face him down the length of the hall.

"I wish to thank you, m'lord, for rescuing me, not once but twice, but now I must decline your hospitality and leave Edinample. I bid you farewell." With a small bow she whirled toward the door again.

"Stop her!" Thane roared, and immediately two men in servant's livery leapt forward to bar the door. Gillian came up short, saw that she could not push her way beyond them, and whirled to face Thane Campbell once again.

"I pray you, m'lord, to let me pass."

"Not until we've talked, Gillian," Thane said, stalking down the hall toward her. Gillian saw the expression on his face, the same he'd turned upon servants and troops when they displeased him. Now that look was turned toward her. She looked from left to right, seeking an escape. The two servants leapt forward to block her flight in either direction, and as quick as a cat's wink she ducked under their arms and scrambled out the door.

"Don't let her leave the castle," Thane thundered, and immediately two guards stepped in front of the castle doors. There was no place for her to go but up the stairs, and up them she went, her hands gathering the limp skirts high so she might not trip, her slender ankles flashing as she nimbly climbed the steps. She could hear Thane approaching and knew it was but a matter of moments before he would reach her. She ducked into a room, slammed the door, and turned the key.

The footsteps on the other side of the door came to a complete stop. She pressed an ear to the door panel. Had he gone on by, or was he there on the other side, waiting for her to put her head out again?

Well, she would stay right here until everyone had given up on her and had gone off to bed, then she would run out of the castle and make her way back to Glenartney. She wasn't ill now, and she would remember to take a warm blanket and food and water to keep her until she found Lachlan. Together they would rebuild Hannah's hut and live there as they had before.

She would be no *baille* of any man's, even of the mighty Thane Campbell. She'd seen how such women were scorned during the days of her father's rule at Edinample. Thane had taken quite enough from their clan; he would not take her honor as well. A small thing, perhaps, but all she had left to protect.

She thought again of the rose gown and felt disappointment sweep over her. She'd thought him a kind friend, but he'd wanted only to bed her. Tired from all the excitement, she made her way to the deep armchair by the fire and curled up in it.

Her gaze roamed around the room, and she realized with a start that it had once been her father's. As elegant as her own room was, this was far grander. Noting the richness of its plenishings, the glint of gold threads woven in tapestries and cushions, the richness of wooden chests with gold drawer pulls, the thick carpet upon the floor, she guessed it belonged to someone of equal importance. Dread washed over her as she realized her blunder. She'd automatically sought a haven here, never once thinking it might now belong to Thane Campbell.

She sat thinking of what her next steps must be. The warmth of the fire and the deep comfort of the chair lulled her. Her eyelids grew heavy and her stomach growled with hunger, for other than that single morsel of meat, she'd eaten no supper. The thought of making her way into the cold night was unappealing when faced with the comfort of the castle, yet she knew she must flee. She'd sleep now, she decided, so she'd be rested later, when she made her escape. She dreamed she was in a roomful of trollops, all wearing rose-colored gowns. Thane himself stood in the midst of them with a gleeful leer on his face. She tried to force her way through the women to get to his side, to tell him she had no wish to be part of his retinue, but all the women were clamoring to be chosen for a night with the laird, so he didn't see her.

"Thane!" She called his name over and over in her dreams, then mercifully awakened, blinking her eyes.

"So you've wakened at last," a voice said. "I've brought the rest of your supper, since you didn't eat downstairs."

Gillian stared at Thane Campbell, who had settled himself comfortably across the huge carved bed, a wine goblet in his hand.

"How did you get past the locked door?" she demanded, turning to stare at the panel that was still tightly closed. The expression of disbelief and betrayal was so evident on her face, Thane's laughter pealed out and filled the chamber. Gillian glared at him, her cheeks reddening.

"You're not the only one capable of witchcraft, lass," he teased.

"Ah, you used the secret—" Gillian bit off her words.

"The secret what?" Thane demanded, eyes narrowing. There was no lingering signs of merriment on his handsome face now. His gaze was stern.

"I—I assume ye have a secret way in and out of yer room that many castles have for the escape of the laird and his family in times of strife." Gillian forced herself to meet his gaze with innocent eyes. Thane studied her face as if measuring all she'd said.

"If you don't remember your clan, how do you remember this bit of knowledge?" he asked softly.

Gillian shrugged, thinking quickly. "Hannah used to tell me stories of the old struggles and of secret passages used by wily chiefs who lived to fight another day."

Her answer seemed to satisfy him, for he sighed and rose from the bed, his demeanor relaxed, but the humor seemed to have disappeared. Moving a small table bearing her supper tray near her, Thane pulled up a stool on the opposite side and settled himself.

"Eat your supper," he ordered, "while it's still warm."

"I'm not hungry, m'lord," she said stiffly, although her gaze wandered to the platter of meat. It had been quite tasty earlier when she'd taken a bite of it, and the bread looked crusty and fresh. A small bowl of butter sat beside it, and her mouth watered.

"Hungry or not, you must eat to keep up your strength," Thane said, and a tiny grin crooked one side of his mouth. "Especially if you plan to walk back t'Glenartney."

"How did you know I planned to do that?" Gillian demanded, and was met with another grin, a flash of strong white teeth in his tanned face, a twinkle of humor in the blue eyes. He wasn't nearly as stern as he liked to appear, she realized, and felt some of the tension leave her.

"I'm beginning to understand many things about you, Gillian," he said softly. "But still I'm puzzled why you would not wear the gown I sent and why you became so incensed at me for doing so."

Gillian gazed down at her hands clasped in her lap. "I understand nothing about you," she began, then raised her head suddenly so her green gaze tangled with his. "Why treat me as a trollop?"

"A trollop?" He blinked.

"Aye, a—a *baille*. Is that why you've rescued me and brought me here, because you wish to make me your mistress?"

Thane couldn't help but flush, for those had been his thoughts exactly, although he'd arrived at them far less cold-bloodedly than it might have seemed. "Nay, Gillian. I brought ye here because ye needed help and ye'd saved my life. Nothing more." Unable to meet her gaze, he got to his feet and stalked around the room, one wide brown hand rubbing at the back of his neck. "How did you come to this conclusion about me?"

"Bridget said—"

"Blast Bridget and her jealous conniving."

Gillian said nothing, for his words had given away full well his relationship with the serving girl.

"You must not believe any word Bridget utters," he said, coming to tower over Gillian and glare at her as if she were the serving girl herself. When Gillian remained silent, Thane sighed and seated himself again, reaching across the table to take one of Gillian's hands in his. The warmth of his touch began its hypnotizing magic on her. She wanted to pull away from him so she might think clearly, but she could not.

"What did she say that got you so upset?" Thane demanded.

"I'm not upset, m'lord," Gillian said instantly. " 'Tis not for me to question your moral conduct. I am but a guest here at Edinample, or at least I thought I was."

"And so you are." His grip on her hand tightened so she nearly cried out, but instantly he loosened his grasp. His fingers stroked her hand as if he feared he'd injured her beyond reason. "You are more than a guest. Edinample is your home now. So I've said and so it will be."

"But as what, m'lord?" she asked stubbornly. She was unaware her bottom lip pouted sweetly or that she looked as demure as a child seated so primly on his chair. Her very innocence was a seduction to him, for he knew beneath the shapeless servant's gown were the soft, round curves of a fully developed woman. Had he not become achingly familiar with them on those rides to Edinample with her cradled against his chest? He would have to be a stone not to remember that feminine softness.

"M'lord?" Gillian said tentatively, and he knew he'd let his mind wander too far. Had his expression given away his thoughts? He thrust himself up from the stool, turning so she could not see the effect of his thoughts upon his manhood. Stalking to the window, he threw open the shutters and stared out at the night.

"I asked you in what capacity you planned to have me here, m'lord," Gillian repeated.

"As a—as a—"

"Sister?" She reminded him of the promise he'd made before.

"Aye, if that is what you wish."

"I do, m'lord," she said, and couldn't keep the relief from her voice.

"Only if you'll agree to wear the gowns I send you," he bartered, and turned at last to face her, a bit of humor on his face once more. "After all, the laird of Glenorchy can't have his sister wandering around in cast-off servants' clothes."

"Better this than the gown you sent me, your lordship," she answered sternly.

Thane's eyes darkened. "Why this stubbornness over a simple gown?"

"Why this insistence I dress as a—a trollop?" she countered, her chin rising again.

"Where is it? I would see this gown you object to so strenuously."

" 'Tis in my room. I will get it for you." Gillian pushed aside the table, preparing to rise and fetch the gown, but Thane clamped a hand on her shoulder.

"Stay where you are and eat your supper, which even now grows cold. I will fetch the gown myself." He strode away and Gillian did as he bade, for her stomach quivered at the thought of food. She'd had an active day and her young body required refueling. Besides, much of the anxiety she'd felt earlier was dissipating in the face of Thane's reassurances. Greedily she began to eat.

He was back, the rose silk clutched in his hand. "What is wrong with this gown?" he demanded. " 'Tis one of the latest fashions."

Gillian was shocked at his claim. She swallowed the

lump of meat and bread stuck in her throat. "You mean that ladies wear gowns like this that show their ankles and display their—their . . ." She gulped, unable to go on.

Thane regarded her outraged expression, his delight in her innocence and backwardness on the subject of fashion evident in his sparkling eyes. "Aye, lass. 'Tis a bit shameful, is it not? But even the court ladies wear such things."

Gillian stared at him doubtfully, remembering the display of rounded bosom. "Even in the winter?" she asked. "Don't they suffer from the ague, displaying so much of their chests to the cold?"

Thane's laughter rang out, and he tossed the gown across the bed. "Point well taken, lass," he said. "I'll see you get something else less immodest."

"Thank ye, m'lord," Gillian said, grinning back impishly. Relieved that the matter was solved and that she would not have to leave Edinample this night, she took up her spoon and finished eating with relish. Thane watched her, an amused smile on his lips. When she glanced up and saw him regarding her so steadily, she flushed and put down her spoon. Her plate was empty anyway. "I—I was hungrier than I thought," she acknowledged.

"Aye, I think you were," he agreed, and removed the tray though he left the table in place.

"I'd best leave ye t'yer rest, m'lord," she said, putting her hand against the edge of the table.

"I thought you might care to play a game with me," he said.

"What sort of game?" she asked warily.

Thane returned with a board filled with ivory and ebony figures. " 'Tis called chess."

"I don't know the game," she said reluctantly.

"I'll teach you."

A shout of laughter came from below. "Don't you wish to go back to your friends?"

"Nay. I'm quite content here with you," Thane replied,

removing his doublet. His masculine figure was more fully exposed beneath the soft fabric of his shift and plaid. She couldn't help but admire his long, muscular legs. "It's pleasant here beside the fire, and I'm tired, for I've had a hard day. We rode to Kirkcaldy to see to the repairs."

"Did you happen to see Lachlan about in your traveling?" she asked anxiously.

Thane shook his head. "I made inquiries, but no one had seen a little hunchbacked man."

"No one *will* see him if he's a mind to keep himself hidden," she said sorrowfully. "I wish I knew he was all right."

"I think he must be, Gillian. He knows where you are. If he wanted to see you, he would come here. Don't concern yerself so for him."

"I can't help it. He's my friend and protector."

Thane regarded her saddened expression and picked up a chess piece. "Come, I'll show you the first move to make. This is a pawn. It is expendable. You may sacrifice this piece at will to gain a more favorable play."

Gillian listened to his words carefully, noting each piece and its particular strengths. She quickly grasped the concept, but her ploys were clumsy, her strategies unsophisticated. Thane offered praise generously.

"May I ask a question without offending?" she asked during a particularly long pause. She'd been ever conscious of the magnetic man sitting across from her. When he moved a piece, her gaze noted the thick-boned wrists with the smattering of pale hair. When he shifted on his stool, she became too aware of the broad shoulders and taut belly, and her imagination flashed back to that moment in her hut when he'd lain unconscious and naked beneath her ministrations and she'd been fully aware of every inch of his masculinity.

"Aye, lass, you can ask me what you wish. I will not be offended," he declared now. His smile lit his handsome features in such a way, she thought her heart would surely stop beating at the glory of it. She swallowed and looked away from him. She must if she were to retain her senses. She was loath to utter the words that pushed at her lips, but some devil inside her needed to know.

"Have you many mistresses, Thane?" she asked, and jerked her gaze up to his face when she heard his exclamation. His face grew red with anger, then slowly the fury ebbed to be replaced by the old shimmering humor.

"Ah, lass, why d'ye ask me such a question?"

"Was it wrong of me to do so?" she inquired innocently.

"Aye, a lady should not ask such of a man."

"Oh."

"Why do you want to know?"

"Bridget said—"

"You were to forget everything Bridget said," he admonished.

She fell silent, distracted. Thane studied her bowed head and sighed heavily.

"I will tell you, for I don't wish you to wonder and perhaps build the number of peccadilloes beyond reason."

"Nay, I will not think of it," she said.

"Aye, you will. You do even now."

"Aye, I do!"

"I've had no more mistresses than most men," he said, somewhat uncomfortable at discussing such a matter with her. Yet he sensed her reasons for wanting to know were tangled up in her dawning awareness of him as a man. His spirits rose at the thought. "Despite what Bridget may have told you, Gillian, I'm not a whoremonger."

"Nay, I don't think of you that way."

"Don't you? Even when you fled the hall earlier?"

She blushed. "Well, mayhap a little."

"D'ye still?"

She raised her eyes to his. "Nay, m'lord."

He wagged a finger at her. "Thane."

"Thane," she repeated.

"Good," he said, and picked up an ivory chess piece. "I've taken your pawn. I believe I have you in check."

"Not yet!" she declared, and made her escape.

"Well done." He applauded and she glowed under his warm gaze. The hour passed. The fire burned down. The hall below grew quiet. Gillian stifled a yawn and Thane leaned back in his chair.

"I've kept you overly long, lass. You should have spoken up."

"Nay, I'm not tired—" A yawn made a lie of her words. Chuckling, Thane rose and removed the table. Taking hold of her hand, he pulled her from the chair. "Go t'bed, lass," he said, gripping her shoulders for a moment and placing a chaste kiss on her brow. Automatically Gillian raised her face to his.

Thane tilted her head backward so their gazes locked. Gillian drew a trembling breath. They stood so close now that her hands came up to rest against his broad chest. Breathlessly she waited, unable to understand or name the aching need that arose in her. Thane saw it reflected in her eyes and felt his own needs soar, yet he remembered her outraged reaction when she'd thought he meant to make her his mistress and he restrained himself.

"Come, I'll walk you to your room." He felt her stiffen slightly, but took hold of her elbow nonetheless and slowly walked her down the corridor to her door. "I'll see that more appropriate gowns are brought to you, but you must promise me to wear them."

"I shall, Thane, if you so command." He caught the impish dimple that flashed in one cheek when she smiled.

"I wager I can't command you, little sister, so I pray you sleep well," he said, and once again pressed his lips to her temple. Her warm scent was nearly his undoing, so he swung around and walked straight back to his room, not even pausing to glance over his shoulder at her before closing his door. Alone inside his room, he shifted his clothes to ease the ache in his groin, stamped to the fire, and rattled the poker in the embers until he'd nearly put out the fire before thinking of adding more wood.

Gillian watched him stroll away and wondered if he was in a hurry to be done with her so he might signal to Bridget or one of the other comely serving wenches to come warm his bed. The thought made her miserable, but she wasn't sure why. If she were to insist that he think of her as a sister, then she must think of him as her brother and such things should not matter to her, but she knew they did.

Everything she'd insisted upon that evening was a lie, for she herself did not want to be a sister to Thane. She wanted so much more, but could she become one of his mistresses? Unsettled by such thoughts, she prepared for bed and pulled the covers high under her chin. She lay listening to the whistle of the wind against the castle wall, and from a distance the muted roar of the waterfall rushing the river into the basin of Loch Earn. A sigh of contentment escaped her lips. She was home, truly home again.

Gillian rose in the morning with renewed exhilaration. The first sight that greeted her was the pile of new gowns draped over a chair. Though simple of design and material and obviously of the quality worn by the serving women, they were nonetheless nicer than any gown she could remember possessing. She chose one of light wool in a hunter green and eagerly pulled it on. It fit her neatly at the waist and bodice and the skirt covered her ankles but allowed the toe of each new slipper to peek out most becomingly. The dark green set off the paleness of her skin and the skirt was full enough to swish about her legs as she walked.

She took extra pains to plait up her hair and secure it around her head before leaving her room. Thane was in the hall below, giving orders to one of his servants before leaving. She called to him and tripped lightly down the stairs.

At the sound of his name, Thane turned around and drew in his breath as he watched Gillian descend. She was even more beautiful in the morning light than she'd been in the firelight. The new gown was well cut for a servant's dress and showed off her trim waist and small, full breasts. Her chin was high, her cheeks blushed becomingly, and her eyes sparkled with spirit. Thane wanted to stand at the bottom of the stairs and catch her to him. She was like some exotic forest creature too wild to tame, yet so achingly beautiful, his heart leapt in his chest.

"Thank you for the new gowns," she said in a rush when she'd reached the bottom of the stairs and stood gazing up at him in a friendly, open manner. He had no wish for her friendship, he thought impatiently. He'd rather have her breathless and flushed with desire, as he himself felt. Still, she expected uncomplicated friendship in return, and so he would give her for the time being.

"This one fits you quite well." He nodded approvingly. "I take it the cut is more to your approval."

She flushed under his indulgent gaze. "Aye, they're quite appropriate."

"For the time being, Gillian." He couldn't help expressing his earlier thoughts. "But one day I vow I'll see you in the rose-colored gown."

"Nay, Thane." She looked up at him quickly and was caught in the heat of his gaze. His true meaning was there in his eyes. Pledge to treat her as a sister he might, but he did not consider her a sister. She caught her breath and felt a giddy heat sweep through her body. "Nay," she whispered, although she knew the words were meant for herself more than for him.

With a final heated glance he swept out of the castle, called to his men, and mounted Bhaltair, whom a stable boy held saddled and ready. Gillian listened to the sound

of hooves against the bailey cobblestones and knew that
what passed between Thane and her would have to be
acknowledged. But the thought was not as distressful that
morning as it had seemed the night before.

Chapter 8

T HE DAYS THAT followed passed in uneventful bliss. Thane and his men rode out each day to check the progress of repairs at the burned villages or to oversee the rounding up of the long-haired, shaggy herds that had roamed the hills throughout the summer. Thane had kept a troop of Highlanders riding the boundaries of the vast Glenorchy holdings. There were no further raids, so tempers began to cool and cautiousness waned. The village men and boys came down from the shieling huts in the mountains, driving fattened sheep and milk cows before them. An air of gaiety seemed to take hold of the people of Edinample and the villages beyond.

In the evenings Gillian went to the great hall to join Thane and his men, and she began to perceive how precarious and uncertain her position was at Edinample. She was not one of the Campbells, therefore she could take no hand in the running of the castle. She wouldn't have known how, at any rate, she decided, for it was a far cry from a humble one-room hut in the forest to a castle filled with hundreds of people, each with his or her own job to do. Still, she saw the waste of goods and manpower and wondered how Thane could sustain such even given his great fortune. She'd learned frugality at Hannah's knee, and the lesson would stay with her the rest of her life.

With no real duties, Gillian found herself with time on her hands. She borrowed one of the books from the library and spent hours practicing her reading.

Now that her mind had been primed, she began to remember the arithmetic taught her and used a piece of charcoal from the fireplace to scratch out the numbers on a flat piece of stone she'd brought from the riverbank. Evenings without Thane passed well enough, though she was left with an aching void that seemed would never be filled.

During the days, as she walked along the riverbank and fields beyond Edinample, she found the familiar plants she'd gathered all her life with Hannah and remembered the richness of those sun-warmed days when the two of them set out on such excursions.

Gillian was lonely for friendship and centered all her thoughts on Thane and pleasing him. Every evening after supper she trailed him up to his room, where he taught her the intricacies of chess. She knew the men and women below believed she'd already become Thane's mistress, and Bridget hissed at her at every passing, but Gillian was too caught in an enchantment to care. And Aindreas, who'd changed his opinion about her, was always there with his funny tales to keep her company when Thane was not about.

Her world seemed filled with sunshine, and she basked in the warmth of it. How different her life had become from the isolation of the Glenartney hut to the hustle and bustle of Edinample and the breathless wonder of Thane's company. That he wanted more than just her company was all too evident in his warm glance and possessive manner, and she had little doubt that he was used to having what he wanted.

That troubled her less than the fact of her own responses to him. She had not forgotten that this was the son of the man who'd destroyed her clan and thus should have been treated as an enemy, but with each day that passed, Thane made himself her friend and mentor, her life and breath. How could she deny him further? More, how could she deny her own heart's desire?

One day, as she knelt in the open meadow before the castle, reveling in the drone of cicadas in the long dried grass and the smell of hot fertile earth beneath her hands, intent on coaxing out the roots of the balsam fir, which would make a fine tea to ease Goody Pott's arthritic aches, she glanced up to see Thane astride Bhaltair, watching her. Man and horse were as still as if struck of stone. The strong sunlight burned behind them, so she had to blink against the diffused rays. Finally he lifted a powerful arm to wave to her, guiding Bhaltair with his knees so that he came forward away from the sun, and the spell was broken.

"Have I found a wood fairy?" he asked, smiling down at her, and his eyes were so warmed with laughter, she much preferred the man over the golden image.

"Nay, Laird Campbell, naught but a humble lass intent upon her business," she answered sassily.

"And what is that business that keeps you here in the sun instead of resting in the shade?" Thane alighted from his horse and came to join her where she sat on her heels in the grass, her skirts spread around her, a small cutting blade in her hands. She wore a rough gown dyed a deep mulberry-wine color and a white apron tied around her slim waist. Her glossy black curls had been temporarily tamed in a single thick braid down her back. Escaping tendrils curled fetchingly around her face. Her lips were as red and inviting as newly ripened berries, and Thane, acting on impulse, leaned forward and kissed her. Gillian didn't draw away, but went very still, like a deer startled to quietness in the forest. Thane drew back.

"I'm sorry," he murmured, fearful he'd undone weeks of patient wooing.

"I'm not," she said, gazing boldly into his eyes. Her cheeks were flushed, her eyes darkened and fathomless.

"Gillian," Thane whispered, and gathered her close, his big hand molding her body against his, his mouth closing over her sweet lips, conquering, claiming, branding her as his. Gillian couldn't deny the passion of his touch, nor did she want to.

Her body swayed against his, fitting itself to his broad chest as if God had designed her that way. Aching nipples peaked against his chest, soft breasts yielded. A wave of fire swept through her, and her arms crept up over his shoulders. Her fingers rose to brush through his golden locks. The feel of him, hard and unyielding, the taste, masculine and earthy and tantalizing, all awakened such a need inside her, she was helpless in its thrall.

Thane's kiss deepened, his lips parting hers, his tongue thrusting against her teeth, nipping at her jaw until she opened to him and he tasted the sweetness beyond, his tongue conquering and subduing hers.

Her world was spinning, and she feared she might twirl away into infinity if she did not grasp tightly the giant who held her. When his mouth had plundered hers and she lay swooning and unresisting in his arms, he lowered his lips to the pale column of her throat and breathed in her musky essence.

"Ah, lass, you tear my soul apart," he murmured against her ear. His breath, hot and raspy, sent a shiver down her spine.

"I am helpless in your arms," she whispered. "Though I tell myself I should not love you, should not desire you in such a shameful way, I can't help myself."

"Ah, lass, 'tis not shameful to feel this way," he whispered, and brushed his mouth across her swollen lips, along her dainty, rounded chin and down to the modest top of her gown. His hands moved to the soft mounds covered by the mulberry worsted. Their giving softness beneath the rough texture of her gown was maddening. His hands fumbled with eager haste at the fastenings of her gown and were rewarded at last with the rough folds sliding away and revealing her pale beauty. Thane paused to gaze at her until her cheeks grew pink and she moved to draw up the bodice of her gown.

"Nay," he said gently, capturing her hands. "Let me look my fill, for never has a man set eyes on such beauty." He raised his gaze to her face, and Gillian thrilled at the passion she saw in his darkened glance. She had the power to move him as he did her, she thought, and her shyness fell away from her, so she dropped her arms from her breasts, revealing herself to his hot gaze.

"I want to taste you, lass," he murmured, bending to brush his hot, raspy tongue across one engorged nipple. Gillian shuddered at the touch. Her breath hissed between her teeth, and she closed her eyes to the sky and mountains so every sense might give itself over to the magic he wrought. Gently he pressed her back in the grass and bent over her.

"So bonny," he murmured, running his hands over her flesh, leaving a fiery trail wherever he touched. She opened her eyes and gazed at him, a golden giant shimmering in the sunlight, then he lowered his head to nestle his face between the full orbs of her breasts and his greedy tongue licked a path to one soft nipple. His strong teeth nipped at her, then licked the pleasure-pain from her and finally sucked until she thought he would draw her very soul into himself.

"I want you, lass," he crooned, "here in the sunlight so I can see the expression in your beautiful eyes when I teach you all the passion and fire between a man and woman." He cradled her head in his big hands, holding her so he could gaze deep into her eyes. His huge body was resting on hers now, the weight of it tempered by the support of his elbows. She felt surrounded by him, secure, complete.

"Aye, Thane," she said, and was surprised at the throaty, breathless tone of her voice. "I want you, too." Her words were innocence and trust, burning him with their wholehearted giving. He captured her mouth with his, his tongue thrusting, his hips moving against her so she might feel the hard rod of desire against her.

Their clothes kept them from that final discovery. Impatiently he reached for the hem of her skirt, but the sound of approaching riders stopped him.

Aindreas and Duncan were upon them before they had a chance to straighten their clothes. Mortified, Gillian clasped her bodice to the front of her chest and rolled away from them. Her bare shoulders and sloping white back bearing the marks of the grass told them the story.

"Sorry, Thane. We've been searching for you, and when we saw Bhaltair, we just rode out without thinking," Aindreas said, and seeing where his young cousin's gaze lingered, Thane moved to shield Gillian from his gaze.

"What is it you want, you dolt?" his words were growled.

Sheepishly Aindreas looked away. He understood now that the woman Gillian belonged to his cousin. Still he couldn't help seeing the physical allure of her, the arching grace of her back and the swirl of black hair that had come loose from its plait. She was a beautiful woman and Aindreas felt desire stir within him for her. He fixed his gaze on the ground at Thane's feet. "James Campbell's son, young Harold, arrived minutes ago from Cutty-bragan. The raiders have struck again."

"God's Passion," Thane swore, and stood up, quickly rearranging his clothes. "How long ago?"

"Early morning, just before dawn," Aindreas said. "James ordered Harold to slip away for help at the first sign of the raid. Their trail can't be too cold yet."

"Aye," Thane agreed, and began buckling on his sword, "but we won't ride to Cuttybragan. We'll head south and cut them off south of the Glenartney forest."

"Are you sure, Thane?" Duncan called. "We don't know for sure they'll go that way."

"We always lose them in the forest. My guess is they have a hideaway somewhere on its edge. We may be able to pick up their trail there. Are the men ready to go?"

"Aye," Duncan answered.

Thane took a step toward Bhaltair and turned back to Gillian. "I'm sorry, lass," he said in a low voice. "I have to go. You see that, don't you?"

"Aye, Thane." She still sat on the ground, though she'd shoved her arms through the sleeves of her bodice and laced herself up. "Don't worry about me. I'll get back to Edinample without harm."

"We've not finished this, you understand?" He stared at her bent head, willing her to look up and meet his gaze. "You'll not leave the castle while I'm gone? You'll wait for my return?"

She looked up then, her eyes widening in under-standing at his worry. "Aye, Thane."

He was unable to leave her like that. His men awaited him. Bhaltair stamped with impatience; still he could not leave her. He strode back to her and lifted her from the ground, his powerful arms pinning her to him, his mouth plundering hers, branding her, making her his woman.

Her knees nearly gave way when he released her. She righted herself and stared at his departing back, her fingers brushing the lips swollen from his kisses. Thane swung into the saddle and turned back to face her.

"Don't leave me, Gillian," he ordered, and kicked his heels against Bhaltair and galloped away. Gillian's heart was filled with joy. She gathered her crimson skirts in her hands and ran after him.

"I'll be waiting for you, Thane," she whispered, because she knew she could never leave him. She belonged to Thane Campbell as surely as did Edinample.

Chapter 9

"*T*HANE, OVER THERE!" Duncan whispered, pointing to the wavery shapes looming up out of the fog.

"Aye, we've found them," Thane muttered. "Pass the word. Don't fire until I tell you. I want their leader alive."

"Aye, Thane." Duncan melted away in the fog as soundlessly as he'd come. Thane watched the approaching riders. Mouth tightening in a thin line of fury, Thane took aim at the horse that carried the first rider.

To his right came a clink of saber against rock. Instantly the lead rider spun his horse away. Thane's shot missed. He brought up his other pistol and fired. The leader swayed in the saddle but did not fall off his mount. Still, Thane was certain he'd struck him.

"Run, lads," the raider called to his men, and mercilessly spurred his horse directly at Thane.

The man's a fool, Thane thought, then quickly changed his assessment, for both his pistols were empty. Thane threw them aside in a clump of heather and reached for his sword, knowing even as he moved that he'd not have time to draw it.

"Hold!" a voice said from out of the mist, and a blade rested against Thane's neck. Bhaltair whickered at the

nearness of the raider's mount. "Still your animal or my
blade will drink Campbell blood," the voice ordered, and
with a pressure of his knees, Thane quieted his stallion.

"Well done, Thane Campbell of Glenorchy." The
words were uttered in a mocking, bitter tone.

"You know my name," Thane said. "I have not the
pleasure of yours."

"You'll know soon enough," the man replied evenly.
"Son of Archibald Campbell, the laird of Glenorchy, and
now laird himself. I remember you well when you were
but a whelp riding at yer father's side." The point bit into
Thane's flesh, raising a trickle of blood.

"I don't remember you, sir," Thane shouted, ignoring
the sword point. "Enlighten me."

"I daresay you don't remember me, for yer father sent
you off to France when he heard a price had been placed
on your young head."

"By whom?" Thane demanded, but at that moment
Duncan loomed out of the mist, his blade slashing downward against the raider's sword arm. Thane yanked on
Bhaltair's reins and the stallion reared backward, carrying him away from the enemy blade. The raider's
sword clattered to the rocks. Cursing, he clasped his
shoulder and dug in his heels so his sturdy pony bolted
away. Immediately he was lost in the mist.

"Are you hurt, Thane?" Duncan called.

"Nay, after the bastard," Thane ordered. He urged
Bhaltair up the slope after the outlaw, knowing that it was
already too late.

"Who are you?" Thane shouted in frustration. "Blast
you!"

No one answered.

Duncan returned, shaking his head. "We've lost them
again, Thane. The mist made it impossible to follow
them, and they know these glens and hills like they were
their own."

"Mayhap they once were," Thane said thoughtfully. "I

think I wounded their leader. Call the men back. We'll camp here and try to pick up their trail in the morning, when the sun rises and burns away this mist."

"Aye." Duncan went off to gather up his men. Thane sat on Bhaltair, straining to see through the mist. Come morning, he knew they'd find no trace of the raiders.

Gillian was beside herself with shame. Aindreas and Duncan had seen her rolling in the fields like a common—Bridget's word came to mind, and she applied it to herself unmercifully—like a common trollop! Bridget had known, had seen through her reticence and pride to the heart of her and guessed what she truly was. She should leave Edinample, go back to the woods, where she would not be faced with temptation, for she clearly had not the character enough to resist. Aye, she was worse than a trollop.

She sighed in exasperation. No one at the castle would come to regard her with trust or admiration if they continued to find her naked in the meadows. She may already have shocked Aindreas with her wanton behavior so he no longer wanted to be her friend. That brought her to the real crux of her dilemma. If Aindreas and Duncan were disgusted at her behavior, how must Thane truly feel?

She'd been so easy, like one of the castle wenches whose services were taken for granted and had no real value. Was this where she was headed? When Thane tired of her, would he relegate her to kitchen duties and share her with the other men? The thought was so repugnant, she cried out in pain. Nay, she'd not mind the kitchen duties, but she'd never go to another man. But in all her anguish, she knew in her heart she'd never be able to deny Thane.

So she put her shame behind her, carried herself with quiet dignity, and went about her normal activity of walking in the bailey, offering her herbs and advice to anyone who ailed. Surprisingly some took her dried potions.

"Mama says ye're a white witch," Peter Krochmal said, walking alongside her. "Mama says you don't do bad things."

"I am not a witch, good or bad."

"Mama says!" Peter insisted.

"In this your mama is wrong," Gillian answered. "I am not a witch."

"D'ye want t'be?"

"Nay!"

"D'ye ever see a witch?"

"Nay."

"I did once," Peter confided. "She was a bad witch and she was old and ugly."

"She may have been old and ugly, but she was probably not a witch," Gillian answered patiently. She liked Peter and normally welcomed his prattling, but today in her preoccupation over Thane, she found herself impatient with the lad. "Peter, there are no witches. None. There are poor, lonely old women without family who become strange in the head and so are accused of being witches."

"If they aren't witches, why do they become strange in the head?"

"I don't know, Peter, but when people grow old, sometimes these things happen."

"You're na old," Peter observed.

"Not yet."

"And you're not ugly."

"Thank you, Peter." Gillian resumed her walk. Peter ran to catch up with her.

"Peter," she asked as they strolled, "where is yer father? I never hear you speak of him."

"He was killed when I was a babe," Peter answered.

"So you never knew him?"

"Nay. Mother tells me he was a very brave man. He

was fightin' off the lowland raiders who'd crossed onto Campbell lands and he was shot in the back."

"How awful!" Gillian said, reminded that Thane had gone to fight off raiders.

"Nay, he was a hero. He died defending his village. I want t'die like that someday."

"Nay, Peter," she cried in distress. "Don't wish such a fate for yourself."

"One day I'll be old enough t'ride with Laird Thane, and I mustn't be afraid of dying."

"You must always be afraid to die," Gillian said. "Didn't God put you on this earth? He would not have you throw away such a precious gift so carelessly."

The boy lapsed into thoughtful silence then. They walked far along the riverbank before Gillian realized the distance they'd gone and turned back. She was surprised suddenly to see people rushing about.

"Mayhap the men are back," she cried, and taking Peter's hand, rushed forward, but as she arrived at the castle gate, she was greeted by the accusing faces of servants and tradesmen.

"So, ye've come back, have ye?" demanded one woman, her arms akimbo. "Aye, and ye'll answer to Muriel for any harm ye've done her bairn."

"I've done no harm," Gillian cried, looking about at the set, angry faces. At that moment Muriel pushed her way through the crowd.

"Peter," she cried, and ran forward to draw her son into her arms. Frantically she hugged him, then drew back to study him, running a hand over his hair, his cheeks, and shoulders as if to reassure herself that he was there and unharmed. Then her gaze fell on Gillian, who stood at one side, watching.

"You," Muriel cried, facing the younger woman. "What did you do with my son that you must take him off? What evil spell have you cast over him?"

Gillian's heart shuddered at the unfair accusation. "I did naught with him but allow him to accompany me."

"I would not have given my son permission to go with the likes of you."

"But Peter said . . ." Gillian turned to look at the boy, who stood shamefaced, his gaze pinned on the ground. "Ah, Peter, you've done me a disservice this day," she said softly. "I did not take Peter against his will, Muriel, and you must ask him how he spent the time."

She turned and strode toward the castle gate, suddenly fearful that the gathering of tradesmen might turn on her and drive her away or throw her into one of the dungeons below Edinample. But the servants parted for her, letting her go unmolested. Behind her came the sound of Peter's high-pitched voice. Gillian didn't look around. Her heart was heavy as she made her way up the stairs to her chamber. How she wished Thane would return.

The next morning she did not walk through the bailey greeting the tradesmen but went off to spend the day alone in the woods near the River Ample. Hunger and fatigue finally drove her back to the castle. Shadows had already gathered in the cobblestone streets before the craftsmen's cottages. Gillian turned toward the castle keep and did not see the figure that broke free of the shadows.

"Gillian!" She turned and waited as Muriel came forward. The laundress paused before Gillian, and stood shifting her weight from one foot to the other while her hands nervously turned the hem of her apron. But her eyes, dark and proud, fiercely met Gillian's.

"Aye, Muriel, what do you wish of me now?" Gillian asked wearily.

"Peter told me about your time together and of your— of your conversation about God and helping people and all."

Gillian remained silent, wondering where all this was leading.

"Peter, he—well, he says he does not think ye're a witch."

"I'm not!" Gillian said quickly. "Not even a white witch."

Muriel studied her face. "Aye, I don't know if ye are or not, but I judged ye wrong today," Muriel said. She took a step back. "Well, g'night."

"Muriel!" Gillian called impulsively. When the other woman turned back, Gillian swallowed. She feared Peter was Thane's son. "I have something to ask, I mean no offense."

"Aye, and what is it?" Muriel asked hesitantly.

"Peter's father. Can you name him?"

Muriel looked at her strangely. "Aye. His name was Charles Krochmal."

Gillian could not hide the relief in her face. Muriel noted it and nodded.

"You thought his father was the laird?"

Gillian was loath to confess her doubts, but Muriel's gaze was too probing and far too wise. "Aye, I thought so," she admitted.

"You were wrong too," Muriel said softly, and it was a while before Gillian realized that was Muriel's apology. Gillian watched her hurrying away down the path back to her cottage.

Thane and his men returned to Edinample two days later, cold, exhausted, and empty-handed.

Twilight lay over the land. The proud, whitewashed stone walls of Edinample beckoned. As they approached the castle, Thane's ill humor vanished upon seeing Gillian standing on the parapets, waving to them. Her black hair had been left unbound, and it blew behind her like raven's wings. He could see the sparkle in her green eyes in spite of the distance, and the bright color in her cheeks. She'd not fled as he'd feared. She was there waiting for him. His spirits soared.

Despite the great stallion's fatigue, Thane urged him

forward, eager to greet Gillian and hold her in his arms. Even then he could taste the sweetness of her kisses and feel the yielding softness of her breasts against him. His loins tightened in anticipation.

He must not make the same mistake he had in the meadow, he reminded himself. Though she'd complied with his every urging, he'd sensed the reluctance in her passion and noted the shame reflected in her eyes when Aindreas and Duncan came upon them. He would be more patient and find the proper moment, when there would be no interruptions, for he would have her capitulate to him without a thread of reserve or shame. It was not enough to win her body, he reflected, he would have her heart and soul as well.

"Thane!" Her happy cry greeted him as he rode into the bailey. Nimbly she scrambled down the narrow stairs from the parapet and ran to him. He dismounted and caught her in his arms, his earlier resolve to go slowly and patiently forgotten in the joy of his reception.

He lowered his head and claimed her lips in a kiss that took her breath away. With a small laugh of embarrassment she stepped back and glanced at the other men milling in the bailey. Some were receiving a similar greeting from the serving maids they'd fancied.

Thane's eyes were all for the dark-haired enchantress standing before him.

"Are you thirsty?" Gillian asked shyly. "I've ordered some wine brought to your room and a hot bath and food, for you must be famished."

"Aye, that I am, lass," Thane replied, staring at her so intently, she blushed, for she knew he hungered for something other than food.

"M'lord," she said, turning away from him. Cursing himself for his clumsiness, he stepped forward and touched her shoulder.

"I'm that sorry, Gillian, if I've embarrassed you, but I

thought of nothing else but you during those cold hours in the mountains."

She turned to stare into his eyes, seeking the truth of his words. What she saw there thrilled her. "And I you, Thane," she said softly.

He'd never known the icy sparkle of emeralds could hold a fire hot enough to sear his very soul, yet her eyes held all that and more. He drew in his breath sharply. "Don't look at me like that, lass," he murmured, "if you don't wish me to continue what we started in the meadow."

"I can't look away, Thane," she said softly.

Duncan had dismounted nearby, and now, seeing the two of them together, guessed at the need between them. "I'll tend t'Bhaltair for you, Thane," he said, and taking the stallion's reins, led him away.

"Will you come to my room with me, Gillian?" he asked, loath to let her out of his sight for one moment. "Will you help me with my bath?"

"Aye, if you wish it," she answered, although her gaze dipped. Thane became aware of his men and servants, some of them casting the two of them knowing glances. Thane turned so his shoulders blocked Gillian from their leering, and with an arm about her waist walked into the castle and up the stairs to his room.

Gillian's step did not falter as she walked beside Thane. She felt his arm, strong and protective, at her waist. She knew what the evening held for them both, and her heart beat inside her chest like thunder. Her head felt tight and her breathing was shallow and rapid, as if she'd run a very long way. At his door Thane paused and glanced at her before turning the handle.

"Are you afraid, Gillian?" he asked in a low voice, his blue gaze intent upon her face.

Gillian swallowed and shook her head. "Nay, Thane. I am not afraid with you."

He gazed into her eyes, as cool and clear as a burn

moving over forest moss on its path from the mountain snows. They reflected perfect trust in him. Thane drew a shaky breath.

"Aye, but *I'm* afraid, lass," he whispered, and bent to claim her lips in a kiss that left them both breathless. His arms folded her close against him, his hands gliding hungrily over her curves.

"Your bath cools even now, Thane," she whispered, and he drew back, chuckling.

"Is that your way of reminding me I've need of a bath, lass?"

"Nay," she said so quickly that they both knew it was true. Their laughter mingled. Thane threw open the door to his room and saw that she had indeed anticipated his return. A warming fire blazed on the hearth and a table had been set to one side with a platter of meats and breads and a flagon of wine. Best of all a tub of steaming water awaited, close enough to the fire that he wouldn't grow chilled as he bathed.

"How did you have time for all this?" he asked, laying aside his outer garments and pouring them both a glass of wine.

"I sent one of the stable boys to the mouth of Glen Ample with instructions to return in all haste upon first sighting you," she recounted proudly. Her cheeks flushed with pleasure that she'd anticipated his arrival and needs so successfully.

"Now, m'lord," she said shyly. "If you don't need me, I will retire to my own room while you tend to your bath."

"You don't want to scrub my back, Gillian?" he asked.

"Certainly I will return and wash your back if you so need." Her head was lowered, but he could see one pink lip was caught between small white teeth.

Suddenly he realized how insensitive he'd been. Though it was often the practice of female servants to bathe their laird and even for some noblewomen to perform such a task upon honored guests, he had once again

overlooked Gillian's inexperience with men and was
treating her as he had Bridget, assuming she would
quickly overcome her inhibitions. He believed she'd not
yet viewed a man's naked body. To do so in such a casual
manner would be difficult for an unbroken maiden.

"I'll send for you when I'm done with my bath," he
said, although he was reluctant to let her go. "Mayhap
you'll join me here for supper?"

"Aye, Thane. 'Tis my pleasure to do so." She met his
gaze, smiling freely, and withdrew from his chambers.

Thane slid into his bath and felt his aching muscles
begin to relax. One ache could not be alleviated by the
warm water. Only Gillian's body could cure that pain.

Gillian was grateful to Thane for releasing her from her
promise. She'd thought she could perform the intimate
task of bathing him. Had she not done so when he lay in
her forest hut, unconscious and dependent upon her skills?
She'd taken liberties then that even now brought a flush to
her cheeks. But this was quite different. Thane's sharp
gaze would be watching her every move, gauging her
every reaction, and she feared she would give herself and
her wayward thoughts away. How could she bathe that
golden skin and not let her fingertips linger upon it? How
could she gaze at the naked length of him and not blush to
the roots of her hair? He would soon guess she was far
more familiar with his body than she had the right to be.

Gillian sat on her window seat and watched the last
glimmer of light on the peaks of Ben Earn die away.
Night had come. From the great hall below came the
ribald laughter of Thane's men and the squeals and giggles of the serving girls as they carried large platters of
food to them. Everyone was happy to see the men
returned, but none as gladdened as she. How eagerly
she'd stood on the parapet watching for the first sight of
Thane on Bhaltair. How proudly she'd watched them
approach. Her world seemed complete when he was near
and desolate when he was gone.

"I think I love the laird," she whispered to a lone star that had appeared in the velvety sky. She thought back of the few discussions she'd had with Hannah concerning the feelings between a man and a woman.

"When the time's right, lass, ye'll know it," Hannah had said, and so had ended Gillian's preparations for what was to come. She shivered, uncertain if she would seem clumsy and ignorant to Thane, for he'd been with many women. She'd drawn this conclusion from the comments made by Bridget and the other young serving girls. All seemed to agree Thane was a skillful and thoughtful lover.

Nervously Gillian paced her room, plucking her skirts into place, smoothing her hair which she'd washed that afternoon with scented herbs. And despite the grumbling of the servants who had to carry up the water, she'd bathed that afternoon as well, taking great pains to remove the grime from beneath her fingernails and scenting her water with lavender. Now, as she'd seen the serving women do when they wanted to look their best, she pinched her cheeks to bring up the color and bit her lips until they were red. Finally sheer nervousness drove her back to the window seat, where she sat watching the moon rise from the distant band of trees and begin its climb in the sky. So caught up in its golden glow was she that she didn't hear the door of her room open or see Thane enter. The first she knew of his presence was when his hands clamped lightly on her shoulders. She jumped, then grew still beneath his touch. Her heart hammered in her chest, but she held her back straight and continued to gaze out at the moon.

"Why sit in darkness, lass?" he asked huskily. His strong fingers kneaded her taut shoulder muscles, and she felt her stiffness melt away.

"I was watching the moon rise," she replied through lips gone dry. Nervously she wet them. "Do you ever wonder if anyone lives there on the moon?"

Thane was silent behind her, considering her surprising, outrageous notion. "Nay, I have too much here in Glenorchy to think about. I dare not consider the moon as well, though in truth, now that you mention it, I wonder if my father ever considered claiming land there." His laughter was rich and self-mocking.

"Didn't you like your father?" she asked, ever sensitive to anything that affected Thane's well-being.

He sighed, and his hands turned her so she faced him. "I don't wish to talk about my family tonight," he protested. "Besides, I've told you more than you'll ever need to know."

"Aye, you have," she acknowledged. "Except about your mother. Bridget says Lady Joan will be coming to Edinample soon." His kiss cut off her words.

He lifted her against his hard, broad chest, his arms like bands of steel around her. She gave herself to the surge of passion that claimed her. Her lips opened beneath his probing tongue, and when the kiss ended this time, Gillian became bolder, pressing her mouth against his, sliding her small tongue inside his mouth, drinking the male essence of him. She was trembling in his embrace and was unaware that her weight rested so completely against him that if he moved away, she would fall to her knees.

But Thane had no intention of leaving her. He scooped her up in his arms, marveling at the light delicacy of her body, and turned to the door. She was hardly aware of their passage through the corridor to his room. When he placed her on his bed, warmed by the fire and their desire, she lay back against the pillows and gazed up at him with complete confidence. Thane hovered above her, his blue eyes licked with an inner flame.

She was like some wild untamed bird, he thought, infinitely beautiful and as difficult to hold in his hand. Yet here she lay, supine and waiting in his bed, her eyes filled with trust and a passion that smote his heart.

"My little wild bird," he murmured. "What we are about to do will cause you pain, but I will try to make it as easy for you as I can."

"I'm not afraid, Thane," she whispered. "You would never hurt me."

"Aye, I'll do my best not to." He removed his shirt and threw it to one side, then kicked off his boots, leaving only his cannons, tubelike breeches, to cover the growing bulge at his groin. Gillian's eyes widened at the expanse of his chest. She felt the blood rush to her head, and she remembered the first time she'd looked at him and felt these strange stirrings. Now she understood what they meant. Then, she'd felt ashamed of her response to him; now she reveled in it, letting him see how he pleased her.

Thane chuckled and lowered himself beside her on the bed, his arms wrapping around her possessively. At once he claimed her mouth in a kiss that never seemed to end except to turn into a moist, hot caress all the way down her throat to the edge of her gown. With a muffled curse he unfastened her simple gown and drew it away, exposing the full pale orbs of her breasts and the puckered dark areolae of her nipples.

Thane hesitated, his eyes drinking their fill, then slowly, almost reverently, he traced a large finger over her soft flesh and around the engorged nipples, making her shiver with anticipation. A soft moan escaped her lips.

"Ah, wild bird. I thought of naught else but this while I was gone. To be shown a bit of paradise and have it snatched away seemed the cruelest of all tricks by the gods."

Gillian remembered that day in the meadow and the shame she'd felt when Aindreas and Duncan came upon them. Her arms automatically came up to shield her breasts from his view.

"Nay, lass. Don't be ashamed of such beauty," Thane crooned, pinioning her wrists against the pillow on either side of her head. He stretched himself over her and she closed her eyes and drew in a sharp breath at the tingling flood of feelings that exploded in her body.

Thane dipped his head and drew one rose-tinged nipple between his teeth, nipping gently so she felt a pleasure so intense, it nearly brought pain. His tongue laved away any real discomfort, its rasping surface causing her to writhe in his embrace. Her breathing became deep and heavy. A lethargy seemed to settle over her so that her movements became fluid and languid.

She felt detached from her body, as if she'd moved into another world filled only with pleasure. With every stroke of Thane's hands and tongue she felt a sense of urgency building within her and a sure knowledge that soon that urgency would cease and she would learn the deepest mystery of all.

"I would see the rest of you, little wild bird," he murmured, and rose to pull her gown from her. She might have felt some reticence in another time and dimension, but not here, not with Thane touching her and holding her this way. He discarded his cannons and stood beside the bed, his golden body outlined by the flame in the fireplace. His manhood was so hard and rigid that he looked made of stone, yet when she put out her hand and touched him, he was hot and leapt against her hand.

"Nay, lass, don't do that now," he whispered huskily as he grabbed her hand. "Or you'll be the undoing of my resolve to make this night pleasurable for you, too."

"But I wish to touch you as you've been touching me," she said innocently.

Thane chuckled. "You will in time, I promise." He placed one knee on the bed and leaned over her. "Tonight I teach you the secrets of a woman's desire. Later I will teach you what pleases me."

"I want to please you now," Gillian insisted stubbornly.

Thane chuckled, his gaze like blue fire over her flesh. "You do, little bird, you do." He ran his hand over her belly and hips as if taking her measure, save that his touch was warm and lingering and awakened new yearnings within her. He lay beside her, alternately kissing her lips and her breasts until she was breathless and unable to offer any sound except a sigh and a moan.

His hands went to the conjuncture of her thighs, searching among the dark curls until he found the tiny bud he sought. Gillian jumped, then automatically spread her legs to accommodate his caress. Her breath came in tiny gasps now. Thane stroked her, dipping and stroking until she felt a tightness begin somewhere deep inside her.

When he judged the moment right, he rose above her, his shaft thick and stiff as he gently entered her. Her moistness was so sweet and hot, he had to strive to control his own need, otherwise he would thrust against her until he breached her maidenhead in a heedless moment and plunge toward the hot core of her.

Slowly he entered, paving the way with kisses and murmured endearments, and when he felt the tight resistance of her maidenhead, he clasped her close and pressed forward, praying he wouldn't hurt her too badly or frighten her for all time. He felt the tear of virgin flesh, heard her muffled cry, the slight withdrawal of her body, then she wrapped her arms around him fiercely and buried her face against his neck.

Her young, strong body began to move beneath his, startling him. Stunned, he acknowledged her generous giving with a deep kiss and his own hard, lean body thrust against her. He'd not expected to receive any satisfaction from this moment. A caring man could not find passion in the pain of a virgin, but Gillian was giving him this gift of herself, of her new, untried body, giving it without hesitation, ignoring the pain.

"My lass, my beautiful lassie," he murmured, and the rhythm of their bodies increased.

The pain had let up, and now she felt only the wonder of Thane's body bound within hers, the thrusting glory of him. She felt as if she were on the slopes of Ben Earn, high above the rest of the world. The air was thin, so she was light-headed, yet still she raced for the top because at the pinnacle was life itself. She felt the cresting wave of their passion, reached for the peak, and plunged over, joyfully.

She didn't realize she was crying until Thane raised his head and peered at her in concern. "Did I hurt you, lass?" he gasped, drawing away. Quickly her arms clamped around him, imprisoning him above her.

"Nay, my love," she whispered. "You've taken me to the heavens and back." He relaxed against her, his breathing ragged in her ear. Their bodies glistened with mingled sweat, which quickly dried so they grew cold. Thane drew a coverlet over them and cuddled Gillian against his side. She curled against him warm and replete, a slight smile on her face as she drifted into sleep.

Thane lay awake, listening to her breathe, now and then running a broad hand down her back just to reassure himself she was finally in his bed. A wild, untamed bird, he thought, yet tame her he would, for she was a prize, even without land or family connections. Even after his marriage to Juliana Cawder he would keep Gillian as his mistress. Juliana would bring him lands, bear him children, and carry on the Campbell traditions, helping him gain new prestige in King James's court; Gillian would give him pleasure and passion.

Chapter 10

A WIND BLEW down from Ben Earn and rattled the windowpanes with the promise of winter to come. Gillian lay cocooned within Thane's warm embrace and thought she'd never felt so cherished and protected. She'd never dreamed even that first night she saw him what ecstasy could exist in the coupling of a man and woman.

Contentedly she drew in a deep breath, taking in the very masculine essence of the man beside her. She remembered the night when he first awakened her to this deep passion, yet he'd held her gently, adoringly, fearful of bringing her pain, but she'd had no fears. She'd guessed that only through that pain could ecstasy be achieved. Her lips curved in one small, knowing smile of a woman who's been well introduced to the intricacies of lovemaking.

She never wanted to leave his side, never wanted to leave Edinample. She would live here forever and grow old with Thane and bear his children and heal him when he grew ill and make him laugh when he grew sad. She would give all she had to offer, holding nothing back. Their sons would look like Peter, strong and sturdy with fair hair and piercing blue eyes like Thane's and one day he would grow up and become laird of the land and all the old feuds and hatreds would be forgotten.

She sighed again, so caught up in her fairy tale she hadn't noticed Thane had wakened and lay watching her through half-closed lids, until she felt the throb of him against her thigh. Quickly she peered into his face, but his eyes were shut tight and his breathing deep. She lay for a bit, considering that he could become aroused even in sleep, then her attention was diverted by his growing member. She felt the heat and weight of his erection against her flesh and longed to touch him, but he had not permitted it the night before.

Now she reached for his engorged member, shyly touching it with her fingertips, and when this elicited no denial from him, she grew bolder, wrapping her fingers around the hard rod, marveling at its smoothness. This had been the source of her pleasure and pain the night before. It seemed to have a life of its own, for it leapt in response to her exploring fingers. She brushed a fingertip across the hot, smooth tip, found the indentation between tip and shaft, and curiously brushed the pebbled surface between the two. To her surprise, Thane let out a deep groan.

"Oh." She drew her hands away and stared at him. His eyes were wide open now and staring at her with a fervor she recognized from the night before. Yet he'd groaned so loudly. "Did I hurt ye?" she whispered.

A smile curved his lips. "Nay, lass, your touch didn't cause me pain," he said, and pulled her against him, his mouth coming down to claim hers. Gillian felt the fires flare to life within her and knew Thane felt the same. He took little time to caress her now, for he sensed she was as ready as he. He positioned himself above her and entered her, still taking care that she was new to this, yet with barely controlled passion. When he felt her moist, hot flesh close around him, his control vanished and he thrust into her.

Gillian's eyes opened wide in surprise. This was different from the night before. As pleasurable as that had been, she sensed this coupling was more urgent. She brought up her knees, wrapping her long, slender legs about his churning buttocks and matched her rhythm to his, taking and giving back as urgently as he. Their mutual climax was shattering, a tearing asunder of body and soul so they were no longer separate beings, but each a part of the other, a melding of their very spirits. And when at last the wonder receded so they could think and act and breathe again, Thane drew back slightly and peered into her eyes, his large thumb slightly caressing her cheek.

"Ah, lass, I've used you hard."

"No more than I wished," she murmured, then could not hide a frown of discomfort.

"I've hurt you," Thane said so contritely, she had to chuckle.

"Nay, I'm not in pain," she said. "I—I must return to my own room."

"Nay, lass!" he cried in dismay. "Why would you leave me now? Are you angered with me?"

"Nay, I could not be angry with you."

"Then why do you wish to leave me?"

Gillian blushed. "I can't tell ye."

"Aye, lass, you can tell me anything." Thane regarded the flushed cheeks. "Ah, my little sparrow, so shy," he teased. "The necessary chair sits yonder in the corner."

"Nay, I'd not use it here," she cried in horror.

"You must or flee down the hall without your clothes." His eyes danced with mischief.

"I—I will wait," she said, sticking her nose in the air.

"Ye can't wait forever," he teased.

Gillian felt pain across her bladder. "Promise you won't look at me."

"I promise," he said with a wolfish grin.

"I don't believe you."

He laughed and turned away. When he heard her scurry across the room, he turned back. She perched on the edge of the necessary chair with such delicacy, his heart swelled with emotions. Observing her in such an intimate act only made him feel closer to her. He wanted to familiarize himself with every part of her, with every beat of her heart, every breath she drew, and yes, even this act as well. When she finished, he threw back the covers and welcomed her back to the warmth of his bed. She leapt into bed, all sweet, delicate limbs and flying black hair, and snuggled against him, seeking his warmth.

"You're not trustworthy, Laird Thane," she complained from between chattering teeth. " 'Tis a fault I wouldn't have guessed you possessed."

"Where you're concerned, I have no honor," he whispered huskily, smoothing his large hands over her back and hips to bring warmth to her chilled flesh. He pushed the thick hair back from her face and licked her cheek, then trailed kisses down to her chin, where he nibbled delicately.

"Do you mean to eat me, Laird Thane?" she asked saucily, holding her small chin so he might have better access. Her giggle was music to his ear.

"Aye, my little wild bird. I've a terrible hunger this morning."

She flinched and pulled back. Her eyes were wide and filled with regret. "I don't think I can again, Thane," she said softly.

His laughter rolled over them. "Aye, lass, I've used you. I expect no more this morning, but I warn you, there'll be many more nights like this one."

"The thought pleases me greatly," she said, and returned his kiss with a fervor that surprised him. He felt his member stir and pushed her away gently.

"Enough, wench," he cried with mock rage, drawing his brows down over sparkling blue eyes. "Ye can't seduce me again. I am an honorable man, a man of character and resolve. I must rise from this bed and be about my business." Her giggles pealed from beneath the tangle of covers as he bounded out of bed and drew on his clothes. A glance back at the bed showed her merry face peering out at him, her red lips smiling, her green eyes sparkling, her black hair tumbling about her bare shoulders.

"Ah, lass, you bewitch me," he said, then lest he be tempted to linger further, he drew on his boots, gave her a quick kiss, and left for the bailey, where he knew his men awaited him.

She never wanted to leave Edinample. She never wanted to leave Thane. This was her home, and now the Campbells would become her people. Old feuds and hatreds would be put aside, forgotten in the glow of Thane's and her love.

So thinking, she set about with renewed fervor to win over his men and the castle tradesmen and women. When Duncan's favored stallion developed a sickness that skimmed over his eyes, she brought him a wash of herbs and urged him to use it. Finally, desperate that his mount was getting no better, Duncan used her concoction and was astounded to find that within days he was able to ride the stallion again. When Peter's new puppy grew listless and dull-eyed, she fed it meadowsweet rolled in bits of lamb she filched from the kitchen, which soon had the puppy frisking about again.

Not all her attempts were triumphs, however. One day she came upon Evan MacGibbon beating his horse unmercifully. Without thinking, Gillian stepped between the whip and the horse, receiving a blow across her chest that ripped the bodice of her woolen gown, so fierce a blow was it.

"What the devil are ye doing?" Evan shouted at her. "I have no wish t'strike ye."

"Don't you?" Gillian asked, holding her gaze steady on his. Evan dropped his gaze first. "Why do you beat your mount like this? He'll not trust you again."

" 'Tis no business of yours why I choose to beat my horse. He's mine and not yours."

"Nay, Evan, he's mine," a voice reminded him sternly. Gillian and Evan whirled to find Thane, who'd been drawn there by the commotion. When he saw the bodice of Gillian's gown had been torn and that her exposed shoulder was already beginning to welt, his blue eyes turned icy and he grabbed hold of Evan's tunic, balling it in his fist and nearly lifting the man off his feet. "You've some explaining to do, man."

Evan had the good sense to look afraid, for he'd seen Thane strike a man down with one fist. Though he knew Thane to be fair, he was never overly lenient with his officers and he never allowed his animals to be treated badly. Evan shuddered. He had struck the laird's woman, albeit unintentionally.

"I didn't mean to strike your lady," he stammered. "I was disciplining m—yer horse and she stepped between us."

"Is this true, Gillian?" Thane asked.

"Aye, Thane," she answered, and had the satisfaction of seeing Thane release the man. "He was beating his horse unmercifully."

Thane glared at Evan. "You know how I feel about that," he said.

"Aye, Thane, but the horse has gone wild," Evan asserted forcefully. "Whenever I try to saddle him, he fights me. Today he stepped on my foot. I'd be no good to you if he broke my foot."

"Aye," Thane said, relenting somewhat, although his eyes still flashed with disapproval. "But the mount has not done that before. Mayhap there is a problem."

"I tell you he's grown stubborn and recalcitrant, like a woman . . ." Evan cast a glance at Gillian. His face grew red and he squared his shoulders.

While the men had been talking, Gillian had been gentling the mount in question, running her hands over his glossy neck and blowing against his nostrils. He was a young stallion, black, and shiny as a new penny. His soft brown eyes reflected pain and wariness rather than the wildness Evan claimed. When he was quiet beneath her touch, she began going over him inch by inch, even loosening the cinch to peer at the mount's belly.

"Ah, here's the reason for his wildness," she called to the men. Thane came to her side and squatted down so he might see. Evan followed suit. Gillian pointed out a long-festering wound beneath the horse's belly. Splinters of wood and bark protruded from the wound.

"You've ridden him through some rough country to cause this kind of wound," Thane said grimly.

"I don't know where he could have gotten such a wound," Evan said stoutly. "How did she know it was there if she didn't put it there herself?"

Thane's eyes blazed with anger. "You mentioned a week ago that you took a shortcut through Ample swamp. There's dead trees and stumps enough there to inflict such a wound if you were not careful in guiding your horse through."

"I took great care, Thane," Evan flared. "D'ye question my horsemanship?"

"Nay, Evan. 'Tis your horse sense I question," Thane snapped. "Even if you used the greatest care, you should have found this wound when you brushed him down. You grew careless wi' the beast, and I'll not have a good horse ruined by such sloppiness. You'll ride Micha from now on."

"But he's old and slow," Evan protested. "How will it look to my men to see me riding such a mount?"

"Aye, Micha is old and slow and experienced. He wouldn't let you lead him into that swamp, much less ride him into stumps. Maybe since you'll be riding at a slower pace, you'll have time to reflect on the best way to treat good horseflesh." Thane waved him away dismissively. Evan cast Gillian a murderous glance and stalked away.

"I fear I've made an enemy this day," she said softly.

"He'll not harm you or he'll answer to me," Thane said. "Now, tell me. Can you do anything to heal this wound? He's a young stallion and one of my best."

"Ah, I'll clean the wound and make a wash of wild plum, but he'll need to have a few days for his mouth to heal."

"His mouth?" Thane frowned.

"Aye," Gillian nodded. "Another reason he is so flighty is that his mouth is sore. Evan is too hard with the bit."

Thane's lips thinned. "I'll speak to him of this," he promised. "Evan is not a cruel man. He's just superstitious, and though he'd ride alone against a hundred men, he's easily spooked. I suspect the night he led his men home across the swamp, he was spooked and drove his men and his horses too hard."

Gillian remained silent, for she remembered that from the first, Evan had expressed his fear and belief she was a witch. Despite Thane's confidence in his captain, she would remain wary of Evan MacGibbon.

"Are you leaving Edinample?" she asked, noting he wore his leather-plaited shirt and riding boots.

"Aye. We plan to ride our southern borders and investigate the progress of the villages the raiders burnt out. Summer is passing and the people must be housed before cold weather."

This was a new image of Thane as laird of Glenorchy. Not only must he be a good protector and governor, but a considerate overseer as well. She felt an irrational sense of pride in him.

"Will you be gone long?" she asked, following as he led the black stallion back to the stables.

"Aye, a week or two." He motioned a stable boy forward to unsaddle the young stallion and gave him instructions that he was not to be ridden for a few days, before turning back to Gillian. Her woebegone expression brought a smile to his face, and he reached for her, pulling her close. "Aye, lass, I feel the same. I'll miss you with every beat of my heart."

"You'll be gone so long, Thane," she whispered, hiding the well of tears by pressing her face against his neck. "Can't you have Aindreas or Duncan ride the boundaries for you?"

"Would that be the actions of a good laird?" he chided her gently. "When I need my Highlanders in time of battles, they come without hesitation. I must see that their needs are met during peace. Do you not see that?"

"Aye, I do," she sighed, "but I don't have to like it." She still hid her face against his shoulder.

He chuckled and took her small chin in his hand and raised her head so he might look into her emerald eyes. The depths of passion he saw there made his heart leap.

"Like a wild bird," he murmured softly.

"Nay, m'lord. My wings have been clipped," she answered. "I lie here in your hand at your mercy." He drew in his breath at her words, so complete were they in their import. Her green eyes darkened until he was reminded of the dark, shadowy trees of Glenartney. He felt her tremble and lowered his head to capture her lips with his own.

"Use me gently, Thane," she whispered, "for my heart is yours."

Though his men awaited him, he could not leave her just yet. A quick glance showed him that the stable was empty. He swung her up in his arms and climbed the ladder to the loft, where he placed her back on the soft clumps of hay. His mouth claimed hers in a searing kiss. She was pliant and eager for him. Their hands fumbled impatiently with their clothes, and he hovered over her, his hardened rod plunging into her without hesitation. She took him readily, her hot, womanly flesh urgent against him. Their climax was quick and shattering, leaving them both gasping for air. When they could breathe again, they laughed, sharing a brief moment of elation at this wondrous thing between them.

"I must go," Thane said, rising to straighten his clothes. He gazed down at Gillian with her crimson skirts about her waist, her pale, slender legs sprawled in abandoned grace, not even bothering to cover the glossy nest of curls. Once she would have blushed and done so, but now she lay propped up on her elbows, smiling up at him, teeth flashing, cheeks flushed, and eyes sparkling wickedly.

"I wish you to remember me, Laird Thane," she said mockingly.

"You witch, as if I could forget you," he answered huskily, and was sorely tempted to linger with her awhile longer. "When I return you'll answer for your wantonness," he warned with mock sternness. Without lowering her teasing gaze, she slowly and provocatively smoothed her skirts down.

"I shall await your return with bated breath," she promised, and laughed at the lust she saw in his eyes.

"Witch!" he spat out, and turned on his heel.

"I think you will not forget me, Laird Thane," she called as he climbed down the ladder. Quickly she scurried after him, for to miss even these final moments together was more than she could bear. While he saddled Bhaltair, she stood plucking bits of hay from their clothing and hair. A somber silence had fallen over them both. All had been said that could be for then, and the moment of parting was upon them.

"I've received word, my mother will be here in a week's time. I'll likely not be back by then. Will you receive her and see to her comfort?"

"I? But is she not mistress of Edinample? I could not presume . . ."

"Mother has never been to Edinample."

"In that case, I shall be glad to do as you ask."

"Go to Micheil for anything you need," he said,

referring to the factor who handled the castle stores. His face grew somber as he took her into his arms for one last kiss. "Farewell, my little wild bird," he whispered.

"Farewell, Laird Thane," she answered, but the wistful softness of the words belied the formality of her good-bye. "Go with God's blessing."

He squeezed her shoulders, the blue of his eyes vivid against his tanned skin. Leaping into the saddle, he urged Bhaltair toward the central bailey, where the other men milled. Aindreas's lips curved in a smile when he noted the bits of hay still clinging to his cousin, and he exchanged a knowing glance with Duncan. Evan sat on Micha, his lips drawn downward in a sneer, and he glared at Gillian, who'd followed and now stood on the steps of the castle keep, her arms hugged about her waist in abject misery. Though Thane had often taken short jaunts for a night or two, she was strangely unprepared for this absence.

"Are all the men ready?" Thane asked, and at Duncan's nod led the way over the gate bridge. Gillian scampered up on the ramparts to watch as long as she could. Thane sat tall and dignified on Bhaltair's back, the two of them a magnificent sight.

When they reached the bend in the road, Thane reined Bhaltair to a halt and turned to wave to her. Gillian's heart soared. He'd known she'd be there. His certainty in her was touching. She waved until they were out of sight, then slowly made her way down to the bailey.

Thane had asked her to see to his mother's comfort, so Gillian busied herself choosing proper accommodations for her, finally deciding on a suite of rooms that looked out over Loch Earn and caught the morning sun. It was a beautiful view and the rooms were spacious, with huge fireplaces to warm each one on a cool evening. The furnishings were not as elegant as they might have been, so she wandered through the other rooms, picking out a table here, a chair there, and went to the kitchen to ask some of the servants to help move the pieces to the east room.

"We'll not do yer bidding. Ye're not mistress here at Edinample." Bridget was the first to rebel. The other servants followed suit.

"But 'tis for the comfort of the laird's mother," Gillian explained.

"The laird didn't tell us this himself," Bridget sniped. Thane had shown no interest in her since Gillian arrived at Edinample, and she'd received no small amount of gibes from the other servants, who'd secretly reveled in her comeuppance.

"I'm sure he meant to tell you," Gillian replied patiently, striving to keep her tone even. " 'Tis not for myself. I but do as the laird has ordered."

Bridget shrugged, her eyes dark and filled with malice. "Then you shall have to move the pieces by yourself," she answered. "For I've received no such orders."

Frustrated by the attitude of the other servants, Gillian went back to the task. Micheil came upon her tugging an ornately carved table down the corridor.

"What are you doing now, Gillian?" he asked with an indulgent smile. He'd come to have a healthy respect for the high-spirited, quick-witted girl. "Have you not enough furniture in your room?"

" 'Tis not for me," she exclaimed, pausing to regain her breath. Her chest rose and fell with each gasp. A sheen of perspiration gleamed on her brow and throat. Springy black curls clung damply to her cheeks. "Thane's mother will be here soon, and I'm trying to make her rooms more comfortable."

"The servants would not help?"

She shrugged. "They don't like to have me tell them what to do, since they consider me little more than a servant like them." Her troubled gaze rose to meet his. "I don't blame them. I'm not certain myself what my position is here."

"Something more than a servant, I'll wager," Micheil said, thinking Thane had indeed left her in an untenable position. Neither servant nor wife, she was doomed to face this kind of dilemma. He could make it a little easier for her, he decided. "Wait here," he instructed. "I'll get someone to move these pieces for you."

"You're most kind, Micheil," she said with some of her old fire. "I wish you better luck than I've had."

Micheil went off and soon returned with one of the stout young lads who carried firewood and otherwise assisted the cook. "You're to stay here and assist Mistress Gillian for as long as she needs ye," he instructed sternly, then to further confirm her raised position, he turned to Gillian. "D'ye wish me to accompany you to the storage rooms when you choose the menu for Lady Campbell's visit?" Though his expression remained untouched by the events around him, his eyes twinkled with a secret message for her.

Gillian stared at him in surprise, then, drawing herself up, answered in her very best imitation of a lady of the manor. "I would appreciate your help," she said grandly. "Mayhap we have something special to whet Lady Campbell's appetite."

"I'm sure we have," Micheil replied evenly, and with a last quelling glance at the waiting servant, took his leave. The rest of the furniture was moved with much less groaning and pain on Gillian's part. The hours flew by as she worked to ready Lady Campbell's rooms, so she was quite startled when Bridget made her appearance to announce Gillian had a visitor.

"A visitor for me? Are you sure there's not some mistake?" Gillian said.

"Aye, the guard said he asked for you. Who d'ye think would come visiting you?"

"Lachlan!" Gillian cried, a smile lighting her face. "Where is he?"

"He waits at the drawbridge gate." Bridget watched her with speculative eyes. "Pray, who is Lachlan, then? An old lover?"

"Nay," Gillian answered, in too good spirits to take offense at her words. "Lachlan is a—a friend." How could she explain about Lachlan? Without waiting for more questions, she ran down the stairs and to the drawbridge at the end of the lower bailey. She arrived breathless and expectant, her eyes sparkling, but no small hunchbacked man awaited her.

"Didn't a man, a hunchback, come to inquire for me?" she asked the guard.

"Nay, none has shown his face this day," the guard answered her indulgently. "Have you a yen for one? They say a hunchback brings luck."

"Word came to the keep that a visitor awaited me here," she said, drawing herself up, for the man's familiar manner offended her.

"Aye, there was a man who said he brought a message, but he waren't no hunchback."

"Where is he?" Gillian asked impatiently, for the thought occurred to her that Thane might have sent a message. Mayhap he'd been injured or delayed or— She quelled her wayward thoughts and fixed the guard with a stern eye while she awaited his answer.

The guard peered along the path. "He was just here," he muttered, then pointed to a distant figure who'd wandered down the path. "There."

Puzzled, Gillian walked along the path, wondering why the messenger hadn't come around to the town gate, which was most often used. A ragged drape of plaid formed a cawl over his head and threw his features in shadow. 'Tis naught but a beggar, she thought, and warily paused some distance back.

"You wished to see me?" she called, and the ragged

beggar raised his head to study her. He had, she realized, been perfectly aware of her approach long before she spoke. Silently he studied her until she felt a shiver of apprehension and turned back toward the drawbridge.

" *'Srioghal mo dhream!"* came the words from her past. Gillian paused and looked around, surprised to hear those words from a mere wanderer. The beggar raised his head, throwing back the dirty plaid that covered him, and stepped toward her. He was much younger than she'd thought at first, with a handsome face and the strong, tall body of a soldier.

"Do you speak to me, my good man?" she inquired sharply.

"Aye, lass, and you heard me right enough. *'Srioghal mo dhream.* Royal is my race! Have you forgotten these words and their meaning after all this time, Gillian Mac-Gregor, daughter of Angus MacGregor?"

"Nay, I didn't forget them," she whispered, looking around frantically to see that they were not overheard. "Nor did I forget that the words are forbidden."

"No man can condemn a MacGregor name and its motto."

"Who are you?" she asked, lips pale and trembling. "How do you know me and my true clan?"

"Aye, Gillian, and have you forgotten so easily your kinsman, Jaimie MacGregor? Didn't I always take you riding on your little pony?"

"Jaimie MacGregor!"

"Aye, himself!" He flipped the plaid aside, revealing the red and green of the MacGregor tartan. His fiery hair flashed in the sunlight, and above a matching beard were the gleaming blue eyes she remembered from her childhood—save now the eyes held a hardness she'd not seen before.

"Where have you been all these years?" She could scarcely believe he stood before her. They'd been children together. He'd tweaked her braids and teased her unmercifully and scoffed when she wanted to tag along after him. He was nearly five years older, which was a lifetime of difference then. Now she saw lines on his face. "Have you been well, cousin?"

Jaimie laughed, a bitter cackle that died as abruptly as it began. "Nay, Gillian, I was farmed out to a clan that hated the MacGregors as much as the Campbells did. Never a day passed that I wasn't cuffed and beaten and made to do the most menial of labor around the castle. I've dug out the cesspools of my enemy and cleaned up his vomit when he drank too much wine and ate too rich a food, while my own belly ached with hunger." He clenched his fists. "I have not been well, my little cousin, but I will be, for now I'll answer to no man and no enemy will make me bow my head again."

Gillian looked away from the furious light that burned in his eyes. "And what of your sister, Robena? Did she fare better?"

"Nay, Gillian. M'proud sister was sent to the MacLarens, where she worked as a servant by day and served as mistress t'old Dugal MacLaren himself by night."

"Oh, Jaimie!" The cry of anguish escaped Gillian's lips as she thought of the proud, high-spirited girl Robena had been. Three years younger than Jaimie, Robena had been far too grand and full of herself to pay much attention to Gillian unless she wanted to play a prank on her father or their nursemaid. Robena and Gillian looked enough alike with their bright coloring and raven hair to be mistaken for twins, and Robena had used that to her advantage to avoid punishment or some unwanted task. But Angus MacGregor hadn't often been fooled, for he had only to look into the eyes of the two girls. Gillian's eyes were clear green, while Robena's were a stormy dark hazel. The manner of the two girls set them apart as well, for Gillian was a warm-hearted girl while Robena was a

tyrant with the castle servants and often struck them when
no adult was about to chastise her.

All this flashed through Gillian's mind as she stared at
her cousin. Those were happier days for them all. "Why
do you come here, Jaimie?" she asked gently.

"To remind you that you are a MacGregor," he thundered. Gillian glanced over her shoulder to see if they
had attracted the attention of the guards. Satisfied they
had not, she turned back to Jaimie.

"I have not forgotten I'm a MacGregor," she said furi-
ously, "nor that my father was hanged from the tower of
Edinample itself. But the past is over and we must look
ahead to the future."

Fanaticism burned in Jaimie's eyes as he pointed an
accusing finger at her. " 'Tis hard to believe you're the
whelp of a man like Angus MacGregor, else you'd naught
be speaking such mewly-mush. You'd have buried the
hilt of yer dagger in Thane Campbell's back."

"He's done no crime against the MacGregors," she
cried, suddenly fearing for Thane's life.

"He claims Edinample Castle for the Campbells—
crime enough. And you!" His tone was contemptuous.
"You would lie with such a man. You're a traitor to your
clan."

"Nay, Jaimie. I'm not. I but struggle to survive in a
world harsh and unsympathetic to any who bear Mac-
Gregor blood. You well know our clan was proscribed.
You were not the only one to suffer hardships because of
it. We can't even speak our own name. I didn't bring that
about, nor did Thane."

"But you've forgotten the need to avenge your
kinsmen," Jaimie said scathingly.

"And what of you, Jaimie? What have you done to
avenge my father's death? He was your chief too."

He relaxed and smiled so disarmingly that Gillian
blinked. This handsome, smiling young man was the

Jaimie MacGregor of her childhood. "It has begun," he said softly. "The MacGregors are rising again."

"What do you mean?" she asked, a shiver running up her spine. Jaimie MacGregor seemed most dangerous when he was being calm and reasonable.

"Why do you come here, Gillian MacGregor, to the arms of your father's murderers?"

"Nay, Thane didn't kill my father and his clansmen. He was but a child in France when it happened. He has told me so himself. 'Twas his father who brought this misery to the MacGregors, and his father died two years ago."

"Aye, Archibald Campbell, a greedy, ruthless bastard of a man who would stop at nothing to get more land and power." Jaimie MacGregor's voice was tinged once more with bitterness.

"Why have you come here, Jaimie?" Gillian asked, hugging herself as if chilled. "Have you come intending to do mischief, because I warn you, Edinample is well guarded, even when Thane is gone."

"And he's gone now, is he?" Jaimie asked quickly.

"Aye, but he's left men aplenty." Gillian felt her heart beating in her chest. "You can't attack a castle by yourself."

Jaimie's lips curved in a feral grin. "Who says I'm alone, Gillian?"

Gillian's eyes grew dark with fear as she studied his smug expression. "You're mad," she cried, and grabbing up her skirt, turned to make her way back along the path to the drawbridge. A hard hand clamped over her arm.

"Nay, cousin," Jaimie said. "I'm not finished with ye yet." He spun her around and slapped her so hard, she gasped for breath. She put one hand against her burning cheek and blinked against the welling tears.

"Why do you strike me, Jaimie?" she demanded.

"To show you, Gilly, the way of things. I am not a child

to be so easily dismissed. Ye can't walk back into that castle and pretend all is well."

"You're the ones who raid our villages," she cried.

"Your villages?" he mocked. He gripped her wrist, shaking her as he spoke. "Are ye so completely a Campbell, then? Has he buried his seed within you so deep that your brain is addled and you no longer think as a MacGregor? You're a woman without honor, Gillian MacGregor."

Gillian jerked away from him, her emerald eyes blazing with a fury to match his own. "You speak of honor, Jaimie MacGregor, without knowing what happened to me. If not for Thane Campbell, I would be dead in the Forest of Glenartney, burned to death by men as steeped in hatred as you are. He saved my life, not once, but twice, and he gave me food and clothes and treats me with respect and gentleness. I—I love this man." His fist struck her to the ground. Gillian tasted blood as her teeth cut into her lower lip. Defiantly she stared up at Jaimie. He had become a stranger to her.

"It will do you no good to beat me, Jaimie Mac-Gregor," she said. "Ye can't change the way I feel about Thane Campbell."

Jaimie bent over her, his handsome face twisted with rage. "Then 'tis better I strike you dead at this moment," he snarled.

Her gaze did not waver. "Do as you must," she said stoically while her heart sent a wild cry of anguish to the south, where Thane rode. Would he grieve for her when he returned and found her dead? Jaimie studied her expression and smiled.

"Did you tell your lover that you're a MacGregor?" he asked softly. He read the answer in her eyes. "So you didn't trust him enough t'tell him that."

"I—I didn't know how he would look upon me if he knew," she admitted, unable to meet Jaimie's fierce gaze.

Suddenly Jaimie squatted before her. His gaze bored

into hers. His tone was menacing and sure. "Thane rides his boundaries to the east or south?"

"He didn't tell me."

"Liar!"

Gillian met his gaze, but he read her deception. Slowly he removed a knife and held it to her throat. "I will not tell you," she whispered tearfully. "You'll kill him."

"Ah!" Jaimie smiled. "The bitch protects her lover." His grip on the knife relaxed. "If I'd wanted to kill Thane Campbell at this time, I've had many chances t'do so. Tell me where he is so I may raid his lands where he is least expecting it."

"I can't betray him," Gillian said.

"If you don't tell me the information, I *will* kill him."

"He's well guarded."

"Aye. Duncan Burnhouse and Evan MacGibbon ride at his side, and of late his young cousin, Aindreas Campbell." Her eyes widened as she considered how well he knew Thane's movements. "There are moments when he relaxes his guard, and during those moments I could easily slip my dirk into his heart."

"Nay," Gillian cried.

"Aye, lass. See this?" He held up a medallion she'd often seen Thane wear. "I took this from around his neck as he slept." He paused, letting the fear build within her. "If you won't serve us for love of your own clan, you must serve us well to save the life of this enemy you lust after."

"What do you wish of me?" she whispered brokenly.

"Food, supplies, weapons."

"I can't get you what you ask," she protested. "I have access to none of those things."

"Aye, there's plenty of what we seek within the castle walls," Jaimie said thoughtfully. "The storerooms of Edinample are deep and rich, and stout weapons are made by the castle tradesmen." His eyes gleamed. "I remember well the hidden gate into the castle. You must see that the door is left unbarred and lead us to the storerooms."

"I—I can't do that!" she turned and stalked away, her back stiff and straight, her head held proudly. Seeing the pride of Angus MacGregor evident in his daughter, Jaimie cursed under his breath. She was a MacGregor, for all her loyalties in the wrong place.

"I'll find another way, cousin," he muttered, "and 'tis sorry you'll be for denying yer own kin this day."

Chapter 11

ANGER AND GUILT dogged Gillian in the days that followed, anger at her cousin for his continued feud against the Campbells, guilt that she'd not stood by her clan as a MacGregor, proud and true. She was surprised by Thane's arrival; he came out of the southeast, entered the castle through the town gate, and was already at the inner bailey before Gillian heard the commotion and went to investigate.

"Thane!" she cried, running to him, her beautiful face was filled with urgency and joy at seeing him, but her eyes, which usually glowed with her every emotion, were guarded in their expression. She threw herself against him, her slender arms going around his waist in a fierce hug.

"Have a care, my little wild bird," he whispered huskily, "else you'll feel the thrust of my desire even here in front of my men."

Gillian blushed but couldn't relinquish her hold on him. "I was so afraid you'd be wounded or—or worse."

"I've returned all of one piece." He chuckled, tugging at her arms. "I would hate to suffer injury in my own bailey." At his words she smiled and relaxed her grip, but he noticed a pensive air about her.

"Is something else troubling you, little one?" he asked,

gently taking hold of her chin and turning her face up so he might study her features. Her full lips pouted prettily, begging to be kissed, but her eyes, dark with secret worries, warned him she was not in a teasing mood. He thought of the laughing girl he'd left, and sighed, hugging her close and turning her toward the castle steps. "Tell me what ails that agile mind of yours."

" 'Tis naught but worry about your mother. She's not yet come, but sent a message that she'd been much delayed and would arrive soon."

"Ah, she will. Dinna worry so. Did you miss me?" he asked softly.

Her arm tightened briefly around his waist. "Ye can't know how much."

All through his bath, Gillian remained melancholy, although she was responsive to his every need before he voiced it. Hot water was brought and scented. Strong, slender fingers massaged his scalp and worked up a scented lather. Soft hands smoothed away the dirt and weariness of his journey. When he rose at last from his bath with the water sluicing around him, she was there with a towel which she'd warmed beside the fire. Her hands lingered over him, drying his back and hips, his chest and legs, and finally his loins. When she raised her head and gazed at him, he saw all her worry and sadness had disappeared. Wicked prisms of light flashed in his eyes, and his lips parted, revealing his strong white teeth. He looked like a sleek wildcat waiting to pounce. Muscles rippled beneath his golden skin as he sprang forward.

Squealing, Gillian leapt aside, but now he had her trapped against the bed. Laughing, she kicked off her slippers and jumped up on the bed, racing for the other side, where she might escape. Thane lunged after her, one large hand gripping a delicate ankle so she sprawled across the bed. He was on top of her at once, pinning her hands on either side of her head, capturing her wriggling body with the solid strength of his own. When she could do no more but lie breathless and suppliant beneath him, he lowered his head and captured her lips. His kiss was thorough, his tongue probing against her soft lips until she opened to him, and with one surrender came all the rest. Her legs parted so he lay between them, his hard rod pressing against her. Heat rose from his intimate caress until she was aflame with desire.

He took her hungrily, for he'd been too long away from her. Her womanly fragrance inflamed his senses. She was a willing partner, matching his fervor with her own. Her hands, her mouth, caressed him, touched him, and sought to erase the troubling guilt that plagued her. Lost in his passion, she forgot her fears for a little while and felt whole and happy, as if once again she'd come home. She rode the crest of their passion and drifted in a dazzling aftermath. Thane was home again. All was well at Edinample.

"By the gods, I'll kill the bastard," Thane shouted, striding from one side of the great hall to the other. His face was dark with fury, his eyes spitting blue fire so that the servants quickly completed their tasks and fled. The castle guards had no such escape open to them. They quelled before their chief, their gazes pinned to the stone floor, their feet shuffling in their discomfort. Gillian chose that moment to enter the hall, but no one seemed to notice her appearance. She couldn't help but feel the anger and tension in the room and wished herself elsewhere. Then she became aware of the gist of their conversation and lingered, sliding into a chair beside Aindreas and Duncan.

"What has happened?" she whispered.

"Someone raided the castle stores last night and made off with food and weapons," Aindreas informed her.

Jaimie! Gillian bit her lip not to cry out his name. "How did they get in?" she whispered frantically. "Was anyone hurt?"

Aindreas cast her a sharp glance. "Nay, lass, have no fear. They but took a few supplies in the middle of the night. 'Tis nothing."

"If 'tis only a small amount, why is Thane so angry?"

"Aye, but Thane doesn't tolerate a laxness of duty, especially for men on watch. It might have been murderous raiders entering the castle rather than thieves."

Gillian turned her attention back to Thane and the two men he was interrogating.

"Which of you fell asleep at his post and failed to see the intruders?" Thane demanded.

"M'lord, we didn't sleep," one man said boldly.

"Silence!" Captain Shiels shouted.

"Let the dolt speak!" Thane ordered, stalking over to glare at the man who stood a full head shorter than he.

The hapless guard swallowed hard. "We did not sleep, m'lord," he muttered. "I remember well, for I lost m'favorite sword with the cast of the die."

"You played dice while raiders crept into Edinample?" Thane exploded.

"Nay, m'lord." The man's companion spoke up. "There's no way anyone could enter the gate without our knowing it, for we played our game on the parapet right above. We could have heard the footfall of a ghost itself if it had come across the bridge."

"Aye, 'tis true," the other man said, nodding vigorously.

"Then they came by way of the town gate," Thane said, turning to the other two guards, who jumped and alternated between looking scared and aggrieved at being so wrongly accused.

"Beggin' yer pardon, Laird Thane, but I've stood guard for many a year at the town gate and there's never been a soul slip through there what never belonged inside the castle." The grizzled, burly man jerked his chin to emphasize his assertion. His younger cohort nodded in agreement.

Thane looked at Shiels. "Then by God's Passion how did they enter the bailey? How could they go right to our storerooms and wreak such havoc without someone seeing or hearing them?" His gaze was fierce as he paced. Gillian's heart beat so hard, she feared he might hear and round on her next.

"Obviously the thieves were led by someone who knew the castle well," Aindreas suggested, and Gillian cursed his quick wit. "Mayhap a disgruntled servant or tradesman?"

"Micheil, is that a possibility?" Thane turned to his factor, who had been quietly standing to one side. Micheil moved forward, his expression thoughtful.

"Aye, I've thought of such," he said. "Mayhap a servant who wished to sell the goods for an extra coin or two?"

Thane regarded the men and slowly shook his head. "Aye," he said wearily, and slumped into a chair. "Or it could be the raiders who've plagued us throughout Glenorchy."

"But no more than one or two men could have entered the castle without someone noticing."

"Aye, mayhap it was so, one or two men dressed as peddlers or tradesmen would have been let through the town gate. If it was our raider from the south, he's done this only to let us know he can enter Edinample at will."

"The devils mock us!" Evan MacGibbon cried.

"Aye, that they do!" Thane answered, his lips thinning in anger. "But we will not be mocked again. From now on we double our efforts to find them. We'll ride south at first light."

"But you've just returned," Gillian cried out despite herself.

"Aye, lass, we patrolled our borders, but now we ride after the raiders themselves."

"What of the MacNabs?" Evan asked. "Dare we ride into their borders without consulting them?"

"We'll consult them, and if they care to ride with us, they may," Thane said.

"Is it wise to leave the castle again?" Gillian said. "What if they come back?"

Thane's attention was drawn to her pale face. "Don't be afraid, lass," he said, and was unaware of how his voice softened. "Aindreas and his men will stay here to supplement the regular guards. You'll be safe enough. I intend to run the devils to ground before they do more mischief."

"But what if you can't?" Though no sound was made by the men present, she felt their immediate repudiation of her words. "What if you're hurt?" she finished weakly.

The men smiled with tolerant indulgence. Even Duncan seemed softened by her misgivings.

"Don't fear for me," Thane said, crossing the room to take hold of her hand. If his men had not been there, he would have drawn her into his arms and held her, running his big, rough hand over her silken locks. Instead, he towered over her, his blue eyes lighting in a smile. "I have the best of the Highlanders riding at my side."

Despite his reassurances, she sensed trouble was ahead and prayed silently for Thane's safety.

She went about her duties for the rest of the day, thinking of little else but that tomorrow he and his men would once again ride after Jaimie MacGregor. She'd seen the anger in Jaimie's face, heard the echo of old hatreds in his voice, and she feared for Thane's well-being more than ever. She must tell Thane the truth, she thought, then he would take her warnings more seriously. Perhaps he would understand that she'd had no choice but to keep her identity hidden. Perhaps he would forgive her.

At any rate, he wouldn't ride off at the break of dawn. She would tell him that night when they were snug in their bed, replete with lovemaking. Impatiently she waited through the long evening, supping with Thane and his men in the great hall, listening to their grim speculations about the identity of the unknown raiders.

"They're like ghosts coming and going at will. No one has ever seen them," Duncan grumbled.

"Nay, I saw their leader," Thane said. He'd been unusually quiet throughout the meal, but now he raised his head and looked about the table at his officers. "We spoke and he claimed t'know me and my father."

"Your father?" Duncan and Evan exchanged glances. "Then he knew you as a boy."

"Aye, so he says."

"A MacGregor!" Duncan and Evan exclaimed in unison.

Gillian jumped at the explosive utterance of her clan's name.

"Aye, so it would seem," Thane said. "He is about my age, so he was but a boy when the MacGregor clan was proscribed."

"Your father was behind their downfall," Duncan said. "He ordered his clan chieftains to provoke the MacGregors at every opportunity, and when the Mac-Gregors retaliated, the earl went to King James himself, requesting letters of fire and sword."

Thane's lips were a thin line as he listened to details about his father's schemes. The duplicity of his father was too hard to bear. "A whole clan wiped out by the greed for power."

"They didn't kill the women and children, only hanged the leaders of the clan," Duncan went on. "The women were branded and cast out. The children were passed around to other clans to be raised."

"I well remember the story," Thane said, nodding his head. "It would seem that one or more of them have grown up with their old hatred for the Campbells still hot in their blood."

"That would explain their getting around the castle guards so easily," Aindreas said. "They would know every nook and cranny of Edinample."

"Aye!" Thane rose, and taking his drinking cup with him, paced behind the table. "And they would know any secret passages into the castle. Captain Shiels, set the men to searching for any secret passageway, doors, caves—anything that would give access to the castle."

"Aye, sir," the captain said, relieved to have the honesty of his men confirmed.

Thane looked along the table at Duncan. "I remember hearing once that the MacNabs were supporters of the MacGregors."

"Aye, so they were, as were the Lamonts," Duncan answered.

Thane thought for a moment. "The Lamonts are too far south to be a base for the MacGregor raiders. They must be on MacNab land somewhere."

Duncan muttered agreement.

Gillian listened to their reasoning, nervously pleating her skirt between her fingers. Now was the time when she should rise and admit her own identity, but she had no wish to brave all the men in the hall, especially in the face of their obvious hostility toward all MacGregors. She would wait until she and Thane were alone.

But later, when they'd retired to their room and Gillian tried to broach the subject, Thane was not inclined to talk. "I've had enough speculation about the MacGregors for one night," he said brusquely.

"But I wish to—"

"Enough!" Thane's voice was sharp, cutting off anything she might have told him. Gillian jumped and looked at him with eyes wide and suddenly cautious. This was the peremptory tone she'd heard him use with some of his men. Now he'd turned it against her, but she'd said nothing to earn his ire. What would he do if he knew the truth? She felt a clutch in her heart and wanted to weep. Thane glanced up in time to see her hastily quelled expression and was immediately contrite.

"Forgive me, lass," he said, coming to take her into his arms. "This has been a difficult day, and I want to be free of worry for a few hours before I must ride out to find the MacGregors."

"If you find them, will you kill them?" she asked in a low voice, for the first time giving some thought to Jaimie and his renegades.

"Aye, if we must, for I fear they will not surrender to us peacefully."

"You must not kill them," she cried. "The feuding will start again."

"The feuding has already started with the MacGregor uprising against my people. They want war. They were always an undisciplined bunch of rabble."

" 'Tis not so!" Gillian cried, and Thane looked at her in surprise.

"And how would you be knowing that, lass?" he demanded, his golden brows drawn down, his gaze blue ice on her. "The MacGregor is a cold-blooded man and he hates the Campbells. He'll kill as many of us as he has the chance to."

"But didn't you tell me, he had you under his blade and yet he hesitated?" she said, unable to stop herself.

"Only to jeer at me, Gillian. If Duncan had not appeared with his sword, I'd be dead now."

An urgent rap at the door saved her from having to answer. Impatiently Thane crossed to throw open the door. Aindreas stood on the other side, his young face pale.

"What is it, Ain?" Thane demanded, taking hold of his shoulder and guiding him to a chair.

" 'Tis your mother," Aindreas gasped. "One of her guards just arrived. They were ambushed on the way here. Lady Joan has been kidnapped."

Chapter 12

"**D**'YE THINK THEY'LL come this way?" Aindreas asked for the dozenth time. Thane no longer bothered to answer.

"They canna travel any other pass if they come from Kilchurn t'the east," Duncan said.

"Mayhap they passed through before we arrived here," Aindreas worried.

Thane shook his head. "Nay, they dinna!" he said with certainty.

Duncan said, "Some of the men call their leader the Red Fox for all that he's so sly and elusive."

"Aye, he is that," Thane agreed. "But a fox can be caught right enough. We have only to set the trap for him. Tonight, I believe, we have one he can't escape." He looked around the pass at the positioning of his men, reassuring himself that the trap was ready to be sprung.

"Aye, the trap is set," Aindreas remarked. "We wait only for the fox."

They'd begun to think the fox had eluded them once again, when near dawn they heard movement on the path below.

With held breaths and tense muscles they waited, unable to tell in the dark night exactly where their quarry was except by the occasional brush of a hoof against a stone or the sighing protest of a horse being urged through the narrow pass.

"Do they have the women with them?" Aindreas asked, straining to see through the black shadows.

"Be still. Don't give us away before it's time," Thane admonished. At that moment the movement along the path ceased. A low, guttural curse sounded and a horse left the path to move back along the line of riders.

"What's wrong? Why have you halted?" a low, rough voice demanded.

"I am tired, sir," a light feminine voice said. Thane's grip on his cousin's arm tightened in a silent message.

"I insist you let us dismount and rest," the voice went on peremptorily. Thane grinned despite himself. Lady Joan being her most autocratic.

"We can't rest here, m'lady," a male voice answered. "The sides are too steep to accommodate a camp. We must ride on through. We can rest on the other side."

"Are you certain?" Lady Joan raised her voice, pitching it higher.

Another rider came along the line in great haste. "Be still!" the rider hissed in a low voice. "Your voices will carry here."

"But, my good man, I insist we rest now!" Contrary to the rider's command, Lady Joan's voice rose even louder and ended abruptly in a stifled cry of pain. Thane leapt to his feet and was pulled down at once by Duncan and Aindreas.

"I'll kill the bastard," he whispered, shaking off their grip.

"Wait until they are farther into the pass and I'll help you," Aindreas muttered in a low voice.

Lady Joan's voice came to them again. "Let go of me, ye're hurting me," she said, and beneath the bravado Thane could hear the edge of fear creeping into his mother's voice. His hands balled into fists.

"I apologize for hurting you, Lady Joan," the voice

said, and Thane recognized it as that of the man he'd confronted on these mountain slopes once before.

"The MacGregor leader," he whispered between clamped teeth. "You'll leave him for the bite of my sword."

"Aye," Duncan and Aindreas agreed in unison.

"I have no wish to cause you pain, Lady Joan," the MacGregor leader was saying. "But we must travel as quietly and swiftly as we can. We'll rest as soon as it's safe for us to do so."

The motion of the horses began again.

"Careful, just a little more," Thane said, peering over the boulder that hid them. The misty shadows parted slightly, and the pale moonlight gleamed down in a quicksilver moment, lighting the scene of horses and men and captives. They had entered the narrow pass completely; there was no going back, for they couldn't turn their horses.

"Now," Thane shouted, leaping from behind the boulder. He had the satisfaction of seeing his troops ride down to close off the pass at either end. The MacGregors were trapped.

Thane saw the sheen of red hair and beard as the leader jerked around in the saddle and took in the Highlanders bearing down on them. "Ride," he commanded. At once they kicked their mounts, and despite the treacherous footing that could lame man and horse, they surged toward the southern exit of the pass.

Thane and his men were on foot, for their horses could never have traversed the sides of the pass high enough to hide themselves. Only those troops at either end of the pass were mounted. Now he could see his quarry escaping and launched himself forward through the air, to fall against a mounted rider. One powerful arm came out to seize the man, one powerful fist drove his blade deep into the man's chest. Claiming the dead man's mount, Thane galloped after the other riders. Meanwhile his men had followed his example and regained mounts while in pursuit.

"Leave the captives," Jaimie MacGregor shouted, and the women were shoved from the path as the MacGregor men thundered past. Struggling to stay on their frightened mounts, they were in danger of being trampled, if not by the fleeing raiders, then possibly by the pursuing men.

"Climb up the sides," Lady Joan ordered Evina and her maid. After sliding from their horses, the women scrambled up the steep, rocky slope until they were well out of danger. Breathless, they crouched, watching the melee below as raiders were caught and quickly dispatched. Lady Joan marveled at her son's fighting prowess. She'd known he possessed it, but never had she witnessed it firsthand. Now she noted with pride that he was as humane as he was skilled, granting life to those men who threw down their weapons and surrendered. But for all his efforts, some of the raiders were escaping.

"Hold that end of the pass," he shouted, but the MacGregor men rode hard at the guards. Horses reared, squealing their pain and terror as the MacGregors boldly charged. They had little to lose, their plight was desperate and so was their fight. The Campbell men couldn't hold back their fierce attack. Swords flashed and Campbell men fell beneath the thrashing hooves.

"The pass is clear!" came the MacGregor cry, and the outlaw Highlanders fled down the narrow gorge. The red-haired leader waited until all his men who had not fallen to the Campbell swords had passed through the gap, then he turned to face his enemy.

" *'Srioghal mo dhream!'* he cried defiantly, holding his sword aloft. The Campbell troops, surprised by such boldness, hesitated, and in that momentary pause the MacGregor goaded his horse and galloped through the end of the pass.

"After them!" Thane ordered, urging Bhaltair forward. They'd barely reached the end of the pass, when a rumble sounded over their heads. Thane felt a shudder of dread race down his back. Like a fool, he'd ridden into a trap as well. The MacGregor men had not failed to set a snare to cover their escape.

"Go back!" he shouted to his troops, and once again pandemonium reigned as men tried to turn their horses in the narrow gorge. Rocks tumbled about them. With horror Thane saw his men and horses being struck down by deadly boulders. Men shouted. Horses screamed. Above it all, Thane heard his mother's horrified cry. Pain exploded in his head, pushing him down. He tried to stay in his saddle, tried to hold onto Bhaltair's reins, but darkness claimed him, so he was unaware that his stallion made a last valiant effort to carry him to safety. A tumbling boulder felled the gallant horse.

"Thane!" Lady Joan cried, having seen her son struck down. At once Duncan heard her cry, and seeing Thane and Bhaltair sprawled on the rocky path plunged forward to give aid without thinking of his own safety. Throwing his own body over Thane's, he sought to protect his chief from the last fall of rock. All around them lay devastation. Some men were fatally injured, their bodies sprawled like broken twigs. Those men who were able-bodied were already hurrying to help their comrades. When the sky stopped raining stones, Lady Joan rushed down the slope and stumbled toward her son.

"Don't come down here, m'lady," Duncan called. He knelt beside Thane, searching for the flutter of a pulse. "He's alive!" he called when he found one.

At his admonition, Lady Joan had paused. Now she rushed forward, clambering over stones and bodies to get to her son. "Thane, speak to me," she called, kneeling beside him and wiping at his bloodied face with the bottom of her gown. Her hair tumbled about her face, her gown was torn and dirty, yet she looked every inch the lady. Tears dampened her cheeks, but her voice was firm when she raised her head and addressed Duncan.

"We must get him back to Edinample. Is Bhaltair badly injured?"

"I don't know," Duncan said, bending to examine the stallion's legs. Bhaltair moved restlessly but made no attempt to get up, for Thane's body lay half on the stallion. "No bones are broken," Duncan said. Spying Aindreas, he waved him over. "Help me move Thane. With any luck Bhaltair can stand up and carry him home."

"Is Thane alive?" Evina Campbell asked. She'd followed Lady Joan and stood to one side, her expression fearful, her shoulders slumped.

"Of course he's alive, you dolt," Aindreas said harshly to his sister. "Nothing can defeat Thane." His young face was starkly pale, which belied his show of bravado.

Carefully they lifted Thane off Bhaltair. At Duncan's urgings the great stallion lunged to his feet and limped about, finally standing on three legs.

"Is he strong enough to travel all the way to Edinample?" Lady Joan asked doubtfully, for she knew the great store Thane set in this horse.

"Aye, he'll have to," Duncan said. They tied Thane into Bhaltair's saddle. The men who'd been killed in the rockslide were placed across their saddles facedown. Several of the horses had been killed, so the able-bodied men walked, giving over their mounts to the badly injured.

"We'll walk as well," Lady Joan said, refusing Duncan's offer of assistance to mount.

" 'Tis not necessary, Lady Joan," Duncan urged her. "We'll be able to move faster if you women ride."

"Aye, you're right, my good man." Lady Joan placed her foot in his hand and let him help her into the saddle. Evina and the maid followed suit on the remaining horses, and they all began their sad journey back to Edinample.

Gillian knew something was wrong, knew it long before she saw the small, bedraggled column move along the path toward Edinample. From the parapet she strained to see Thane seated astride Bhaltair, but the great stallion appeared riderless.

As the party drew closer, she could see that Thane sagged over Bhaltair's neck. Gillian was reminded of that first night when they brought Thane to her, all gored and bleeding from his wounds. Beside her, Odaria, the cook's assistant, threw her apron over her face and began to weep.

"What is it?" Gillian asked as the other women gathered around Odaria.

" 'Tis her man. He's come back dead," Bridget snapped as if it had all been Gillian's fault, and in her own guilt Gillian quietly accepted their blame.

"I'm sorry, Odaria," she murmured, and turned away, going to her room to check her supply of herbs. When she had gathered and dried them, she'd thought she'd never have the chance to use them. That she had now seemed a guidance from God himself, for she'd readily spied a number of injured men. Taking her bag of herbs and fresh linen cloths, she hurried down to the bailey to await the arriving party. They limped over the gate bridge and into the bailey. At first Gillian had eyes only for Thane, and hurried to Bhaltair's side. His face was deathly pale, his eyes closed. When she called his name, he made no response.

"He's badly injured," she said to Duncan with a catch in her throat. She was unaware her gaze darkened with unspoken accusations. Why hadn't Duncan guarded Thane against injury? Was that not his responsibility? Wearily the warrior nodded as if accepting her blame.

"Aye, he'll need all of yer skill, Gillian." He motioned two of the castle guards forward and directed them in lifting Thane from Bhaltair's back.

"What happened that so many are injured and killed?" Gillian asked. Aindreas had come to help his sister and aunt alight, and he turned a bitter smile on Gillian.

"It seems our wily MacGregor fox is slier than we credited him," he said, and explained briefly about the rock slide. "They rigged it deliberately so they could loosen the rocks down on the heads of anyone who pursued them."

Gillian's face was pale with anger as she listened.

Aindreas indicated the two women who had alighted and now stood beside him. "This is Lady Joan and my sister, Evina," he said.

Gillian's eyes widened momentarily, then she curtsied. "Welcome to Edinample, Lady Joan," she murmured. "I'm sorry you've met with such hardships on your journey, but I've readied a room for you and the servants have warmed the sheets and are bringing a supper and a bath." She smiled at the young woman who'd stood silent, her pale blue eyes assessing Gillian with some hostility.

"I'm happy to meet Aindreas's sister," Gillian said sincerely. "I hope we will be friends." She dropped a small curtsy. "A room has been prepared for you as well. Now, if you'll excuse me, I'll see to Thane's injuries."

"But, my dear, we have a surgeon for that," Lady Joan said.

"Aye, and good he is at his craft," Gillian acknowledged. "But I've gathered some fresh wild lettuce, which will be good to pack the wounds and ease the pain."

Evina's face wrinkled in distaste. Lady Joan regarded Gillian thoughtfully.

"By all means, child, be about your business," she said finally, and with a quick bob Gillian sprinted away down the corridor, unaware of how elegant her slender figure appeared even in its humble servant's garment.

The next hours passed in a haze for Gillian as she worked beside Shadwell, trying to alleviate the suffering of Thane and his men, trying to save them from death. Thane had not regained consciousness since he was injured, and she hovered beside his bed, patiently forcing gypsyweed tea between his lips, her own lips moving in silent prayer. He had to live. She could not bear it if he died.

In her anguish she cursed Jaimie MacGregor and all the MacGregors who rode with him and loosened the rocks down on Thane and his men. When she stood over the injured troops, listening to their moans of pain, she knew hatred for her cousin.

Using every skill at her command, calling on every scrap of knowledge Hannah had lent her, she sought to give them some comfort with her potions and had the satisfaction of knowing she'd succeeded with all save Thane. She was not alone in her vigil and prayers. Shortly after the party had arrived, Gillian looked up to see Lady Joan standing at the foot of her son's bed, her face somber.

"Will he live?" she asked Shadwell.

"I don't know, m'lady," he answered. "No bones were broken, but something inside him is amiss and I can't fix it."

"Oh, dear God," Lady Joan whispered, and swayed on her feet. Gillian leapt forward to lend her strong young shoulder and lead her to a chair.

"You should not be here, Lady Joan," she said. "You've been through a terrible ordeal yerself. You need to rest."

"But he's my son," Lady Joan protested, and Gillian said no more. How could she expect Lady Joan to leave Thane without knowing if he lived or died, when she herself could not. So the two women watched over him through the night, sometimes sharing their tears, sometimes sitting in mutual silence, their hands clasped together for strength.

Near dawn Thane stirred and groaned. At once Gillian was at his side.

"Thane, beloved," she whispered through a fresh surge

of tears. "Do you hear me? Open your eyes and let me know you're all right."

With a moan Thane raised his golden lashes, revealing narrow wedges of blue, clouded by pain. Gillian smiled despite herself.

"You're awake," she cried, and threw herself across his chest. Thane felt the silken brush of her black tresses, caught the perfume of her hair, and fought back the dark shadows that crowded around him. One arm was bound to his side, but the other was free and he used it to gather her closer.

"I didn't think I would see you again," he whispered hoarsely.

"I feared the same," she answered. "I prayed that God would watch over you."

"And so he has."

"Of course. Otherwise you wouldn't be lying here with your body all bruised and battered."

Thane laughed, then stopped abruptly, pulling in his breath against the sharp pain that ripped through his chest. "Have I broken ribs?" he asked.

"No broken bones."

"Then God must surely have protected me," he said softly. "When I saw the rocks hurling down on us, I thought I had glimpsed my last of this world."

Gillian's arms tightened fiercely, and she hid her face against his shoulder.

"Aye, lass, have a care or you *will* crack my ribs," he said, and immediately she released him.

"I'm sorry. I'm that grateful to have you back." She twined her fingers in his and let her tears fall unchecked. Thane drank in the sight of her.

"Never have I seen a sight so pleasing as your bonny face," he whispered. Gillian smiled through her tears, then carefully lowered her mouth to his, taking care not to cause him more pain, yet unable to deny herself the touch and taste of him. A discreet cough at the foot of the bed drew them apart.

"Lady Joan," Gillian cried, her smile radiant. "Forgive me for not coming for you. He's awake."

"So I see," Lady Joan said, and turned to her son. "I'm afraid I dozed for a while, but this child hasn't stopped fussing and worrying over ye since our return. You've been in good hands."

"Shadwell has tended the most," Gillian said modestly.

"Where is the good physician now?" Thane glanced about the room.

"He's in the barracks with the other injured men," Gillian answered.

"Did we lose many?" Thane's voice caught at the thought of the men he'd led into the MacGregors' trap.

"It seems so," Lady Joan answered. "Many were injured. Duncan was strong for us though, for he quickly led us back to Edinample before the kidnappers could rally and attack us again."

"Aye, Duncan is a cunning man," Thane said, then pushed himself upright in the bed. "I must go down and see t'my men."

"Thane, you can't move," Gillian admonished.

His mother hurriedly came around the bed to press against his shoulders. "You must stay here until whatever injuries you've sustained have healed some."

"Nay, Mother. My men need t'see that I'm alive." He pushed himself out of bed and stood, swaying.

"Don't be such a fool," Gillian cried. "You must go back to bed at once. It will do your men little good if you drop dead on the doorstep of Edinample."

"Aye, if I were in danger of doin' that," Thane answered harshly, for he would not have Gillian speak to him in such a tone in front of his mother. But Gillian had her dander up and was in no mood to placate his manly ego, when only hours before she'd feared for his very life.

"If you go down to the barracks now," she intoned, her

arms crossed over her chest, her mouth set in a stubborn line, "you'll go without me, and if you have need of nursing, don't expect me to put the pieces back together again. If you're so pigheaded and dunderheaded that you would try to walk about so soon, you deserve whatever happens."

"That's quite all right by me," Thane snapped, aggrieved by her peremptory tone. He reached for his cloak and felt a dizziness seize him so that he toppled to the floor. Gillian rushed over to him. Lady Joan hovered above.

"See what you've done," Gillian shouted. "I say you'll not go down t'the barracks t'night. No, and mayhap not tomorrow either. You'll stay right here in this bed until you're well." She wrapped his arm over her shoulder and tugged at his big frame, but could not budge him.

"See what a lot of trouble you've become," she fussed. "I shall have to wake someone to come help me fetch you back to your bed."

"I'll help, Gillian," Lady Joan said, and the two women set about getting the large man back onto his mattress. They were breathless and sweating with the exertion by the time they had him tucked in again. A white line of pain rimmed Thane's mouth.

"You must stay here tonight," Gillian said, and Thane nodded his agreement. Satisfied, Gillian stepped back, but Thane's hand shot out and took hold of hers.

"Don't leave me, little wild bird," he pleaded softly, and her heart melted in her chest. Sinking down on the edge of his bed, she smoothed his hair back from his forehead and crooned a wordless tune while her fingers stroked his cheeks. Thane closed his eyes and sighed. Within minutes he was sound asleep again, but this time the women knew it was a healing sleep.

Lady Joan stood at the foot of the bed, watching her warrior son, marveling at the way this gentle girl had alternately scolded and soothed him. What had Thane called her? His little wild bird? Lady Joan smiled. She'd often hoped her son would find a woman he could love with all his heart, but she'd feared he was too like his father and the other Campbell men, too preoccupied by their ambitions to open themselves to love, to do so. She thought of Juliana Cawder, to whom Thane had betrothed himself. What would become of that alliance now?

Chapter 13

T HE DAYS THAT followed were filled with joy and
sorrow, joy that Thane had survived, sorrow that
too many Campbell men had died or been crippled from
their injuries in the rock slide.

Desire for revenge against the MacGregor raiders ran
high. Walking in the bailey, Gillian often heard the Mac-
Gregor name vilified, and she turned aside with grief in
her heart. Even in the village, sentiment ran high and
those who would not normally have spoken to her now
approached to inquire how the laird was doing and to
offer their services should he or Duncan plan to ride out
after the raiders again. If she'd once meant to tell Thane
the truth of her identity and of Jaimie's visit, she no
longer thought to do so now.

Lady Joan and Evina brightened her days. Looking at
the petite Lady Joan, Gillian could hardly believe she'd
given birth to such a giant as Thane. Yet so completely
were they alike in coloring and expression that Gillian felt
drawn to Thane's mother.

Though an elegant and proud noblewoman, Lady Joan
reminded Gillian in some ways of Hannah. Each woman
had been wise in the ways of her world, each had
achieved a certain acceptance, a serenity of life. Hannah
had been her teacher during her years in the Glenartney

forest and now Lady Joan unknowingly be
teacher at Edinample. Gillian observed her every
movement, from the mocking lift of one golden
to the refined sway of her skirts and her unhurried

At first, too busy with her self-imposed duties of
assisting with the injured men, Gillian had little time to
engage in conversation with the ladies. But as Thane's
fever burned out and he opened his eyes and croaked out
demands for food and water, the urgency with which
Gillian attended his needs lessened somewhat.

"My child, he's resting easily now. Indeed, it's a
healing sleep and you must take some time for yourself. I
insist," Lady Joan had said when Gillian finished bathing
Thane's body with cooling herbal water and stayed until
he drifted into a deep sleep.

"I'm not sure I should absent myself," Gillian said
doubtfully. "He asked after his men and Duncan was
forced t'tell him the truth. He was quite upset. What if he
awakens?"

"We'll have a manservant sit with him, and should
Thane stir, the man will fetch us at once." Lady Joan's
smile faded. "You look tired, child. You need t'rest yourself a bit or you'll be ill. And what would we do without
you?"

Gillian shrugged her shoulders, uncomfortable at Lady
Joan's praise. "I didn't do so much."

"Aye, child, you did. You've stayed at Thane's side
nearly every moment, leaving it only t'tend his men."
Lady Joan studied the lovely pale face and the tumble of
black curls and wondered about this beautiful girl who
seemed to have become so much a part of her son's life
and of Edinample itself. Impulsively she placed an arm
around the young shoulders and turned Gillian toward the
door of her own chamber.

"I've ordered a bath brought to your room and I've sent
over some of my very own French lavender to scent the

water. Go and soak yerself and dress in something pretty."

Loath as she was to leave Thane's side, the thought of a hot bath made Gillian's weary muscles tremble in anticipation. "Thank you, Lady Joan," she murmured, taking the older woman's hand and dropping a light kiss on the back in an age-old sign of reverence and respect. "You are a kind, gentle lady."

"Nay, Gillian, don't you understand it's you who's kind and gentle? Now go have your bath and come to supper with me in the sitting room. I have no wish to brave the rugged male company in the hall tonight."

"Aye, I will," Gillian said gratefully, for she felt far too tired to face the noise and crowd in the hall.

The water was heavenly, the light fragrant scent of the French lavender rising around her with the steam. She washed her hair and rinsed it in the scented water, then lay back against the sides of the tub, feeling her muscles relax. The warm water lapped against her bare skin in a most seductive fashion, and she thought of Thane as he had been in his bed this very day when she bathed and shaved him.

Later, sitting by the fire, she spread her hair to dry, weaving her fingers through it to loosen the tangles. When it hung soft and warm against her neck, she took up a brush and plied it until her unruly tumble of curls were tamed into some kind of glossy order, bringing the sides up into a knot at the back of her head while the back hung down to her narrow hips. Peeking into the small hand mirror Thane had given her, she tried to guess what Lady Joan might think when she saw her.

"Aye, 'tis too late to make a good impression now," she muttered to herself. "The fine lady has seen you in your work clothes, soiled and dirty, looking like a servant." She put away the mirror and went off to the sitting room. On her way she couldn't help but stop in to check on Thane. He lay as before, deep in slumber, his large body sprawled in total surrender, his breathing deep and untroubled. As Lady Joan had promised, a manservant sat on a stool nearby.

"The laird's restin' like a wee babe," he said in a low voice and with some pride as if he himself had brought about such a miracle. "Your medicine worked its magic on all the men."

"No magic," Gillian said dismissively. "It was only a few herbs. I wish I could have done more to ease their suffering."

"Their wives and they will thank ye," the man commented, and Gillian went away with a lighter heart for his words.

The sitting room was on the floor above the main hall. She found Lady Joan seated before the fireplace, working at a fine cloth with brightly colored silk threads.

"Ah, there you are, Gillian. Come in. We've been waiting for you," Lady Joan called in her soft, cultivated tones.

"I'm sorry if I've taken overly long," Gillian said, entering the room and dropping a curtsy. As usual, she felt awkward and unrefined in the presence of the noblewoman. For the first time she saw Evina seated in the window seat, a pout on her pretty lips. When the auburn-haired girl saw Gillian, she frowned.

"Have I interrupted?" Gillian asked, perceiving Evina did not wish her there.

"Nay, child," Lady Joan said, rising and coming toward her with a hand extended. "Have I not invited you to join us? Evina and I were just saying how delighted we are that you're here, weren't we, Evina, dear?"

Evina looked taken aback, then hastily replaced her petulant look with a smile of welcome. Rising, she too came to greet Gillian. "Aye, delighted," she said, and when her eyes met Gillian's, they held only friendship. Gillian smiled, grateful to be welcomed so warmly.

A servant entered the room with a tray and moved

toward a table that had already been set with cutlery and with stools placed around. "Ah, the food is here and I'm absolutely famished," Lady Joan said. "Gillian, sit here by me, and, Evina, my dear, you may sit there across from us." Obediently the girls took the seats she'd indicated and the servant set out plates of hammered silver and platters filled with meat, cheese, vegetables, and sweet breads. Goblets were filled with wine, and, at last, the servant bowed and left them.

"At last we have a chance to get to know one another better," Lady Joan said. "What a homecoming this has been, first with the kidnapping and then with the injuries of Thane and his men."

Gillian flushed with remembered guilt over the kidnapping. In the past few days, as she'd busied herself with nursing Thane, she'd managed to forget about it. Now it was back and must be dealt with. "I hope you were treated decently by the kidnappers."

"They were a bunch of outlaws—uncouth, unwashed renegades." Evina exploded. "They have no decency in them."

"Nay, Evina, 'tis not true," Lady Joan remonstrated. "We were treated well enough considering the circumstances. They didn't kill any of our men. They saw to our comforts as best they could. We had food and wine to drink and frequent rests." Lady Joan smiled, displaying a dimple in one cheek. "Of course, I required frequent rests." Laughter danced in her eyes momentarily as she thought of the helpless lady she'd played as a delaying tactic.

"Still, I would not have it happen to me again," Evina said grudgingly.

"Gracious, child, nor would I," Lady Joan said lightly. "I was quite stunned when the kidnappers loosened the stones down on the heads of Thane and our troops."

"It must have been truly frightening," Gillian said, and

hesitated before asking her next question. "Were any of the outlaws killed?"

"Aye," Evina said quickly. "Thane and his men set a trap, and when the outlaws entered the narrow passage, they fell upon them with swords and hacked them to pieces."

"Evina, do be still," Lady Joan reprimanded. "You've frightened Gillian."

Evina glanced at Gillian's pale face. " 'Tis just as well you were not there," she exclaimed, "if even the telling frightens you so."

"I—I was but thinking of the lives lost," Gillian said lamely. "Did anyone get the leader?"

"The leader?" Evina asked puzzled. "I didn't see him in the melee. Perhaps he ran away."

"He didn't," Lady Joan said. "He was a brave, handsome man for all his ruthlessness in the end. When he saw only death awaited them in the narrow passage, he charged straight toward the other end of the gorge, leading the rest of his men t'safety, and he didn't leave the gorge himself until he was sure they'd all escaped."

"Why, Lady Joan, you sound as if you admire him!" Evina stared at her wide-eyed.

"Nay, neither that," Lady Joan replied easily. "But I recognize chivalry and bravery even in my enemies." She smiled at Gillian. "But we didn't invite you to sup with us so you might hear of our adventures. Tell me, dear, who are your people and how did you come to be here at Edinample?"

So Gillian told Lady Joan the story of her rescue and how Thane had brought her to Edinample. Lady Joan shook her head sympathetically.

"So you don't remember your clan?" she inquired. "How very sad, my dear."

Gillian looked away, unable to meet her kind gaze.

"You must consider us your family, is that not so,

Evina?" Lady Joan said, including her niece in her warm smile.

"Aye, I've always wanted a sister," Evina said, taking hold of Gillian's hand. Her blue eyes were clear and friendly. Gillian's heart swelled to bursting at such warmth.

"I don't know what to say," she stammered. "You fill my heart with things I can't express."

Lady Joan laughed. "Don't try, lass. Your expression says it all. Now, let's talk about more practical things, shall we?" She lifted her wine goblet, and the ruffle of her sleeve fluttered prettily. Lady Joan fixed Gillian with a measuring gaze. "My dear, have you no other clothes than those of a servant?"

Gillian shook her head.

"Thane, that great lout, didn't give you some finer gowns?" Lady Joan asked, and so richly indulgent was her tone when she spoke of her son, Gillian guessed there was no insult intended by her words.

"Aye, he did," she said quickly, for she herself would do nothing to discredit Thane. " 'Tis my own fault that I didn't feel comfortable in such finery."

"Pray, why not, lass?" Lady Joan inquired. "I've never known a female who didn't love pretty gowns and fripperies. Was the gown so terribly displeasing?"

Gillian blushed to think she must be critical of a gift. "The gown was far more—daring than I am used to," she said. "A-and Bridget, the servant who brought it, said it was the gown of a—a trollop."

"A trollop?" Lady Joan repeated the word gingerly, striving to repress her humor, for the young woman seated before her was earnestly somber, her gaze cast down to the floor, her cheeks and brow pink.

"A—a *baille*!" Gillian said in a low voice. "A mistress."

"Aye, I well know what a trollop is," Lady Joan said.

"But you *are* one, Gillian," Evina burst out, her voice

surprisingly harsh. At Lady Joan's sharp glance, she looked chagrined. "A *baille*, I mean, not a trollop," she said lamely.

"I am neither!" Gillian flared, then faltered. "At least I don't think of myself as such."

"There is a world of difference between a trollop and a mistress," Lady Joan said firmly. "One is shameless while the other gives her loyalty to one man much as a wife does." Still, Gillian looked so miserable that Lady Joan reached across and squeezed her hand. "Do you love my son, lass?" she inquired softly.

Immediately the proud head came up and green eyes as brilliant as emeralds gazed at her with all the fire and passion a mother could hope for her son.

"You need not answer. Once again your eyes tell me the answer." Lady Joan sighed and glanced at Evina, who'd listened avidly to the conversation. Lady Joan had a hundred questions she wished to ask Gillian, yet she could not do so in front of her niece.

"Well, we've gone somewhat afield," she said, patting Gillian's hand before folding her own primly in her lap. Immediately Gillian followed suit, and once again Lady Joan was forced to hide her smile though her heart warmed for this beautiful girl.

They dined then, and afterward, Lady Joan said, "You look tired, child. Don't sit by Thane this night. He is recovering. Go to your own bed and get the rest you so richly deserve."

"Aye, m'lady," Gillian replied with a little curtsy. "I'll just look in on him before I retire. I bid you good night and thank you for your company at supper."

"It was my pleasure too, Gillian," Lady Joan said.

"I'll walk with you," Evina said, putting down her napkin and following Gillian.

In the corridor Evina took hold of Gillian's hand as they walked along. "I'm so glad you're here, Gillian," she said lightly. "I was so dreading this visit with naught t'do but sit and sew with Lady Joan."

"Oh, but she is wonderful company," Gillian replied, unable to bear any slight to her heroine. "She's so kind and intelligent and so gracious. I wish I could be like her."

"Aye, she's all that and more," Evina said, although her voice held less sincerity than it had before. "She's truly a great lady, but I wished t'have the company of someone my own age, and ye were here. I know we'll be dear friends in no time."

"I've never had a friend of my own age before," Gillian murmured.

"Never?" Evina asked in amazement.

"Never." The two girls looked at each other, then hugged, giggling suddenly in their nervousness.

"I'll be your friend forever," Evina vowed.

"Will you do me a favor, then?" Gillian asked, and Evina frowned slightly to think their friendship would be so quickly tested.

"I will try," she said tentatively.

" 'Tis a great favor to ask, I know," Gillian rushed on, "and may be impossible, but I would have you help me learn to be a great lady like Lady Joan."

"A lady?" Evina repeated, relieved that the favor had been so simple. Then the enormity of the request hit her, and the naïveté of the beautiful girl. A smile curved Evina's mouth, and for a moment something about the smile troubled Gillian, as if the other girl might be laughing at her, but then Evina put her arm about Gillian's shoulder.

"Of course I'll help you," Evina said softly. "Being a great lady is really rather easy. We'll start first thing tomorrow."

"Oh, thank you, Evina," Gillian said as if a great weight had been lifted from her, and in fact it had, for the arrival of the two women had shown her clearly how lacking she was in refinement and manners.

The two girls had moved down the long corridor and now paused before Thane's chamber door. "Well, I'll bid you good night," Gillian said. "I wish to see to Thane."

"Aye, you're a good healer," Evina said, erasing the tight lines about her mouth with a broad smile. She squeezed Gillian's hand and released it, taking a step backward. "Good night, friend."

"Good night, friend," Gillian responded, and with a full heart opened the door to Thane's room, closing it quietly behind her.

Chapter 14

"**W**HEN WILL YE tell her the truth?" Lady Joan stood over her son's bed and glared at him.

"I will tell her when I feel like it, Mother," Thane answered. His face was dark with fury that she would speak to him of such a matter. " 'Tis unseemly for you to broach this subject with me."

"No more unseemly than is your behavior. Yer bride-to-be comes in less than a fortnight to visit her future home. How will she feel if she finds your mistress about?"

"What do you know of it, Mother?" he demanded angrily. In a rage he threw aside the covers, retaining only enough to shield his nakedness from his mother's eyes, and stalked behind a screen.

"I know all I need to know," Lady Joan retorted. "You've taken a poor, naïve orphan of a girl, brought her here to Edinample, and set her up as mistress. This is intolerable, Thane. You can't let things stand as they do."

"Nor will I, Mother. But at the risk of hurting you, I must remind you that Father kept his mistresses at Kilchurn. 'Tis the way of men." At once he regretted his words, for his mother's face grew pale.

"Forgive me, Mother. I didn't think it would cause you pain to speak of such things since you've spoken so frankly with me. You never seemed to mind that Father had his women within the castle, and I assumed there was never any love between you."

"And so there was none," Lady Joan admitted in a soft voice free of bitterness, for she'd years before come to terms with the ways of men and how deeply they wounded a woman's heart. She would not have that happen to Gillian or Juliana if she could help it. "A woman always minds, for such behavior is an affront to her very womanhood. And to be forced to pretend that she knows nothing of the willing creatures kept on the side like sweetmeats in the guise of serving women or seamstresses is the worst affront of all."

"But you went about so cheerfully," he said, emerging from behind the screen fully clothed. His face was pale, though, from the bent of their conversation or because he was too soon out of his sickbed, she was uncertain. She forebore to order him to return to his bed, for she knew it would do little good.

"There are many things in a woman's heart you don't know," she answered, turning away from him to look out the window at the loch gleaming in the morning sunlight. "Have you considered Gillian in this matter?" she asked, swinging about to confront her stubborn son.

"Gillian?" he asked with some surprise. "What is there to consider? She is safe and well cared for here at Edinample. She is happy."

"Is she?" Lady Joan paced toward him, and for a moment he had a vision of a tigress about to pounce, so set was her expression. "Will she be happy when Juliana arrives and she learns you're to be wed to her?"

"She'll understand, Mother."

"Nay, Thane, you make yourself the fool if you believe that. You've not even spoken to the girl to prepare her. You must do that, else Juliana's coming will be a blow from which her pride may not recover."

"She loves me, Mother, why do you speak of pride?"

Lady Joan stared at him, shock paling her face. "You're aware of her feelings for you, yet you don't tell her the truth of your plans. You're a blackheart, Thane, and I never thought to feel shame for you."

"There's no need now," he snapped. "You've gone off all pious and preachy, but what's between Gillian and me remains that. She doesn't expect me to marry her. She's without name or land or prospects. She's grateful for what I give her now. She demands no more."

"She demands no more because she trusts you," Lady Joan railed. "She's too unworldly to realize the way of things, that a woman needs a dowry to make a worthwhile marriage."

Lady Joan's words reached through his denial, and he slumped down on the side of his bed. "Aye, Mother, I realize I've not done fairly by her, but I could not ignore my feelings for her. I've never known a woman like her. She's . . ." He shrugged, unable to name the feelings he had for Gillian, for he'd denied them even to himself.

"Do you love her?" Lady Joan asked. Thane's head jerked up, and he glared at her with icy blue shards.

"Love?" he demanded, leaping to his feet and pacing about the room. He'd donned a jerkin of dark embroidered cloth with the rolled pickadil hem at the shoulder and waist, and a simple pair of cannons rather than the loosely fitting padded slops most men favored. The tight-fitting cannons hugged his slender hips and showed his muscular thighs to full advantage. Below the knee he'd pulled on a pair of dark silk hose and shoved his feet into unadorned square-toed leather shoes. Not for her son the laces, ribbons, and rosettes other men of nobility affected in their wear. Though his face was pale and his eyes burned a bit too brightly so that she suspected he was still touched by fever, his movements were vigorous, his glance abrupt and scathing.

"Don't speak to me of love, Mother," he snapped. " 'Tis a word giggled over by milkmaids who tumble with the dandies in the hayloft. If you ask how I feel about Gillian, then I will tell you, I find her comely. She's gentle and sweet and good."

"Aye, she's all of that and more," Lady Joan said. "She's of uncommon wit and moral character. She didn't come to your bed as easily as one of those milkmaids, I'd wager. She possesses the pride and sensitivity of a noble-woman, and in truth, you can't be sure she is not one."

"She has no knowledge of her clan," he said, although it was obvious his mother had already learned much about Gillian.

"Aye, so she claims," Lady Joan said.

Thane whirled to look at her. "Don't you believe her?"

"Nay, son, I don't," she said enigmatically. "Did you stop to think she may have no lands to offer for dowry because you have them already?" Before he could demand more of her, she left the room, moving with all the regal grace that Gillian so admired and tried to emulate.

Left to chew over all she'd said, Thane paced his room, then in a pique decided to go to the barracks and visit his wounded men. Perhaps if they saw for themselves that he'd rallied, they would do so as well. Besides, he had a need for the simplicity of male companionship at this moment. Women, with all their complicated emotions and mysterious moods, made him feel tired.

Yet, as he ran down the stairs, he heard Gillian's laughter in the great hall and detoured to peer in as she and Evina played at some game. He stood watching her, seeing the glossy curls brush over her shoulder and tumble down her back, alive and inviting to a man's hand, the pale, flawless skin, the faintest blush on her cheeks, and most of all the glitter of her eyes, like green stones of the highest value. He knew how they caught the light and sparkled with mysterious depths that hypnotized a man's body and soul.

"Let me try," Gillian cried, and lightly sprang to her

feet. Extending her arms, she bobbed a deep curtsy, wobbled, and went sprawling to her knees in a tangle of petticoats. Once again the peal of her laughter came to him, lighthearted and happy. He remembered pulling her into his sickbed last night. He remembered the feel of her soft body beneath his that morning before she left his room, the taste of her sweet mouth, and the sound of her voice, husky from sleep, whispering words of love that had enflamed his soul.

He turned away and stamped outside. He refused to acknowledge that he'd taken what she'd so freely given and not acted honorably in return. He'd always known he'd have to tell her of his plans to wed Juliana Cawder, but he'd procrastinated. Now he acknowledged his mother was right. He could no longer put off that disclosure. He cursed beneath his breath and wondered what had prompted Robert Cawder and Juliana to visit Edinample at this particular moment.

He was not to be rushed. Perhaps he'd extend the time of their betrothal to the following year. Like as not, Sir Robert would not mind, for his daughter was still a bit young, barely fifteen by his reckoning.

That's what he would do, he decided. He'd send word to Sir Robert at once and delay their arrival for several months, perhaps until spring. Feeling he'd found a solution to his troubles, Thane whistled and went off to see to his men.

The days had passed in a haze of happiness. She should have guessed, Gillian thought later. The gods had decreed she was not to know peace and contentment for long. Though Thane had informed them that Sir Robert Cawder and his daughter would not be visiting until spring, Nessa had worked diligently on Gillian's new gowns and two were ready save for the hemming, while the third, a luxurious pink satin that Lady Joan had chosen, was promised to be ready within a day or two.

During the myriad fittings required for such gowns, Gillian and Nessa had become good friends. Though a seamstress and maidservant, the Highlander woman was proud and opinionated. Nessa often sat with the women at night when they retired to the sitting room. Her nimble fingers never faltered, nor did her equally agile mind fail her when Lady Joan and Evina spoke of Scotland's nobility.

As Lady Joan's servant, she'd traveled a great deal and her knowledge of people was insightful and often funny. She'd even accompanied Lady Joan to Edinburgh and observed King James and his court. With a few words or the waggle of her eyebrows she could communicate her opinion of the strict Protestant king and his pious court. At first Gillian feared Nessa's outspokenness would anger her mistress, but soon she noted that Lady Joan was as amused by her servant's outrageous comments as the rest of them.

The days were spent in learning the intricacies of curt-sying, good table manners, the playing of card games, and the making of witty conversation while plotting to scalp an opponent's queen. Gillian was so immersed in her new activities, she did not at first notice Thane's chagrin.

"You never seem to have time for me, lass," he complained one night when she'd come to his bed.

"But I'm always here for you, Thane," she said lightly, snuggling against him.

"That's not what I mean," he grumbled petulantly. "You're always off with Evina or sitting with Mother or having Nessa flit about you measuring and plotting."

"She's making new gowns for me," Gillian protested. "Your mother's been most generous."

"Aye, and well she should be since it's my coin she spends."

"Oh, I didn't know. I'm so sorry. I shall tell Nessa to stop sewing at once."

"Nay, lass, I don't begrudge the coin to buy you new

gowns. I should have seen to it myself, but I know nothing of women's garments and geegaws. 'Tis well enough my mother has chosen to oversee the task."

"I would not have you angered with me, Thane," Gillian said, her body warm and supple beside his.

"I'm not, lass, as long as you come to me in the night." He rolled her on top of him, pressing her hips so he might grind against them and thus show her his need. His kiss was deep and demanding.

"If you're not angry with me, m'lord Thane," Gillian persisted when he'd released her mouth so she might draw a breath, "then what has your temper up so?"

He rolled away from her and stared up at the ceiling. "I'm not angry at you, little wild bird," he sighed, "but there is something I must tell you, something I don't like."

"Aye, then tell me," she said dropping a light kiss on his lips. Her hair, blue-black silk, brushed across his skin bringing a shiver of passion. He reached for her again.

"There's time enough for the telling," he said huskily and drew her beneath him. His big hands caressed her body with such thoroughness all thought left her head and her demand he tell her now was lost in the heat of their desire. Afterward they lay in drowsy completion, unwilling to talk after all they'd savored. Sleep claimed them and the moment passed.

One morning as Gillian left Nessa after a fitting, a servant came to tell her that someone was asking for her at the bridge gate. All the blood seemed to flow from her head, and she felt dizzy.

"Did they give a name?" she inquired.

"Nay." The servant shook her head and turned back toward the kitchen.

"Where is Laird Thane?" Gillian called.

"They've ridden off to do some hunting in the Glenartney forest," the servant answered rather sullenly, for she'd not yet accepted the fact she must treat Gillian as she did the noblewomen.

Gillian flung a cape over her shoulders, for the day had dawned cool with the hint of an autumn chill, and hurried through the upper bailey to the bridge gate. As before, there was no sign of anyone lingering near the gate, but on the distant path strolled a hooded figure. Not wishing to call attention to her visitor, Gillian hurried along the path.

"Jaimie, you can't come like this," she hissed when she was close enough. "If you're discovered, you'll be killed."

The figure spun about and flung back the hood. Gillian gasped and came to a halt, her mouth agape, her eyes wide.

"Robena MacGregor," she gasped, staring at the dark-haired woman before her. The face was so like her own, the hair a dark cloud about her shoulders, the curve of her jaw and arch of a brow, save the eyes, which were dark to Gillian's green ones. Robena's eyes held much bitter knowledge, and there was a fineness to her features, lines at the corners of her mouth that spoke of grief. " 'Tis like looking in a mirror."

"Aye, you've the look of the MacGregor about you. Jaimie said it was so. We might be sisters, so nearly do we match, save you've still a sleek youthfulness to you that I've long since lost. Life has not yet treated you harshly, fair Gillian." Robena's lips curved in a bitter smile. One eyebrow rose mockingly. "But then, 'twas always the way for you."

"Jaimie told me of your misfortune when the clan was proscribed. I'm sorry, Robena, but we all suffered great losses. Have you forgotten my father was hanged?"

"Nay, but Jamie seems to think you've forgotten such treachery." Light flared behind Robena's dark eyes. "I told him not so for our wee Gillian. She was always loyal and helpful. She will continue t'be so."

Gillian drew herself up, knowing this little speech was

but a forerunner for a request for something. "Aye, I am loyal to my friends and loved ones," she said. "And that loyalty extends to Thane Campbell and the people at Edinample. He saved my life. He's brought me home again to Edinample, and I will do naught to harm him and the others."

"We didn't ask you to harm the Campbell laird," Robena said softly. "We ask only for your help. We've need of more supplies and weapons. The winds grow cold in the mountains. Soon it will be winter, and men without food for their bellies grow impatient to return to their land."

Gillian was silent for a moment, imagining the desperate need of Jaimie and the other MacGregors. She could not turn away from their hunger and cold, yet she remembered well the broken limbs she'd tended when Jaimie treacherously let down the rocks on Thane and his men.

"I will not help," she cried. "Do not come to ask me again. 'Tis dangerous for you and for me."

"For you as well?" Robena asked, startled by her declaration. "Then you've still not told Thane Campbell you're a MacGregor?"

"I meant to," Gillian said in a low voice, "but there is much anger against the MacGregors since Jaimie's wicked trap. Many men were killed and lamed by it."

"Aye!" Robena smiled. "I take good news back t'my brother."

"The devil take you and Jaimie," Gillian cried. "He has a bitter heart filled with hatred and murder. I'll do naught to help you in your cause."

Robena's eyes narrowed, flashing angrily. "You do as we wish, Gillian," she warned, "or you'll feel the revenge of the MacGregors."

"Don't threaten me, Robena. I'm not a small child to be frightened by you nor by Jaimie." She whirled and strode along the path toward the bridge gate.

"Heed my warning, Gillian," Robena called. "If you don't open the secret door to us this night, you'll be punished."

Gillian didn't look back. She was sickened by the hate she saw in Robena's eyes. She thought of Thane. The feud between their two clans would never end, and where would that leave her? Jaimie or Robena would come again, their demands more urgent, their cunning more bold, and soon she would be found out as a MacGregor. How would Thane look upon her then? Would his blue eyes darken with desire for her, would his big hands brush across her with tender protectiveness, would he hold her through the night and whisper words of passion?

She ran across the bridge gate as if pursued by demons, and entered the middle bailey just as the courtyard filled with riders and packhorses. Surprised, for no guests were expected, she stood to one side, watching as a tall, elegantly dressed man dismounted and turned to help a young girl from her horse. Lady Joan had come out onto the castle steps and held out her hands in welcome. Thane stood to one side, his face dark with anger. Gillian was too far away to hear their words, so she pressed closer.

Standing beside Lady Joan, Evina glimpsed Gillian in the crowd and came down the steps to take her hand, her lips curving in a sweet smile.

"Come, Gillian," she urged, "you're just in time. Thane's bride has arrived."

Chapter 15

"**D**ON'T JEST WITH me, Evina. I'm not in the mood," Gillian said, turning away from Evina's triumphant smile.

" 'Tis not a jest, I assure you," Evina said. "Didn't Thane tell you he was betrothed to Juliana Cawder? He has been for some five years now, since she was but ten years old. She brings with her the lands and status of the Cawder clan."

Gillian gazed into Evina's eyes and read the truth of what she said. She felt the blood drain from her head and feared she might fall down beneath the hooves of the milling horses into the dung and mud.

"Didn't Thane tell you this?" Evina insisted, her voice soft with sympathy. "You poor lass." She patted Gillian's arm pityingly. "How could he be so cruel?"

A thousand questions crowded against Gillian's lips, but she would not ask them of Evina. Thane! She must speak to Thane. He would tell her this was not so or that he'd changed his mind. He could not love this girl, who was little more than a child still. Likely he would tell them he had changed his mind. That was the reason for the fury she saw on his face. It would be all right. She must not panic.

She pressed her cold fingers against her mouth to halt

any whimper, and without speaking to Evina again ran through the crowd and out of the bailey. She had to get to her room, so no one could see her cry. For the first time since entering Edinample, Gillian felt keenly that she was the outsider, unwanted and out of place. She closed herself away in her room and sat on her bed, waiting for the tears to come, but a numbness had settled over her and she could not weep.

She had no idea how much time had passed. She was closed in a cold, lonely place that gave no light and no hope. Stubbornly, fingernails biting deep into the flesh of her palms, she waited for Thane. He would come to her. He would make everything right again. She believed in him. She trusted him. When a soft knock sounded on her door, she was startled from her cocoon of misery and flew across the room to throw open the door.

"Thane!" she cried, and the light went out of her eyes when she saw Nessa standing in the entrance, her arms filled with the gowns she'd sewn.

"At Lady Joan's bidding, I've just spent the last two hours hemming these gowns," she said, entering the room and spreading the beautiful garments on Gillian's bed. "She feared you might not join them because you lacked proper gowns. I'm to help you dress for supper."

"I can't go down!" Gillian cried, recoiling as if she'd been requested to touch a snake. "Didn't Thane send a message to me?"

Sadly Nessa shook her head, her face filled with sympathy. Abruptly Gillian turned away, unwilling to have the serving woman see her humiliation.

"Lady Joan says you must dress and join them for supper," Nessa said. "That's why I've worked so hard t'finish the gowns, so you'll be able to present yerself proudly to the guests."

"Proudly?" Gillian said bitterly. " 'Tis not fine satins and pretty gowns that give one pride or take away the sting of betrayal."

"Aye, child, you've learned this news of Thane's betrothal most cruelly, but 'twas not his intention. I heard him tell his mother he planned to postpone his wedding to the Cawder wench until spring, and he had sent word t'her father not to come to Edinample at this time."

"He did?" Gillian said, hope rising within her. "Mayhap he has no intention of marrying her."

"Ah, lass, lass," Nessa said reprovingly. "Don't raise your hopes like that. Ye'll only know more pain in the end. Thane will marry the Cawder lass because she's the only heir to lands and titles that the Campbells have coveted many a year."

"But would he if he didn't love her?" Gillian asked, unwilling to have her hopes dashed.

"Aye, he would," Nessa said firmly. "The gentry dinna think of love in choosing their mates. The wedding vows are but tools to acquire more lands, more power, more prestige."

Gillian's face grew pale, and she slumped on the edge of the bed.

"Ye poor wee thing," Nessa said, crossing the room to touch the girl's shoulder, the most she could offer in the way of comfort. Her features grew stern and she drew her shoulders up stiffly. " 'Tis the way of things. Surely you did not think the laird would wed you, a nameless orphan with no land or titles. He's taken you as his mistress, 'tis the most you can hope for."

"Nay," Gillian cried out her denial.

"Aye, lass, look on this as it truly is. You've no prospects but your beauty, and with it you've bound the laird of one of Scotland's most powerful clans to you. You and any child you have, though he be a bastard, will never want. Even Lady Joan acknowledges you and bids you to her table in the presence of the Cawders. With her as your champion your position is further strengthened. Juliana could never have you put aside, a fact that will rankle in years t'come."

"I have no wish to spite a young girl who expects to be a bride. If what you say is true, if Thane truly plans to wed with her, then I'll leave Edinample." Her voice broke on a smothered sob. "But I would hear this from Thane's own lips."

"Aye, he owes you that much." Nessa nodded.

"Will you tell him I would see him?" Gillian pleaded in a tearful voice.

"Aye, lass. I'll get a message t'him, though in truth, it may take a time for him to come. He entertains Sir Robert Cawder." Nessa paused. "If 'tis any comfort, he's barely cast a glance at his bride-to-be though she be a comely lass. 'Tis Aindreas who's set himself to entertain her."

"There is no comfort for me this day," Gillian whispered in anguish. Nessa shook her head at the girl's plight and went off to carry a message to the laird. Beneath her breath she muttered a curse for the perfidiousness of all men.

Nessa had barely left the room before Thane appeared. He entered without knocking and halted to study Gillian as she huddled on the window seat, her tear-blurred gaze fixed on the reflection of sunlight on the loch. She was unaware of his presence until he took a step forward, and she whirled, her expression unguarded. Thane saw the paleness of her features and the eyes nearly black with despair.

"Ah, lass," he said, crossing the room in long strides to catch her up in his arms. Gillian drew a breath of relief, tears sliding from beneath her closed lids. It had all been a misunderstanding. "I would have spared you from this if I could have," he whispered, his strong arms encircling her protectively. "My messenger to Robert Cawder didn't reach him in time. They'd already set out for Edinample."

"Then 'tis true? You plan to marry Juliana Cawder?"

"Aye, it's true enough, lass," he murmured regretfully. "But I didn't mean for you to find out like this. I planned to tell you this winter, so we could make plans and I could find a place for you to reside."

"A place for me?" she drew back. "You mean I'm not to remain at Edinample?"

"Not after I wed. 'Twould be too much an affront to my wife and her clan. Her father would na hear of such a discourtesy to his daughter, and Sir Robert is a powerful man. I wish to be an honorable son-in-law to him."

"And is it honorable to keep a mistress, a *baille*, even as you pledge to honor and love his daughter?" Gillian stared at him as if she'd never seen him before. He had the grace to look shamefaced.

"I know 'tis hard for you to understand. You're unworldly about such things, but most men keep a mistress. Sir Robert knows this and would not object as long as we were discreet. God's Blood, I've never intended to be anything else, but you turn my head in such a way, I forget all else."

"And like most men, you planned to keep me as your mistress, albeit discreetly?" she asked in a voice that sounded strangely hollow to her own ears. Her heart, she was sure, had ceased beating, and she felt numb.

"Aye, do you doubt me?" He reached for her urgently, his face a mixture of outrage and reassurance. "Lass, my little wild bird, do you think I could leave you now that I've found you? You belong to me."

Gillian jerked away from him, stepping back and facing him with cold determination. "I belong to no one but myself," she snapped.

Thane gazed at her with some exasperation and impatience. "I know you're hurt. I canna blame you for your anger, lass, but I know no other way t'do this. I've pledged to marry Juliana Cawder from the time she was ten. I can't take back my pledge, even if I were so inclined, and I am not. Juliana brings land and troops with her. I've need of this alliance." Gillian remained silent. "Lass, you didn't think I would marry you? You have no land, no title, no clan. I'll protect you and care for you all your life, but I must marry a woman of substance."

Each word fell like a blow against Gillian. "Do you love her, m'lord?" she asked piteously, and hated herself for this futile effort.

"Love? I don't know about love, but if you mean does she please me as you do, then I must answer nay and nay again. None could do that but you." His expression was earnest.

"Do you find her bonny?" Gillian persisted, looking for some small comfort.

"Aye, she's bonny enough for a child," he answered honestly. "But her figure is only half formed. Her breasts are little more than buds."

"You've noticed them, then?" Gillian's voice cracked with a combination of pain and anger.

"Aye, I'm a man, and if she's t'be my wife, I would know of such things about her."

Gillian took a deep breath and drew herself up. "I understand, m'lord," she answered.

"Ah, lass, I knew you would when you had time t'think on it." He came forward, arms outstretched for her, but she moved away, out of his reach.

"Aye, m'lord, and I pray you'll understand when you hear what I must do." Her head was held high and proud. He'd seen her in many moods—gentle, contrite, frightened, brave, and loving—but never with such dignity.

"What must you do, lass?" he asked gently, knowing she'd undergone a terrible shock that day. He'd make it up to her, he vowed. He'd find her a castle of her own, he'd fill it with treasures, and he'd clothe her in the richest gowns and baubles. A smile curved his lips as he thought of all he'd do to please her, but before he could offer her reassurances of his intentions, she'd crossed the room and stood with regal grace and grim determination.

"You've asked what I must do, m'lord," she said in a quiet voice that sounded ominous by its lack of inflection.

"I was not raised t'be any man's *baille*, and now that I know your true intentions, I will leave Edinample."

"Gillian," Thane cried in disbelief. "You must be daft, lass. You can't leave."

"I can and I must," she answered.

"Why?" Thane demanded, and his voice was rough with anger, his blue eyes flashed, his features were harsh, but she was not to be intimidated. She raised her chin and kept her peace.

"Is it because you think to force me into marriage?"

"Nay, m'lord, I would not think to do such mischief with the mighty Laird Thane Campbell." Her lip curled with contempt. He was tempted to strike her, but held back. She was not like other women. He must handle her carefully. She would calm down and see there was no other way than this.

"I can't marry you, lass," he said kindly. "You must accept that. If we're to be together, it must be as it is now. There's no other way."

"Nay, m'lord," she said forcefully. "You misspeak. Since I don't wish to marry you myself and don't wish to be associated with you in any further manner, I will leave at first light."

"You'll not!" Thane roared, his patience gone. His hands clenched into fists. "I tell you now, Gillian, you'll not leave Edinample."

"Am I your prisoner, then, m'lord?"

Thane clenched his teeth in frustration and forced his voice to a calmer level. "No, lass," he said, trying to take her into his arms, but she held her body rigid, her arms crossed over her chest, sharp elbows jutting. "Don't be like this. Don't you remember how it is between us?" His hand brushed across her hips and down to the conjuncture of her thighs. He cupped her mound, feeling her heat even through the cloth of her gown and petticoat. In spite of her anger, Gillian felt the instant flare of response to his touch and forced herself to stand cold and unresponsive.

"I will try never to remember again," she said, "for such thoughts would be wicked, m'lord."

"Damn you," Thane cried, jerking away from her. "What goes between a man and woman can't be wicked."

"When the man is to be married to another lass, then 'tis wicked," Gillian replied evenly. She turned away, unwilling to see the anger in his face. She was shaken by this encounter and was unsure how much longer she'd be able to hold her own. "Now, if you'll excuse me, m'lord, I wish to be left alone to make my preparations to quit Edinample on the morrow."

His hand clamped down on her shoulder, spinning her about. His fist balled in her hair, tilting her head back so she had no choice but to look into his eyes, sharp with fury. His lips, thinned in anger, sent a chill of fear through her.

"Would you use your superior strength against me, m'lord?" she whispered.

"Aye, Gillian, make no mistake I would, for you'll not leave Edinample unless I tell you so."

"And will you strike me as you might your dog or servant if I don't obey?"

His grip on her lessened and he pressed her against him, burying his face in her hair, inhaling the scent of her, the silken texture drawing him in like a moth to flame and in the end driving him nearly to madness for want of her. "I don't wish to hurt you, little wild bird," he whispered against her temple, "but I will not let you go. Don't think to escape me."

He drew back then and looked deep into her eyes. "I see Nessa has brought your gowns. I would have you dress and come down to sup with us and meet our guests."

"Are you not fearful of offending your bride-to-be and her powerful faither?"

"They'll never know. I'll claim you're a ward of Mother's."

"Then you will lie about me," she said sadly. She heard his sigh, felt it in the deep intake of breath.

"There are no easy answers here, Gillian," he said wearily. "The tale will do for now."

"I will save you the need, m'lord. I'll not show myself before your guests. 'Twould be the most discreet way."

"I don't want you up here alone," he said gently.

"I must become used to it," she answered. "Is this not what a mistress must do, wait, alone and unacknowledged?"

She saw how her words cut him and was glad, for she bled as well and she knew no way to extricate them from this web of deceit. She took a step backward. "You'd best return to your betrothed, m'lord," she said, knowing she turned the knife.

"Don't try to leave, Gillian," he warned. "I'll have guards placed at your door."

"They won't keep me," she said with such finality, he knew it was so.

"Don't go this night," he pleaded, and when she made no answer, he turned blindly and left the room.

Nessa came to her next to hold her head while she wept and wipe her tears and utter wordless sounds of comfort when they both knew she could never be comforted from this pain. A sound at the door made Gillian spring up, believing Thane had returned and not wanting him to see her despair. Lady Joan entered the room.

"Gillian," she said in a voice warm with affection and concern. "My dear child," she said, smoothing a tendril of hair from Gillian's dampened cheek. "There are no words for your suffering. I warned Thane it would be so when you found out the truth, but men have a way of ignoring what they don't wish to deal with."

"He knew all along that he would marry someone else," Gillian said bitterly. "Then why did he dally with me?"

Lady Joan sighed deeply. " 'Tis a dishonorable thing

my son has done to you and he is not a dishonorable man. If it comforts you, I believe he harbors deeper feelings for you than his bride-to-be will ever know. 'Tis a shame, for she's little more than a child, and like you doesn't know the ways of the world."

"If she's so young, why would her father agree to her being wed?" Gillian asked distractedly, though in truth she had little care for Juliana Cawder, for she would take her rightful place at Thane's side as his wife.

Lady Joan sighed and perched on the side of the bed. "This alliance between the Cawders and the Campbells is strongly desired on both sides. Such alliances are made through marriages."

"Aye, so Thane told me."

Lady Joan stared at Gillian's set face, and a glimmer of understanding nudged its way into her thoughts. She sighed.

"I am no longer Thane's concern," Gillian said, leaping to her feet and starting to pace the room.

"Nay, child, you are, as you are mine." Lady Joan paused, watching the young figure move restlessly, the tumble of black curls swinging about her shoulders with every turn. "I will make you my ward, Gillian, and take you back to Kilchurn with me."

"I will not go," Gillian answered. "I wish to be done with the Campbells."

Lady Joan's lips tightened at the unintended insult. "I don't blame you for yer feelings," she said softly. "But ye can't cut off your nose to spite your face."

"Ye've been most kind, Lady Joan," Gillian said reluctantly.

" 'Tis not kindness that prompts my offer, Gillian," Lady Joan said, seizing upon the hesitation she sensed in the girl. " 'Tis guilt that my son has treated you so shabbily. I would try to make up for it. I beg you, be kind in return, Gillian," Lady Joan said quickly. "Allow me to sponsor you. You can stay with me at Kilchurn until you decide what you wish to do."

"Aye, I will do as you ask," she said finally, for in truth she was uncertain how to go about making her way in the world, alone and penniless.

Lady Joan sagged, visibly relieved at her decision. "We must remain at Edinample for a few days during the Cawders' visit. I know 'twill be hard for you, but I can't leave. It would be bad manners."

"I'll stay out of sight until we depart," Gillian answered dully. Lady Joan's heart went out to the girl. She remembered her pride and grace as she moved about tending Thane and his injured men. Now she sat with shoulders slumped, head bowed. Crossing the room, Lady Joan placed a hand beneath her chin and raised Gillian's head so she could gaze into the dark emerald eyes.

"You're not the one to be ashamed, lass," she advised. "You've not done anything wrong. Lift your head up, don one of the gowns Nessa's brought you and come down to sup with us. Dinna let Thane see you slink away from Edinample in humiliation."

"Ah, and so I will," Gillian said. "I will be so beautiful that Thane will want t'weep t'think of having lost me."

"Aye, good for you, lass," Lady Joan said. "I will leave Nessa here t'help you. If you've need of anything, come to my room. I have combs and veils and jewels."

With a swish of scented skirts, Lady Joan left them, hurrying along the corridor to her own room, where she wished to take time with her own toilet. She'd thought not to see Robert Cawder until spring, yet here he was at Edinample, his slender figure elegant and alluring in his simply cut suits, his gray eyes warming each time he glimpsed her. Lady Joan sighed with pleasure at the feel of her own warm blood singing through her body.

Left alone in the entrance hall, Gillian drew a deep breath, feeling her lungs push against the constricting whalebone, and when she'd counted to ten once and then once again, she moved forward as if in a dream. She swept into the great hall and paused, blinking against the noise and bright candlelight. The hall grew silent, as if all had been but waiting for her appearance.

The onlookers seemed to hold their breath. Gillian paid them no heed, nor did she notice the small girl seated on the dais at Thane's side. She saw only Thane, the glitter in his eyes, the dumbfounded look on his face, the stain on his high cheekbones, for they told her more clearly than words that he desired her and found her beautiful.

He loves me, she thought elatedly. *He may not know it yet, but he loves me.* Head high, she swept forward, moving gracefully down the hall to greet the laird and his betrothed.

Chapter 16

HER ELATION WAS short-lived. As she moved along the tables toward Thane, she heard the murmur of voices and knew the speculation that ran high among the onlookers. Here was drama. Thane's mistress and his betrothed were meeting for the first time, and people waited with bated breath to see the outcome. Lady Joan's eyes signaled courage and caution to Gillian, and she smiled slightly to reassure her.

Still, when she'd come to a stop before the head table and turned to gaze at Juliana Cawder, she was hard put not to give way to gnashing her teeth and tearing at her hair in despair, for Thane's betrothed was the most delicately beautiful creature Gillian had ever seen. Her eyes were of the same shade of blue as Thane's. Twisted braids the shade of moonbeams trailed along her temples and held back the silvery gloss of her hair. Her skin was porcelain with a kiss of blush on each smooth cheek, her features as dainty as a rose newly bloomed. She was tiny with delicate hands and a graceful throat that flowed downward to the slightly rounded curve of her childlike chest.

Why, she truly is a child, Gillian thought dimly, and her gaze flew to meet Thane's. Like those around them, he waited for her first reaction, his gaze hungry as he took in the low-cut bodice and the smooth plumpness of her breasts. Her head held regal as a queen's, Gillian curtsied low before him.

"Pray, forgive me for not joining you and your guests sooner, m'lord," she said softly. "I fear I suffered from a strange malady."

"I hope you're recovered sufficiently now," he said stiffly, his glittering blue gaze capturing hers for a brief moment and taking her breath away.

"Aye, I'm quite myself again," she answered, meeting his gaze unflinchingly. She turned to the young girl seated at his side. "And this, I trust, is your betrothed?"

"This is Juliana Cawder," he answered brusquely. "Lady Juliana, this is Gillian, my mother's ward."

Gillian curtsied again. "Welcome t'Edinample," she said. "I hope you'll be happy here."

"Thank you," the girl said in a voice that was light and silvery as a bell on a clear, cold morn. "It is welcoming to see another young face. Now there are three of us. I hope we shall be good friends."

Gillian was quite taken aback by the girl's good manners and warm words. "It is my devoutest wish."

"This is Sir Robert Cawder," Lady Joan said. "We've left you a seat next to him."

"I'm most happy to meet you, Sir Robert," Gillian said, and took the chair Lady Joan had indicated. Sir Robert Cawder was a handsome man, vigorous and strong despite his years. He sported a small pointed beard as white as his hair, and his clothes were more sumptuous than anything Gillian had seen Thane wear, though she didn't think Sir Robert a dandy. There was a careless ease about him that said despite the elegance of his attire, he gave it little regard. Still, the ruff at his neck and the ruffles at his wrists and knees were immaculate.

"It seems I have been most fortunate this night, Mistress Gillian," he said with a slight bow.

"Why is that, m'lord?" she inquired.

He looked surprised. "Why, to have been seated next to such a beautiful young woman." He noted the blush on her cheeks. She was not being coy, she'd truly not guessed his meaning. He rose and held her chair, then reseated himself, taking care to move the tails of his coat out of the way.

"You are far too kind," she muttered, feeling awkward.

"If truth be kindness, then so be it," he remarked. "Have you been long here at Edinample? Lady Joan said nothing of you when she passed through Cawder."

"Only for a few weeks," Gillian replied, suddenly nervous. "Laird Thane was good enough to take me in when—when my home was burned."

"And what castle are you from?" Sir Robert asked in some alarm. "I've heard of none burning recently."

"Nay, 'twas not a castle in which I lived," Gillian replied hastily, and paused, wondering if she should go on and explain about the hut in the forest.

"Ah, well, 'tis good enough for that, at least," he replied, "although I'm sorry to hear you're homeless. Will you make your home here at Edinample?"

"Nay, I travel t'Kilchurn with Lady Joan when she returns there," Gillian replied, and saw Thane's head rear up at her words.

"Gillian is welcome to stay at Edinample as long as she wishes," Thane said implacably. "I don't wish to see her leave." A silence fell over those who sat nearby. Juliana glanced curiously from Thane to Gillian and back again. Her face was expressionless, but Gillian sensed her puzzlement. Sir Robert too seemed troubled by something.

"M'lord is most gracious, but since Lady Joan has invited me to join her at Kilchurn, I plan to make the trip there with her."

Thane fiddled with his knife, then, sensing he'd left his guests in some disquiet, he shrugged. "Gillian has a way with the healing herbs," he said lightly. "When I was gored by a wild boar, she sewed up my wounds and made me well again. And when the MacGregor outlaw let loose a rock slide on the heads of my men, she once again helped nurse them back to health. I shall miss her if she goes."

Once again came the awkward pause, while those seated about fixed their gazes on their plates and searched frantically for something to say. Sir Robert came to the rescue.

"So you've had trouble with MacGregor outlaws," he said. "I've heard you had reivers, though I'd not heard they were MacGregors. I thought the clan disbanded some years ago."

"Ah, why they should rise again now is something I don't readily understand," Thane said with some frustration evident in his voice, "save that the whelps they farmed out to other clans have come full grown and seek to avenge their clan's proscription."

"One can hardly blame them," Sir Robert remarked casually, and Gillian warmed to him.

"Aye, I would do the same if it were my clan," Thane acknowledged. "Still, I can't be lenient with the poor bastard, for he's killed several of my men and kidnapped my mother and Evina."

Sir Robert's gaze turned to the end of the table, where Lady Joan sat. "Aye, I would not be lenient with them over that," he answered. "You were not hurt, m'lady?"

"Thane and his men rescued us too quickly for harm to be done to me or my party," Lady Joan said, and blushed beneath Sir Robert's warm gaze.

"Still, I would have you well-protected on your trek back to Kilchurn. Who's t'say he will not kidnap you again?"

"Aye, 'tis true," Lady Joan replied evenly.

"Will you go t'Edinburgh, m'lady, for the winter court?" Sir Robert asked, and talk began to flow easily. Gillian listened to the latest gossip and speculation about the English queen's health and the new title their own king might well inherit.

Gillian felt quite giddy trying to keep up with the conversation. Finally Sir Robert turned to her. "What think you, Mistress Gillian. Have you any desire to go to court in Edinburgh?"

"I have never considered the possibility," she replied truthfully. "Is it very grand?"

"Not as it once was," Sir Robert answered. "King James and his wife, Anne of Denmark, are far more austere than our past nobility. Some think he means to earn his sainthood, save that his wife has produced seven heirs for him in the thirteen years of their marriage, so he can't be too saintly." Sir Robert tweaked his eyebrows and Gillian laughed despite herself.

"I think I should not like to be nobility," she said finally.

"And why is that, lassie?"

"I should not want others t'speak of me so intimately."

" 'Tis the way of man to look upon what his fellow man is doing and to comment upon it."

"Still, it must be hurtful at times."

Sir Robert regarded her solemnly. "Aye, I suppose it must be, lass. What makes you so sensitive to the hurts of others? Have you been the subject of cruel gossip?"

"Oh, I—nay, m'lord," she answered quickly, and looked away, for she would not have him see her lie. Sir Robert was far too quick-witted, she decided, and vowed to steer clear of his company until she'd left Edinample.

"What think ye of young Thane Campbell?" Sir Robert asked her bluntly, catching her unawares. She drew a breath and pressed her fingernails into her palms to still her trembling.

"Why d'ye ask me this question, m'lord?" she asked.

"I would have ye tell me, will he make a good husband for my daughter?"

"I would not know, m'lord," she answered, striving to still the flutter of her pulse in her throat.

"Come now, surely ye've formed an opinion of yer host. Will he treat her roughly or will he be kind?"

Gillian drew a breath. "He will not beat her," she whispered, "nor will he speak unkindly to her." She pressed her hands together in her lap. "He will protect her and rescue her from danger and give her his castle and"—she swallowed hard and forced herself to go on—"and his name and his sons." She bit her lip and fell silent.

"You don't speak of loyalty and faithfulness," he pointed out. "Will he give her those or will he betray her?"

Gillian jerked her head around to stare into his eyes. He knew of her role in Thane's life. Color suffused Gillian's cheeks. "I can't say, m'lord," she answered softly. "Nor can I promise to watch out for your daughter's happiness, for I shall be far away by the time of their marriage."

"I see." Sir Robert nodded his head. "I wish you well in your travels."

"Thank you," Gillian said, and pushed back her chair, preparing to rise. "If you will excuse me."

A noise erupted in the outer hall, causing every gaze to turn toward the great doors. Evan opened the doors and strode through.

"What is that racket?" Thane called with some irritation.

"M'lord, 'tis the villagers come t'talk with ye. They say 'tis a matter of some great urgency."

"Can't it wait until our meal is finished?" Thane demanded, but the roar increased in the outer hall. Suddenly the doors were pushed open and men and women streamed in, their eyes widening as they took in the sumptuous hall and generously laden tables.

"What is the meaning of this?" Thane demanded, jumping to his feet.

"M'lord, I pray ye excuse our intrusion." A man

stepped forward, his hat in hand, his head bobbing nervously. "I am Cliff Canmore of Edinample village."

"Why do you break in on us when we have guests?" Thane demanded.

"M'lord, we've come t'warn ye, ye have a witch in yer midst," the man said dramatically.

"A witch you say?" Thane roared while from all around him came murmurs of outrage. Thane's gaze flickered to Gillian and away, deliberately scanning along the table at his guests. "I see no witch, man!" he proclaimed.

"Aye, m'lord, and they hide themselves well wi' pretty faces and lovely bodies, so no man can see the black heart within."

"Did you say one of my guests is such?" Thane demanded. "You dare to offer an insult to Sir Robert and his daughter, Lady Juliana?"

"Nay, m'lord," the man cried, beginning to twist his cap in his hands. " 'Tis not that lady."

"My own mother, then," Thane continued, unrelenting.

"Nor yer mother," the man stammered.

"Then I bid you be gone before I take such an offense at your words that my blade must speak my fury."

"Nay, m'lord," the man cried, backing toward the entrance. "I but come out of concern for my laird. 'Tis the dark-haired wench known as Gillian what's been seen this very evening in her coven of witches."

"Nay!" Gillian cried, and would have leapt to her feet but for Sir Robert's strong hand on her arm.

"Don't draw the attention of your accuser, lest you give him more ammunition against you," he whispered. With languid grace that belied any sense of peril, Sir Robert got to his feet. "What a pretty show you and your Highlanders put on for us, Lord Thane."

" 'Tis no show, m'lord," Canmore exclaimed, aghast that his word might be doubted, for he held a high status within the village. " 'Tis the truth of it, and I have witnesses who saw the witch and her cronies with their own eyes."

"Then bring these witnesses forward and let them speak their piece, then let's be done with this travesty."

"Bring Mistress Beathas and her daughter Leana," Canmore ordered, and the crowd at the door parted and two women clasping each other for support came forward. The eyes of the younger woman rolled in her head as if she were unable to settle on one face. Her mother gripped her by the arm.

"We are here, m'lord," the woman said, and though her voice was faint with nervousness and fear, her resolve was clearly set. She looked around the table of noblemen, and when her gaze fell on Gillian she shrieked and hid her eyes behind the end of her shawl. "There she is, m'lord. The black witch." She began to rock back and forth and let out a loud wail, and her daughter joined her.

"Silence!" Thane ordered, and at once the two ceased their caterwauling. "These are serious charges you level against my mother's ward," Thane said into the hush. The women began to babble, and with a swift slash of his arm Thane motioned them to silence.

"I would have you tell me one at a time what you've seen," he ordered, and the older woman raised her head, and taking great care her gaze did not fall on Gillian, began to relate her story.

"We were caught late in the Forest of Glenartney," she began. "Our cows had wandered or been seduced away, so we went in search of them. Well inside the forest we glimpsed a light through the trees and feared it might be that of reivers who had stolen our cows and had stopped to kill and eat one of them."

"So close to the village and to Edinample itself?" Thane asked in amazement.

"We don't know how a reiver would think, m'lord," she answered meekly. "I am but a poor widow with little knowledge of the ways of men—"

"What happened then?" Thane demanded, cutting short her self-pitying whine.

"My daughter is far braver than I, m'lord, and she's a bit of the fire in her, so she says if 'tis reivers, she'll teach them t'take the cattle of a poor widow when they can take the fatted ones of the laird what has so many, he would not miss a few." A crafty look had come upon the woman's face. "These are not my sentiments, m'lord, but those of my daughter, who sometimes speaks rashly."

"Aye, that she does," Thane said, scowling. "Be done with your tale."

"I was that scared, I didn't want to go with her. I would have been well content t'leave them t'my cows, but she was my daughter, after all, my own child, and I could not leave her. So I followed behind her and we crept close to the light. When we arrived, we saw they had made a fire on a hillock and were crouched about it, uttering their blasphemous curses."

"Ye can't know what they were saying," Thane said dismissively.

"Aye, m'lord, I did," the woman cried with such conviction, all around the table awaited her answer. Seeing she held their attention, the woman preened a little, then, remembering the seriousness of their plight, she scowled and hurried on. "If I tell you the rest, m'lord, you must promise me protection from the witch. Me and my poor daughter, who even now can't speak for the fright she's had." The girl in her arms shivered and whimpered, her eyes vacant. "Ye must promise me, m'lord, you'll not let her hurt us."

"I so promise, woman, go on!" Thane roared. His hands were clenched into fists and he dared not look at Gillian, so great was his concern for her.

Satisfied that the laird would keep her safe, the woman continued. "We must have made a noise, m'lord, for suddenly the figures 'round about the fire grew still and turned as of one mind and body to look at us. 'Twas then my daughter lost her tongue and could not speak. Evil their faces were, m'lord, with great hooked noses and fire where their eye sockets ought to be. And this one"—she waved vaguely in the direction of Gillian—"this one sprang up. Her hood flew back and I saw her face."

Robena! Gillian thought. In her distress over Juliana's arrival, she'd nearly forgotten that it had been only that morning when Robena had come to the bridge gate to see her. She understood all too well what had happened. Robena had met with Jaimie and his men in the Forest of Glenartney, and Beathas and her daughter had come upon their campfire. But she could not explain this to Thane, Gillian realized, for to do so would require revealing her kinship with the very men who had killed and maimed and kidnapped. She sat silent while Beathas continued with her terrible accusations.

"Aye, her face was the most terrible of all," Beathas said. "She opened her mouth and called great curses down on us, ordering the other witches and warlocks to capture us. We turned and ran, m'lord, and only by the grace of God did we stumble out of the forest and make our way back t'the village."

The woman fell silent, stroking Leana while she sobbed piteously on her mother's shoulder. All around the tables, people sat stunned and quiet. Thane knew Beathas's tale had made a great impact, and he must do something to discount it.

"How long ago did this encounter happen, Mistress Beathas?" he demanded.

"Only the time it took us to come from the edge of the Glenartney woods, m'lord," she answered. "We came straightaway and told Mr. Canmore, for I guessed he'd know what to do."

"I brought them directly here, m'lord," Canmore said. "I felt certain ye'd want t'know of the danger among ye."

Thane turned to Gillian. His expression was grim, his

eyes dark with anger, whether at her or at the two women, Gillian was uncertain.

Gillian was aware of Sir Robert rising from his chair. "You've just encountered this spirit within the past hour, my good woman?"

"Aye, yer lordship," Beathas replied eagerly. " 'Twas the woman who sits beside ye now."

"But that can't be true," Sir Robert said. "For Mistress Gillian has been at my side for the past hour."

"Aye, and before she come down t'the great hall, she was in her room all afternoon and I was with her, helping her t'bathe and dress." Nessa spoke up from the servants' end of the table.

"I tell ye, I saw her," Beathas cried sullenly. "I am not a false sayer, m'lord."

"Nor do we accuse you so," Thane answered crisply, barely able to hide his elation at Sir Robert's and Nessa's recounting of Gillian's presence in the castle. He smiled faintly at the old villager.

"We question only whether you might have fancied you saw Gillian in the forest, for obviously she could na be there and here at the same time."

"Mayhap she slipped away, m'lord," Canmore said, seeing the doubt that had risen in the faces of the listeners.

"Still, she would not have time to travel to the Forest of Glenartney and back again to present herself here properly gowned and coiffed."

A shrill moan escaped Leana. "The witch flew." She spoke up for the first time.

"You seem to have regained your speech at an appropriate time," Thane snarled.

"Let her speak, m'lord," Canmore said. "We would know the truth of it."

At his nod, Leana continued. "I saw her flying through the air on the branch of an ash. Her black hair fanned out behind like—like the wings of a raven."

Thane's heart stopped beating for a moment, for how

often had he seen Gillian's hair flare just so, and he'd likened it to a raven's wings.

" 'Tis naught but your imagination," he scoffed.

"I've seen her cast her witch's spells before, m'lord," Leana cried. "When I've walked by the riverbank, I've seen her there gathering her special herbs and casting her spells."

Gillian sprang to her feet. "I can't remain silent, m'lord, and let such lies be told about me." She turned back to her accuser. " 'Tis true I gather herbs and use them to cure the villagers. You've come to me for the healing plants yourself, Beathas."

"Aye, that I have," Beathas cried out bitterly, "but little good they did. And now ye've stolen my cows."

"Did I not give you pine leaves boiled in vinegar for your toothache and you told me it took away your pain?" Gillian demanded.

The old woman looked chagrined at being caught in a lie. Her daughter raised her head and stared at Gillian with hate-filled eyes.

"I saw ye wi' my own eyes," Beathas replied. "Ye stood at the edge of Canmore's fields and blinked his cattle. They would have died if I had na warned him in time and he had not burnt the thatch from his roof beneath their noses. Now they wear red rags, so ye can't harm them again."

"Aye, and when I crept upon her at the river," Leana cried, "I saw her decorating her fingers with witches' bells and singing one of her chants. Every now and then she stopped t'laugh, a most awesome sound."

"I know she's a witch," Beathas intoned. "For I remembered my grandmother telling me an old remedy. I boiled the green juice from the inner bark of the elder and bathed my eyes in it, so my vision was cleared and now I can see witches when no one else can. 'Tis how I knew she was a witch from the first moment of her coming to Edinample."

"So you're one of the miserable fools who've spread such vicious rumors about her," Thane cried.

"I but warned my neighbors," Beathas declared. "I would not have her hurt them."

"Have a stout heart, lass," Sir Robert whispered to Gillian. "And you have no qualms that you might be a witch without your full knowledge?" Sir Robert asked.

"Nay, m'lord, I am not," Gillian said so earnestly, he allowed a small grin to light his austere features.

"Then I may have a solution," he said, and once again got to his feet. "I don't believe this woman to be a witch as you claim," he said with such firm conviction that Beathas and Leana fell silent. "At any rate, there is one way to prove her innocence." He summoned his manservant and whispered instructions. Immediately the man left the room.

"Ye've been bewitched by her, m'lord, just as our laird has," Beathas said with something less of the conviction she'd shown earlier.

"I think not, my good woman," Sir Robert answered. "I am not a man to be so easily bewitched." His servant returned almost at once, carrying a black bundle. Sir Robert held the bundle aloft so all might see.

"I hold in my hand a Bible, which as ye all know bears the word of our Lord. No witch would deign even to touch its covers, for to do so would bring instant and damnable death to her. Even for a witch to gaze upon such a holy book can strike her blind and take away her evil powers." He turned to Gillian. "Tell me, lass, would you be willing to look upon this Bible, to place your hand upon it at the risk of death if you be a witch, and would you swear t'God Almighty himself and to those gathered here this day that you are not a witch?"

"Aye, m'lord, with a full and innocent heart," Gillian cried with some elation, for it seemed at last that Sir Robert had hit upon a solution that would clear her from this awful indictment.

"So be it," Sir Robert declared, and taking Gillian's hand he led her off the dais to the center of the hall, where he left her while he carried his bundle around so all might see it truly was as he claimed. With the silk covering once more in place, he returned to Gillian.

He raised the bundle before her eyes. "Knowing that the sight of this holy book might strike you blind and strip you of your powers if you be a witch, Mistress Gillian, I ask you, do you wish me to show it?"

"Aye, m'lord," she cried fervently. "I am innocent of these charges."

Sir Robert nodded and flipped away the black silk, revealing the leather-bound Bible. Gillian's gaze did not waver from it. Deliberately Sir Robert opened the covers and regarded the ornate handwritten Scriptures within. Gillian's gaze remained unflinchingly on the open book. A murmur rose around her, but she glanced neither to the left or right.

"Will you place your hand upon the Bible, Gillian, and swear to the Almighty Himself that you're not a witch?"

Calmly Gillian placed her hand on the open Bible. "I so swear it," she said. They stood for a full minute of revelation.

Beathas licked her lips and earnestly willed that God should strike the witch dead and thus prove she'd spoken the truth. Thane was full of gratitude for Sir Robert's ingenuity. Lady Joan smiled as she watched the elegant white-haired man. She felt a flutter in her heart and wished she were alone with Sir Robert so she might properly thank him for this good deed.

"She has passed the test," Thane said, "which should be proof enough to you that this woman is not a witch. Now I bid you return to your homes and let's have no more of this nonsense."

"Aye, m'lord," Canmore said, feeling foolish. He turned an angry glare upon the two women.

"But I tell you, laird, we did see a gathering of witches

in the forest and this woman was there. Oh, her hair was not bound up and she did not wear the fancy gown she does now, but I would swear on my husband's grave, 'twas her we saw."

"Be gone with you," Thane roared. "And no more tales or I'll have your tongues cut out and fed to the geese for their silly quacking."

Beathas and Leana exchanged worried glances and quickly left the hall, Canmore following close behind. Only Thane's command halted their flight. "Canmore! Since you've assigned yerself spokesman of this delegation, I bid you to put a stop to this tongue-wagging of witches and spells. It does no good for the villagers."

"Aye, but, m'lord, in truth it does, for if a man's cow dies or his child takes sickly or his fortunes are lost—"

"If a man looks for an excuse, then he must surely be lacking within himself," Thane interrupted. "See that these rumors die down."

"Aye, m'lord," Canmore said, and quickly exited. When the door was closed behind them, everyone exchanged glances and let out sighs of relief and trills of laughter.

"Well done, Sir Robert," Lady Joan called.

"Aye, I have not heard of this means of identifying a witch," Aindreas called. He cast a quick smile at Juliana, and she dimpled prettily.

"In truth, I don't know if 'tis," Sir Robert admitted.

"Then here's to your quick wit, Sir Robert," Thane said fervently, for he'd not known how to protect Gillian from the accusations.

" 'Twas my pleasure to help so beautiful a lady," Sir Robert said, bowing extravagantly to Gillian. She inclined her head graciously, as she'd seen Lady Joan do on occasion, and took his hand so he might lead her back to her place at the table.

"Pity the woman's accusation has no truth to it," he said, his eyes twinkling. "I would beg you make me a love potion so I might draw the attentions of my lady fair."

"Alas, m'lord, such charms seldom work," Gillian said. "They are but the superstition of milkmaids." She glanced at Lady Joan, who was coquettishly studying them from behind the lacy edge of her fan.

"Mayhap all you need to win your lady fair is but the courage to approach her, m'lord," she said teasingly.

Sir Robert threw back his head and laughed. He was a most handsome and distinguished man, Gillian saw, and perfect for Lady Joan. "Aye, lass, you're not only bonny but astute as well. Tell me, dare I have any expectation with the lady? Has she spoken my name or uttered my praises in an unseemly manner?"

"Nay, m'lord," Gillian answered honestly. "But it seems that Lady Joan holds her own council about deeply felt matters, so the fact that she has not uttered your name at all may tell more than anything she might say."

Eyes twinkling yet again, Sir Robert bowed. "Then I take heart at your words," he said. "You've given me hope."

"Nay, Sir Robert, you've given me hope with yer kind protection," she answered quietly, and slid from her chair. "I'll bid you good evening."

"Must you go?" he asked quickly, his eyes filled with warmth and concern.

"I think it best if I retire now," she said, unaware of how forlorn her words sounded.

"I would speak to you on a matter," he said before releasing her hand. "Will you take a walk about the grounds with me?"

"I can't promise you a love potion," she teased, throwing aside her melancholy in the face of his persistent friendship toward her.

The corners of his eyes crinkled as with a smile, but his gaze remained somber. "Perhaps upon yer arising?" he suggested, and she nodded. "Good night, lass," he said, and released her hand with another slight bow.

Wondering what Sir Robert wished to discuss, Gillian made her way from the hall, looking neither to the left or right. She thought she heard Thane calling her name, but she didn't look back. That part of her life was finished now. She lifted her skirts and ran, holding her breath, until she was alone in her room and no one could see her tears or hear her anguished sobs.

Chapter 17

THERE WAS TO be no morning rendezvous with Sir Robert after all. Thane had arranged a hunt, Sir Robert explained in his hasty note, and the Cawder nobleman considered it bad manners to refuse. With a sigh of relief Gillian went back to bed, huddling beneath the covers. Steeped in misery, she spent the day in her room, wanting to avoid all who knew the truth of her position at Edinample. Late in the afternoon, when the shadows were settling in the corners of the bailey and a chill had crept in the windows so servants hastened to close the shutters and stir up the fires, a familiar knock sounded at her door. Her heart leapt into her throat. She remained seated at the window, her eyes turned to the heavy oaken door and the lock she'd so carefully turned.

"Gillian, open the door," Thane called. "I would speak with you."

Every nerve in her body urged her to throw open the door, to take what comfort Thane offered, accept whatever explanation he made, live with whatever promises he could give. But stubborn pride, born she knew not where, kept her silent and still. If she could not be his wife, she would not be his mistress. Some innate part of her knew she had a greater worth than that. After a while his footsteps moved away down the corridor.

In the days that followed, Thane made no further attempt to speak to her, nor did she present herself in his company, remaining in her room and taking her meals in the kitchen with the servants.

At midday of the third day Lady Joan arrived followed by a servant bearing a tray. "I thought I might find you mooning about here in your room," she said briskly. "Nessa said you didn't go down for breakfast and ordered none brought up. Now 'tis past noon! Trust me, child, this is foolish."

"I don't feel hungry," Gillian said, but Lady Joan ignored her, motioning to the servant to arrange the tray on a table near the window. " 'Tis a lovely day. We'll look out on the loch as we eat. That will do nicely." She dismissed the servant and filled a plate, placing it on the opposite side of the table before filling one for herself. Gillian had no choice but to settle onto the window seat and take up a spoon.

" 'Tis cook's best barley stew," Lady Joan said, crumbling a bit of bread into her bowl. She honored her silence until Gillian had spooned down most of the stew and nibbled at the cheese and pears. The girl's color, she noted, was somewhat better. At last she could hold her patience no longer and fixed Gillian with a stern eye. "You can't hide away like this, child."

Gillian drew a deep wavering breath. She'd held her feelings too long. "I can't bear to face Thane, for I'm that hurt and angry at him."

"Rightfully so." Lady Joan nodded. "His behavior has been outrageously bad, and I've told him so, if that makes you feel any better."

"Nothing can make me feel better," Gillian wailed, getting to her feet and pacing the length of the room.

"Have ye missed yer menses?" Lady Joan asked softly. Gillian returned to her seat and met Lady Joan's gaze.

"Nay, m'lady. My monthly bleeding has come and gone."

Lady Joan couldn't hide her relief. "For a moment I feared—"

"I'm not with child," Gillian said quickly, and suddenly wished with all her heart that she was. At least then she'd have someone to love, someone who belonged to her and whom no one could ever take away.

Lady Joan watched the troubled young face and could almost read the longing in the girl. "Such will come to you at the proper time," she said sympathetically, "when it will not bring you shame." She paused, choosing her next words carefully. "You might have influenced your cause with my son had ye been carrying his bairn."

Gillian's head came up, her eyes widened. "I would not trap him so to marry me," she answered. "He must choose me of his own accord, and he has not." She leapt to her feet once more. "I don't mean to rush you, Lady Joan, when you've so recently come to Edinample, but when will we be leaving for Kilchurn?"

"I can't go while we have guests. Besides, Sir Robert has offered to act as escort for us should we change our minds and decide to winter in Edinburgh. Would you like to go there?"

"I've never been to Edinburgh, m'lady," Gillian said. "I don't know if I would like it or not, but it is away from Edinample, and so I will travel most gratefully wherever you choose." Nessa entered the room, bringing with her two more of the gowns she'd been assigned to make for Gillian. She spread them across the bed. Gillian paid them scant attention, but Lady Joan nodded her head in approval.

"Well done, Nessa. You'll have an extra coin or two for all your trouble."

"Thank you, m'lady," Nessa replied calmly, for she was used to such largesse.

"Gillian is going for a walk," Lady Joan said. "Are Evina and Juliana about? Perhaps they can join her."

"Nay, m'lady. They've long since returned from their

walk. Lady Juliana has gone to her room t'rest at the behest of that dragon who serves as her nursemaid, and Evina has gone to the village again."

"The village?" Lady Joan raised an eyebrow in inquiry.

"I don't know why," Nessa answered her unspoken question. "She's spent a lot of time there these past three days."

"I hope 'tis not to do mischief," Lady Joan replied cryptically.

Gillian glanced at her in surprise. Did Lady Joan distrust her niece?

Lady Joan turned and smiled at Gillian. "I've need of fresh verbena. Will you not gather some for me?"

"Aye, m'lady, but why do you need it?" Gillian blurted out. "As I recall, the leaves of the plant have little use except that they're believed to have powers of attracting a lover." Lady Joan's blush was uncharacteristic and wholly endearing. Gillian looked at Nessa, who'd turned aside to hide her grin.

"I'll willingly collect the verbena for you," Gillian said somberly, and then, not wishing to offend the lady who'd shown her such kindness, she bolted from the room. She couldn't withhold a chuckle as she made her way from the castle and out the bridge gate.

Lady Joan and Sir Robert were obviously attracted to each other. Despite their age and position, they approached their relationship with the same temerity as a young, untried swain and his maiden. She rounded a corner and came face-to-face with Thane. Her smile died away and she stared at him in consternation. His features were haggard, his blue eyes tormented. His lips thinned as with anger when first he observed her lingering smile.

"Do you find this time humorous, then, Gillian?" he demanded. "Are you so frivolous, then? Do you feel no shame for the pain you cause me?"

"Aye, I feel shame enough," she snapped, "for the fact I was foolish enough to be misled. Dinna speak to me of shame, Thane Campbell. 'Tis not I who acted dishonorably in this affair." She wheeled away from him. His hand shot out to catch her wrist. She felt the fire of his touch.

"Lass, don't grow bitter against me for this. I can't change the way of things."

She turned back to face him, her hand still captive in his. Her gaze was scornful. " 'Tis a thing of your own making. No one else can change it," she cried, yanking her hand away. She ran across the bailey, her heart pounding painfully in her chest.

She feared he might follow her, but when no sound of pursuit came to her, she slowed her pace and admitted she'd secretly wanted him to come after her. She'd wanted him to touch her, to hold her and press kisses over her eyes and cheeks. God help her, she'd wanted him so, she'd had to run from him in fear she would throw herself against him and agree to anything he wished. She would not be his *baille*. She would not. Yet the alternative was so painful, she quailed at the thought of it. Could she continue through life without seeing him again, without knowing his embrace, without sharing his passion?

She set her feet along the river path and soon her young muscles moved with fluid, easy grace. Her spirits lightened, and she found comfort in the scolding song of the wren and the antics of the tree creeper that scampered in and out of the oakwoods in its quest for food. She plucked purple heather and tucked it in her hair.

"Oh, how beautiful," a voice said, and Gillian swung around to find Juliana Cawder standing on the path. Once again Gillian was struck by the innocent beauty of the young girl. No wonder Thane wanted her as his wife.

"The heather looks wonderful against your dark locks. I've often wished I had hair of such color."

"Surely, you jest. Don't you know how rare is the color of your hair?"

"Aye, I've been told often enough," Juliana replied, "and I see how men look at me, as if they've a great hungrying for lamb stew." She made a face, and Gillian was startled to laughter.

"There, you *do* laugh after all," Juliana cried.

"Why would ye think I did otherwise?" Gillian asked, suddenly nettled that the girl had found her wanting in some way.

"Well, judging from what happened in the great hall the other night, there's little enough for you to find amusing," Juliana observed. "And Evina said—" She paused. "Well, it doesn't matter what someone says about us, does it? Only we know who we are really."

"You sound uncommonly wise for a lass of yer age," Gillian observed wryly, wondering despite herself what Evina had said of her to this innocent creature.

"Aye, I think so." She paused. "Tell me, do you think the laird is a handsome man?"

Gillian swallowed. "Handsome enough," she muttered.

"I suppose he is, but he's so big and fierce and he never smiles, even when I make a witty remark. He's not at all like his cousin, Aindreas."

"That's true enough. Aindreas is a bit of a flirt and he's lighthearted. But then, he doesn't have the responsibility that the laird does."

Juliana sighed. "The only time I see the laird's face soften is when he looks at you," Juliana said, gazing directly at Gillian. Her childlike features were perfectly serene, and she seemed untroubled by her observation.

"Laird Thane rescued me from a horrible death and brought me to safety here at Edinample."

"How romantic!" Juliana cried, clapping her hands together. Her eyes shone brilliantly. "Did he ravish you in payment for his good deed?"

"Nay," Gillian cried, aghast. "Thane is an honorable man."

"So I've heard," Juliana said almost petulantly. "In fact, I've heard naught else over these past five years, save how virtuous and goodly he is."

"You must be pleased to have such a man as yer betrothed," Gillian reminded her tartly.

"I suppose I should be," Juliana said thoughtfully. "But he does na look at me the same as he looks at you. I don't think he loves me."

"He will," Gillian assured her, wondering why it had been left to her of all people to reassure this girl of Thane's love. "He must have time to come to know you."

They walked for a while in silence, contemplating their conversation. The walls of Edinample were just ahead when Juliana spoke again. "Do you love Thane?"

Gillian gasped at the unexpected question. "You're rude to ask such things," she stammered.

"Aye, Sophie, my nursemaid, often tells me so," Juliana replied calmly, "and I don't wish to offend, but you both look so sad, especially when you look at each other, that I can't help but think some feelings exist between you."

"You're quite in error, m'lady," Gillian said stiffly. The bridge gate was before them now, and Evina rushed from the castle.

"Juliana, I've looked all over for you," the flaxen-haired girl cried. "I didn't know you would want to go for another walk again this afternoon, else I would have stayed and gone with you."

" 'Tis no matter," Juliana said dismissively. "I found Gillian, and she's wonderful company."

"Thank you, m'lady," Gillian said, bobbing slightly. " 'Tis my pleasure."

"Did you take her to the Fairy Baking Stone?" Evina asked jealously. She'd so far not deigned to greet Gillian.

"Nay, I thought you'd done so by now," Gillian answered, and Evina had the grace to look uncomfortable.

"I'll take you there tomorrow," she said to Juliana. Gillian turned away, hurt by the slight, for Evina had pointedly not invited her to join them.

"Gillian!" Juliana called, and Gillian turned to face her

again. "Will you go with us tomorrow? I see that you gather plants as you walk. I know something of the healing properties of some plants, but I'm woefully ignorant of much. Will you not come and teach me?" Her beautiful pale eyes were sincere.

Gillian wanted to refuse but couldn't. She found she'd enjoyed Juliana's constant chatter and quick intellect. Now she nodded at the girl. "Aye, I'll come tomorrow." Over Juliana's shoulder she saw Evina's smile twist into a pout.

Gillian turned toward the bridge gate.

"Why did you ask her to join us? Don't you know the kind of woman she is?"

"Yes. A nice one," Juliana said, and stalked away from Evina. Gillian hid her bitter smile and started back.

"Gillian!" Thane called when he saw her approaching across the bailey. "I've brought someone to you, though I'd not have brought him like this if I could have helped it." He carried something large cradled in his arms.

She was close enough now to see a humped back and rough red hair and beard. "Lachlan!" His blue eyes were closed and dried blood stained his clothes and pale face. Her heartrending cry captured the attention of Sir Robert, Duncan, and the other men in the bailey. Silently they watched as the beautiful young woman ran to Bhaltair's side, her arms reaching up for the ugly little man.

Thane laid Lachlan in a patch of grass and Gillian knelt beside him, using the hem of her skirt to wipe his bloody brow. She half sobbed, half crooned to him as her hands flew over his body, searching for wounds. She was unaware of how her behavior might seem to others.

"Take him into the castle," he ordered, and two Highlanders came forward and picked up the crippled man by his short legs and his arms.

"Have a care," Gillian cried, unaware that tears streamed down her face. She followed the soldiers into the castle.

"Where do you wish us to take him, laird?" they asked.

"We'll find a pallet for him in the servants' hall," Thane said.

"Nay, take him to my bedchamber. I can attend him better there," Gillian ordered.

The two Highlanders exchanged glances but carried him up the stairs with Gillian trailing close behind. Thane stood in the hall below, watching. He sensed the surprise Gillian's loving greeting of the hunchback had caused among his superstitious Highlanders. Impulsively he mounted the stairs after her.

"Place him on my bed," Gillian was instructing the soldiers when Thane arrived at the doorway of her room. The two men looked troubled.

"Then where will ye sleep?" one of them asked.

"It doesn't matter. 'Tis easier for me to tend him here, and he'll be more comfortable." Gillian threw back the covers of her bed and turned to look at the men. "Why are you hesitating?"

"We don't know if Laird Thane wishes this," the outspoken one mumbled. Thane stepped into the room.

"Aye, I do," he said calmly. "Place him on the bed as Mistress Gillian has requested."

"Aye, sir," the man answered. "We just weren't sure if the arrangement met with yer approval."

"It does," Thane answered, "since Mistress Gillian has no need of this bed. She will sleep in my room tonight."

Gillian opened her mouth to protest, but an outcry at the door stopped her.

"Didn't I tell you she was his mistress," Evina's voice demanded of the silvery-blond girl standing beside her.

"Juliana, 'tis not as it seems," Gillian said quickly. "Thane misspeaks himself."

"There is no need to deny it," Thane said firmly. "The whole castle knows Gillian is my mistress."

"But no more," she cried, anger racing through her.

"How dare you name me so to your betrothed. You do us both an injustice."

The two men who'd carried Lachlan up stood with open mouths, listening to this scandalous talk between the gentry.

"Be gone with you," Thane shouted at them, and they scrambled from the room. Thane rounded on Gillian. "You were right in that I sought to protect you, lass," he said. "You've made such a fuss over the hunchback, even bringing him here to your bedchamber. Don't you see how some will look upon this?"

Gillian's brows drew together in perplexity. "Lachlan is my friend, my brother. We were raised together by Hannah when all else turned their backs on us. I would gladly give him my bed."

Juliana advanced into the room, her smile gentle. "Aye, I can see well the reasons for your affection for this poor creature," she said softly. "But don't you see the reason for Thane's trying to protect you? They whisper in the village that you're a witch even now and to have a rumor that you share your bedchamber with a hunchback would only add fuel to their rumors."

Gillian's anger at Thane died away, and she might have told him so except that Lachlan groaned and thrashed about. Gillian rushed to his side.

"Lachlan, dear friend," she cried, bending over him. "You're safe now. You're among friends. Thane has brought you to Edinample. No one can harm you here."

The little man groaned again but did not open his eyes. Gillian sprang up and rushed to fill a bowl with warm water and gather up linen for bandages. Without sparing a glance at those who filled the room, she knelt and began bathing the hunchback's ugly, misshapen face, murmuring a soft, crooning sound that made Thane's heart wrench with jealousy.

"I'll send Shadwell to help tend him," he offered. "In the meantime, my men and I will return to Glenartney in the hope of finding the man who did this." Troubled, he turned to Juliana and Evina.

"We'll leave Lachlan in Gillian's capable hands," he said, and escorted them from the room. In the corridor he paused, waiting for Evina to return to her room before facing Juliana. "I'm sorry for any distress I may have caused you in there, m'lady."

"You caused me no distress, Thane," Juliana replied serenely. "I see before me a man who is kind and protective of those he loves." Her cool, pale eyes regarded him without rancor. "Since it is already so stipulated that I become your bride, I'm happy to see these softer sides. Perhaps one day we'll grow to love each other and you'll protect me as you've done Gillian."

For the first time since her arrival, Thane considered the child bride that was to be his. She was a beauty, an unblemished peach nearly ripe for the plucking, and if a man were patient enough to wait, he'd have a rare beauty.

"You are far wiser for your years than one might expect," he said softly.

Juliana nodded her head slightly. "Thank you, m'lord." Unhurriedly she drew back, then walked down the hall with regal dignity.

Gillian worked over Lachlan, washing his wounds and binding them before she was finally satisfied she'd done all she could.

When Lachlan was once again dressed in a new linen shirt, she sat back and watched the ugly features for any sign of returning consciousness. Her efforts were finally rewarded, for Lachlan opened his eyes and lay staring at Gillian with wonder growing in his eyes.

"I'm at Edinample," he croaked, and beamed his appreciation of that.

"Lachlan, praise be t'God. I feared you might be dead."

"I feared the same when Jaimie MacGregor ran me through with his sword."

"Jaimie did this to you?"

"Aye, he wanted me to trick you into helping them into the castle through a secret passage."

"Aye, a hidden door in the siege tower," Gillian said. "But I fear to do as he asks. He's done a great deal of mischief. He kidnapped Lady Joan and wounded Thane and killed many of his men. I cannot help him."

"Aye, well I knew you would not!" Lachlan said, and coughed, his chest wheezing as he fought to draw a breath.

Gillian smoothed his brow and felt the fever burning through him. "Jaimie can't hurt you again. Thane will not let him near us."

Lachlan nodded and closed his eyes, concentrating on the drawing of each shallow breath so he would feel no pain. Gillian sat beside him. The fever was taking hold and she feared he'd not be able to throw it off. A sound at the door caused her to turn.

"Oh, Gillian," Evina said. "I've come to apologize. I'm feeling that bad for the way I acted before. I don't wish to give up being yer friend." She came forward to take Gillian's hand. Her lips curved in a sweet smile and her eyes were as warm and friendly as they had been when first she offered friendship.

Gillian stared at her, seeing the girl's fickle nature better now.

"I fear we have no future as friends," she said, firmly withdrawing her hand from Evina's. "Soon I will leave Edinample and I will never return. Concentrate yer efforts on pleasing Juliana."

" 'Tis more than I can bear t'think I've lost yer friendship." In a flurry of petticoats she ran to the door and was gone.

Gillian dismissed the woman from her thoughts. Lachlan's fever had worsened and he'd begun to toss about on the bed. She would try some of the fruit of the fresh jaundice berry she'd gathered that afternoon. She turned to the small table that held her willow basket, but it was gone. Puzzled, she looked around, but it was not in the room. Quickly she began to search.

Evina hurried through the lower bailey, wrinkling her nose at the smells from the stables, blacksmith, and tannery. Leaving through the town gate, she made her way down to the village and on to the pasture beyond, where milk cows grazed. Gillian had told her once that the roots of the yellow broom could sicken a cow and even bring death.

Glancing around furtively to ensure no one was observing her actions, she drew the roots from her pocket and held them so the cows might chomp on them. When the roots had been devoured, she smiled and dropped the little willow basket she'd carried from Gillian's room.

Chapter 18

LACHLAN WAS WORSE. The fever had taken his mind, so he babbled of things she'd never known and wished she'd never heard, of cruelties he'd borne all his life and the pain such rejections had brought him. Gillian sat beside his bed and wept for him.

Nessa came upon her. "What is it, lass. Has yer hunchback died?"

"Nay, though I fear he might," Gillian sighed, wiping her eyes. "His fever grows worse and I can't find my basket. I gathered some jaundice berry this morning and I'm thinking it might bring down his fever."

"Can you gather more before the light is gone?" Nessa asked, and with a start Gillian noted that the sun had dipped and dark shadows were already sliding along the passes of Ben Earn and Meall Odhar. "I'll stay with him while ye're gone."

"Thank you, Nessa," Gillian cried, leaping up and throwing a shawl over her shoulders. "I'll go directly there and back."

"I'll keep close watch over him. Be gone with ye," Nessa ordered, and Gillian ran down the stairs and across the bailey, keeping watch for the missing basket as she went.

The light was fading far quicker than she'd thought.

She'd have to hurry or be caught outside the castle gates after dark. Her steps were swift upon the well-worn path leading to the river, and so intent was she on her task, she didn't notice the hooded shadow that sprang from the bushes and reached for her until she felt the cruel grip close over her arm.

"Where do you hurry so, little cousin," a familiar voice demanded, and Gillian drew back, unable to shake the hand on her wrist.

"Robena!" she cried, her heart thudding heavily in her chest. "You frightened me. Why do you slink about here?"

"Ah. I am with my brother," Robena said, and smiled. The beauty of that smile had once dazzled any man who saw it, Gillian remembered, but now its bitterness twisted the lovely face into an ugly mask.

"Jaimie is here?" Gillian gasped. Frantically she looked around, "Where is he?" she cried.

"He is hiding," Robena said serenely.

" 'Tis well he does, for Thane and his men are searching for him, even now, for his murderous deeds. He nearly killed Lachlan. How could he take a sword to an unarmed cripple?"

Robena shrugged. "Winter comes. Time is running out. Jaimie grows impatient. The hunchback would not do as Jaimie asked."

" 'Tis no reason to kill him," Gillian answered. "Any sympathy I might have had for Jaimie and his cause I don't entertain now. He's gone mad with his hatred."

"Have a care, cousin. 'Tis my brother you call mad."

"And mad he is. So are ye if ye think t'continue as ye are. There is no hope for yer cause, na by robbing and killing of innocent people. That's what caused the king t'turn against the MacGregors in the first place."

"Bah! Jaimie has sent me t'give ye a message. What he has done to the little hunchback, so he will do to the laird and his family if you don't help him."

"How can I help him?" Gillian cried. "I have nothing to give him and no influence with the king to have our clan reinstated."

"Aye, well he knows. But the MacNabs have given him sanctuary and the MacLarens and others, too, have offered him and his men a home among them."

"Then what more does he want? Why is he wounding helpless people and uttering threats?"

Robena regarded her for a moment. "Remember my brother is a proud man and he will not go empty-handed with a ragged, starving army. He wishes more arms, food, and clothing, mayhap a few cattle to take with him."

"I can't give him these things," Gillian snapped, her green eyes flashing.

"Nay, but you can help him attain them. Jaimie will come to the secret door tonight. You must open it for him."

"I will not."

"You will, for if you don't, I will slide my blade between the ribs of the fine lady you mimic so, or mayhap the untried young lass from Cawder Castle who would take your place in Thane's bed." She laughed at Gillian's shock over her familiarity with the castle household. "Aye, I know it all. I have a reliable source for information from within the castle itself."

"A spy?" Gillian cried. "Then why have you need of my help?"

"She is not familiar with the castle as you are, cousin."

"She?" Gillian asked.

Robena's eyes darkened at her slip. "Aye, 'tis a woman, for in the end 'tis always the woman who bears the pain when the laird's eye turns away from them, and 'tis the woman who seeks her own revenge."

"Bridget!" Gillian whispered.

Robena's laughter was almost gay. "Enough!" she snapped. "Jaimie will be at the castle wall tonight." She swirled the cape around her and disappeared so quickly into the darkening brush that Gillian blinked and for a moment considered the possibility that Robena was indeed a witch.

The air had grown chilled and the light was nearly gone. Gillian hugged the shawl about her and raced along the path to the riverbank where she'd found the jaundice berry. Hastily she tore away branches bearing the purple berries and turned toward the castle. As she neared the gate, she saw that villagers were gathered along the path, bearing lanterns. Their pale lights wavered in the dark, strangely unwelcome beams of light. Gillian paused, catching her breath.

"There she is," someone called, and the villagers turned toward her. "There's the witch. Don't let her get away."

At their words Gillian dropped the branches of jaundice berry and turned to run, but the villagers were upon her, grabbing hold of her arms and her hair so she was held captive. Gillian screamed.

"Take her to the riverbank above the falls," Canmore shouted, and of one body they lifted Gillian and half dragged, half carried her along the path to the spot designated.

"Thane!" she cried. "Thane, where are you?"

"No need to cry for the laird now," Beathas called gleefully, her eyes gleaming with malicious triumph. "You'll have to answer for yer wickedness."

"I'm not a witch," Gillian shouted, but her words were lost as hands tore at her clothes and hair, fists landed on her back and shoulders.

The villagers had become a mob intent on one thing only: her death. Suddenly a light gleamed and Lady Joan stepped forward to confront the mob. Juliana and Nessa stood beside her.

"What are you doing with Gillian?" she called. "You will release her at once."

"Nay, m'lady, you can't stop us now," Canmore cried out. "We've proof enough she's a witch."

"What proof?" Lady Joan demanded.

"Three milk cows fell sick and died but within the past hour, and we found her willow basket discarded along the way with all her evil potions within."

"I pledge on all that's holy that I am not a witch," Gillian said, voice breaking. "I don't know how my basket came to be there, but I didn't walk by the pasture today."

"Aye, ye don't have to walk there to do your mischief," Beathas cried. "We know you're a witch, for you fly through the air on an ash branch and you bed with a hunchback to produce more of your spawns of the devil."

"Lachlan is as a brother to me. He can't help the way he looks."

"If you be not a witch, then settle it once and for all," a man cried. "Take the test to prove your innocence."

"Did I not touch the Bible and swear on it as to my innocence before all?"

"It was but a trick," Beathas cried. "There be one sure way."

"Aye, bring the witching stool," someone shouted, and the mob surged forward again. "Take her to the river."

"You can't have a trial like this," Lady Joan called out. "You must wait for the laird to return." No one listened. They carried Gillian down the trail to an eddy pool and pushed her down in the soft mud.

"I have the stool," a villager cried, running forward. "Have ye cut a pole?"

"Alais is doing so," Canmore cried, and the sounds of an ax at work on a sapling came to them. In mere minutes the sapling pole was passed forward and the stool tied to it. Lady Joan and Juliana pushed their way through the crowd. Nessa trailed behind.

"Canmore, I command you to stop this foolishness," Lady Joan ordered. "If you continue with this travesty, I will name you to my son and you alone will stand responsible for this."

Canmore hesitated. Lady Joan never lifted her compelling gaze from his. Finally he nodded and turned to the other villagers.

"Let her go," he called. "We must leave the matter t'Laird Thane." The mob sent up a roar of protest.

"He'll let her go as before."

"He's under her spell as it is."

"Kill her now!"

"You have the stool and the pool is yonder. Prove t'her ladyship that what we say is true. If the girl be innocent, the water will show that right enough."

"Yes, give her the test. If she survives it, we'll have proof she's a witch." The mob was united in its purpose.

"God's Passion," Lady Joan cried, and the mob fell silent in awe to hear such a genteel woman curse. "Are ye saying she must die in order to prove herself innocent, but if she survives the test, she'll be burned as a witch! What madness is this? She must die either way!"

" 'Tis the way of things, m'lady. Stand aside," a harsh voice called, and once again the mob took up the cry. Without further ado they tied the stool to the log they'd brought. The contraption was anchored over a boulder so it might be raised and lowered at will. Rough hands swept Gillian forward, pushing her down on the stool. The pond glittered before her, black and menacing. For the first time, she screamed.

"Ah, hear her witch's shriek?" Beathas gloated. "She knows she can't pass this test."

A bag was drawn over Gillian's head. She bucked against the restraining hands, whipping her head from side to side in an effort to discard the bag, but she was held firmly. Ties were drawn tightly around her throat, securing the bag so she could scarcely breathe. Ropes were placed around her, pinning her arms to her sides.

Soft hands were suddenly there, slender arms encircled her shoulders.

"Don't do this, I beg you." Gillian heard Juliana's voice pleading and marveled at the young girl's bravery in facing the mob. "She's not a witch. She's good and kind. You're making a horrible mistake."

"Stand aside, lass," someone said cruelly.

Juliana gasped. The comforting arms were torn away from Gillian and she perceived the young girl had been pushed aside.

The first shock of cold water took her breath. Gillian felt the water rushing about her, felt it invade her ears so she nearly fainted at the chill. Then came the panic and terror as her lungs ran out of oxygen and she struggled not to gasp in water. Blackness danced on the outside of her consciousness. Thane, she called wordlessly, and felt a moment's comfort at the memory of him. It enabled her to push aside the panic, to concentrate on maintaining what little air she still possessed. When she knew she could hold it no longer, she expelled it slowly, giving up a prayer for mercy to her almighty God. At that moment the men above raised the stool. Gillian felt the water sluice away from her and gasped in air. The wet bag filled her mouth, so for a moment she feared it had cut off all chance of breathing, then her lungs filled with air.

"See, she truly is a witch. She still breathes." The shouts came from the shore.

Frantically Gillian shook her head in denial.

The stool plunged downward again, barely giving her time to snatch a breath. The water was less cold now. Her body was becoming numb. She fought less than before. Her thoughts turned once again to Thane and the happiness she'd known with him. Images of his laughing face passed before her. She did not fight the darkness as it claimed her this time, but welcomed it, for within its cold depths she thought she might find peace at last.

She was unconscious when they raised the stool the

final time. She sagged on the stool, only the ropes holding her upright.

"Aye, look, she's dead," Muriel Krochmal cried. "She were no witch after all." She looked shamefaced, remembering Gillian's kindness to her son. Slowly she backed away from the crowd and turned toward the castle.

"You've killed her," Lady Joan cried. "Bring her to shore."

The men leapt forward to pull the witching stool to dry land as instructed. They fumbled with the wet knots, and Gillian tumbled forward onto the grass.

"Take that bag from her head," Lady Joan snapped, and hands pulled away the black cloth. Juliana was the first to kneel in the grass beside Gillian and smooth back the wet strands from her pale face. Nessa pulled off her shawl and knelt to cover the slight figure.

"God have mercy on your souls," Lady Joan said to the milling villagers who began to draw back, suddenly in doubt of their accusations, suddenly remembering as they looked at her lying on the ground in her wine-red dress that a witch would never wear red as she'd done. It was a color to ward off witches.

Thane galloped into view, his face awful to see, his eyes promising the fires of damnation to any who stopped him. The villagers parted and Thane reined in his great black stallion, flinging himself out of the saddle before Bhaltair had even slid to a halt.

"Gillian!" he shouted, running to gather her in his arms. His anguished gaze studied her face for any signs of life. One big hand came up to smooth the wet strands from her cheeks as tenderly as mother with child.

"Gillian, lass," he whispered. "Don't die, little wild bird." His voice broke, and cradling her against his chest, he raised his face to the heavens in a silent plea. He gave no heed to the tears that rolled down his cheeks. Even the heartiest villager turned away, unable to bear the torment upon their beloved laird's face and the knowledge they'd been the cause of it.

Kneeling beside them, Juliana studied Thane's face and knew with a certainty that touched her heart that Thane Campbell loved this clanless waif with all his being. He would never feel that way about her, she was sure, and furthermore, seeing the bright hot light of their love, tragically as it had ended, she knew she would never settle for less for herself.

Horses could be heard along the path, and Aindreas and Duncan rode into the clearing. At once Aindreas's gaze sought out Juliana, and when he caught sight of her, he slid out of his saddle and hurried toward her. Juliana met him halfway. Willingly she went into his arms, feeling them close about her protectively.

"Are you safe, lass," Aindreas inquired against her temple.

Wordlessly she nodded. "I am now," she murmured, and his arms tightened about her.

A commotion sounded behind them and they turned back to Thane and Gillian.

"Her eyelids fluttered," Lady Joan cried joyously. "Thane, she's alive."

There was muttering among the villagers. "She's alive. The witch is alive."

Before the cry could build, Nessa stepped forward and faced them all, her head high as she gazed at them with contempt.

"Ah, she lives after all," she said, "but not because she's a witch. 'Tis more because the good Lord has seen fit to undo the work of the devil you've started. This is a goodly lass. Never have I seen her work a spell or do an evil deed. I've made gowns for her and helped her dress and undress. Never have I seen the mark of the devil upon her.

"She was raised in the forests by an old woman. She learned the ways of the woods and the plants and animals and she learned kindness and gentleness. You've cut her heart time and again with your accusations. I've seen her weep from the slights you've bestowed upon her, but never did she return your words with bitter ones of her own."

"I tell ye, I've seen she's a witch," Beathas said. "Did I not bathe my eyes with the green juice of the inner bark of the elder tree so I might see witches when naught else can?"

"Enough!" Thane roared. He rose, lifting Gillian in his arms. Her head lolled back so all could see the paleness of her features, the black, silky lashes lying along cheeks that held no color. "Even now, when she barely clings to life, you argue and accuse. Be gone with you, and if you ever raise your voice against her again, I'll have you put out of the clan."

His angry gaze raked around the circle of faces, then he turned back toward the castle, carrying Gillian as carefully as if she were the most fragile of all treasures. She moaned and turned her head, seeking warmth and reassurance in the strong hollow of his shoulder.

"Thane," she whispered.

"Aye, lass. I have you. You're safe with me," he said, and cursed himself that he'd allowed this to happen.

When Shadwell was finished with his teas and potions and poultices, he was none too gently guided from the room and instructed to go along and tend to Lachlan. Lady Joan, seeing her son's desire to be alone with Gillian, quickly said her good-byes and left, taking Nessa with her. When they were alone, Thane perched on the edge of the bed and gazed at Gillian. Her face was still pale, although a little color had returned to her cheeks and lips. A frown marred the perfection of her brow.

"Are you in pain, lass," Thane whispered, bending over her.

Her dark lashes swept upward and she gazed at him with eyes of deep forest green.

"Nay, m'lord, I'm not in pain," she answered softly, and shivered. "I can't throw off this chill."

Thane straightened and began divesting himself of his clothes. When he was naked, he drew back the covers and slid into the bed beside her, then reached for her. Willingly Gillian went into his arms. Thane gathered her close, his large hands molding her body against his possessively.

"I'll never let you go, lass," he sighed against her lips.

"And I'll never go," Gillian vowed, and moved her head so his lips might follow the line of her chin. His gentle kisses fell like a healing rain on her eyelids and cheeks. He'd meant only to warm her and cuddle her, but the feel of her beside him, the fear that he'd almost lost her, awakened such a strong desire within him that his manhood grew, gouging into her belly so that she laughed and grasped it in her soft hands.

He thought to make love gently, only to assuage their need and no more, but she would not be satisfied with his gentle touch. She demanded more from him, her kisses tempting, teasing, seducing with a sweet fire that drove his senses from his head. They mated with all the fire and abandonment they'd always shown, hungry from their abstinence, freed from their anger and misunderstanding and able at last to admit to themselves and each other that nothing, nothing else mattered in the world but their love.

Chapter 19

GILLIAN WOKE IN the middle of the night, haunted by the horror of the evening past. She crept closer to Thane's sleeping body, wrapping her arms around his waist and drawing comfort from his warmth. Something nagged at the back of her mind, something left undone, something that would bring danger to her—no, not to her, to someone she loved.

Lachlan! she thought, and sprang up. The cold floor seemed to burn her feet. Taking up a candle, she tiptoed from the room. The chilled air in the corridor crept around her bare ankles and made her shiver. She longed to return to the warm bed and Thane's embrace, but knew she couldn't sleep without seeing how Lachlan fared.

Quietly she opened the door and raised the candle so she could peer into the dark shadows. A sudden rustling sounded in the bed.

"Who's there?" a familiar voice cried out.

" 'Tis only me, Lachlan." She hurried over to reassure him. "I can't sleep for worry of you. Do you still have a fever?" She moved across the room and raised the light so she could see him better. He lay on his back. His forehead and cheeks glistened with perspiration; his feverish eyes gazed up at her in helpless resignation. He was ill, but she had no herbs to cure him.

"Lachlan," she cried, kneeling. "My basket is here! But it was not here before, else I would have seen it. Canmore and the others said they found the basket near the pastures where the milk cows died. Who would have brought it back here?" Lachlan regarded her silently. "Did you see anyone enter and leave the basket?"

"Only the lass with hair like mine."

"A girl with red hair?" She remembered the times Lady Joan and Nessa had commented on Evina's trips to the village. Lachlan moaned and shivered in his bed.

" 'Tis no matter now," she said quickly, "for look, there's jaundice berry here. I'll make a tea for ye. It will surely help yer fever and make ye sleep." She hurried to the fireplace, where a kettle of water sat on the hearth. Adding herbs to the kettle, she placed it over the coals, then filled a cup with the hot brew and brought it to Lachlan. She held his head so he might sip the tea.

When she was certain he was resting well, she took up her candle and cautiously made her way down the stairs. She pushed away any doubts that plagued her now. She could not even think of Evina or puzzle over her role in the villagers' accusations. She would deal with that later. First she must open the door for Jaimie and Robena. Only after they'd gathered the necessary supplies could they be gone from Edinample forever. She had set a course of action, and she must follow it, trusting in Jaimie's honor.

Yet how could she trust a man who would plunge his sword into the body of a cripple, a lesser man than he? She paused, gripping the railing while she fought back tears. Lachlan would not like her to think him a lesser man, nor would he have allowed Jaimie and his men to treat him as such. He would have taunted and strutted and dared. Aye, if the truth be told, Lachlan might well be part of the blame for what happened. She had to cling to that hope and believe Jaimie still had some honor left, otherwise she must fear that one day he would run his sword through Thane as he'd so often threatened. Either way, hers was the devil's choice.

The bailey was silent and black beneath a cloud-filled sky. Gillian stumbled on the path. There were no guards about, which made her pause for only a moment. Hazily she remembered Thane ordering the guards doubled, or had that been a dream? She peered around the square. No shadows moved. Not even a hound let out a warning cry. If she stood here longer she would lose her nerve, she reflected, and ran across the open grass to the siege tower. Once inside the round turret with the door closed behind her, she drew a trembling breath and clasped her hands in silent prayer. Let this be the right decision and let Jaimie keep his pledge to leave Edinample.

Memories of her childhood tugged at her as she made her way through the narrow winding corridor to the panel behind which the door was hidden. The thick oaken bar resisted her efforts, but she threw her weight against it and felt it give. She flung open the door, and at once Jaimie and his men poured into the tower.

"What took you so long?" he hissed. "I'd given up on you." He motioned to his men, who silently filed past.

"I had to wait until all were sleeping," she whispered, noting the number of men and the weapons they carried. "Now gather what you need and go quickly, as you promised."

"I made no such promise, little cousin," Jaimie said absently, and instructed his men to quit the tower and spread out through the castle grounds. They moved as silently as wraiths, their grim purpose obvious in their expressions.

"But Robena said you but needed enough supplies and goods to start anew in Ireland."

At the mention of her name Robena entered the tower, her lips curved in a triumphant smile. "You were always the trusting one, Gillian," she mocked. "We're MacGregors. We'll never give up MacGregor lands."

"Then ye never intended to leave Argyll?" Gillian cried.

"We're descended from kings and our home is here in the Highlands. Our lands were bestowed on us by Alexander II in his conquest of Argyll. None can take them from us."

"Why are you here now? What do you want at Edinample?" She knew before she saw the feral grin on his face. He'd brought too many men to simply steal supplies. "You plan to take the castle tonight and you've tricked me into helping you. God's mercy on your soul, Jaimie MacGregor." She turned toward the door, but he was too quick for her, grabbing her arm and dragging her back.

"Have you told anyone of our presence?" he demanded roughly.

Numbly she shook her head. "Only Lachlan."

Jaimie looked startled. "Ah, the little hunchback. He lives, then."

"Barely. Even now he lies in the castle with a fever and infection. He may yet die."

Jaimie looked only mildly regretful. "Robena, keep our little cousin here. Don't let her raise an alarm until we're ready." His eyes were hard with purpose. "Mayhap you'll use this time to reflect, Gillian. You've no reason t'feel you've betrayed your lover. 'Twould have been a betrayal to your clansmen if you'd not helped us. Stay here with Robena, and when I've taken the castle, I'll decide whether to pardon ye or not."

"Jaimie, these people are good and innocent. You promised me once you would not take lives," she cried, clinging to his arm.

"Aye," he said impatiently, shaking her off. "MacGregor lives, but as many Campbells will die this night as my blade can find. And Thane Campbell will be the first."

"Nay," Gillian cried, but he'd already sprinted up the stairs and out the door into the bailey. Gillian tried to follow, but Robena dragged her back and slapped her smartly on both cheeks.

"Ye'll stay here, little cousin," Robena said, shoving Gillian down on the stone floor, "and you'll make no sound or my blade will silence yer traitorous cries."

Gillian huddled on the floor and strained to hear sounds without. All was silent. She swallowed the bitter gall in her throat. "Robena," she pleaded. "'Tis not too late. Don't you see that what you do is treason to the crown? 'Twas King James himself who gave these lands to the Campbells. Jaimie can't take them back by force. Even if he succeeds in capturing Edinample, he'll not be able to hold it. King James will send his forces. He will not abide his noblemen being so treated."

"You seem t'know much about the king's wishes," Robena mocked. "Do you share his bed as well?"

"I know only what every Highlander should know about his king. James will not abide a ragtag band from a broken clan to defy his orders like this. Jaimie places his own head in a noose."

"Little you know of such things," Robena said. "Be still."

"I beg you, listen to reason."

Robena's blade appeared almost magically at Gillian's neck. "And I beg you, cousin, be still with your prattling. I would not like to answer Jaimie should he return and find you dead."

Gillian fell silent and watched Robena as she paced nervously. Shouts came to them and the clang of steel against steel. Robena's eyes gleamed with pleasure.

"So it begins," she whispered. "The MacGregors take back what is theirs by right."

"At what cost?" Gillian asked bitterly. "You've changed, Robena. You've become hard and evil, you and Jaimie. I don't remember you being as you are now."

"Aye, I've changed," Robena snapped, her eyes flashing. "Mayhap when I live in a castle again and wear pretty gowns and have servants t'dance attendance on me, mayhap then I'll be simpering sweet and maidenly fair, but until then I am not afraid to wreak vengeance on my enemies." Suddenly she laughed. "Aye, you didn't sound so ladylike yourself, Gillian, when they dunked you in that pool. I heard you pleading for your life and I thought my work was well done."

"You caused the rumors about me?"

"Aye, some! When that old crone and her pie-eyed daughter came upon Jaimie and me in the woods and sounded the alarm that 'twas you, I thought to take away all suspicions about us by spooking the ignorant fools into believing you're a witch."

"But how did you get my willow basket to leave it by the pasture gate?" Gillian asked, barely able to believe the malice her cousin had shown her.

"Nay, little Gillian. I didn't do that mischief. You've an enemy in the castle." Robena smiled.

A sound at the door caused Robena to whirl. One of Jaimie's men staggered through, heading for the secret door. "The battle is over," he cried. " 'Twas a trap they set for us." Robena turned back to Gillian, raising the knife with single-minded purpose.

Instinctively Gillian leapt for the hand that held the knife, jerking Robena off guard. The two girls rolled on the stone floor, each struggling for the knife. Dimly Gillian perceived the door was flung open and someone had entered.

The knife went flying out of Robena's hand. Robena sprang to her feet, intent on retrieving her weapon. Gillian struggled upright, equally intent on stopping her. She was sure Jaimie's men would intervene before she could reach the knife, but she had to try.

"God's Teeth, Thane, there're two of 'em," Duncan Burnhouse cried, and Robena and Gillian ceased their struggling and stared at the men. Gillian read the rage in Thane's eyes, the dark fury at her betrayal. He would never forgive her for this. At that moment, when all stood hesitant with shock, Robena leapt forward, shoved Gillian toward Thane and Duncan, and fled through the secret door.

"After her," Thane roared.

"Thane, 'tis not as it s-seems," Gillian stuttered, but he thrust her into the arms of one of his guards.

"Hold on to her. Don't let her get away," he ordered, and followed after Duncan.

"Thane!" Gillian whispered through her tears, and allowed the guard to lead her out into the bailey, to join the other MacGregor prisoners. Sir Robert and Lady Joan stood on the castle steps, bewildered. Gillian hung her head and did not look at them. She was too ashamed. Earlier in the evening Lady Joan and Juliana had begged so eloquently for Gillian's life from the mob. Now Gillian stood before them a traitor.

Gillian and the rest of the prisoners were taken to one of the dungeons on the lower level, although thankfully not to the infamous bottle dungeon, where many a man had ended his days. Neither Jaimie nor Robena were among them, so Gillian could conclude only that they had escaped or been killed.

The prisoners were a ragged and dirty lot, their lean bodies bearing the marks of their spartan existence in the hills. Now they huddled together in silent bunches with little to look forward to but a hangman's rope. Gillian's heart went out to them. They were MacGregor men one and all, with a thirst for their birthrights.

Through the long night they awaited their fate, expecting at any moment to be taken out to the hanging wall. The stone cell was dank and chilled. Gillian huddled against it and dozed fitfully. Finally at first light Thane and his officers arrived, spreading out to face the prisoners. Gillian studied the somber faces of Duncan, Evan, and Aindreas before turning her attention to Thane's stern features. His eyes were like dark flint, unreadable, unyielding. When his scanning gaze lighted on her, his expression grew harsher, and she knew there would be no mercy from him that day. She shivered despite herself.

"Captain Shiels, escort the prisoner Gillian MacGregor to the great hall and keep her there."

"Aye, sir!" Shiels said, and led her out of the cell and up the stairs. She kept her head high, wrapping her tattered dignity around her with a trembling heart. But when she reached the great hall and felt the warmth of the blaze burning in the huge fireplace, she almost threw herself onto the hearth.

"Warm yourself, mistress," Shiels said not unkindly. "The laird will be here shortly."

Only when he'd left the hall and set a guard outside the door did she creep forward and draw what comfort she could from the flames. An hour dragged by. Huddled on the hearth, she dozed. Suddenly the door was thrown open and Thane strode in. Immediately Gillian sprang to her feet and turned to face him.

His gaze pinned her like a helpless butterfly, and she paled despite her resolve to be brave in the face of his condemnation. Nothing could have prepared her for the coldly quiet voice that sent shivers of alarm along her spine.

"Why did you betray me?" he inquired as if asking her what herbs she'd gathered on her walk. He settled himself in a chair and gazed at her as though studying an insect scudding down a stalk. This was the Thane she feared— cool, restrained, unreachable.

"What possessed you to leave my bed and sneak down through the night to open Edinample to my enemies?" he persisted.

Gillian blinked against the tears that stung her eyes, all pride and dignity gone now. "I didn't wish to betray you," she said in a low voice.

"Are you not a MacGregor?" he shouted, slamming his

fist down on the table so his silver flask danced across its surface.

"Aye, I am a MacGregor born!" she said with a return of some old pride.

"And didn't you lie to me about who you were?" Thane got to his feet, too unsettled to remain sitting.

"Aye, m'lord." Her voice remained steady, but inside she quivered with a mixture of shame and defiance.

"And all the while you lived here under my protection you spied on me for your murdering cousin, Jaimie Mac-Gregor." His words stung her, his hand lashed out to point an accusing finger at her. So outraged was he, his eyes flashed blue fire.

"Nay, Thane, I never spied against you," she whispered. The sight of her pale, trembling lips nearly undid his self-righteous anger.

"We caught you in the tower," he shouted, and turned away from her. "Aye, so much is explained now, the manner in which the MacGregor leader learned of my mother's arrival and the way he seemed to know where we'd be when we didn't know ourselves." He whirled around to face her, and his fury was back full-blown. "How could you lie with me, then help them? They were set on murdering everyone in the castle. Is that what you wanted?"

"Of course not. I—I thought only to protect you," she cried in defense.

"By opening the doors to our enemies?"

"Jaimie promised not to harm anyone. He said he only needed supplies enough to go to Ireland to start afresh. He—he said he would kill you if I did not help him."

Thane was silent for a long while, studying her face. His lips curled in contempt. "A pretty story, to match all your other lies."

" 'Tis true, I promise you," Gillian cried, going forward to place a beseeching hand on his sleeve.

"It seems MacGregor promises are not to be believed!"

Scornfully he shook her aside and bent over the table, resting his weight on his two outstretched hands. Every line of his body bespoke a pain and fury that could barely be borne.

Briefly she sensed the despair he felt, for it mirrored her own. "Thane, I love ye," she whispered. "If ye canna believe any other words I say, believe these. I would give my own life t'protect ye. I would not have betrayed ye for any other reason than that I was led t'believe 'twould save yer life."

Thane did not answer. He seemed made of stone, yet she saw a muscle tremble in his cheek. Finally he straightened and turned to face her.

"I should have let them drown you," he muttered, and his face was so set, it seemed a mask. "By all rights I could hang you and none would blame me."

Gillian's heart raced. "Is that what you intend to do with Jaimie's men?"

"Those who did not bend a knee and pledge allegiance to me as their new laird. The number was surprisingly small. So much for MacGregor pride."

She was not afraid of dying, she realized, not if she must live without Thane, but she couldn't bear the thought that her life would be ended by his command. Did he hate her so much now? "And me?"

"You'll not hang! You've done your work here well. You've ingratiated yourself into the hearts of too many people." His words made her spirits rise a little. He didn't hate her, then.

"My mother is one whose heart is broken by your treachery. She's pleaded with me to show you mercy." He turned away from her and paced to the fireplace. "Sir Robert has added his voice in your defense, as has my bride-to-be." He whirled and glared at her. "You've worked your spells to good advantage."

Something in his gaze changed. She felt her heart

respond to it, but then his demeanor hardened. "Mayhap you're a witch after all."

No words he uttered could have hurt her more, and well he knew it, for he turned away so he wouldn't see the pain flit across her face. He went on in that unfamiliar, cold voice. "And so between us, a solution has been found."

Gillian's hopes sank even more. She guessed this would not be a solution to her liking, but by her own actions she'd lost any right to choices. Thane Campbell was the law in this land, and she was his to do with as he chose. She was barely aware of a door opening somewhere behind her and others entering the hall. Silently she waited for Thane's sentence.

"You made plans some time ago to travel to Edinburgh."

"I—'twas when I found out about Juliana and I wanted to leave Edinample," she said softly, remembering the night just past, when he'd rescued her from the mob and carried her to his room and cradled her against his chest. She'd thought then never to leave, even to remain as his mistress if nothing else. That decision seemed a lifetime away.

Thane continued as if she hadn't interrupted him. "You will go to Edinburgh as planned," he said tonelessly. "Funds will be placed at your disposal for as long as you have need of such."

"I don't want your money."

"You will obtain a room in Edinburgh, perhaps seek a position or find a rich tradesman and marry. Regardless of what your future holds, you are never to return to Edinample."

"Never to see you again?" she whimpered, hearing the finality in his words, seeing it in his face, feeling it in her heart.

"Never to see me again!" he said, and turned away from her.

She trembled so, she feared she might fall down, yet she crept across the room and reached out a hand toward his broad, implacable back. "Thane," she whispered brokenheartedly. "Can't you forgive me?"

"Forgiveness for a MacGregor? A fool's request. Be gone from my sight, ye witch." He kept his back to her so there was nothing more to do, nothing left to say. She glanced at Sir Robert and Lady Joan, who stood to one side, observing all that had occurred. Neither spoke to her as she left the hall, but she thought she saw a glimmer of sorrow in their eyes.

Silently Sir Robert watched Gillian pass by, her shoulders hunched in pain, her face so pale, one might have thought her a ghost. When the door closed behind her, he strode toward the towering blond Highlander.

"You were uncommonly harsh with the lass," he rebuked Thane mildly.

"She's a traitor, a spy, and by rights I could have taken her life, so I'd say I was quite lenient with her," Thane said, his voice savage. He regarded the elegant nobleman who would one day be his father-in-law. "You seem overly concerned as to her well-being. Mayhap you've fancied her yourself and but take this opportunity to win her."

"You dishonor my intentions, Lord Thane," Sir Robert roared.

"Thane, you forget yourself," Lady Joan cried, coming forward.

"If you were anyone else, I'd demand you answer on the field of honor for your insult," Sir Robert said sternly. "Only this dear lady's presence restrains me from challenging you."

"Don't speak to me of honor at this moment," Thane cried, and with a savage motion swept drinking goblets and candlesticks from the table. The items fell to the floor in a clatter of noise, which seemed to bring some surcease of pain, for he looked at Sir Robert and grimaced.

" 'Tis no matter of honor, sir, for she is not a true lady, but a trollop to be passed from one man to the next. I give her to you, but warn you guard your house and your heart. She's devilishly appealing and has not one ounce of loyalty. You'll find her pleasing enough in bed, if a trifle modest, although as we now know she's a good actress and such modesty may be only a ploy." In his anger he did not notice how his mother's face blanched with outrage.

"I never thought to see the day I would find my son a fool," she said, her eyes snapping. She left the room, her back ramrod straight, her head high.

Sir Robert knew Thane's words were uttered from the deepest recess of his suffering; still, he grimaced disapprovingly. "I've not yet had the opportunity to talk to you of another matter," he said sternly.

"And what is that, sir?" Thane asked wearily, his anger fast disappearing, leaving behind only a great searing torment. Absently he brushed golden tresses from his brow and searched among the debris for an unbroken drinking goblet.

"I regret to inform you that my daughter, Juliana, declines to become your wife. I will honor my daughter's wishes."

" 'Tis not the way of things, Sir Robert," Thane reminded him. "She is but a woman and has no right to make such a decision on her own."

"Aye, so it is thought, but Juliana is an exceptional young woman, Thane. If your head had na been so full of another, you might have seen her value. She's well read and intelligent and comely. But most of all she has an uncommonly sensible head on her shoulders for a woman."

"I've sent Gillian away," Thane said thickly, giving up his search for an unbroken goblet. "Mayhap, in time—"

"Nay, lad," Sir Robert said, and his voice was filled with kindness. "You'll not forget Gillian soon. And I would not have my daughter face the certainty each day that she's not loved. I will not fight the laws governing the dowry and lands in this case, since 'tis my daughter and I who break the betrothal pledge. I will pay for this breach of contract with a portion of the lands ye covet."

"I've not acted honorably myself in this affair," Thane acknowledged stiffly. "I'll require no recompense for dissolving the contract."

Sir Robert nodded, some of his respect for Thane Campbell redeemed, but the laird seemed not to notice or care about his guest's opinion. He bellowed for a servant to bring him wine and a goblet.

"We'll leave in an hour's time," Sir Robert said, and turned away from the unhappy man.

"Robert, what are we to do?" Lady Joan cried the moment he entered the room. She'd been pacing the floor with some agitation and now threw herself forward, stopping just short of falling into his arms. Sir Robert gripped her elbows and gazed down at her exquisite face.

"Shhh, my dear," he said reassuringly. "I'll take Gillian to Edinburgh with Juliana and myself. Time will cool Thane's fury. Perhaps then he'll see things from Gillian's side a bit."

"I doubt it," Lady Joan said. "He's as stubborn as his father in some things. Oh, Robert, why didn't that child tell him who she was in the very beginning?"

"Aye, it was a grievous error on her part," Sir Robert acknowledged. "Mayhap it would have made no difference in the outcome."

"Her cousin would have had no hold over her," Lady Joan replied, wringing her hands.

"Perhaps. At any rate, her motives were of the purest. She sought only to protect the people she loves."

"And she does love us, fiercely so," Lady Joan said, her voice husky.

"She's a bonny lass," Sir Robert reflected. His gaze swept across Lady Joan's face. "Now we must speak of our own affairs," he said firmly. "I fear events force me to declare my feelings for you, dear lady, in a hasty fashion, but they are no less constant."

Lady Joan blushed prettily, her golden lashes dipping before she raised them to gaze into Robert's eyes. Their clear blue depths revealed to Robert all he needed to know of her feelings.

"My dear and beautiful lady," he murmured, and lowered his head to claim her lips with his own.

Gillian went to bid her last farewell to Lachlan. He was awake, his eyes clear of any sign of the fever, though he was still weak.

"I am not abandoning you, dear friend," Gillian said, sitting beside him and taking his thick hand in hers. "As soon as you're well enough to travel, you must come to Edinburgh and live with me."

"In Edinburgh there are more people to laugh and tease me for being an ogre. I can't live there. 'Twould crush my soul."

"But what will you do?" Gillian asked fearfully.

"I've rebuilt the Glenartney hut and am living there. When I need supplies I venture into the villages and trade my carvings for food and such."

"Oh, Lachlan, why didn't you tell me? I'll come home with you and I'll take care of you and we'll be as happy as before."

The hunchback shook his head. "You weren't happy there. You were lonely and restless. Nay, lass, you must go to Edinburgh. If you're not happy there, you can come back to Glenartney."

Gillian smiled in grateful acceptance of his words and squeezed his hand. "Good-bye, Lachlan." She left him with a kiss on his rough cheek, and he lay a long time in his bed, fists clenched as he cursed the gods that did not allow him to be a whole man. If he were, he would fight Thane Campbell for this pain he had caused

Gillian, then he, Lachlan, would take her back to Glenartney and make her his wife. He turned his face to the wall and swallowed the bitter dregs of the dream that could never be.

Within an hour the packhorses were loaded with trunks and supplies. Sir Robert's party was saddled and prepared to leave. Seated atop a handsome gray, Gillian gazed around, hoping for a final glimpse of Thane. Juliana perched on a sleek black mare, her skirts spread along its flanks, her face pale and drawn. Her teeth worried her bottom lip, then suddenly she smiled. Aindreas rode into the courtyard, his troops behind him.

"I thought to accompany you partway, Sir Robert," he called, his auburn hair glinting in the sunlight. "We've not yet caught the MacGregor leader."

"Aye, we'll be pleased with your company, won't we, daughter?" Sir Robert asked. He was rewarded with a brilliant smile from Juliana who glowed as only a woman in love can.

Evina stood on the upper balcony, watching the preparations below, elated at the news that both Juliana and Gillian were leaving Edinample. She would have Thane to herself and time to make him love her. She'd be Thane's wife, as she'd always dreamed of being, and mistress of Edinample. There was plenty of time and she would find a way, as she always did.

Mounted, Gillian felt the weight of someone's gaze and turned in her saddle, glancing up. Thane stood on a balcony overlooking the bailey. His eyes were overly bright and his step unsteady, so she discerned he had taken too much strong drink. Still, she read in his gaze the same hot passion they'd always shared.

He still desired her, she thought, and gazed into his eyes, trying to convey the love she bore him. His lips curled contemptuously, and he turned to one side, his arm sweeping a voluptuous blond woman closer. Bridget's triumphant laugh rang out before Thane's lips settled over hers. Gillian could watch no more.

The order was given and the line of riders moved forward toward the bridge. Gillian did not look back as she rode away from Edinample.

Chapter 20

*S*PRING HAD COME to Scotland. Salt-laden winds blew off the Firth of Forth, fresh and pleasing to the cheek. They carried the exotic promise of faraway lands and rousing adventures. Sighing, Gillian strolled down Princes Street, intent on the gardens, but ending up instead on Castle Rock, the hill upon which Edinburgh Castle stood. From there she had a view of the firth and the city itself.

She thought back to the summer before and her brief sojourn at Edinample. How happy she'd been! How bright and perfect the world seemed. She missed seeing the snow on the mountains and smelling the tang of pine from the Forest of Glenartney and hearing the roar of the falls at the River Ample. Most of all she missed the hustle and bustle of Edinample and the wild anticipation that Thane might ride into the bailey at any moment and take her into his arms. Was Thane still there? Had he chosen another wife since Juliana had refused him? What of Jaimie?

Near tears she left the hill and made her way along Princes Street to the square where Sir Robert kept Cawder House. Juliana met her at the door.

"Where have you been?" she demanded. "Have you

forgotten we're to go to Holyrood tonight to take supper with the king?"

"Oh, I had forgotten," Gillian answered, removing her wraps and hurrying up the stairs behind Juliana.

"You must look especially beautiful tonight," Juliana said.

"Why, are ye ashamed of me?"

Juliana turned around and glared at Gillian, the question hanging between them. "Do you think so little of my character, Gillian MacGregor?" she demanded.

"Nay, and I withdraw my question," Gillian said. "I'm just in a mood today and I take offense at everything."

"Don't take offense until I give it," Juliana stated saucily, and taking Gillian's hand, pulled her the rest of the way up the stairs and into her room, where the two quickly became immersed in an assortment of gowns and petticoats. Only later, when she was relaxing in a tub, did Gillian realize that Juliana had neatly sidestepped her question as to why she must look especially beautiful on this night. No doubt Juliana was intent on matchmaking again, a role that had occupied much of her time since their arrival in Edinburgh. In love with Aindreas, who was enjoying an extended visit, Juliana wanted everyone around her—especially Gillian—to know the same kind of blissful happiness.

Later, when they descended the stairs and noted the expressions on the faces of Sir Robert and Aindreas, they felt their efforts had been worthwhile. Juliana was as beautiful as an ice princess in a gown of pale blue silk with her pale hair piled high on her head and the white lace ruff framing her face.

If Juliana was ice, then Gillian must surely have been fire. She shimmered in an old-fashioned samite silk of rose shot through with both silver and gold threads. Even the whalebones of the stomacher could not disguise her willowy shape or the fullness of her breasts. The neck was cut low with an open lace-edged ruff to frame her face, and her glossy black hair was arranged in a tumble of curls atop her head. Sir Robert thought she'd never looked more beautiful, and even Aindreas, whose gaze could barely leave Juliana, had to acknowledge Gillian was breathtakingly beautiful.

"Thane will eat his heart out this night," Aindreas remarked. Juliana pinched him and he glanced at her, startled.

"Did you say Thane?" Gillian asked in some consternation.

"Aye, Gillian. He will be there tonight. It seems he's captured your cousin Jaimie at last, and has brought him to Edinburgh to be executed."

"Oh, no," Gillian cried. Aindreas had earned himself another pinch from Juliana.

"Couldn't you have kept this news until a later time," she hissed.

"I'm sorry, love," Aindreas whispered back. "My brain is too besotted by the sight of you to think straight."

Somewhat mollified, Juliana brushed her hand over his as if to smooth away any hurt she might have inflicted.

"Do you wish to stay behind tonight?" Sir Robert asked Gillian, who looked stricken.

"Nay, Sir Robert," she said with a shaky smile. "I would not have us pass up this opportunity to dine with King James. Soon he will be off to London." She paused and turned back to Aindreas. "Will Lady Joan be accompanying her son?"

"Aye, my aunt has arrived as well," Aindreas said, looking to Juliana as if for guidance as to how much more to reveal. "Evina has accompanied them."

"I see," Gillian said, and her heart squeezed painfully. She'd heard little past the words of Thane's arrival. In a daze she followed the others out to the carriages and remained dolefully silent on the ride along the Royal Mile to Holyrood.

"Don't torture yourself so," Sir Robert whispered in

her ear. "Mayhap he has forgotten his anger. Now, smile, my dear, for 'tis truly an honor to be invited to the king's court, and you're uncommonly bonny this night."

Gillian tried to take heart at his words, but her pulse hammered in her ear so she could scarce think.

Holyrood Castle was an imposing affair, as befitted a king's residence, with pale gray stone walls, soaring towers, and elaborate outerworks. The palace was ablaze with lights, an unusual occurrence for the austere court. Within the castle they were led up the long staircase to the oak-paneled galley lined with delicately carved heraldic shields of the Stuarts.

Gillian's gaze searched through the regally garbed gathering of noblemen, seeking one golden head towering over the rest. When she caught a glimpse of Thane, she felt her heart lurch in her chest. She'd never seen him dressed in such splendid attire.

His doubtlet was of black velvet edged with gold piping at the shoulders and down the front. For his appearance before James and his court, Thane had chosen to wear the fashionable padded breeches known as slops. His strong calves were clad in fine hose; slops and hosiery were of the same color and ornamentation as the doublet, a dramatic contrast to his tawny hair and glittering blue eyes.

Only when she'd looked her fill did she notice that Evina stood beside him. She was wearing an elaborate gown of green taffeta with a stomacher and ruff of yellow silk. Her auburn hair was piled high in the latest fashion, and Gillian grudgingly admitted to herself that the girl looked fetching.

"She looks like a bawdy!" Juliana whispered in Gillian's ear.

"Nay, we must not deny her beauty," Gillian said, but she had to swallow hard against the knot in her throat. The crowd shifted, giving them a view of Lady Joan. Gillian was aware of a sharp intake of breath on Sir

Robert's part and turned to look at him. His gaze was fixed on the petite lady, who seemed transfixed herself. Gillian gazed at them and smiled with the knowledge of how they cared for each other.

"Gillian, there's something I must tell you," Juliana said at her elbow. "I've been a dunce not to do so before. Aindreas wanted to, but I feared to bring you pain. Now I see, 'tis crueler not to have told you. Gillian, are you listening?" But Gillian's attention was caught elsewhere.

As if sensing the tension, Thane turned and his gaze fastened unerringly on Gillian's, as if no one else were in the room. His eyes were the darkest blue, his expression somber. Gillian saw the longing in his face, the flare of passion, and her heart soared. He still desired her. Nay, there was more than desire in his eyes. They carried a message of love. Laughter bubbled in Gillian's chest. Her face lit with joy.

He still loved her. Thane loved her! Of their own accord her feet moved, carrying her across the room to him. She pushed her way through the crowd and floated to a halt just inches from him, so close she could inhale his masculine scent, feel his body heat.

Her gaze was blinded to all save him, the shape of his lean jaw, the curl of his pale lashes against sun-browned skin, the thick muscles of his neck, the set of his shoulders and tapering line of his hips. His essence seemed to coil inside her like a living, pulsing thing, reminding her of the torment and beauty of their passion.

She was unaware that Sir Robert and the others had followed.

"Thane." She whispered his name. He reached for her hand, clasping it possessively, desperately, as a drowning man would.

"Gillian," he murmured. "Ye're more beautiful than I remembered."

"And you," she said, thinking how inane the words their lips spoke, when their hearts communicated in a language so profound, she could have wept for the beauty of it.

A movement at their elbows broke the spell. Evina had pushed herself forward.

"Well, Gillian, what are you doing here?" she demanded in a tone that plainly implied she thought the other girl out of place in such a noted gathering. Gillian barely spared her a glance, concentrating instead on Thane's face. His expression had become closed once again, shutting her out. Gillian's heart lurched painfully. What had brought about this change, when only a moment before he'd seemed ready to declare his love for her openly. Inside she began to shake, and she feared her knees might give way. Upon seeing her stricken expression, Lady Joan stepped forward.

"Gillian, child, you look stunning. That gown is magnificent."

"Aye, it is," Evina echoed. "How on earth are you able to afford such a gown on the allowance Thane gives you?"

Gillian's cheeks colored at the insult. She had never accepted a penny of the funds Thane had allotted for her use. By the look in his eyes she knew he was all too aware of that fact. His lips tightened in anger.

"Be still, Evina," he said.

"You dolt," Aindreas echoed. Evina glanced at her brother and turned back to Gillian, a spiteful smile on her lips.

"I'm sorry if I've offended you," she said with no effort at sincerity. "I'd forgotten you were once Thane's— friend. When Thane and I are married, I must learn to accept my husband's acquaintances, whether I approve of them or not."

"You and Thane are to be married?" Gillian whispered.

"I was about to tell you," Juliana whispered.

"Aye, Thane asked me and I've accepted," Evina rushed in. "We're to be married at Edinample in the summer. Mayhap you can come?" Once again Thane's lips tightened. A bit of color brushed his high cheekbones, but Evina seemed not to recognize these signs of his barely leashed rage.

"I—I wish you well," Gillian managed to say. A band had tightened across her chest. She longed to flee, but concern for her cousin's well-being held her.

" 'Tis said you've brought Jaimie MacGregor to Edinburgh to be hanged?" She gazed into his blue eyes, looking for some flicker of compassion. There was none.

"Aye, the MacGregor renegades have been broken."

"What good, then, to take his life?" she asked. "Can't he be exiled to Ireland?" Her soft voice wound around his heart, and he longed to grant whatever she wished, but he could not. Slowly he shook his head.

" 'Tis out of my hands now. The decision belongs to King James."

"Can't ye beg for clemency for him?" she insisted. Bright spots of color stained her pale cheeks. Before Thane could answer, Evina stepped forward, grasping his arm possessively.

"You have no right to ask such a favor of him," she cried.

"Aye, I have no right," she said wearily. "If you'll excuse me, please?" Without waiting for further pleasantries, she turned and fled across the ballroom.

"Gillian," Thane said sharply.

Dimly she was aware of his pursuit and knew she could not face him again. Darting into an alcove, she waited until he hurried past, then quietly slipped out a side doorway.

In the slim hope of obtaining a fare, a row of rented carriages waited outside the castle gate. Gillian leapt into one and ordered the driver to take her back to Edinburgh. The thought of returning to Cawder House gave her little comfort, so she asked to be taken to her favorite place at Castle Hill, which overlooked the Firth of Forth.

* * *

"Where is she? I demand to see the little witch. You can't protect her, Sir Robert." Evina's face was livid. Sir Robert and Juliana exchanged glances over the breakfast table and turned back to the woman who'd burst into Cawder House unannounced.

"Pray, of whom do you speak?" Sir Robert inquired gently, although the thin line of his lips should have warned his unwanted guest she'd overstepped the bounds of courtesy. Sir Robert had been infuriated to learn of Thane's betrothal to this woman.

"I do not understand it myself," Lady Joan had confided when they'd had a chance to slip away and share a few stolen kisses and speak privately. "He says only that he will do what honor demands."

Now Sir Robert glared at Evina, striving to keep his own anger in check. "This intrusion is rather unseemly," he mildly rebuked her. "Will you calm yourself, have a cup of tea, and tell us again what is troubling you."

"So you can have time to whisk her away, or has Thane already done that?" Evina demanded stridently.

"Why would you think Thane has been here to take Gillian away?" Juliana demanded.

"Because he ran after her last night, making a fool of me in front of the whole court, and he didn't return. I know they were together all night."

"You are quite mistaken. Gillian is upstairs in her bedchamber," Juliana said. "I peeked in on her myself on my way down to breakfast."

Evina blinked and seemed at a loss for words.

"Now, I suggest, my dear young woman, that you take yourself back to your lodgings. Your betrothed will appear in good time."

Evina glared at them as if certain they were playing a trick on her, then turned and flounced out of the room. They heard the angry slam of the door and breathed a sigh of relief.

"By the gods, I'm happy to see her gone," Sir Robert retorted.

"Father." Carefully Juliana wiped her mouth and placed her napkin beside her plate while her mind scrambled for the right thing to say. Was Gillian with Thane as Evina charged, or had something happened to her?

"What is it, child?" Sir Robert demanded with uncustomary brusqueness.

"Oh, Father, Gillian is not here," she said at last. "She didn't return home last night. I hoped she might be with Thane, and in truth she may be."

"That scoundrel," Sir Robert cried, pushing back his chair. "How could he compromise her in this manner?"

"What can we do?" Juliana asked helplessly.

"I'll find the young laird and see that Gillian is safe with him. Once that's assured, I'll demand he declare his intentions for my ward, and if his intentions are not honorable, I'll take my blade to him."

"Oh, Father!" Juliana cried with some alarm. "He's a far better swordsman than you."

"Don't worry, pet," Sir Robert said, patting her shoulder. "I was a fair enough swordsman in my day."

He hurried out of the room and ordered his horse saddled and brought around. Juliana lingered in the breakfast room, fretting, until she heard a rattle in the front hall. She hurried there, hoping Aindreas had arrived. He'd know what to do. Mayhap he could ride after her father. But when she entered the hall, she gasped.

"Gillian," she cried upon seeing the other girl. "What are you doing here? We thought you were with Thane!"

"Nay, why would I be?" Gillian asked. Her face was pale, her eyes like gleaming green coals, filled with pain, and Juliana's heart wept for her.

"Evina came and said Thane had not returned to the castle. We thought he was with you."

"I walked along the shoreline, trying to determine what

I must do. I fear I've ruined my slippers." Her voice was so filled with misery that Juliana hugged her.

"Father has gone to find Thane, and he was fairly angry with him for compromising you so. I fear he might even call him out."

"Juliana, we must stop him," Gillian cried.

"Lady Joan and Thane are lodged at Holyrood. Father has no doubt ridden there. Go change your wet slippers and I'll order the carriage." The girls sprang into action. By the time the Cawder carriage had been brought around, Gillian had changed from her ball gown into a plain day gown of brown silk with a white lace ruff. Tendrils of hair tumbled from the elaborate coif she'd worn the night before, but there was no time to have it redressed. Hastily she pinned on a soft-brimmed hat. The girls leapt into the carriage and directed their driver to Holyrood at top speed, arriving there only to be told Thane had ridden out at dawn. They were escorted to Lady Joan's guest chambers.

"Lady Joan, I've come on a matter of some importance," Gillian said.

"I've heard that Thane snatched you away last night. 'Twas shameful behavior on his part, and I must apologize. The court has talked of little else this morn. Evina is quite upset about it, yet what else must she expect? Surely she doesn't think Thane is about to marry her out of love."

"Why has Thane chosen to wed his cousin?" Juliana asked.

"I don't know for sure, but I have my suspicions."

"None of that matters now," Gillian said, although she would have liked to find out more about Thane and Evina's betrothal. "I've come about a different matter."

"What is it, lass?"

"The rumors are wrong, Lady Joan. I eluded Thane and went to a secluded cove, where I often go to meditate.

Now Sir Robert believes Thane compromised me and may challenge him in swordplay."

"Surely not," Lady Joan replied. "Robert is far more level-headed than that."

"I fear not in this matter," Juliana replied. "Though Father feels himself skilled enough, he has not the strength of Thane."

"We must find them and stop this nonsense before one of them kills the other." They hurried through the corridors and down the staircase just as Evina emerged from one of the rooms below. Her expression darkened when she saw Gillian.

"So, you think to slither your way back into the family," she cried.

"I can't talk to you about it now," Gillian answered breathlessly. "Do you know where Thane has gone?" She paused to grip the stair railing and gazed down at the woman she once thought her friend.

Evina's gaze flitted to Gillian. "Why do you ask?"

"Because we must find him and right some misunderstandings." Evina's face paled at Lady Joan's words. Slowly she backed away from them, rage distorting her features as she glared at Gillian. "You'll not have him," she cried.

Suddenly she raised a finger and pointed at Gillian.

"There she is," she cried. 'There's the witch!"

"Evina, what are you saying, lass?" Lady Joan demanded.

"I've seen her cast her spells," Evina continued to shriek, so all came running to see the commotion.

"She's got the evil eye and she puts spells on people," Evina called. "She flies on the branch of an ash."

Queen Anne herself strode through the arch and looked about with a reproachful air. "What is the meaning of this noise?"

" 'Tis the witch, mum, 'tis the witch!" Evina wailed.

"My god, Evina. You will not do this thing," Lady Joan

swore, but she was too late. Evina's mischief had been done. Queen Anne's face grew mottled, and she cowered back.

"Guards, arrest this woman," she cried.

"Nay, mum, she's not a witch," Lady Joan said, but her cries were lost in the bedlam as ladies-in-waiting screamed with terror and threw up their hands to ward off the accused witch's evil eye. Castle guards grabbed hold of Gillian. She struggled . . . to no avail.

Chapter 21

ALL MET UP simultaneously. Sir Robert had located and was just confronting Thane, when the carriage bearing Juliana, Aindreas, and Lady Joan rolled up.

Sir Robert's eyes widened in alarm at the sight of Lady Joan, so great and obvious was her distress. "What is it, my dear? What's amiss?"

" 'Tis Gillian. Evina has accused her of being a witch, and she has been carted off by the castle guards."

"By all that's holy, I'll wring Evina's neck," Thane cried.

"Aye, and I'll help ye," Aindreas declared.

"What are we to do?" Lady Joan asked. "You know what they do to witches. King James has a passionate fear of them and is fanatical about burning one and all. Oh, Thane, how can we stop them from doing this to her?"

"They won't, Mother, not unless they burn me first," Thane declared. He took Sir Robert aside, whispering to him hurriedly. Finally he said, loud enough for the others to hear, "Sir Robert, return to Holyrood and request an audience with King James. I'll be there as soon as I can—with proof of her innocence," Thane declared, and sprang into his saddle. Sir Robert ushered the others into the carriage and Aindreas took his mount. They rode at full tilt to Holyrood, where Sir Robert used his influence to request an audience with the king himself, only to be told the Lord High Chamberlain, the Duke of Lennox, was handling the case against the MacGregor witch.

Frustrated, they were left to cool their heels in the Lord High Chamberlain's anteroom. Thane had arrived with a reluctant and caped figure in tow before they were shown into Lord Lennox's offices.

"Sir Robert, I understand you're here to see me on a matter of some urgency," Lennox said without preamble, eyeing the large number that followed the nobleman, for none of them would be left standing outside when they might add something in Gillian's defense.

"Aye, m'lord, and we're most grateful you've consented to see us," Sir Robert began tactfully, but Thane pushed himself forward, his jaw jutting belligerently.

" 'Tis about the woman Gillian MacGregor," he said urgently.

"Ah, yes, the woman who's been accused as a witch," Lennox replied. "She is at this moment being questioned at Edinburgh Castle."

"Questioned or tortured?" Thane demanded, eyes flashing. His fist came down on the corner of Lord Lennox's elegant desk.

Lennox gazed down his patrician nose at him. "Is this the way you Highlanders are taught to behave before your king?" His pale eyes were icy.

"King? I see no king present, unless you have such ambitions yourself, m'lord." Thane's eyes snapped with rage.

Sir Robert tugged at his sleeve. "Have a care, lad. 'Twill do Gillian no good to anger the king's high lord."

"I'd advise you to listen to Sir Robert, Laird Campbell. His words are wise. I have the ear of the king himself. I've had better men than you executed for less effrontery."

"M'lord, I pray you forgive this young man. He's but riven with grief and doesn't know what he does." Sir

Robert spoke up now. "Could you tell us precisely what the charges are against Gillian MacGregor?"

Lennox seemed only slightly mollified. "She's been charged with witchcraft. 'Tis said she's caused village cows to sicken and die, kidnapped village children, that she's been seen in two places at one time, and been observed flying through the air on an ash branch."

"Lies, all lies!" Thane stated.

"And from whence came these charges?" Sir Robert inquired, keeping an eye on Thane, who had drawn back and now paced like a caged beast. Lennox sent him a wary glance.

"Sir Thane's kinswoman has raised the cry."

"Surely you don't mean poor Evina Campbell?" Sir Robert asked, and hid a smile behind his hand.

Lennox regarded him with some surprise. "Aye, that's the wench."

"But, my dear Lennox, I urge you have a care you're not made the laughingstock of Edinburgh. Don't you know, this poor lass is touched in the head? She believes the most outrageous things."

"I've not heard this about her," Lennox replied. "In fact, I'd been informed she's betrothed to Thane Campbell himself."

"Well, there you see," Sir Robert said, looking at Thane as if sharing some humor. "Thane Campbell and Evina are cousins and can't be married," Sir Robert continued.

" 'Tis well known if cousins are distant enough in blood, they may marry," Lennox said, glancing at Thane.

" 'Tis true, but I ask you, m'lord"—Sir Robert nudged Lennox slightly as if sharing a bit of logic man to man— "why would a man take his own cousin to wife when he can look outside his clan and increase his holdings? She's no great beauty, you may have observed."

Lennox rubbed his chin and regarded the two noblemen. "You have a point."

"Besides, m'lord," Sir Robert continued, "I have a way to prove that Evina Campbell is a troubled woman who makes false accusations about those around her."

"What is this proof?" Lennox asked, and Sir Robert could see the same question in Thane's eyes.

"The young woman in question has made an accusation against the young Campbell laird that he has gotten her with child, yet she's a virgin."

"Sir Robert!" Thane said warningly.

"And you say you can prove this?" Lennox asked curiously.

"Better yet, m'lord, the king's own physicians can prove it. They have only to examine the young woman to see that her maidenhead is intact."

Thane looked nervously about. It was not at all certain she was a virgin—but a suspicion borne in the last few days and supported by his mother. He had been drunk and had no memory of spending the night with Evina. He thought he'd gone to bed with Bridget. But, when he'd awakened in the morning Evina had been with him, naked and purring. He'd told this to Sir Robert earlier. However, he had more confidence in another direction. "M'lord," he said, "I have proof that Gillian MacGregor is not a witch."

Lennox studied the blond giant before him. "And what is your proof, Laird Campbell?" he inquired warily. For the first time since entering the suite, Thane's lips curved in a genuine smile. Quickly he crossed to the women who stood near the door. Taking hold of a shrouded figure, he pulled her forward.

"You say one of the accusations against Gillian Mac-Gregor is that she had been known to be in two places at one time. What say you to this?" With a flourish he threw back the cowl that hooded the woman's face. All in the room gasped. Lennox's eyes narrowed.

"What witchcraft is this?" he demanded.

"Not witchcraft, m'lord. Merely a kinswoman who

bears a strong resemblance to Gillian MacGregor. May I present Robena MacGregor?"

Lennox studied the raven-haired woman before him, rubbing his chin as he circled her and stopped before her to peer into her face. "The resemblance is uncanny," he muttered. "Ah, I see the difference now." He whirled to face Thane Campbell. "You make a good case in your defense for Mistress Gillian," he said, strolling to his desk to scribble on a piece of parchment. He sanded, sealed, and handed it to a hovering secretary with a few whispered words of instructions. The man nodded and exited the room. Lennox settled himself behind his desk and regarded Thane inscrutably.

In this game of nerves Thane knew he was outmaneuvered. "What say you, m'lord?" he demanded in a quiet voice that bordered on pleading.

"I say I must see the two together, and so I have instructed my guards to leave at once for Edinburgh Castle to fetch the accused woman. In the meantime I've also sent word to your kinswoman that she's to join us and make her accusa—I say, Laird Campbell, where are you going?"

Thane halted at the door only long enough to address Lennox. "I'll travel with your guards to Edinburgh Castle to fetch Gillian MacGregor."

"How do I know you will not whisk her away out of our hands," Lennox protested.

"I give you leave to forfeit all the Campbell lands if I don't return with her," Thane said, throwing open the door.

"Aye, and Cawder lands as well," Sir Robert said, stepping forward. His words gave Thane pause as nothing else could have under the circumstances. His blue gaze held Sir Robert's, and words were communicated between them that none other in the room could hear or understand. Thane knew Sir Robert had made the magnanimous offer to insure he did indeed return. Thane might forfeit his own fortunes, but never would he cause the loss of Cawder lands.

With a slight nod Thane left the room and strode down the hall to catch up with the guards. Astride Bhaltair, he urged the party toward Edinburgh with far greater speed than the Holyrood captain would have executed had he been on his own.

Thane's impatience was even greater once they reached Castle Hill. In the distance he could glimpse the field where witches and heretics were burned. Great scorched pilings stood in blackened appeal to a cloudless sky.

"Take us to the chambers where you keep Gillian Mac-Gregor," Thane demanded once they'd entered the fortress castle and stood before the prison guards.

"Do as m'lord commands. Here is the order signed by Lord Lennox," the Holyrood captain said, handing over the proper paperwork.

"Yes sir, at once, sir," the guard stuttered. "But the witch is—is—"

"What? Speak up, man," the Holyrood captain snapped.

"She's being interrogated at this very moment, sir."

Dread swept over Thane. He reached forward and grabbed hold of the man's neck, applying pressure so he could scarcely breathe. "Take us to her at once!"

"Aye," the guard answered, looking from his superior to the fine laird with the crazed look in his eyes. "Follow me." Grabbing the keys, he scurried ahead in case the towering Highlander took it upon himself to show his strength yet again. Thane and the captain followed on his heels. The guard led them down a dank, narrow flight of stairs and through a corridor that was dark and cold. A woman's scream echoed through the cramped stone passages. Thane cursed and sprang forward, a broad hand on the guard's back pushing him forward until they came upon a stout oaken door that stood open. The scream sounded from within. With a growl as deep and ferocious as the fiercest beasts of the Forest of Glenartney, Thane ran into the cell, his gaze taking in all at once the tableau of Gillian strapped into a chair, her tormentors hovering over her. Her pale cheeks were marked by tears, her beautiful emerald eyes were glazed with pain, her white teeth bit cruelly into her lower lip to still yet another outcry. Her long, slender hands were cruelly twisted in an iron device once called pilliwinks, which Thane knew could break and hopelessly maim her. He hardly noted the identity of the two men who were so intent on increasing the pressure on her twisted fingers that they did not notice his presence, until his great hands clamped over their shoulders and spun them around. With a mighty heave he butted them together so their heads cracked, and they fell to the floor in a stupor.

Gillian's gaze was uncomprehending at first, as if she couldn't believe he was truly there. "Thane," she whispered brokenly.

"Aye, 'tis I," he reassured her, set on freeing her hands from the torturous screws. She made a sharp intake of breath as if he'd hurt her more, and in frustration he turned to the guard who'd brought them down. "Take them off her," he ordered, his hand reaching for his dirk. "And by the heavens, if you cause one moment more of pain, I'll slit your throat where you stand."

Pale and visibly shaken, the guard sprang forward to do as he was bid. The moment the iron shackles fell from Gillian's hands, Thane scooped her up, holding her tightly against his chest.

"Lass, are you all right?" he demanded. "I could not get here any sooner."

"You're here now, 'tis all that matters," she answered, laying her head against his shoulder. Her injured hands, swollen and red, were cradled against her waist.

"They'll pay for what they've done to you."

"They've broken no bones yet. You came in time," she

whispered. "Take me away from here, Thane. I'm afraid."

Her whimper broke his heart. He'd never known her to express this humbling fear. In the face of danger and hatred, she'd always retained her quiet courage.

" 'Tis no cause for fear now, my little wild bird. No one will hurt you again whilst I draw a breath." He carried her back along the corridor they'd traversed and out into the sunlight.

"Bring a carriage," he ordered, and the Holyrood captain motioned forward a rough cart that was used to transport prisoners. There were no cushions to soften the jolting ride. Thane glared at the captain, who shrugged and shook his head.

"I'm sorry, m'lord. We have no other."

Thane climbed on the cart and sat on the floor, cradling Gillian in his arms. "Tie Bhaltair behind," he ordered. "And tell the driver to go slowly so as not to jar us, else I'll cut loose the horse and yoke him in front."

"Aye, m'lord," the captain said, and gave the instructions. Slowly they made their way back to Holyrood. Thane saw that Gillian's face was gravely pale. Despite his admonitions, the rough cart jolted over the rutted road, now and then eliciting a low, pain-filled groan. Thane tore away his neck band and tenderly wrapped her injured hands in the soft, fine cambric. The action brought a smile to her lips.

"You tend me now, my love," she whispered.

"Aye, I should have tended to your needs better, lass. I was too blinded by the cursed greed of the Campbells and thought I should marry for lands and wealth. I will never let you suffer again," he vowed, burying his face in the dark, glossy curls he loved so much. He smoothed the strands from her face, gazed into the emerald depths of her gaze, and tasted her sweet mouth once again, all the while cradling her slim body against his protectively.

Despite Thane's efforts, Gillian insisted she was

capable of walking to the High Lord Chamberlain's apartment. Juliana and Lady Joan threw themselves on her when she entered, their warm hugs and happy cries filling her heart with joy. She'd not been forgotten. Her friends had fought for her release. Despite the seriousness of the accusations, she felt an uplifting of spirits.

Thane lost no time in venting his rage toward Lennox. "Did ye order the use of pilliwinks on her?" he demanded, fists balled, teeth bared.

Lennox looked alarmed. "I did not order such devices used. There were other ways to question Mistress Gillian, witnesses to be brought forth to support the claims. We would not have resorted to torturous devices until all other avenues had been exhausted." A portly man entered the room. Grateful for the distraction, Lennox angled toward him.

"Ah, Lord Yarwood, you've come at last. I would have you look at Mistress Gillian's hands and see what can be done about them. She's undergone a grievous punishment."

At once the physician moved forward. A chair was brought for Gillian to be seated and the makeshift bandage Thane had affected was removed. Carefully the physician examined the swollen fingers, nodding and humming in some private consultation of his own.

"There are no broken bones," he decreed finally. "I shall dress them so as to give her less pain. In a few weeks she'll be good as new."

"There, you see, no harm done," Lennox stated. Sir Robert's hand on Thane's arm saved the High Lord Chamberlain from receiving a thrashing. Lennox prudently removed himself to safety behind his desk. "Shall we proceed while Lord Yarwood bandages your ward's injuries?" he inquired of Sir Robert.

"By all means," Robert said, although his own lips were thin with anger.

"Mistress Evina, will you step forward, please, and

have a seat," Lennox ordered, and Evina, who'd remained quietly in the background since Gillian's arrival, took the chair he indicated. All eyes turned to her. Thane's hands clamped protectively over Gillian's shoulders, giving her support, offering his strength. Gillian drew a trembling breath and faced her accuser.

"Evina, why do you make such claims against me? Do you hate me so?"

"I didn't hate you until I discerned you were a witch," Evina said, but her voice did not carry the conviction it had when she'd made her outcry that morning.

"You well know, I am not a witch," Gillian replied evenly.

"So you have stated, young woman," Lennox replied, "and now we will have the truth of it all." He motioned to a guard, who brought Robena MacGregor into the room. Robena stood beside Gillian. Evina gasped and gripped the arms of her chair.

Lennox studied the MacGregor women. "Remarkable," he said, then turned to Evina with such firmness of purpose that she blanched beneath his glare. "Now, tell me, Mistress Campbell, what were your accusations again?"

"I—I didn't know she had a kinswoman," she stuttered.

"Did you not?" Lennox demanded. "While I awaited your arrival, I had a most interesting conversation with Robena MacGregor, and she tells me you came upon her in the woods and at once recognized that she was not Gillian, but in fact that you, not knowing she was a Mac-Gregor, engaged her in mischief against Gillian Mac-Gregor. She claims you deliberately roused the villagers at Edinample to burn Gillian MacGregor as a witch."

"She lies. I didn't!" Evina cried, leaping to her feet. " 'Tis but a cruel trick they play upon me, your lordship."

"Is it, Mistress Campbell, or is the trickery being done

by you to rid yourself of a rival for your cousin's affections?"

Evina's expression was stricken with guilt. "Nay, m'lord," she whispered, sinking back on the seat. Her pale glance darted about her gathered kinsmen. "Lady Joan?" she appealed. "Don't you believe me?"

"I've never believed Gillian to be a witch, Evina," she stated with such conviction that Gillian wanted to hug her.

"Your word is most gravely in question here, Mistress Campbell," Lennox went on. "And it has been put to me that you are a habitual liar, even going so far as to play a cruel hoax upon your own cousin in claiming he spawned a child upon you. Is this accusation true?"

"Aye, m'lord," Evina cried, gripping the carved arms of the chair where she sat. "I carry his seed. He can't refuse to marry me."

"And well he should not, if what you say is true. That is what we are about to prove, Mistress Campbell. Now that Lord Yarwood has finished tending Mistress Gillian, he is prepared to examine you as to this point."

"What?" Evina leapt to her feet again, but swayed as the full significance of what was about to happen registered. "M'lord, I beg you," she whimpered, her face blotched with patches of red. Freckles stood out in bold relief, brown and ugly. Fear seemed to have sucked away all youthful vitality, so the bones of her jaw and nose jutted prominently.

"The time for charges is done. Now you will either prove those charges or retract them. If you will be so good as to follow Lord Yarwood into the adjoining room?"

Evina's eyes widened. Her lips were pale, "I refuse to submit to such—such indignities."

"You have no choice, my dear," Lennox said, sounding somewhat bored by this time with the whole affair. Languidly he motioned forward two of Queen Anne's ladies-in-waiting. Taking hold of Evina's hands, they led her into the adjoining bedchamber. Lord Yarwood, clearing his throat to denote his displeasure at having his afternoon tryst with a notorious beauty delayed, followed the ladies. Gillian exchanged bewildered glances with Lady Joan. Juliana grinned gleefully. From beyond the closed door they heard the screams and shrieks of a distraught Evina.

"What is this about?" Gillian whispered.

"It seems Evina's schemes are about to come to naught," Juliana said, hugging her raven-haired friend.

They heard the angry sputters and cries of outrage from beyond the door.

"Poor Evina," Gillian whispered, shivering slightly. Thane looked into her beautiful face, seeing the marks of weariness and pain, and wondered at her generosity.

"She's not suffering as she caused you to suffer," he said, and pulled her close against him.

In a short while Lord Yarwood returned to the room, drying his hands on a linen towel.

"How did you fare?" Lennox demanded when the physician remained silent.

"The young lady didn't wish to cooperate," the portly doctor said, taking the wine Lennox offered and downing it in one gulp.

"Surely, you did not let that stop you?" Lennox asked with a raised eyebrow.

The physician shook his head. "Nay, I had her held down and completed the examination." He paused to sip his second glass of wine. Suddenly Thane felt a savage pleasure at Evina's outrage.

"And?" Lennox was growing nearly as impatient as Thane, who'd just barely managed to contain his temper.

"And the lass still has her maidenhead. As tight as a drum it is."

Sir Robert smiled knowingly. Thane gravely nodded, all his late and new suspicions confirmed.

"Well, m'lord, we've proven the unworthiness of the

accuser, not once, but thrice. Now will you release my ward to me?" Sir Robert inquired evenly.

Lennox frowned. "Bring the wench to me!" he roared. One of the ladies-in-waiting went to fetch Evina. Eyes red from crying, Evina entered the room and stood before Lord Lennox, her head bowed.

"Will you tell me the truth now, Mistress Campbell," Lennox demanded. "Or must I go to greater lengths to determine it for myself."

"Nay, m'lord," Evina wept piteously. " 'Tis true I lied. I—I but wished to— I love Thane Campbell as no other ever could. He should have wanted to marry me!"

"Bah, take her out of here. She is to return to her father at Kilchurn immediately. Be assured that a letter will be sent informing your father of this incident. Know too that I speak for the king and queen when I say you are herewith banned from court, nay, even from Edinburgh."

"M'lord?" she whispered, not believing her ears, so low had she fallen. Even her father, with all the powerful Campbell connections, would be hard put to make a suitable marriage for her with this scandal hanging over her. "M'lord, when may I come again to court?" she pleaded.

"Never!" Lennox said cruelly. "Now, be gone from my sight. You've taken enough time from the king's business."

Lennox turned to Gillian. "I'm sure the king would like to compensate you for your ordeal, Mistress Gillian," he said with surprising graciousness. "If there's anything I can do . . ."

"I believe there is, your lordship," Thane said. Surprised, Gillian glanced at him. "Jaimie MacGregor is lodged in Edinburgh Castle as a prisoner. I believe it is the wish of Mistress Gillian that he be set free and allowed to sail to exile in Ireland."

"Is this so, Mistress Gillian?"

"Aye, m'lord, 'tis most surely so." Her face glowed.

"But as I understand, he is an outlaw who's plotted against the king."

"Not against the king, m'lord," Gillian said quickly, "only against the law that took MacGregor lands and made him an outcast. He was most sorely used by the clan that took him in, and his heart grew bitter. Perhaps in Ireland he can make a new life and find peace for his tortured soul."

"You plead his case most engagingly, lass," Lennox said, not without some warmth. He turned his attention to Thane Campbell, taking in the Highlander's hard, muscular body and the quick intelligence in his blue eyes. When he removed himself and his court to England, King James would have need of the support of such men as this. Not only did Thane Campbell possess the strength of a powerful clan behind him, but a steadfast loyalty for which the Highlanders were well known.

"The prisoner is yours, Thane of Glenorchy. What do you think of freeing him?"

"I will bow to m'lord's wishes," Thane said.

Lennox sat thinking, then abruptly nodded. "So be it, then," he said. "Though I will not have this man left in Scotland to rouse his broken clan against the king."

"I will personally place him on the first ship to Ireland," Thane promised.

"Then it seems we've settled this matter once and for all." Lennox got to his feet, every inch the High Lord Chamberlain. "James will be leaving in a few weeks for England. Do either of you wish to be among the noble families to accompany him?"

"Nay, m'lord. We'll be occupied with weddings." Sir Robert's hand closed over Lady Joan's.

"What about you, Laird Campbell?"

Thane looked at Gillian. "I've a wish to return to Edinample and wed Gillian MacGregor," he said.

"The king's best wishes to you all," Lennox said

absently, and waved his secretary forward to show them out. In the anteroom Gillian turned to her cousin.

"Thank you for coming t'rescue me, Robena," she whispered. "You can't hate me if you'd do so."

Robena's smile was cryptic. "I sought only to save Jaimie's life," she answered. She turned her dark gaze on Thane. "I will attain passage on the *Flying Rose*, as you've instructed."

Without hesitation he brought out a leather sack heavy with gold coins and handed it over. Robena took the sack and hid it within the folds of her cape.

"The other half will be paid you the moment before the *Flying Rose* sails. I'll bring Jaimie there at high tide," Thane answered.

"Then our business is concluded," Robena said. Her head was held high with the old arrogance Gillian remembered from long ago, in a better time for them all.

"I wish you safe journey, Robena," Gillian said softly. "May God be with you in your new life."

Robena scoffed, nostrils flaring. Her dark gaze fixed on Thane's face. She pulled the hood over her head and moved purposefully toward the stairs.

Gillian felt a sadness settle over her. For better or worse, these were the last of her kinsmen, and she would never set eyes on them again. Thane sensed her melancholia and scooped her up in his arms. Effortlessly he strode along the corridor and down the long flight of steps.

"I can walk, m'love," she murmured in halfhearted protest.

"Aye, lass, well I know. But I've a need to hold on to you now. Do you mind?"

"Nay, Thane," she whispered, placing her face against his jaw and drawing a deep sigh of contentment. "Did you mean what you told Lord Lennox? Do you plan to wed with me?"

"Aye, lass, with indecent haste."

"But, laird, I don't possess an acre of land for a dowry." Her eyes flashed with mischievous lights.

"Don't mock my foolhardiness, lass," he pleaded. His own gaze darkened. They had arrived at the carriage now. Lady Joan and Juliana were already there, waiting for them. Still, he held her. "Will you be my wife, Gillian MacGregor?" he asked thickly.

"Aye, Thane of Glenorchy. I have naught to bring as my dowry save my heart, which is so filled with love for you, it can scarcely beat."

" 'Tis all I need of you, lass," he whispered, and his lips claimed hers. They neither heard nor saw the people around the carriage cheering for them. They were one again, one heart, one soul, and neither God nor the devil could separate them—ever.

*You won't want to miss
this fabulous novel by*
FERN MICHAELS

SERENDIPITY

As a naive and pregnant seventeen-year-old, Jory Ryan found herself in a loveless marriage to lawyer Ross Landers, scion of a prominent publishing family in Philadelphia. Fleeing to Florida, Jory transformed herself into a successful and glamorous journalist. Now, six years later, Ross sends for Jory to finalize their divorce. Caught in a vicious family power struggle, Jory must confront her painful past to find new love and true happiness.

ON SALE NOW
wherever books are sold.

THE BRIDE OF PENDORRIC

The words "till death do us part" take on a new meaning when Favel Farington arrives at her new husband's ancestral home and finds a crypt filled with Pendorric brides who all died so mysteriously...and so young.

THE BLACK OPAL

Abandoned as a baby, the exotically beautiful Carmel March must return to Commonwood, her childhood home, to uncover the dark secrets that will free her to find the love she has been searching for.

THE CAPTIVE

Saved from certain death by a handsome and mysterious stranger, Rosetta is bound by a consuming passion that will take her all over the world to rescue this man who has become her love's captive.

THE DEMON LOVER

Kate Collison's miniature portrait of the powerful Baron de Centeville brings her fame and fortune. But her feelings for the baron will bring pain and heartache until she learns to fight him with his own weapons.

THE HOUSE OF A THOUSAND LANTERNS

Drawn into the world of Chinese art trading, Jane Lindsay will travel halfway around the world to unravel the mystery of the House of a Thousand Lanterns and find true love.

MY ENEMY THE QUEEN

It was the lovely Lettice who married the Earl of Leicester, whom Elizabeth I loved. And it was Lettice who was the mother of the Queen's beloved Earl of Essex. It was always Lettice, the constant spoiler in the triangle of love surrounding Elizabeth....

THE JUDAS KISS
Pippa Ewell traveled to the Bavarian Kingdom to forget the handsome stranger who had stolen her heart and to find the truth behind her sister's death. But can rekindled love save Pippa from her sister's tragic fate?

THE KING OF THE CASTLE
The moment Dallas Lawson set her eyes on the notorious Comte de la Talle, she knew she would never willingly leave his legend-haunted chateau. But her passion might cost her life.

LORD OF THE FAR ISLAND
Rescued from a bleak future, lovely Ellen Kellaway journeyed to the Cornish island of her enigmatic new guardian, Lord Jago Kellaway. Drawn to Jago, Ellen must confront a terrifying past to let love reign on Far Island.

MENFRAYA IN THE MORNING
The great house of Menfraya was a refuge for Harriet Delvaney during her childhood. When she returns to Menfraya as a bride, Harriet is engulfed in a family legacy of jealousy and murder that threatens her sanity and her very life.

ON THE NIGHT OF THE SEVENTH MOON
Helena Trant is enchanted by the Black Forest and its legends of love. But her newfound love will come at a dangerous price and plunge her into a nightmare of betrayal and revenge.

THE SILK VENDETTA
Lenore Cleremont is at the center of a deadly family rivalry as two brothers vie for her love and threaten to destroy everything she holds dear.

SECRET FOR A NIGHTINGALE
Tragically widowed, Susanna Plydell fulfills her ambition of becoming a nurse. Yet in the midst of war and bloodshed, she cannot forget Dr. Damian Adair, the man who haunts her dreams and holds the key to a most sinister secret.